Quicksilver & Shadow

Quicksilver & Shadow

Collected Early Stories, Vol. 2:
Contemporary, Dark Fantasy,
and Science Fiction Stories

Charles de Lint

SUBTERRANEAN PRESS · 2005

FIRST EDITION

ISBN
1-59606-003-4

Subterranean Press
P.O. Box 190106
Burton, MI 48519

email:
subpress@earthlink.net

website:
www.subterraneanpress.com

Contents

Here We Are Again

I'm going to assume that if you've bought this book, the second volume in a series of early short story collections, then you've probably got the first volume, so I'm not going to repeat the apologia from its introduction. And actually, unlike that first volume, I still like many of these stories. A few, I wouldn't rewrite even if I had the opportunity and time, because they do the job just as they are.

Oh, that's not to say there aren't a few clunkers. There's a reason no one bought "From a 24" Screen" and it's not just because the shadow of Stephen King lies so heavily upon it. Let's face it, this story misses the mark on all the things that make — not only a King story but — any story work.

But sometimes shadows are a good thing. "The Soft Whisper of Midnight Snow" was certainly influenced by Charles Grant, though what I took from him was the idea of a quiet story still having impact, and the evocative title of which Grant is such a master (though he also came up with one of the funniest: *668: The Neighbor of the Beast*).

And some — like "The Face in the Flames" — have their heart in the right place, but I simply didn't have the chops to pull it off the way it should have been told. For one thing, if I was writing it today I'd strip away the mindless monster/elemental aspect in that story. And in fact, now that I think of it, I remember working on a longer version of this at one point, turning it into a novel that went for about 100 pages before I gave up on it, though part of the reason might also have been that my agent at the time convinced me that

9

rock'n'roll novels simply don't work. I guess he'd never read George R. R. Martin, or John Shirley, or any number of other authors who did make the concept work.

But more on that aborted novel some other time. For now, here are a few thoughts concerning the stories at hand:

Bordertown

"Stick" and "May This Be Your Last Sorrow" appear here, even though they were recently reprinted in my Viking collection *Waifs & Strays,* simply because I wanted to have one place where all my shared-world Bordertown stories were collected together. Mind you, to get all the resonances in "Berlin," you really should read Midori Snyder's "Demon" (which was the second story in *Bordertown*). It would come after "Stick" and before "Berlin."

"Stick" was my tip of the hat to British accordion player John Kirkpatrick and the other musicians who brought Morris dance music kicking and screaming into the rock world with albums like *Morris On.*

"Berlin" has a musical origin, too, growing partly from Leon Rosselson's classic song "The World Turned Upside Down." But it also has its origins in the Diggers of Toronto who provided food as well as medical and legal aid for street people in the summer of 1967. I had more than one meal on the lawn outside their house on Spadina, and helped pick up food and serve it a time or two as well.

Another tip of the hat you'll find in "Berlin" was to Andrew Vachss. Berlin's junkyard friends were inspired by the character of Mole in his Burke books, which is kind of funny, actually, since it was through Andrew reading "Stick" in the Bordertown books and contacting me that we became friends. I went back to the junkyard in *Someplace to Be Flying* with a more overt homage, though to date only a few readers have noticed, or at least written to mention either.

The last influence was Midori's character of Koga from the aforementioned "Demon." There are other writers' characters drifting through "Berlin" (there was much borrowing going on while we were writing these stories) but Midori letting me use Koga was what sparked the whole idea of the dragon protectors, which plays such a pivotal part in the story.

I would have liked to explore those characters more, but by the time I was asked to do another Bordertown story, the nameless street urchin from "May This Be Your Last Sorrow" wouldn't leave my head.

And now I have my own made-up city to play in...

Science Fiction

When it comes to "A Tattoo on Her Heart" and "Raven Sings a Medicine Way, Coyote Steals the Pollen," well...

As you've probably noticed by now, myths and folktales fascinate me — not only for their content, but for how they came to be. Though my stories usually juxtapose old mythic matter with the modern world, or enthusiastically embrace what Jan Harold Brunvand calls "Urban Legends" — contemporary folktales and myths — I've occasionally, as in the following stories set long after a worldwide disaster, dabbled in the origins of myths as well.

Still, these are rare excursions for me. The only other published one that comes immediately to mind is my novel *Svaha* (1989), which, come to think of it, might very well take place in the same futuristic setting as "A Tattoo on Her Heart," albeit in a different city.

The story of Malii and the moccasins that the old man relates in "Raven Sings..." is a retelling of a traditional Blackfoot Trickster tale.

CRSO

Actually, the idea that I would call some of these stories science fiction is really kind of laughable. If anything, they're science fantasy, from the Andre Norton school of writing. Full of earnest world-building, based on nothing else but the idea of "that would be cool." But while the storylines of stories such as "The Lantern Is the Moon" are still rather linear, they're a far stretch from the heroic fantasy stories presented in the first volume of this series, and I still rather enjoy the characters.

And I should quickly mention that my saying "the Andre Norton school of writing" and then mentioning what I see as weaknesses in my stories, has nothing to do with Norton's work and everything to do with my not paying enough attention in class, a failing that dogged me all through high school as well...

"Songwalking the Hunter's Road," while still somewhat under the influence of Andre Norton, is leavened with equal helpings of imagery based on the music of Marc Bolan and Robin Williamson. And while there's another telepathic sidekick, this time he lives inside the protagonist's head.

The Shift Worlds

Back when I was writing many of these stories, the big influences were the pulps. Often the pulp writers would write connective stories, so most of the short fiction I was writing at the time was conceived as possibly being part of a series. The more I wrote, the less I followed up on that, because I found it far more interesting to deal with new characters and new settings in each story. (Something that obviously changed again when I started doing stories set in Newford, but I digress.)

Anyway, while all these science fantasy stories were conceived as possible series, only these two Shift Worlds stories went further than one story.

I got a kick out preparing "The Dralan" and "The Cost of Shadows" for this collection, because it reminded me of the days when artist John Charette (you saw his work in Volume 1), writer Charles Saunders, I and a few other folks used to hang out and swap our stories and art.

One of the people I palled around with in those days was a fellow named Roger Camm. I met Roger at a shopping center called Billings Bridge, here in Ottawa: I worked in the record store, he worked in the bookstore. We liked a lot of the same books and movies, and while Roger didn't really write a lot, he was always full of great ideas.

I don't remember exactly how we came to collaborate on these two stories, or even who did what on them, but I'm pretty sure all the smart tech stuff and martial arts expertise is his, with the writing being mine. I had read some science fiction (Andre Norton, Clifford Simak, Roger Zelazny) but Roger had a huge familiarity with the field and a head that just naturally set up problems and then worked them out.

These days he uses those smarts in the computer field, but hopefully he'll enjoy revisiting these old stories when he gets his contributor's copy of this book.

CRLO

One last thing: perhaps one of you can help me. As I mentioned in the first volume of this early short stories series, there is an unpublished novelette I'd like to include in one of these collections, but unfortunately, I've long since lost touch with my collaborator on it. His name is Jim Coplin and back in the seventies, he was writing as "J. E. Coplin." If any of you know how I can get in touch with Jim, please let either me or the publisher of this book know. Hopefully we'll then be able to include that story in the third and last volume.

CRLO

If any of you are on the Internet, come visit my home page at www.charlesdelint.com.

Charles de Lint
Ottawa, late autumn 2003

Contemporary & Dark Fantasy

The Soft Whisper of Midnight Snow

Night.

The fields lay stark as a charcoal drawing — white drifts, the black clawed talons of the trees, the starlight piercingly bright. A gust of wind-driven snow swirled across the nearest field and he was there again. A shape in the twisting snow. A whisper of moccasins against white grains of ice. One step, another. He was drawing closer, much closer. Then she blinked, the snow swirled with a new flurry of wind, and he was gone. The field lay empty.

Tomilyn Douglas turned from the window and let out a breath she hadn't been aware of holding. The cabin was warm, the new woodstove throwing off all of its advertised heat, but a chill still scurried down her spine. She walked slowly to where her easel stood by an east window, ready to make use of the morning light. Her hand trembled slightly as she flicked a lamp switch and studied the drawing in its pale glow. It twinned the scene she had just been witness to, complete with the tiny shapeless figure, its details hidden in a swirl of gusting snow.

This morning she'd thought it had been a dream, that she had only dreamed of waking and seeing that figure in the snow, moving towards the cabin. Her fingers smudged with charcoal, she'd stood back and smiled with satisfaction at the rendering she'd done of it, that momentary high of a completed work making her a little dizzy until she'd had to go sit down. A useful dream, she'd thought, for it had left her with the first piece of decent work she'd completed

17

since Alan...since Alan had gone. It was an omen of things to come, of a lost talent returned, of an ache finally beginning to heal.

Tomi flicked off the light and the room returned to darkness. It'd been an omen all right, she thought. But she was no longer so sure that she understood just what it was that it promised.

CREAD

"This is where the dream becomes real," he'd told her when they bought and fixed up the cabin. It was meant to be only a temporary arrangement. The cabin stood on a hundred acres of bush land south of Calabogie. Alan had the blueprints all drawn up for the house they would build on the hill behind the cabin. It was his dream to build a home for them that would be the perfect design. The house would grow almost organically from its surroundings. A stand of birch grew so close to where her studio would be that she would feel as though she was a part of the forest, separated only by the glass walls of the room. Solar heating, a vegetable garden already planned out, enough forest on the land that they could cut their own wood...Self-sufficiency was to be the order of the day and she loved him for it. For the house, for the land, for the dream, for...for his love.

They could afford to live out of the city. They were both established in their careers—architect and artist. Alan's clients sought him out now, while her work sold as quickly as she could paint it. They were the perfect match for each other—she loved it when people told them that, because it was true. For eleven years...it was true. But the dream had become a nightmare.

Last spring the foundations of their dream house were a scar on the landscape, like the scar on her soul. The forest began to reclaim its own. By the time the snows came this year, the sharp edges of the foundations were rounded with returning undergrowth. The scar she carried had yet to lose its raw edges.

CREAD

Morning.

Tomi bundled up and went out into the field, but if last night's visitor had left any tracks, if he hadn't just been some figment of

18

her imagination, the night's winds had dusted and filled them with snow. She stood, the wind blowing her brown hair into her face, and stared across the white expanse of drifts and dervishing snow-eddies to study the forest beyond the fields. The quiet that she'd loved when she moved here from the city, that she'd slowly come to love again as she dealt with her pain, disturbed her now. Too quiet, she thought, then she spoke the clichéd words aloud. The wind took them from her mouth and scattered them across the field. Shivering, Tomi returned to the cabin.

She spent the day working at her easel. Sketch after sketch made its mysterious passage from mind through fingers to paper. And they were all good. No, she amended as she looked them over while having a mid-afternoon soup-and-tea break. They were better than good. They were the best she'd done in over a year, perhaps better than before Alan —

She shut that train of thought off as quickly as it came. She was getting better at it now. But while she thrust aside the ache before it could take hold, she couldn't shake the uneasiness that had followed her through the day. Night was coming, was almost here. Just at dusk it began to snow. Tiny granular pellets rasped against the door, rattled on the roof. She wanted to turn all the lights on so that she'd be blinded to the night outside, but not seeing made her more nervous. One by one she turned them off, then sat in the darkness and looked out over the fields at the falling snow.

ભ

One day he just never came home. She could draw up that day in her memory with a total recall that always struck her as a sure sign that she was still a long way from getting over it. He left in the morning to do some work down the road at Sam Collins' place — Sam having helped them when they were having the foundation poured. When he still wasn't back by dinnertime, she gave Sam a call, but he hadn't seen Alan all day and, no, he hadn't been expecting him.

That night wasn't the worst one in her life — those had come after, when she knew — but it was bad. She hadn't been able to do anything but worry, staring at the phone, waiting for him to call. She tried some friends of theirs in the city. No luck. She thought of calling the police, hospitals, that kind of thing, but knew for all her worry that it was too early for that. Then around eleven o'clock the phone rang, startling her right out of her seat with its klaxon jangle.

"Alan?" she cried into the mouthpiece. "Alan, is that you?" The words came out in a rush like they were all one word.

"Whoa, Mrs. Douglas. Slow down a bit. This is Tom Moulton." Her relief shattered into pieces of icy dread.

"Sorry to be calling you so late, but I was talking to Sam a few minutes ago and heard you were worried about your man. Thing is, I saw your jeep parked out on 511, a couple of miles down from my place. I knew right off it was yours, but I figured you all were out for a little hike or something, you know what I mean?"

She called the police then, and they began a search of the surrounding bush. It wasn't until a couple of days later when she had to go to the bank that she discovered half the money in their joint account had been withdrawn.

CREO

Night.

The snow had tapered off, but the wind was still shaping and reshaping the drifts around the trees and fence posts and up against the cabin. Tomi was half-hypnotized by the movement of the snow. Time and again she thought she saw the figure, but it was always just a shadow movement, a tree branch, a fox once. Then just as she was ready to give up her vigil, something drew her face closer to the window and she saw him again.

He was closer still. Not moving now, just standing out there in the field, watching the cabin. Tattered cloth fluttered in the wind, muting his outline against the snow. He was still too far away to make out details, but something about the way he stood, about the way he held himself erect, not hunched into the wind, told her that he wasn't who she'd feared he'd be. He wasn't Alan.

"Who are you?" she whispered. "What do you want from me?"

She didn't expect an answer. He was too far away to hear her. There was a thick glass pane and an expanse of white field between them. There was the wind and the gusting snow to steal her words. She wanted to shout at the figure, to run out and grab him. The window frosted up under her breath. She cleared it with a quick wipe of her hand, but in the time it took the figure was gone again.

Hardly realizing what she was doing, she grabbed her coat and a flashlight and ran outside, stumbling through the snow to where he'd stood. When she reached the spot there was no sign of him, no tracks. The field was virgin snow all around her, except for her own ragged trail from the cabin.

She began to shiver. Returning to the warmth of the cabin, she closed and bolted the door. She tossed her coat onto a chair, the flashlight, never used, on top of it, then slowly made her way to her bedroom. She began to undress, then stopped dead as she glanced at the bed. A long raven's feather lay on the comforter, stark and black against its flowered Laura Ashley design.

"Oh, Jesus."

On watery legs she walked over to the bed, stared at the intrusion, unwilling to touch it. He'd been inside. Somehow, while she'd been out looking for him, in those few moments, he'd come inside. Slowly she backed out of the bedroom. It didn't take long to search the cabin.

There was the main room that included her studio and the kitchen area, a bathroom, and her bedroom. She was alone in the cabin. In a trancelike state, she investigated every possible hiding place until she was positive of that. She was alone inside, but he was out there. What did he want? What in God's name was this game he was playing?

She was a long time getting to sleep that night, starting at every familiar creak and groan of her cabin. When she finally did sleep, restless dreams plagued her, dreams of shapeless figures and clouds of ravens' feathers that fell like black snow all around her while she ran and ran, trying to catch an answer that was always out of reach. Underpinning her dreams, the wind moaned outside the cabin, whispering the snow against its log walls.

CR&SO

The deed to the cabin and its land was in her name and, once the initial shock was over, she was quick to remove what money remained in their joint account into one under her own name. She kept thinking there was some mistake, that this wasn't happening to them, to her. But as the days drifted into weeks, she had no choice but to accept it. To believe it, even if she couldn't understand it.

At first she was confused and hurt. Anger was there too, but it came and went as if of its own will. Mostly she felt worthless. If they'd been having fights, if there'd been another woman, if there'd been some hint of what was coming, maybe she could have accepted it more easily. But it had come out of the blue.

"It's him," her friends tried to convince her. "He's just an asshole, Tomi. Christ, he never had it so good."

Neither had she, she'd want to say, but the words never got beyond her thinking them. He'd left her and she knew why. Because she was worthless. As she tried to lose herself in her work during the following weeks, she saw that her art was worthless too. God, no wonder he'd left her. The real wonder was that he hadn't left her sooner.

And even later as she, at least intellectually, came to realize that it *was* him and not her worthlessness that had made him leave, emotionally it wasn't that easy to accept. Emotionally, she retained the feelings of her own inadequacy. She'd stare into a mirror and see her face drawn and pale with her anxiety, the brown hair that framed it hanging listless, the body that could have been exercised but instead had been let to sag.

"Who'd want me?" she'd ask that reflection and then would retire deeper into the shell she was building around herself. Who'd want her? She didn't even want herself.

ᘓᘔᘯ

Morning.

Tomi had the jeep on the road and was halfway to Ottawa by the time the nine o'clock CBC news came on the radio. She turned it off. Her own troubles were enough to bear without having to listen to the world's. But once she was in Ottawa, she didn't know why she'd come.

She'd had to get away from the cabin, from the figure that haunted the fields outside it, from the black feather that was lying on the floor of her bedroom, but being here didn't help. There was too much going on, too many cars, too many people. She almost had a couple of accidents in the heavy traffic on the Queensway, another on Bank Street.

She'd been planning to visit friends, but no longer knew what to say to them. Running from the cabin wasn't the answer, she realized. Just as withdrawing from the world after Alan had left hadn't been an answer. She had to go back.

CR£O

That first spring alone had been the worst. She hadn't been able to look at the foundations without wanting to cry. Unable to paint, or even sketch, she'd thrown herself into working around the cabin, fixing it up, removing every trace of Alan from it, putting in a garden, buying a new woodstove, discovering talents she'd never known she'd had. She might not be able to keep a husband or express herself with her art anymore, but she could handle a hammer and saw, she could chop firewood, she could do a lot of things now — do them without ever worrying about whether or not she was capable of them.

The first night that she made a vegetable stew with all the ingredients coming out of her own garden, she celebrated with a bottle of wine, got very drunk and never once wanted to cry. She stood out in the clear night air and looked up to the hill at the foundations and was surprised at what she found in herself.

The ache was still there, but it was different now. Still immediate, but not quite so piercing. She might not be able to paint yet, but the next day she took out her sketchbook and began to draw again. She wasn't happy with anything she did, but she wasn't discouraged about it anymore either. Not in the same way as she'd been when Alan had first deserted her.

CR£O

Night.

Tomi had forgotten how quickly it got dark. She'd decided to return to the cabin, but since she was in town anyway, she thought she might as well make a day of it. It went by all too quickly. From grocery shopping to haunting used bookstores and antique shops, it was going on four o'clock before she knew it. By the time she was fighting the heavy traffic on her way home, it began to snow again, big heavy flakes that were whisked away by the jeep's wipers but were building up rapidly on the road and fields. When she reached old Highway 1 going north from Lanark, she was reduced to a slow crawl, even with the jeep's four-wheel-drive. The buildup of snow and ice made for treacherous driving, especially on roads like this without as much traffic.

After Highway 1 turned into 511 and crossed the Clyde River, the driving grew worse. Here the road was narrow and twisted its way through the wooded hills that were barely visible through the storm. The wind drove the snow in sheets across her windshield. The jeep ploughed through drifts that had already thrust halfway across the road in places.

Not far now, she told herself, and that much was true, but a half mile from the laneway leading in to her cabin, the road took a sudden dip and a sharp turn at the same time. She was going too fast when she topped the hill and hit an icy patch. Already nervous, she did the worst thing possible and instead of riding the fishtail and easing out of it, she slammed her foot on the brake.

The jeep skidded, came sideways down the hill and missed the turn. Its momentum took it through and then over the snow embankment until it thudded to a stop against a tall pine. The shock of the impact brought all the snow down from its branches in a sudden avalanche.

Panicked and shaken, Tomi snapped loose her seatbelt and lunged from the jeep. The snow came up to her hips as she floundered through it back to the road. She was breathing heavily by the time she reached it, the cold air hurting her lungs. When she looked back, she saw the jeep was half covered with the snow that it had dislodged from the pine.

She was never going to get it out of that mess. Not without a tow truck or tractor. But she couldn't face seeing to that now. She wasn't far from home. She could walk the half mile easily. Trying to ignore the chill that was seeping in through her clothes, cold enough to make even her bones feel cold, she forced her way back to the jeep, fetched her purse and groceries, and started the short trek home.

The snow was coming down in a fury now, the wind slapping it against her exposed skin with enough force to hurt. Neck hunched into her coat, head bowed, she trudged up the road, fighting the steadily growing drifts. The half mile had never seemed so long. Her boots — fine for town, but a joke out here — were wet and cold against her feet. The stylish three-quarter length coat that was only meant for the quick dashes from warm vehicle to warm store couldn't contend with the bone-piercing chill of the wind.

She got a scare when she stumbled and fell in a sprawl on the highway, her grocery bag splitting open to spew its contents all around her. But she was more scared when she found she just couldn't get up to go on. The shock of the accident and the numbing cold had drained all her strength.

She could lie here and, with the poor visibility, the snowplow would come by and bury her in the embankment, never knowing that its blades had scooped her up and shunted her aside. Or a pickup could come by and run her down before its driver even realized what it was that he was about to hit.

Right, bright eyes, she thought. So get the hell out of here.

She managed to sit up and tried to scrape together her scattered groceries, but her fingers were too numb in their thin gloves to work properly. What a time to play fashion horse, she thought hazily. But then again she hadn't been planning on playing the arctic explorer when she'd set out this morning. What a dramatic picture this would make, she decided. The woman fallen in the snow, her groceries scattered around her, the wind howling around her like a dervish...

She blinked her eyes open suddenly to find that she'd laid her head down on the road again as she'd been thinking.

This. Wouldn't. Do.

She forced herself back up into a sitting position. Screw the groceries. If she didn't get out of here quickly, she wasn't going to get up at all.

But the cold was in her bones now. Her teeth chattered and her jaws ached from trying to keep them from doing so. Her hands and feet just felt like lumps on the ends of her arms and legs. She realized with a shock that she was almost completely covered with snow. Only her upper torso was relatively free, the snow covering it having fallen off when she sat up.

Up. That was the ticket. She had to get up, put one foot in front of the other, and get herself home. She tried to rise, but the cold had just sapped something in her. There'd been a lot of times over the past spring and summer when she'd simply wanted to die, but now that it was a very real possibility, she wanted to live with a fierceness that actually got her to her feet.

She tottered and took a couple of steps, then fell into another drift, frustrated tears freezing on her cheeks. Which was weird, she thought, because the snow actually felt warm now. It was cozy. Just like her bed in the cabin. Or the big easy chair in front of the woodstove...

As she began to drift off, the last thing she saw was a dark shape moving towards her through the billowing snow. Incongruously, for all the howling of the wind, she heard a rasp of bead and quill against leather, a whisper of moccasins against the crust of the snow, smelled a pungent scent like a freshly snapped cedar bough, and then she knew no more.

CRSO

She blinked awake. The air was thickly warm around her. She was lying on something soft, cozily wrapped in a covering of furs. Dim lighting spun in her gaze as she sat up. When her head stopped spinning, she stared groggily about herself.

There was a fire crackling in front of her, its smoke escaping upward through a hole in the roof. Roof. Where was she? The walls looked like they were made of woven branches. She could hear the wind howling outside them. Movement caught her eye and she looked across the fire. He'd been sitting so still that she hadn't noticed him at first, but now he leapt out at her with a thousand details, each one so clear that she wondered how she could have taken so long to see him there.

He sat cross-legged on a deerskin, the firelight playing on his pale skin, waking sharp highlights in his narrow features. His clothing was a motley collection of tatters. A black shirt, decorated with bone. A gray vest, inlaid with beadwork, quills and feathers. A raven's skull hung like a pendant from his neck in the middle of a cluster of feathers and shells. He wore a headdress, again decorated with feathers and bones, that lifted high above his head in the shape of a pair of horns. She thought of the wicked queen in Disney's *Sleeping Beauty* looking at those horns, or of Tolkien's high born elves, taking in his pale features. But there was more of the Native American about him. And more than that, a feeling of great sorrow.

"Who…who are you?" she asked. She spoke softly, the way one might speak to a wild animal, poised for flight. "Why were you watching my cabin? What do you want with me?"

She knew it had to have been him.

He made no reply. His eyes seemed all white in the deceptive light cast by the fire, all except for their pale gray pupils. His gaze never left Tomi's face. She was suddenly sure that she was dead. The plow *had* come by and scraped her frozen body up from the road, burying it under a mountain of snow. He was here to take her to…to wherever you went when you died…

"Please," she said, fingers tightening their grip on the fur covering. "What…what do you want with me?"

The silence stretched until Tomi thought she would scream. She plucked nervously at the furs, wanting to look away, but her gaze seemed to be trapped by his unblinking eyes.

"Please," she began again. "Why have you been spying on me?"

He nodded suddenly. Movement made the bones and quills click against each other.

"Life," he said.

His voice was husky and rough. He spoke with a heavy accent so that Tomi knew that whatever his native language was, it wasn't English.

She swallowed thickly. Fear made her throat dry and tight.

"L-life?" she managed.

She looked for the door of the lodge, trying not to be too obvious about it. She didn't know if she'd have the strength to take off, but she couldn't just stay here with…with whatever he was.

He pulled a strip of birch bark from under his tunic and took a charred twig from beside the fire. With quick deft movements he began to sketch on the birch bark. Curiosity warred with fear inside Tomi and she leaned forward. When he suddenly thrust the finished drawing at her, she floundered to get out of the way, then chided herself. So far the stranger hadn't hurt her. He'd brought her in from the cold and snow, bundled her up in his furs, saved her life…And the drawing…it was good. Better than good.

Tomi taught art from time to time, week-long courses at the Haliburton School during the summer, a few at Algonquin College in Ottawa. Not one of those students' work could hold a candle to the lifelike sketch of a snow hare that her curious host had thrust at

27

her. His quick deft rendering of it was what she always tried to instill in her students. To go for feeling first. She smiled to show she appreciated it.

"It's very good," she began.

"Life!" he repeated.

Taking back the drawing, he blew on it, then laid it on the ground beside the fire.

Fear clawed up Tomi's spine again as the lines of the drawing began to move, to lift three-dimensionally from the birch bark. A hazily-shaped hare sat there, its outline smoky and indistinct. Nose twitching nervously, it regarded her with warm eyes. Her fear died, replaced with wonder. She reached out a hand to touch the little apparition, but it drifted apart like smoke and was gone. All that remained was the birch bark that it had been sitting on. It's surface was clear, unmarked.

"You," her host said. "Your breath."

"I...I can't breathe like...like..."

"You must."

"I can't breathe—"

Suddenly the lodge was spinning again. The fire turned into a whirlpool of glittering sparks that twisted and danced like snow-driven wind. Tomi's words froze in her throat. Gone. It was going. It was—

CR£O

—gone.

"—can't breathe..."

Something was shaking her. She blinked rapidly, trying to slow down the spinning.

"Miz Douglas? Miz Douglas?"

The world came into focus with a sharp snap. A face was leaning into hers. For one moment she was back in the storm, or the storm had torn apart the strange man's lodge, blowing everything away, then she recognized the face. Sam Gould's strong features were looking down into hers. Worry creased his lined features. He looked at a loss.

"Sam...?"

"It's me, Miz Douglas. Found you lying out on the highway. You're damned lucky I didn't run over you with the plow, I'll tell you that."

"You...found me...?"

Then the lodge, the man — that had been a dream?

"Sure did. Funny thing — thought I saw someone standing beside you, just when my high beams picked you out, but that must've been you standing for a moment, just before you fell. Hell of a storm, though, and that's a fact. Had a look at your jeep, but it's in too deep for me to do much about it till the morning. I'll come round with the tractor then, if you can wait."

"I...I can wait."

"Not much damage, considering. Headlight's gone on the driver's side. You might want Bill Cassidy to have a look at that fender. I figure he could straighten her out for you, no problem."

"There was...someone standing...?" Tomi managed.

"Well, I thought there was, I'll tell you that. But it was just a trick of the light, I'd say. Storm can fool you into thinking you're seeing just about anything sometimes."

"Yes," Tomi said slowly.

Like what she'd thought she'd seen.

A dream. Just...

"Anyway, I brought you up to your cabin," Sam continued. "Thought you might'a had a touch of frostbite on your wrist there, but I wrapped it up tight and kept it warm. The skin wasn't broken, so it'll be all right. You were lucky, and that's a fact. I coulda plowed you right up into the bank and no one would've known to go looking for you till your jeep was spotted in the morning. I put you to bed, but 'cepting your boots and coats, I didn't...you know..." He blushed. "I just covered you up, Miz Douglas."

"Thank you, Sam." Tomi sat up slowly. "You saved my life."

A dream?

Sam shuffled his feet. "Guess I did at that. I woulda called up an ambulance, but by the time it would've got here, well...I did what I could, I'll tell you that. You want I should call up the doc now, Miz Douglas? Or maybe get someone to stay with you for the night?"

Tomi shook her head. "I'll be all right, Sam. But thank you."

Just a dream?

"My pleasure. I'd best be going now. Weather's not getting any better and I've got a load of plowing still to do. Keep me busy most of the night, I'll tell you that."

Tomi started to get up, but Sam laid a hand on her shoulder and gently pressed her down.

"I can see myself out, Miz Douglas. You just lie there and take her easy. I'll lock up and be back in the morning with the tractor. You just get some sleep now. You've been through a rough time, and that's a fact. Sleep's the best thing for you now."

Tomi nodded and laid back, knowing that he wouldn't go until she did. She listened to him clomp across the hardwood floors in his work boots, heard him tug on his parka, the sound of the zipper, the door opening.

"I'll see you in the morning!" he called, then the door slammed shut.

The door handle made a click-click noise as he checked to make sure it was locked. Silence then for a time. Except for the wind. The snow being pushed against the cabin, the windows. The big snow-plow starting up. Gears grinding as they changed. The truck backing out of her lane. Silence again as the sound of its engine was swallowed by the wind.

Tomi stared at her ceiling.

Just a dream?

She listened to the wind and the whisper of the snow against the windowpanes and logs outside. She might have drifted off, she wasn't sure, just dozed there, until suddenly she had to get up, had to see, *had* to. She padded out of her bedroom into the main room of the cabin. Sam had left the lights on and she turned them off, one by one, then went to stand by the window.

The snow was still falling, the wind blowing it in great sweeps across the field. She stared out at the field, willing her stranger to be there again, for it not to have been a dream. She wasn't sure what she wanted, what she expected. She had been frightened in the lodge, but remembering it now, there had been no reason for fear. Just the strange man with his totemic clothing, and the drawing that came to life with a breath, with just a whisper of air drawn up from his lungs...

She moved to her easel and turned on a light, aiming it so that it pooled over the easel, leaving the rest of the room in shadows. From the closet, she took out a virgin canvas, a sketching pencil, her acrylics. The sketching went easily. Background first, light, hazy as though seen through a gossamer curtain of falling snow. Then the figure. But close now.

She knew his features and quickly sketched them in. Left their look of sorrow, but imbued them with a certain air of nobility as well. She made the clothing not so ragged, not so tattered. The totemic raven skulls, feathers, beads and quills, came readily, leaping the gap from memory to canvas with an exhilarating ease.

Oh, lord. This was what it felt like. This was what she'd missed, what Alan had stolen from her, what the stranger had given her back.

She didn't know who or what he was, realized that it didn't matter. Dream or real, it didn't matter. Some spirit of the winter, of the snow and wind, or of the forest…or a creation of her own blocked creativity. It didn't matter.

When the sketching was filled in as much as she needed, she moved straight to the acrylics, mixing the paints and applying them, scarcely paying any attention to what she was doing. Her subconscious remembered, her fingers remembered. She only had to give them free rein. She only had to breathe life into what took shape on her canvas.

God. To have forgotten this…to have lost it…

She leaned close as she worked, mixing colors on the seat of the stool, too enrapt in her work to search for her palette. The shades came easily. The painting grew from the rough black and white sketch into a being almost composed of flesh and blood, almost as though she was back in his lodge, seeing him across the fire, the light playing on his features, his steady gaze never wavering from hers. She listened to the wind, to the hiss and spit of the snow against the windows, and smiled as she worked.

CRSO

It was long after midnight, but still far from dawn, when the main figure was completed and she only had the background to fill in. Her gaze locked to the gaze of the figure in the painting as she brushed in the pines and cedars behind him, the swirl of the snow as it gusted through the trees, across the field. But for all the movement in the background, the figure in the foreground was still. Only his eyes spoke to her.

Her fingers were cramping when she heard, under the moan of the wind and the whisper of the snow, the sound of her locked door opening. A draft of cold air touched the back of her neck as the wind entered, the wind and something more, something she had no name for, but she knew she owed it a debt.

It didn't matter what he was—her imagination running wild, or something out of the wild night sparking her imagination. She was repaying what he had recovered for her from that first moment she'd seen him in the field, just a dark shape in the blurring snow, repaying what had been lost and now regained with life.

The door closed, but she didn't turn around. The painting in front of her was like a mirror and she continued to breathe on it as she finished the last cedar.

Scars

They first met when she materialized on the old Morris chair that his grandmother had left him.

She lounged back against the corduroy cushions, one leg cocked jauntily over the chair's arm. Her hair fell in old-fashioned dark brown ringlets framing an oval face. She was barefoot, dressed in faded jeans and a sweatshirt with a stylized comic book woman drawn on it mouthing a word balloon that read, "I can't believe I forgot to have children." Her skin was darkly tanned, for all that it was the middle of winter, and scrubbed clean—even the soles of her feet. Her best features were her eyes—they were gold and green, almond-shaped and large. Right now they sparkled with barely-contained amusement at his reaction.

"Who...What...?"

His jaw felt slack and he couldn't seem to control it enough to do more than splutter a few words. Every other muscle in his body was as rigid as a steel rod.

"I thought you'd be more articulate," she said.

"You...you just..."

She swung both feet to the floor and leaned towards the couch where he was sitting, one hand proferred. "My name's Suzanne."

He shook her hand automatically. Its warmth and obvious substance just had time to register before she let go and was leaning back in the Morris chair again.

"Well," she said, "I can see we're not going to get very far tonight."

"You…"

"I'm Suzanne," she repeated. "Like in the Cohen song, remember it?"

"Sure. But…"

She shook her head. "This is no good. I'll meet you tomorrow — by the river."

He heard an echo of that Leonard Cohen song —

Suzanne…taking someone down to the river…

— and then she was gone, leaving behind a faint impression in the cushions and a scent of lilacs in the air.

"Jesus Christ," Colin Horne said softly, staring at the empty chair. "I'm losing my mind."

CRSO

Things that made no sense just irritated Colin. By the time a half hour had passed, he'd managed to convince himself that he'd nodded off on the couch and dreamt the whole thing. But the Leonard Cohen reference remained to tease him. He got up and rooted through his albums until he found that 1968 gem, Cohen's first album. When he put it on and that mournful voice came out of the speakers, he felt like he'd fallen into a time warp. It was all so long ago. He could hardly remember that time when poetry was more important to him than anything.

It was in the late sixties. He was just a kid then, in his mid-teens, living a bohemian existence. He'd hated his father. The two of them fought constantly — verbal wars where nobody won. The old man died when Colin was fifteen, but Colin left home and hit the streets anyway, as if he could sense the old man looking at him from beyond the grave. To spite him, Colin lived on the streets with only his poetry and his music to shelter him from the world.

They weren't bad times. A whole generation had taken a long hard look at their parents' values and were searching for an alternative as well. Or just making a statement. Finding themselves. Love-ins and be-ins. Drugs to open up your mind and others to close it down. And there was always the music to point the way.

Dylan and the Beatles. Hendrix and Joplin. And there was always the poetry.

There were a lot of poetry readings in those days — at Le Monde in a church basement on Metcalfe, and at L'Hibou on Sussex. They were both long gone now — the latter's space taken up by trendy boutiques. Colin had read some of his own work in them, but mostly he just listened or took part in that silent communication between printed page and mind. On the road with Jack Kerouac's fiction, Cohen's novel *Beautiful Losers* stuck in a back pocket. Howling with Ginsberg. Lawrence Ferlinghetti. Tuli Kupferberg. Gary Snyder. And Burroughs.

Where were they all now? Some of them gone. But Ginsberg still did the college circuit with his harmonium and that halo of frizzed graying hair. Burroughs never stopped writing. Kupferberg had reformed the Fugs with Ed Sanders for at least one album. Cohen had a new album, too, but you could also see him playing a villain on *Miami Vice*.

That just about said it all. And it summed up Colin Horne's own contribution to the world's literature and his dedication to a bohemian lifestyle as well. Because he hadn't touched his guitar in years. The books in which he'd carefully handwritten his poems were collecting dust on a bottom shelf behind a row of best sellers. He lived in a nice apartment and worked nine-to-five for the federal government, supervising clerks who spent all day checking people's tax forms to make sure they'd put their name and other pertinent information in the proper box.

The A side of the album came to an end with "Sisters of Mercy." There was a click as the tonearm returned to the armrest. Then silence. He was too depressed to listen to anymore. There was no sister of mercy around to offer him any comfort — unless that was what his odd visitor had been.

Suzanne.

Down by the river.

CR&O

Colin went down to Windsor Park after work the next day. It was just past five and the sky was darkening. Staying lighter every night. Winter was ending, though you couldn't tell it by looking out across the frozen Rideau River. There was still some open water, black against the white ice. Ducks swam in it, or dozed off by the edge of the ice, bobbing in the current.

If you kept your attention focused narrowly enough, it was easy to pretend you were anywhere but in a city. You could ignore the vehicles on the bridge where Bank Street crossed the river with four lanes of traffic. The residential streets of Ottawa South behind, or Billings Bridge Shopping Centre and the suburbs across the river, were easy to forget, if you just watched the black water, the white snow and ice, the ducks swimming, the bare limbs of the trees.

He wasn't sure what he was doing here. He didn't really expect to meet last night's midnight visitor, but —

"Hello, sailor."

Colin jumped. "Jesus, you startled — "

He broke off in mid-sentence as he completed his turn. She was back, big as life. Dressed only in jeans and a torn Corey Hart T-shirt, barefoot in the snow. He reached out a gloved hand to touch her shoulder. He had time to feel that she really did have substance, then she moved a step away, smiling.

"What...*are* you?" Colin asked.

From somewhere she produced a plastic bag filled with bits of bread.

"I'm sort of like an ambassador," she said as she began to scatter the bread on the ice. "A messenger."

"From whom?"

"Look," she said instead, pointing at the ducks.

A couple of them had noticed her offering and were waddling across the ice towards them. Suzanne flung out more bread and soon the whole flock was on its way, lurching and wobbling like drunkards across the ice. Their raucous approval of the feeding filled the air.

"I love the way they walk," she said.

Colin touched her arm. "Do you have a message for me?" he asked. "Who's it from?"

She turned at his touch. A sudden oppressiveness filled the air. It lifted the hairs at the nape Colin's neck.

"It's from your father," Suzanne said.

"My...father...?"

She nodded. "He wants you to let him go."

36

"Go? Go where? For God's sake, woman, my father's been dead for almost twenty years. He can't go anywhere."

"That's why you have to let him go."

"There's something not right here," Colin said. "I'm not stopping him from going anywhere. I know things were bad between us when he was alive, but I grew up — you know? I understand now that it wasn't me he was really pissed off with. He had a high pressure job where he had to keep a lot of people happy. There was a lot of stress. It had to come out somewhere and it just happened to come out on me because I was acting like such a little shit at the time. You see? I stopped hating him a long, long time ago."

"I know," Suzanne said. "So now it's time to let him go."

"I don't know what you're talking about."

"Think about it," she said, and then she was gone.

"Wait!" Colin cried. "You've got to tell me..."

Up on the path that wound through the park, following the contours of the river, a couple was standing. They looked down at him, obviously nonplussed at his behavior. The woman had a bag of bread bits for the ducks in her hand. The man took a step forward to stand between Colin and his companion.

Colin's voice trailed off. He felt like a fool, shouting at the air. He had the sudden urge to explain everything to these strangers, but he fought it down. Instead, he trudged off through the snow, making for his apartment. The oppressiveness that had touched him just before Suzanne gave him her message followed him home. It was like a shadowy ghost at his heels, watching his every move. It was like a scar on his soul. Colin knew it wanted something from him, but he didn't know what it was. Didn't know if he had it to give.

CRSO

That night he took Suzanne's advice and stayed in, thinking. He brought out more of the old albums, hoping they would help. Except for a few cuts like "The Jeweler," Tom Rapp and Pearls before Swine didn't stand the test of time. The rest of their music just sounded wimpy. Especially the old ESP albums. ESP...Charles Manson had recorded an album for that label, back before he whacked right out.

37

The night seemed to thicken at the windows as he thought of Sharon Tate's killer. He shivered and put on another album.

The Byrds were better — the early albums when Roger McGuinn was still Jim McGuinn, before he'd "gone to Rio," before Gene Clark quit the band because he didn't like flying. Colin didn't blame Clark. Not when he thought of the roll call of plane crash fatalities. Buddy Holly and the Big Bopper. Glen Miller. More recently, Stan Rogers, Ricky Nelson, Stevie Ray Vaughn...

He took off the Byrds in the middle of "Eight Miles High" and finally settled on Tim Hardin. "Black Sheep Boy." "Red Balloon." "Reason to Believe." They weren't great poetry, but they had an honesty to them. And they helped to keep his mind from morbid thoughts. From the scars of his life. Except that was just what Suzanne wanted him to do. To think. Of the past. Of scars. Of the dead.

Everything he'd told her was true. The relationship he'd had with his father was so bad that they couldn't be in the same room for more than a couple of minutes without fighting. One or the other would pick away at the scabs of a hundred old arguments, until the wounds were open and bleeding. And then they'd shout, each trying to outdo the other. And then the hurting would begin.

But he had come to terms with it. He'd accepted the blame for what he'd done through those bad years. He'd come to understand the stress of the job that his father had been under — tensions that were only aggravated by a son who fought his every word. Colin had moved through and past the pain to discover that his father had been a fascinating stranger that he would now know only through the secondhand memories of others.

Born of a mixed Dutch and Japanese heritage, his father had been raised in Sumatra. He'd been a merchant marine. During the Second World War, he'd been incarcerated in a German prison camp. After the war, he'd emigrated to Canada, working in the Arctic as a bush pilot. The man's whole life had been an adventure. Colin could only be proud of all that his father had been and done. But he would never know him. He would never find out if the two of them could have grown past the anger to respect each other. To be friends.

That was the worst of it. He would never forgive the old man for dying before they'd had a chance to...to...

Colin stared out through the window of his apartment. The night swarmed dark against its panes. It fed the dull ache that had started up between Colin's temples. There was something hungry, waiting for him in the darkness. He stared at the night for a long time, then slowly rose and went into the washroom to get something to ease his headache.

Suzanne was sitting on the edge of the tub, wearing a bright yellow tube top and a pair of faded cutoff jeans. The look in her eyes was sympathetic.

"I've figured it out," Colin said as he shook a couple of Anacin into the palm of his hand. He swallowed them with water taken directly from the tap, then closed the seat of the toilet and sat down on top of it. "It's my resentment—right?"

Suzanne nodded.

"I never really thought about it," Colin went on, "but I guess I've been carrying it for a long time."

"Twenty years."

"That's a long time," Colin said. He gave Suzanne a sharp look. "But what made him wait so long to send you?"

"The newly dead aren't always that ready to go on," Suzanne explained. "Sometimes they'll hang on to anything that ties them to what they knew, rather than take the next step. It's not even fear so much—at least not a fear of what might be waiting for them. It's for what they might become. What they'll lose. Some individuals have such strong personalities that they'll do anything to keep from losing who they are."

"Is that what happens?" Colin asked. "We stop being ourselves?"

Suzanne shrugged noncommittally.

"Can't you tell me what happens? Where we go?"

"There's only one way to find out," Suzanne said, "and it's a one-way trip, Colin. Are you ready to take it?"

Colin shook his head quickly. Neither spoke for long moments.

"Where do you fit in?" he tried then. "I mean, are you a ghost, or did my father...I don't know...did he make you...?"

"I just am," Suzanne said. "I help the dead cast loose their ties to their former lives. And, no," she added, reading his face. "I don't bring them their deaths."

Another silence lay between them, long and drawn out. Finally Colin shifted uncomfortably.

"So," he said. "When can I see him?"

"See who?"

"My father."

Suzanne shook her head. "It doesn't work that way, Colin. You have to just let him go."

"But I want to talk to him. I want to tell him I'm sorry. I want to know what he thinks of me, if we could have been friends..."

His voice trailed off as Suzanne continued to shake her head. Behind her, he could sense a gathering of shadows—that presence he'd sensed earlier, both threatening and patiently waiting. Was that his father? He wanted to call out to it, but something in Suzanne's eyes clove his tongue to the roof of his mouth and he couldn't speak.

"Think about it," she said, as she'd said before, and once again she was gone.

CRSO

After a sleepless night and a morning spent at work where he couldn't concentrate for a moment, Colin left the Taxation Centre early and walked home along the river. He'd bought some dinner rolls at the cafeteria before he left and he stood now where Suzanne had met him the day before, shredding the bread and tossing the bits to the ducks. He felt her presence without having to turn.

"I thought about it," he said.

"And?"

He turned finally to look at her. Today she had her hair up in a loose bun. She wore a loose plaid shirt tucked into a jean skirt. Her feet were still bare. In the snow.

"I can't see him again," Colin said, "because that'll just be something else to hold him here."

Suzanne nodded. "The more commerce the dead have with the world of the living, the less chance they have to go on. And they must go on. If they remain, they haunt the living as ghosts, until finally they fade and simply dissipate. There's nothing left to go on."

"And you can't tell me where they go on to, can you?" Colin asked. "You can't tell me if it's a better place or a worse place?"

"Or even a place at all."

Colin busied himself with the ducks for long moments, shredding the rolls with cold fingers and tossing the bits out to them.

"If he goes on," he said finally, "I'll never know if we...if he would've liked me, will I? I'll never find out if we would have been friends."

Suzanne nodded.

He could call his father back, Colin knew now. He could call back the ghost right this minute and get the answers to all his questions. He could *feel* his father's presence, just waiting for the call. But Colin knew that if he did that, it would doom his father.

Colin was never going to know now, but that knowledge didn't hurt as much as he thought it would. He'd realized last night that this was his one chance to do something positive in the relationship he'd had with his father. With his father's memory.

"I'm letting him go," Colin said softly.

Although he'd made the decision last night, the words still fought to stay in his throat. They came out in a rusty croak, but his companion heard him. She gave his arm a squeeze. Colin continued to feed the ducks. He felt Suzanne go—in the same way he'd been aware of her appearance earlier. Throwing the last of his food to the ducks, he turned to where she'd been standing.

There were no prints in the snow. He might have imagined the whole thing—every one of her appearances. He caught movement from the corner of his eye. Looking in its direction, he saw a tall, middle-aged man in a gray tweed overcoat standing on the pathway that followed the river. The man's hair was black, his complexion dark. He lifted his hand in a slow wave. When Colin responded, the figure faded, gradually, like a Hollywood special effect.

Colin smiled. When a personality was strong enough, who knows what it could do? It could go on, to wherever it was that we all go when we break our last bonds with the world we leave behind, but no matter what Suzanne said, it might be strong enough to leave a message behind before it departed all the same. And not be bound to this world. Maybe the answers to questions were as important to those personalities as they were to the living they left behind. All Colin knew was that a great weight he'd hardly been aware he was carrying until Suzanne had come into his life, had now lifted.

"So long, Dad," he said, and he started for home.

Maybe he'd pick up his guitar when he got back, or try to write something. Suddenly it seemed he had a lot he wanted to say.

We Are Dead Together

The ideal condition
Would be, I admit, that men should be right
   by instinct;
But since we are all likely to go astray,
The reasonable thing is to learn from those
   who can teach.

—Sophocles

Let it be recounted in the *swato*—the stories of my people that chronicle our history and keep it alive—that while Kata Petalo was first and foremost a fool, she meant well. I truly believed there was a road I could walk between the world of the Rom and the *shilmullo*.

We have always been an adaptable people. We'd already lived side-by-side with the *Gaje* for ten times a hundred years, a part of their society, and yet apart from it. The undead were just another kind of non-Gypsy; why shouldn't we be able to co-exist with them as well?

I knew now. I had always known. We didn't call them the *shilmullo*—the cold dead—simply for the touch of their pale flesh, cold as marble. Their hearts were cold, too—cold and black as the hoarfrost that rimmed the hedges by which my ancestors had camped in gentler times.

I had always known, but I had chosen to forget. I had let the chance for survival seduce me.

43

"Yekka buliasa nashti beshes pe done gratsende," was what Bebee Yula used to tell us when we were children. With one behind you cannot sit on two horses. It was an old saying, a warning to those Rom who thought they could be both Rom and *Gaje,* but instead were neither.

I had ridden two horses these past few years, but all my cleverness served me ill in the end, for they took Budo from me all the same; took him, stole his life and left me with his cold, pale corpse that would rise from its death tonight to be forever a part of their world and lost to mine.

For see, the *shilmullo* have no art.

The muses that inspire the living can't find lodging in their dead flesh, can't spark the fires of genius in their cold hearts. The *shilmullo* can mimic, but they can't create. There are no Rembrandts counted in their ranks, no Picassos. No Yeats, no Steinbecks. No Mozarts, no Dylans. For artwork, for music, for plays and films and poetry and books, they need the living—Rom or *Gaje.*

I'm not the best musician in this new world that the *shilmullo* tore from the grave of the old, but I have something not one of them can ever possess, except vicariously: I have the talent to compose. I have written hundreds of manuscripts in honour of my patron, Brian Stansford—yes, that Stansford, the president of Stansford Chemicals—in every style of music. There are sonatas bearing his name and various music hall songs; jazz improvisations, three concertos, one symphony and numerous airs in the traditional style of the Rom; rap music, pop songs, heavy metal anthems.

I have accompanied him to dinners and galas and openings where my performances and music have always gained him the envy of his peers.

In return, like any pet, I was given safety—both for myself and my family. Every member of the Petalo clan has the Stansford tattoo on their left brow, an ornate capital "S," decorated with flowered vines with a tiny wolf's paw print enclosed in the lower curve of the letter. Sixteen Petalos could walk freely in the city and countryside with that mark on their brow.

Only Bebee Yula, my aunt, refused the tattoo.

"You do this for us," she told me, "but I will not be an obligation on any member of my clan. What you do is wrong. We must forget the boundaries that lie between ourselves and the *Gaje* and be united

44

against our common enemy. To look out only for yourself, your family, makes you no better than the *shilmullo* themselves."

"There is no other way," I had explained. "Either I do this, or we die."

"There are worse things than death," she told me. "What you mean to do is one of them. You will lose your soul, Kata. You will become as cold in your heart as those you serve."

I tried to explain it better, but she would not argue further with me at that time. She had the final word. She was an old woman—in her eighties, Papa said—but she killed three *shilmullo* before she herself was slain. We all knew she was brave, but not one of us learned the lesson she'd given her life to tell us.

Sixteen Petalos allowed the blood-red Stansford tattoo to be placed on their brows.

But now there are only fifteen of us, for protected though he was, three *shilmullo* stole Budo from me. Stansford himself spoke to me, explaining how it was an unfortunate accident. They were young, Budo's murderers, they hadn't seen the tattoo until it was too late. Perhaps I would now do as he had previously suggested and bring my family to live in one of his protected enclaves.

"We are Rom," I had said.

He gave me a blank look. "I'm a busy man, Kathy," he said, calling me by my *nav gajikano*—my non-Gypsy name. "Would you get to the point?"

It should have explained everything. To be Rom was to live in all places; without freedom of movement, we might as well be dead. I wanted to explain it to him, but the words wouldn't come.

Stansford regarded me, his flesh white in the fluorescent light that lit his office, small sparks of red fire deep in his pupils. If I had thought he would have any sympathy, I was sorely mistaken.

"Let Taylor know when you've picked a new mate," was all he said, "and we'll have him—or her—tattooed."

Then he bent down to his paperwork as though I was no longer present.

I had been dismissed. I sat for a long moment, ignored, finally learning to hate him, before I left his office and went back downtown to the small apartment in a deserted tenement where Budo and I had been staying this week.

Budo lay stretched out on newspapers before the large window in the living room where Taylor and another of Stansford's men had left him two days ago. I knelt beside the corpse and looked down at what had been my husband. His throat had been savaged, but otherwise he looked as peaceful as though he was sleeping. His eyes were closed. A lock of his dark hair fell across his brow. I pushed it aside, laid a hand on his cold flesh.

He was dead, but not dead. He had been killed at three a.m. Tonight at the same time, three days after his death, his eyes would open and if I was still here, he would not remember me. They never remember anything until that initial thirst is slaked.

His skin was almost translucent. Pale, far too pale. Where was the dark-skinned Budo I had married?

Gone. Dead. All that remained of him was this bitter memory of pale flesh.

"I was wrong," I said.

I spoke neither to myself, nor to the corpse. My voice was for the ghost of my aunt, Bebee Yula, gone to the land of shadows. Budo would never take that journey — not if I let him wake.

I lifted my gaze to look out through the window at the street below. Night lay dark on its pavement. *Shilmullo* don't need streetlights and what humans remain in the city know better than to walk out-of-doors once the sun has gone down. The emptiness I saw below echoed endlessly inside me.

I rose to my feet and crossed the room to where our two canvas backpacks lay against the wall. My fiddlecase lay between them. I opened it and took out the fiddle. When I ran my thumb across the strings, the notes seemed to be swallowed by the room. They had no ring, no echo.

Budo's death had stolen their music.

For a long moment I held the fiddle against my chest, then I took the instrument by its neck and smashed it against the wall. The strings popped free as the body shattered, the end of one of them licking out to sting my cheek. It drew blood.

I took the fiddle neck back to where Budo's corpse lay and knelt beside him again. Raising it high above my head, I brought the jagged end down, plunging it into his chest —

There!

The corpse bucked as though I'd struck it with an electric current. Its eyes flared open, gaze locking on mine. It was a stranger's gaze. The corpse's hands scrabbled weakly against my arms, but my leather jacket kept me safe from its nails. It was too soon for him to have reached the full power of a *shilmullo*. His hands were weak. His eyes could glare, but not bend me to his will.

It took longer for the corpse to die than I had thought it would.

When it finally lay still, I leaned back on my heels, leaving the fiddle's neck sticking up out of the corpse's chest. I tried to summon tears — my sorrow ran deep; I had yet to cry — but the emptiness just gathered more thickly inside me. So I simply stared at my handiwork, sickened by what I saw, but forcing myself to look so that I would have the courage to finish the night's work.

Bebee Yula had been a wealth of old sayings. "Where you see Rom," she had said once, "there is freedom. Where you do not, there is no freedom."

I had traded our freedom for tattoos. Those tattoos did not mean safety, but *prikaza* — misfortune. Bad luck. We were no longer Rom, my family and I, but only Bebee Yula had seen that.

Until now.

ᘓᘓᘔᘓ

I had a recital the following night — at a gala of Stansford's at the Brewer Theatre. There was a seating capacity of five hundred and, knowing Stansford, he would make certain that every seat was filled.

I walked from the tenement with my fiddlecase in hand. A new piece I'd composed for Stansford last week was to be the finale, so I didn't have to be at the theatre until late, but I was going early. I stopped only once along the way, to meet my brother Vedel. I had explained my needs to him the day before.

"It's about time," had been his only response.

I remembered Bebee Yula telling me she would not be an obligation on any member of her clan and wondered if the rest of my family agreed with her the way that Vedel seemed to. I had always told myself I did what I did for them; now I had learned that it had been for myself.

I wanted to live. I could not bear to have my family unprotected.

Many of the legends that tell of the *shilmullo* are false or embroidered, but this was true: there are only three ways to kill them. By beheading. By a stake in the heart. And by fire.

What Vedel brought me was an explosive device he'd gotten from a member of the local *Gaje* freedom fighters. It was small enough to fit in my empty fiddlecase, but with a firepower large enough to bring down the house. Five hundred would burn in the ensuing inferno. It would not be enough, but it was all I could do.

I embraced Vedel, there on the street, death lying in its case at my feet.

"We are Rom," he whispered into my hair. "We were meant to be free."

I nodded. Slowly stepping back from him, I picked up the case and went on alone to the theatre.

I would not return.

ᴄ୫ᴇᴐ

Let it be recounted in the *swato* that while Kata Petalo was first and foremost a fool, she meant well.

Even a fool can learn wisdom, but oh, the lesson is hard.

Death Leaves an Echo

For Dean
who never tires of reminding us
that there's more
than just the darkness

and for Gerda
who taught him that

Our echoes roll from soul to soul,
And grow forever and ever.

—from "The Princess,"
Alfred, Lord Tennyson

ONE

1

If he hadn't been so tired.
If he hadn't been so angry.
There was time for recriminations and regrets, all the time in the world, just not enough time to brake before the Pinto's wheels hit the black ice and the car went sliding off the highway, heading

straight for a bare-limbed elm tree standing there at the side of the road like it was just waiting for him.

He'd passed it hundreds of times before along this stretch of road, never really giving it much thought. It was just there, greening in the spring, ass-bare in the winter. But now all he could think was, why didn't the Dutch elm get you too, you smug bastard? Because the score was coming up fast: elm tree, one; Shiel, a big zero. End of story.

There was time to think of that.

All the time in the world.

We're into slo-mo now, he realized. A tacky video effect. The last scene of a *Miami Vice* rerun, everything slowing down until a freeze-frame, then "Produced by Michael Mann" spread across the screen. Fade to black. Commercial.

But there weren't going to be any freeze-frames here — just a fade to black, game over. He was going to ram that sucker, no question. All he could do was stare at it, his head a jumble of raw terror and the most inane extraneous thoughts a dying man could imagine. Aware of everything, but helpless to do a thing. Hands fried to the steering wheel, knuckles white, as the car took its own head like a runaway horse. A sudden cramp knotting the muscles of his calf as he pumped the brake pedal. Wheels locked, tires sliding on that black ice.

It wasn't like he hadn't known. The traffic report he'd just finished listening to as he left Ottawa had ended with a warning of black ice in outlying districts. But was he paying attention? Not likely. I'll just take the black ice, thanks, and maybe one of those little aperitifs when that elm turns me into pâté.

There was no flash of his life going past his eyes. But he did think of all the late nights he'd been putting in for the past couple of weeks, getting the store ready for Christmas, and then tonight Anderson calling him, telling him he wanted an inventory done tonight after closing hours, no ifs, ands, or buts. The fat prick. It took five hours — four listening to his staff bitch about another late night while he went through the bins with them, another hour on his own tallying up the results and phoning them in.

And the reward? No overtime pay, because he was the manager and on straight salary. But we've got this nice elm tree, wrapped with a ribbon, and it's got your name on it.

The Pinto left the road, hit the ditch with a bone-rattling jolt, and kept going. Slo-mo time still holding fast. It took an hour for the wheels to lock. Another hour to slide the twenty yards or so towards the ditch. Maybe forty-five minutes in the ditch with that elm tree looming up.

All the time in the world.

No time at all.

I want that freeze-frame, he told the elm.

But then the bumper of the Pinto kissed its trunk. The slow-mo was gone now. Everything turned to a blur. Bark spraying. Headlights shattering. The front of the car folding in like an accordion—can you play "Lady of Spain?" The engine coming through the dash to sit on his lap. His head going straight for the windshield.

He had time to think of Annie. His wife. Waiting at home for him because she'd finished work hours ago.

Better me than her, he thought. If one of us had to go, I thank you God for picking me.

Because there was no way he could live without her. He could call up her features without even trying. The big dark eyes. The waterfall of dark curls, half of them going gray though she wasn't even thirty yet. That sweet quirky smile...

His face met the windshield. Skin broke. Blood sprayed. The windshield turned into a spiderweb just before it shattered. And then—

2

"Jesus!"

Michael Shiel sat bolt upright in his bed, eyes flared wide but unseeing, bedclothes clinging to his sweaty body like a second skin. His chest hurt and he was hyperventilating. A headache drummed behind his eyes as though he'd really hit that windshield. He could actually *feel* the glass embedding itself in his face for long seconds after he'd woken.

Just a dream.

Slowly he calmed his breathing, wiped the sweat from his face with an edge of the sheet. His head still ached—a sharp fiery pain like someone was digging around in back of his eyes with a dull knife.

"Jesus," he said again.

Softer now. Voice full of relief.

Still moving slowly, he swung his feet to the floor and padded across the room toward the door. He needed a painkiller something bad. His pace slowed as he reached the door, an abrupt sense of wrongness nagging at him. He turned and looked at the bed.

"Annie...?"

The bed was empty.

He flicked on the light. Not only was the bed empty, but it was just a double, not the king-size that he and Annie owned. There was no old housecoat of Annie's hanging on the back of the door. Her dresser was gone, along with the makeup always scattered across it and her jewelry box. The print she'd bought at the last Ottawa Christmas Craft Fair that hung over the bed was gone too.

But it was still their bedroom. No question. It was the same room he'd gone to sleep in. What was changed was that Annie, and everything connected with her, was gone.

You're still dreaming, Shiel told himself as he leaned weakly against the doorjamb. The headache worsened. I've got to still be dreaming. Because how could she be gone — Annie and everything she owned? Maybe Annie could walk out and leave him —

(no way, absolutely no way, they were still in love after five years)

— but take everything with her without waking him? Exchange their bed for another while he was in dreamland, ready to say a too personal how-do to a great big frigging elm tree?

It was impossible.

He rubbed his face. His head pounded. Wake the fuck up, Shiel, he told himself. But he could close his eyes and nothing changed when he opened them to look around himself again. Annie was still gone, and everything she owned with her. Like she'd never been here. Like she'd never existed in the first place.

He slammed his fist against the doorjamb — the sudden sharp pain momentarily overcoming the raw ache behind his eyes — but all he got for his trouble was a sore hand to add to the headache as it kicked back in with renewed fury.

If I'm not dreaming, he thought, each word slow and settling with frightening clarity in his mind, then I've lost it. It's time for the men in their white coats to come and take me away.

He pushed away from the doorjamb and slowly walked around the bedroom, fingertips brushing the dresser top, the night table, the end of the bed. He recognized the bed. It was the one he used to have in his old apartment on Fifth Avenue before he'd met Annie. The dresser dated from that time, too, but they hadn't traded it in on a larger model like they had the bed.

And Annie's dresser was really gone. There weren't even any indentations on the carpet to show where it had stood.

This was worse than the nightmare that had woken him. A hundred times worse. It was his worst fear come true.

Everybody was afraid of dying. Nobody wanted to bite the big one, though eventually we all did. Every one of us, old and young, big and small, sick or healthy. Some sooner than others, but like taxes, it wasn't something that would ever go away. You lived with it, but it sat way back in your head, on hold. You couldn't do anything about it, so to keep you sane, your mind let you worry about other things instead. Minor annoyances. Less final traumas. Like getting stuck in traffic, gaining a few pounds, having an argument at work, whether or not your relationship was going to last...

Shiel sat on the bed and cradled his face in his hands. Christ, Annie. Couldn't we have talked it out?

A dry sob shook him. One heave of his shoulders. Headache burning at the back of his eyes. Hand still stinging from where he'd hit the doorjamb. Slowly he raised his head.

No way. No way she'd walked out on him. No way it was *possible* for her to have taken all of her stuff while he was lying here asleep. How the hell could he *not* have woken up when the beds were exchanged?

(then what...?)

Either he was crazy, or something weird was going down. Something very weird. And since he didn't feel crazy...What was it Sherlock Holmes used to say? When you have eliminated the impossible, whatever remains, *however improbable,* must be the truth.

Right.

Eliminate the impossible.

Their marriage wasn't on the rocks. In fact, things just kept getting better between them. Maybe back when they first got married, when a hundred and one minor arguments came and went while they were still adjusting to living with each other, it could have been possible. But not now. Christ, he would have *known* if there was something wrong.

(wouldn't he?)

He wasn't dreaming.

(was he?)

He looked around the room, his gaze doing a slow pan. The way things looked — the *absence* of Annie's things — sure made it seem like a dream, but it wasn't likely. You didn't dream headaches like this, did you? You didn't —

Eliminate the impossible, he reminded himself.

So if she hadn't left him, and he wasn't crazy or dreaming, then what did that leave?

Someone fucking with his head.

Shiel stood up. Not Annie. He couldn't believe that of her. But then who? And for Christ's sake, why? It wasn't like he had any particular importance in the general scheme of things. He wasn't a nuclear physicist. He didn't have anything to do with national security. He wasn't important at all. Just an ordinary joe, managing a record store, trying to put the bucks aside to open his own store. Married, no kids, but happily married all the same. Wife worked for Statistics Canada, clerical work, nothing important.

So why would anybody bother to play games with them?

He left the room and wandered through the house that they had bought and renovated three years ago. It was on Highway 4, between Franktown and Perth, which made for a forty-five minute commute since they both worked in Ottawa, but it was worth it to them for the feeling it gave them of living in the country. Not like it was anything particularly special, just an old place sitting on the highway, a nice lot behind it sloping down to pasture land.

He'd had friends whose family had a cottage near Perth where he'd spent a lot of weekends back when he was growing up. He'd passed this place coming and going he didn't know how many times, the whitewashed walls with the paint peeling, untidy lawn. But for some reason the old house had always appealed to him. When it came up for sale, he couldn't believe that all it was going to cost them was the back taxes and whatever it cost them to renovate the place.

He went from room to room, remembering the work they'd done on it — mostly just the two of them — but the place was like a crypt now, every trace of Annie was gone. From knickknacks she'd picked up at some of the local flea markets, to her grandmother's wing-backed chair that was supposed to be standing by the hearth. The chair sitting there now was one he could remember throwing out three years ago — another souvenir from his apartment on Fifth. It had been reupholstered — the pattern of the fabric the same as the one he'd considered for it before he decided the chair wasn't worth the trouble. Not when they had Annie's furniture too.

(Annie)

Not a trace of her left. From the carpet in the dining room to her favorite cast iron frying pan. Whoever'd done this number on him had been very thorough. He pulled aside the sheer in the living room window and saw only the Pinto out in the lane. Her Honda was gone, too.

That was when he started to get the shakes — a trembling that began in his legs and arms, traveling all through him. He wrapped his arms around his chest, shivering, teeth chattering.

(Annie)

Eliminate the impossible.

Fine. Sure. No problem. But *this* was fucking impossible. People didn't just disappear along with everything they owned. How could anybody be that thorough in so little time? How could he not have heard?

He went into the kitchen and took a bottle of Jameson's from the cupboard, pouring himself a shot. The whiskey went down like a small fire, hitting his stomach and sitting there, setting up a dull warm glow. It helped ease the shakes. Not much, but it helped. He poured himself another shot.

Eliminate the impossible?

No can do. We're back to dreaming or the fruit farm, because none of this can be real.

He stared at the amber liquid in his glass for a long moment, then downed it and moved to where the phone sat on the kitchen table. Finger still trembling, he dialed up seven digits, then listened to the ringing on the other end of the line.

3

Back to slo-mo, Shiel thought. The pauses between each ring seemed to last a good ten minutes, the rings themselves were long klaxons that hurt his teeth, but finally the connection was made.

"Hlrmph?"

"Randy. It's Mike."

A long pause ensued, followed by, "You got any idea what time it is?"

"No, I—"

"Three-fucking-ayem, buddy."

Shiel had been working at pulling his thoughts together, wanting to sound sane in the middle of all this insanity. He was going to lay it out the way it had happened, nice and easy—

(slo-mo)

—but it didn't work out that way.

"She's gone," he blurted. "Annie's gone, Randy. I fell asleep and when I woke up, she was gone—along with anything that ever belonged to her."

Another long pause, then, "Annie who, Mike?"

"Don't fuck with me. My wife Annie. Look I know it's late, but—"

"You don't have a wife."

Shiel was staring across the kitchen, looking at the Braun blender on the counter, seeing it, but it wasn't really registering. As Randy spoke, the blender blurred in his sight.

"Randy…"

He couldn't finish. The walls of the kitchen seemed to be closing in on him. His headache was a sharp whine of pain. The receiver shook in his hand.

You don't have a wife.

What the fuck was going *on?*

"Mike? You still there?"

"Yeah," he said dully.

He closed his eyes and could call up Annie's features without even trying. Met her in the late spring of '81, lived together a year before they got married. Church wedding and didn't she look just like an angel coming up the aisle? Married five years.

You don't have a wife.

If it was a conspiracy, then — not only Annie, but his best friend was in on it, too.

"Hang on, buddy," Randy was saying. "I'll be right over."

The connection went dead, the dial tone harmonizing with the whine in behind the back of his eyes. He laid the receiver in its cradle, fumbling it before it went into place.

You don't have a wife.

I'm losing my goddamn mind.

4

"Who was that?" Janet asked sleepily as he hung up the phone.

Randy Sullivan turned to look at his wife where she was lying beside him, head turned away from the light on the night table on his side of the bed.

"Mike," he said. "Sounds like he really tied one on last night."

He drew back the sheet and got out of bed, body still feeling thick with sleep. Janet rolled over to look at him, eyes closed to slits against the light.

"What are you doing?"

"He sounds like he's in really bad shape," Randy said as he put on a shirt. "Said something about his wife walking out on him."

Janet sat up. "But Mike isn't married."

"I know that and you know that, but right now, Mike doesn't know that."

"He's a confirmed bachelor."

"We only report the news, babe. We don't make it."

He tucked in his shirt, zipped up his jeans. Janet shook her head.

"I didn't think he was much of a drinker either," she said.

"He's not. So if he tied one on, it's probably hitting him harder than it would us confirmed alcoholics."

Janet laughed. Between the two of them they were lucky if they could put away more than a pair of beers each in an evening. Her smiled faded.

"You be careful out there. The roads are supposed to be treacherous…"

Randy leaned over to kiss her good-bye. "Yes, Mama. I'll take the pickup."

"And mind you don't wake the boys."

Randy chuckled. Tod and Benjy could sleep through an explosion.

"That's a big ten-four," he said. "Don't wait up for me."

"Just be—"

"Careful. Gotcha."

He closed the bedroom door and walked down the hall, work boots in his hand, pausing only in the bathroom where he had a leak, then reached into the medicine chest and took down the little bottle of valium that the doctor had prescribed to him the last time he'd had a muscle spasm in his back. Could be Mike would be needing something like this to calm him down. Though if he'd been drinking it probably wouldn't be a good idea to mix the two. Still…He put the pill bottle in his pocket all the same.

He waited until he was by the front door before sitting down on the stairs and putting his boots on. For all the way he'd played things down with Janet, he couldn't shake a very serious worry about the way Mike had been going on. He'd never heard Mike sound quite so out of it before. And what the hell made him think he was married anyway?

Annie. Right. Maybe Mike had picked her up in some bar after work last night, brought her home, and now she'd taken off, grabbing herself a few bills from his wallet on the way out.

Only one way to find out.

Shaking his head, he shrugged on the heavy plaid work shirt that was hanging by the door, checked its breast pocket for keys, and headed out to the pickup.

5

The first thing Randy said when Shiel met him at the door was, "You look like shit, man."

Shiel grabbed his arm. "She's really gone—like she never existed."

"Okay. Slow down. Let's get some coffee brewing."

Randy led the way to the kitchen. His gaze fell on the whiskey bottle, then quickly slid away.

"Three shots," Mike said. "That's all I've had."

Randy shrugged. "I didn't say a thing. Grab yourself a seat, buddy, and I'll do the honors."

Shiel returned to the kitchen table while Randy put on some water, got filters out of a cupboard, ground coffee from the fridge. He brought the pot over to the table, along with a couple of mugs.

"Okay," he said. "Tell me about it."

Shiel began with his nightmare, then followed through. Randy listened, getting up once to fetch the kettle when it was boiling and some cream from the fridge. He poured them both a mug and shoved one across the table to Shiel.

"We've been friends a long time, right?" he said. "We go back — what? Ten, twelve years?"

Shiel nodded.

"And I've never shitted you, right?"

This time a shake of the head.

Randy sighed. "So I'm telling it to you straight now, Mike. I don't know any Annie. So far as I know, *you* don't know any Annie — at least not since I've known you. And you sure as shit have never been married."

All Shiel could do was put his head in his hands. The room had become a blur again. The whine behind his eyes sharpened.

"What...what is it then?" he asked in an empty voice. "Am I going nuts?"

When there was no reply, Shiel finally looked up to meet Randy's gaze. There was pain in his friend's eyes, and a very real sympathy, but there wasn't what Shiel was looking for. There was no "April fool, man" — never mind it was the middle of November. No "Guess we can't pull a fast one on you, Mike ol' buddy."

"I don't know what's going on," Randy said.

Shiel bowed his head. "Jesus," he said numbly.

"I don't know what to say," Randy went on. "I can see you believe what you told me, but Christ, Mike. I know you've never been married. Janet knows it. So maybe we're nuts. But I look around this place and I don't see anything different. And like you said — how the hell could anyone switch beds on you while you're fast asleep on one of them? It just doesn't work that way."

Shiel nodded slowly. "You're...guess you're right."

"Maybe if you get some sleep...?"

Sleep. Shiel felt hysterical laughter building up inside him. Sure. My nonexistent wife's disappeared, I'm not playing with a full deck anymore, and I'm supposed to get some sleep? Like it's going to change anything? Like I'm going to wake up and everything's going to be normal again?

"Sure," he managed. "I'll try to get some sleep. Listen, Randy. Thanks for coming over."

Randy fumbled the pill bottle out of his pocket. "You're not supposed to mix this with alcohol, but if you took one it probably wouldn't hurt."

Valium. Right. Veg out.

"Thanks," he said again, taking the bottle. He set it down very carefully beside his coffee mug. "You should probably get yourself on home, Randy. Sorry to get you up with all this...you know...all this craziness."

"That's what friends are for."

"Well, I sure appreciate it."

Randy finished his coffee and stood up. "You sure you're going to be okay?"

You don't have a wife.

(like fuck I don't)

"Yeah. I'll be okay."

He walked Randy to the door and stood there, watching until the pickup's taillights faded in the distance. Then he slowly closed the door.

6

He didn't take any of the Valium. He didn't have any more of the whiskey either. He put the bottle away, poured himself another coffee, then cleaned up Randy's mug and the pot. He felt like he was working under remote control. One part of him trying to put a damper on the screaming fear that whined through his head, wailing on the same frequency as the ache behind his eyes; the other part was a handy-dandy robot, compulsively cleaning up table and counter.

Yo! Get yours today. No muss, no fuss. A little screwed up in the head, sure, but hey. It's only a robot.

He sank into a chair in the living room, sloshing coffee on the rug as he started to get the shakes again. He managed to put the mug down before he spilled the rest of it.

Oh, Jesus. What was he going to do?

There was a book he remembered reading not too long ago. *Communion.* All about how little spacemen, or elves, or who-knew-whats, were experimenting on humans. Taking them away to some shiny place—a spaceship if you went the UFO route, elfland if fairies were more your thing—and checking them out. To fill in the blank time when you were under their control, they pumped up your head with fake memories so that you wouldn't remember where you'd really been, or what they'd been doing to you there.

Guy who wrote it claimed it was true.

But then so did the old ladies who saw Elvis at a séance.

Except what if there really *were* UFOs? What if they'd taken him away and fucked up when they were laying in the new memories they'd left him? Or what if they'd taken Annie and then given everybody else fake memories—like that she'd never existed in the first place?

And they'd just forgotten him.

The scariest thing, he realized as he was thinking about all that, was that he was actually giving it some serious consideration.

You are gone, he told himself. Right off the very very deep end, pal, and maybe you're never coming back. But then he thought of—

(Annie)

—and he knew that real or not, there was no way he'd give up his memories of her. Or stop looking for her. Because she *had* been real. And if she wasn't, then nothing else meant shit anyway.

TWO

1

He fell asleep in the chair, waking up the next morning, stiff and with a crick in his neck. But at least the headache was gone. Only so was Annie. Still gone. And that was because—

(You don't have a wife.)

He squeezed his eyes shut and counted slowly to ten. Backwards. Breathing deep and slow. Trying to calm himself. When he opened his eyes again, he checked the time—just going on to nine—and went into the kitchen to use the phone. She'd have been at work for about twenty-five minutes by now.

He knew the number off by heart and dialed it quickly. The receptionist answered, saying good morning in both English and French.

"I'd like to speak to Anne Shiel, please," he said.

There was a moment's pause as the receptionist went through her directory to track down the name.

"I'm sorry, sir, but we don't have anybody by that name working here."

Shiel swallowed thickly. "Try Anne Lancaster," he said, using his wife's maiden name.

"No one by that name either, I'm afraid," the receptionist replied after another look through her directory.

That shaky feeling returned to Shiel as he sat there at the kitchen table, grip tightening on the phone receiver. He wanted to scream at the voice on the other end of the line, but he kept his voice as level as he could.

"Thanks...thanks very much for your time."

He hung up before the receptionist could reply.

Stay calm, he told himself. It had been a long shot anyway. If Randy couldn't remember her, why would he think they would where she'd worked? But he'd had to give it a try. Nobody said it was going to be easy.

In the back of his mind a voice whispered. Stop playing around, Shiel. Check yourself into the Royal Ottawa now. Let the doctors handle your problems, because your mind's gone, solid gone.

He called the store and got his assistant manager Sarah Talbot on the line. Dedicated Sarah. She looked like she'd stepped straight off the cover of a Sex Pistols album jacket with her spiked black hair, five earrings to an ear, her leathers and studs and torn T-shirts, but she had an overachiever's sense of responsibility that went straight against the grain of her image. He told her he wouldn't be in today, hung up and dug out his address book.

The number for Annie's parents wasn't in it anymore.

He looked the number up in the phone book — J. Lancaster, still at the same west end address that he remembered — and started to dial, then cut the connection and cradled the receiver. No, he'd see them in person, not try to get through this on the phone. He wanted to see their faces when he asked them about Annie, not give them the chance to just hang up on him.

He rubbed his cheek. Shower and shave. Put on some fresh clothes and get out there. Right. Just as soon as he collected the energy to get up.

His gaze traveled the kitchen. So familiar, but everything was changed. Like a familiar picture that someone had taken an airbrush to, erasing something here, something there, leaving gaps and holes that you wouldn't notice unless you were familiar with the photo in its original state. Annie's set of *Country Living* magazines were gone from the rack by the window overlooking the backyard. The cookbooks on the sill had been reduced to only those that he'd ever bought. Annie's collection of antique folk art — the wooden geese, cats and the like, all brightly painted, that had filled the walls, balanced in nooks and crannies...they were all gone.

Shiel laid his head on his arms at the table and stared bleakly into an unseen distance.

Jesus, Annie...

2

He could remember a couple of nights ago, sitting here at this same table with her. She was looking at the newspaper, reading an article about a national cemetery that the federal government was considering in the east end. A number of prominent Canadians had been polled on the idea — from Margaret Atwood and CBC journalist Barbara Frum to research scientist Dr. Gerhard Herzberg — none of whom expressed a great deal of interest.

Shiel hadn't read the article himself — talking about death and dying always bothered him — but it had sparked a conversation between them about what they'd like to have done with their own bodies when they died.

"I guess I'd like to be cremated," Shiel had said.

"And what about your ashes?"

"Oh, you could put them in a jar and keep them by the bed." He'd laughed a little uncomfortably. "Naw, I'm just kidding," he added.

Annie had laughed with him, but then she'd asked, "Why do you say that?"

"I don't know. It'd be a little creepy."

"Do you think I'd be scared of your ghost?"

Shiel hadn't had an answer for that.

"If there really are ghosts," Annie said, "the best thing that could happen to me if you died was for some part of you to come back and stay with me."

But I don't even get that, Shiel thought, still sitting there at the kitchen table, head cradled on his folded arms. I get zip. A big blank void.

You don't have a wife.

He felt like he was caught up in some schlocky AM tune. *Woe is me. My baby's gone and I can't get her back.* Except his baby only existed in his mind. How would that play on AM? *A lot of you folks out there got the same problem? You wake up in the middle of the night and find out you imagined the last six years or so of your life?*

He sat up and shook his head. It —

(Annie)

— wasn't a lie. His wife's features swam in his mind. No way the memories were a lie.

He got up to take his shower, glancing out the front window as he went by it. He caught a glimpse of something through the boughs of the tall scraggly cedar hedge that separated the highway from the front lawn. Sunlight flashed on something metallic. There was a car parked there. Somebody having engine trouble? Maybe a flat tire? But as soon as he opened the front door, the car pulled away.

He ran to the highway, but the car was gone before he could get a clear glimpse of it. Standing there in just a shirt and jeans, feet bare, shivering a little in the cold morning air, he realized that he'd just been handed the first tangible evidence that he wasn't losing his mind. Someone had been watching him, watching the house. There could have been a lot of reasons for it — everything from someone looking to buy a little rural real estate to a thief casing the place — but with Annie's disappearance, it didn't take much for Shiel to put it together.

Whatever the reason, no matter how crazy it made him feel, there *was* a conspiracy going on. Someone had stolen his wife. Taken her away, and along with her, everything that had belonged to her, right down to the memories that other people had of her. To have been so thorough they'd have to have been keeping tabs on him and Annie for a very long time.

I don't know who you fuckers are, he thought, or why you're playing this game with us, but I'm going to find her. And I'm going to find you. Don't even think that I won't. And when I do, you're going to regret the day you ever started messing with us.

The anger that filled him as he went back inside to take his shower felt very good. A lot better than that shaky feeling that had been feeding on him ever since he'd woken up last night to find Annie gone.

3

"Yes?"

John Lancaster looked the same as ever, a tall salty-haired general practitioner who Shiel had often thought bore more than a passing resemblance to Albert Einstein. Annie's father. He hadn't approved when Shiel and Annie had first begun seeing each other and was only won over when he realized that whatever his own personal opinions of Shiel, this was the man his daughter had chosen to be her husband and nothing he could do or say would change that.

Standing on the porch of the Lancasters' west end home, Shiel hesitated for a long moment before replying to his father-in-law's brusque question. There was absolutely no recognition of him in Lancaster's eyes. The man deserved an Academy Award for the performance.

"I'm here about Annie," Shiel said.

"I'm afraid I don't follow you, young man. Annie who?"

Shiel shook his head. "It doesn't work, John. I *know* she's real, so tell me what's going on. For Christ's sake, will you give me something?"

"Give you something?" Lancaster asked, looking confused. "Are you asking for money?"

Jesus, Shiel thought. The man had it down aces. Not a flicker of give.

"Anne Lancaster. Your daughter. I want to know where she is."

"I don't have a daughter, Mr...?" His eyebrows rose questioningly.

"Shiel. Mike Shiel. Your son-in-law."

Lancaster shook his head slowly. "I'm not certain what you're referring to, Mr. Shiel. As I have no children, I certainly don't have any in-laws. I'm afraid I'm going to have to ask you to leave."

He started to close the door, but Shiel stepped forward, wedging his shoulder up against it. "Not so fast, John. I'm serious. I want some answers and I want them now."

"I don't know you and I don't have a daughter, Mr. Shiel."

"Bull!"

"I am trying to be polite, but—"

Shiel wanted to grab him by his lapels and give him a shake. "Look," he said, trying to maintain some kind of calm. "All I'm asking is for you to give me a break, okay? I've been going crazy ever since I woke up and she was gone. If I could just know that she was all right, it'd help. Not much, but it'd be something."

There was a momentary sympathy in Lancaster's eyes, but it was the kind of sympathy one felt for a stranger. The victim of a car accident. Or a skid row bum looking for a handout.

"I'm sorry, Mr. Shiel, but I really don't know how I can be of any help to you."

"Just tell me where she is. Give me that much."

"I don't know who 'she' is. Now if you'll excuse me, I have—"

"Don't cut me off like this!"

Easy, Shiel tried to tell himself. Turn down the volume. But he knew it was all pointless. This officious bastard wasn't going to give him zip.

"You seem to be under some strain, Mr. Shiel," Lancaster was saying, "so I'll forgive you your outbursts, but I really must ask you to leave now."

Shiel stared at him. "Enjoying this, are you?"

"I beg your pardon?"

"Giving me the runaround. I'll bet you just about laughed yourself sick when they came around to put you up to this. You finally get to put the shaft to me."

"You've tried my patience too far. Remove yourself from my—"

"Will you cut the crap, John? I can buy there being some government connection, so that's why they played dumb where she works. I can maybe even buy Randy's stonewalling, though that hurts. But you're going to give me something. I'm not leaving until you do. I mean, don't you care? She's your fucking daughter!"

Lancaster drew himself up straighter. "I don't care for your familiarity, Mr. Shiel, or your crude language. And I certainly don't care to be harassed in my own home. Now either remove yourself from my property, or I'll be forced to have the police come and remove you."

"Fine," Shiel said, stepping back from the door. "Call the cops. I've got a missing person to report anyway. And it's going to look awfully funny when they find out it's your daughter who's missing—the one you claim you never had. So I'll just sit myself down here on your steps and wait for them to come."

"I don't think you'll find things quite so amusing once they arrive," Lancaster said before he shut the door firmly in Shiel's face.

Shiel stared at the door's brass knocker for a long moment, then turned and sat down at the top of the porch stairs. He looked out at the street. This wasn't going any better than it had with Randy, he realized. What was it going to take to break through these people? What kind of a hold did whoever was responsible for it all have over them?

He was still working at it when the blue and white police cruiser pulled up to the curb in front of the Lancaster house.

4

Detective Sergeant Ned Meehan looked up as his partner approached his desk in the squad room at the main police station downtown on Elgin Street.

"Did you pull his sheet?" Ned asked.

Ernie Grier nodded. "No priors. Everything else checks out. He's the manager of the Hot Deals record shop on Rideau, lives out of town—on Highway 4, out near Franktown. Only thing that doesn't fit is his missing wife. He never had one—never been married."

"Psychiatric history?"

"Nada."

"Wonderful. What about the woman — this Anne Lancaster. Does she exist?"

"John and Frances Lancaster never had a daughter and none of the hospitals in town have a record of her birth. No record of public school attendance. Carleton U says no one by that name ever picked up a BA from them or even attended classes. If she exists, it's only in his mind."

"Only in his mind," Ned repeated. "Christ. What do you make of him?"

Grier pulled a chair over to Ned's desk and settled down in it. "I don't know. Seems normal enough except for this business with his nonexistent wife. I feel kind of sorry for the guy."

Ned tapped a pencil on the desk and nodded thoughtfully. "Yeah. I know what you mean." Sighing, he rose from his chair. "Guess I'll go talk to him again."

5

It hadn't yet registered with Shiel that he could be in a lot of trouble.

About all he had going for him was that he'd been polite, keeping his temper in check, when the two uniformed officers had arrived at the Lancaster house. But while it depended on the Lancasters as to whether or not there'd be charges laid against him, there was also the possibility that the detective who'd interviewed him earlier would suggest that he undergo psychiatric evaluation. And if whoever was behind this conspiracy continued to be as thorough as they'd been so far, there was a strong possibility that he'd find himself checking into someplace like the Royal Ottawa whether he wanted to or not.

That's where the crazies went. Off the street where they couldn't do any harm.

You don't have a wife.

Maybe that wouldn't be such a bad idea. Because if he *was* losing it, that'd be the best place for him.

He hadn't been booked yet, or put in a holding cell, but that wasn't to say it wouldn't happen. Right now he sat alone in a small cubicle of a room, somewhere in the labyrinth of Ottawa Police headquarters. The only furnishings were the chair he was sitting on, a table, and another chair across from him. The detective who had interviewed him had brought him a coffee before he left. That was twenty minutes ago. Since then, nothing.

They were leaving him here to stew, he realized. Maybe they were watching him from some hidden camera. Maybe they were in on it —

He shivered. Don't even think about that, he told himself. Things were bad enough as they were, without letting paranoia dig its claws into him. Except was it still paranoia when everyone you knew *was* conspiring against you? Because it was either that, or maybe the aliens *had* landed and for one reason or another, they just hadn't done a good enough job in messing up his head.

Maybe the cops were calling them in right now to finish the job.

Oh, Jesus. Give me a break.

Again, just like last night, what scared him the most was that he was half-serious in considering something just that flaky. He wondered if he should have told the detective about the car he'd seen parked across from his house this morning. All he'd seen then was a flash of red metal. But he'd seen it again today. Just as the cops were pulling away from the curb in front of the Lancasters' place. A red Toyota followed them downtown. Same color of red as the one out by his place.

He hadn't been able to make out much of the driver — the guy was wearing a baseball cap with the brim pulled low and shades — except that he was clean-shaven. But he had memorized the license plate number.

Should he give it to the cops? Or was he really pulling at straws? Who was to say the person owning the Toyota didn't just live down the street from the Lancasters and happened to be going downtown at the same time?

Paranoia was saying it wasn't.

There's no such thing as coincidence, he remembered reading somewhere once. Only connections you haven't figured out yet. He wasn't sure if he bought that. Christ, he wasn't sure of anything anymore.

When the door opened, he looked up sharply, heart drumming, but it was only the detective coming in again. Round two.

"So what's the verdict?" he asked, trying to keep his voice light.

The detective sat down across the small table from him. "We've checked on this Anne Shiel, nee Lancaster."

"And?"

"She doesn't exist." *You don't have a wife,* Shiel heard in harmony to the man's words. "The Lancasters have no children. We checked with all the hospitals, plus the public school you said she attended, Carleton U, and Stats Canada. No one's ever heard of her."

"But *I* remember her," Shiel said. "I remember six years of being with her. Am I nuts?"

The detective studied Shiel's face. "I don't know, Mr. Shiel. What do you think?"

I think it's all bullshit, Shiel wanted to tell him. I think you're screwing me around just like everybody else is. I think maybe I am nuts. Christ, I just—

"I don't know," was all he said. "The memories seem so real."

The detective nodded sympathetically. Ease off, Shiel told himself. You don't want to be put away right now. Not until you know the truth. For Annie's sake, as much as your own.

"So what happens now?" he asked.

"The Lancasters aren't pressing charges and we've got no reason to hold you. But I want you to promise me you'll leave them alone— and that goes for Stats Canada and anybody or anyplace else where you might think to go looking for this...ah, woman. I don't want to see you in here again, you got me?"

What if she was your wife? Shiel wanted to ask, but he just nodded his head.

"I understand. I'll let it go."

"You do that." The detective rose. "Come on. I'll get you out of here."

6

The brisk November felt clean in his face as he stepped out of the police station onto Elgin Street. Someone had brought his car here from where he'd parked it on the Lancasters' street. He got in, dutifully put on the seatbelt since he was sitting right here in front of the copshop, and started it up. Looking back at the glass doors and windows that walled the Elgin Street side of the building's foyer, he saw the detective standing there, still watching him. Putting the car in gear, he gave the detective a nod and drove off.

The detective lifted a hand, but his expression never changed.

Once he was on Elgin, driving north, Shiel realized he didn't know where he was going. Or what to do next. Forget it. That's what everybody was telling him. Randy, the cops, even a part of himself.

You don't have a wife.

"Shut up," he told the voice inside him that kept repeating those words. "Just shut up."

Not five blocks from the police station, he pulled onto a side street and parked. Getting out, he fed some change into a meter, then headed for the public phone he'd spotted on the corner. He'd promised not to go see anybody else looking for Annie, but he hadn't said anything about calling.

All the numbers he wanted were missing from his address book. They were all Annie's friends — or people he'd met through her. He looked them up in the phone book then tried them, one by one.

"Hello, Cathy? This is Mike here. Mike Shiel. Annie's husband. What's that? Annie Lancaster. What? Oh. I guess I got the wrong number. Sorry to have bothered you."

They all went the same.

He stood there, leaning his head against the glass, staring out at the street, trying numbers until he ran out of change. Finally he hung the receiver in its cradle and went back to his car. There was a parking ticket sitting under the wiper.

"Thanks a lot," he muttered as he stuffed it into his pocket. "I really needed this."

A woman walking by gave him an odd look. He nodded to her, but she quickened her pace and hurried by.

Right. Start talking to yourself like all the rest of the loonies do. Is that how they end up in rags and on the street? Part of their life disappears and they fuck up the rest of it looking for the part that went missing?

It could happen to him then. All too easily. Because he couldn't see himself going back to work and serving customers like nothing had happened. What no one seemed to understand was that *everything* had happened to him. Nothing could be the same again. Not with Annie gone.

He got into his Pinto and looked around himself. No red Toyota. He hadn't seen one the whole time he'd been in the phone booth either. He checked the time. Past noon. The bars were open.

Might as well start my new life out right and get plastered, he thought, because there sure as shit isn't anything else I can think of to do right now.

You don't have a wife.

Damn straight. Not anymore. But I had one, pal. I don't care what anybody says. I had Annie. Someone took her away. Someone's cleaned the slate on her life like she never existed. But I knew her. She's real to me.

Gaze blurring, he rubbed his eyes on the sleeve of his jacket and drove away, north again on Elgin, heading for the Market and all its bars.

THREE

1

Halfway through his first beer, Shiel realized that coming here had been a mistake. He was in the Lafayette on York Street in the Market. It was one of the oldest taverns in the area, a serious drinking establishment that bore about as much resemblance to the trendy singles bars that had been springing up in the area in the last few years as a mongrel dog did to a purebred prize winner. They shared a certain genetic makeup, but you'd be as apt to find a yuppie in the Laf as you'd find any of the welfare cases in here sipping wine in one of the polished chrome and glass places over on William Street.

Yeah, Shiel thought, I fit right in. Just another loser. Except the people in here shared a certain camaraderie from which his sports jacket and clean jeans excluded him. And he wasn't a drinker anyway. Never had been. All sitting here was going to do was swap his AM "My Baby's Gone" blues for the twang of a Merle Haggard tune.

*Oh, I'm a trucker cowboy and the spacemen stole my red-hot momma, uh-*huh.

He played with his beer bottle, widening the circle of its condensation on the tabletop, and thought about the detective who'd interviewed him. The thing he hadn't been able to explain to the cop was, if he was making all this up, then how come he knew the names and addresses of all these people that Annie had known? It wasn't just a matter of picking names at random from the phonebook. He'd *known* the people—never mind that they didn't know him. Knew where they lived, what they did.

So was he turning psychic as well as psychotic? What do you say, Mr. Policeman? You got a reasonable explanation for that one?

He couldn't blame the detective, though. The guy'd just been doing his job—and being very pleasant about the whole thing, when you came right down to it. If Shiel had been behind the counter of Hot Deals and someone came in off the street to lay this kind of a trip on him, he'd have ushered the guy out the door just as politely, but firmly. He'd have laughed about it with Sarah or whoever else was on the floor at the time, and then forgotten about it, only pulling the memory out the next time he and some of the other record people in town got together and started swapping loony tune stories about the weirdos they got in their stores.

And what about the guy? If it was real for him—what the hell would he do?

Come down to the Laf and get plastered, probably.

Shiel took another swig of his beer.

"Want a Penny for your thoughts?"

Shiel turned to the source of the voice and blinked. Standing beside him was a woman as out of place in the Laf as he'd be in a corporate boardroom. Long blonde hair, deep blue eyes, with the kind of figure that would turn heads for two blocks down any street. Her features weren't classically beautiful—striking rather. The kind that made a billboard model look too bland.

She was wearing a black flounced skirt and a cream camisole under a stylish red leather jacket, dark stockings and high heels. The sort of woman that the beer companies liked to pretend would fall all over you if you just drank their brand of beer, but not the kind of woman you found in a place like this.

"I think you've got the wrong guy, lady," he said.

And besides, I never pay for it, he added to himself. Maybe he was being unfair, but what else would someone looking this good

73

be doing in the Laf? No matter how hard the city council and the cops tried to clean up the area, the Market was still hooker heaven.

She laughed and sat down at his table. "I know what you're thinking, Mike."

"How the—"

She laughed again—a nice warm laugh, deep and throaty. "You don't remember me, do you?"

I should, Shiel thought. How did you forget someone who looked like she did? But he shook his head.

"1973? Philemon Wright High School?"

This happened to Shiel all the time. People knew him, but he could never connect a name to their face, where he knew them from, *if* he even knew them half the time. It came from working in retail for so many years. You saw such an endless parade of faces that they all blurred together after awhile. Usually he just played along— "Right, yeah, now I remember"—but he wasn't up to bullshitting today.

"Sorry," he said. "My mind's in neutral."

His lack of recognition didn't seem to faze her in the slightest. "I'm Penny Moore. I used to take the same North American Lit class as you did—with Mrs. Armstrong. We used to call her Phyllis Strongarm—remember?"

Penny's name still didn't ring a bell, but Shiel found a smile. "Yeah, I remember. She was a bulldog about homework. So what's—"

"A nice girl like me doing in a place like this, offering myself up for your thoughts?"

Shiel was surprised that she'd actually pulled a genuine laugh out of him. "Something like that."

"I was out shopping and happened to see you come in. I..."

She ducked her head for a moment, hiding a blush, Shiel realized, behind that mane of blonde hair. When she lifted her head again, she had a funny look in her eyes.

"This is going to sound really stupid," she said, "but I used to have a terrible crush on you back then, so when I saw you come in here a few minutes ago I—oh, I don't know. I just wanted to say hello. To see how you were doing."

"I can't believe I don't remember you."

"Well, I looked pretty different back then. I guess I'm what you'd call a late bloomer. I was pretty dumpy looking, my hair was this stringy mouse brown…"

Her voice trailed off. Shiel just sat looking at her, unsuccessfully trying to match her up to one of the kids he'd gone to high school with.

"God, you must think I'm really dumb."

Shiel shook his head. "No. I'm just…going through some weird shit lately."

"Oh. Well look, maybe this isn't a good time to be bugging you then. I can just—"

Shiel caught her hand as she started to rise. "No, please. I could use some company." He let her hand go. "Only not in here. I thought I'd come in and drown my sorrows, but I'm not much of a drinker, and this place is just making me feel worse. Do you feel like having some lunch?"

"If you're sure I won't be getting in your way."

Shiel shook his head. "Like I said, I could really use some company."

Penny gave him a bright smile. "Where do you want to go?"

"I don't know. Why don't we just cruise up William Street and see what appeals to us?"

Shiel was startled when they reached the sidewalk and Penny took his arm. You've got a wife, he told himself. Someone stole her, but you've still got a wife.

Penny turned to him, a guileless look in those deep blue eyes. "What have you been doing all these years?" she asked.

2

"You were never the kind of guy that I thought would ever have sorrows that needed drowning—at least you weren't in high school."

They'd found a place on William Street. It was after the lunch hour rush, so they'd managed to get a good table by the window and a waitress who was still running on her morning charm. A couple of hours earlier, in the chaos of the lunch crowds, it might be a different story, but right now they almost had the place to themselves. The coffee they ordered came immediately, the sandwiches hot on its heels.

"I'm kind of surprised myself," Shiel said.

"Want to talk about it? I'm an expert on hard luck stories that make good."

"You look good, but I still can't place you. Are you sure we were in the same class?"

"Oh, I'm sure." She pulled her hair tightly back from her face. "I used to wear this ponytail that was drawn back so tight it hurt. Plaid skirts way past my knees with white blouses. Carried a sucksac. Brown plastic rims on my glasses..."

She let her hair go and it fell back around her neck in a thick wave the way hair does in shampoo commercial, but not before a younger image of her flashed in Shiel's mind. He remembered her now. Take away the contacts and makeup, lose a few years and put those pounds back from the right places to the wrong ones, drop the dye job and perm, and you had her. Penelope Moore. The class lump. The only girl in school who never attended one dance in the company of a member of the opposite sex. Shuffling through the halls, clutching her briefcase of books, glasses askew, shoulders stooped, looking at the floor...

"You remember," she said dryly.

He glanced up, embarrassed. "Guess we gave you a pretty hard time."

Penny shook her head. "You never did. You never spent any time with me, but you never dumped on me either. I had this fantasy back then that you'd ask me out, but..."

She gave a shrug that was meant to be nonchalant, but Shiel caught the tension in it. Some hurts you never lost, no matter what you made of yourself, no matter how things changed.

"Looks like you're doing pretty good for yourself now," he said.

It seemed an inadequate thing to say, but it was all he had. Remembering her now, thinking about how it must have been for her, he could empathize with how she must have felt.

"Oh, I worked at it," Penny said. "Believe me. But back then I just...let myself go, I guess. It wasn't all my fault. I didn't have a father — did you know that? I mean, my mother was never married and I've no idea to this day who my father was."

Shiel shook his head. "I didn't know."

"Well, it's not such a weird thing these days, maybe, but back then it wasn't something you talked about at all. When we moved to Hull my mother just let on that she was a widow and you can bet I never told anybody about it. Didn't have anybody to tell. Anyway, she ended up getting some strange ideas — my mother. Didn't want what had happened to her to happen to me. So she made sure that I always wore clothes that weren't in fashion, wore the ugliest glasses she could get me, kept my hair back, fed me lots of sweets so that I'd put on weight...

"She meant well, I suppose. She just didn't want any guy to think I looked good enough to take out, much less make out with. What happened between her and my father, having me on her own — her parents basically disowned her — it left her very bitter, but very tough as well. She made do and she made sure that I didn't stray from the straight and narrow."

"Jesus."

Penny smiled. "I can handle it now — talking about it, thinking about it — but it was tough back then. I didn't help myself at all either because I ended up with this real lack of confidence problem. When it came to self-esteem, I didn't even know what the concept meant, much less try to build it up in myself."

"I'm surprised you're not more bitter."

"What good would it do?" Penny asked.

Shiel nodded. "What turned you around?"

Her face clouded for a moment, but then that bright smile was back again. "Had a moment of satori, I guess. I was finished with high school, planning to go to university — in Ottawa, naturally, because my mother would have died if I'd left home to go live on campus somewhere. I was feeling probably the lowest I'd ever felt when I finally realized that the only way I was ever going to be happy with myself, with life, was if I did something about it.

"So I did."

"And very successfully," Shiel said. "I mean, looks shouldn't be everything, but — "

"If you can't be happy with yourself — and in this society, that means looking good as well — then nobody else can help you. I worked hard at it, Mike, but it was worth it. Not just because I could look in the mirror and be happy with the woman I saw looking back at me, but because I really did learn that we *are* what we make ourselves — nothing more, nothing less. It's easy to blame somebody else for your problems — like I used to blame my mother, or the kids that made fun of me — but when you get right down it, you've got to start with yourself.

"I did go to college — in Toronto. I took up acting for awhile, appeared in some commercials, then I got into journalism, worked on a few of the dailies in T.O. and now here I am, starting a new job with *The Citizen* on Monday morning."

She grinned suddenly. "God, listen to me. I must be boring you stiff."

Shiel shook his head. "Not at all. I'm just feeling guilty, I guess, for the way I was back then — ignoring you and everything."

"You and everybody else. But don't be, Mike. The change had to come from —" she laid a hand against her chest " — inside me first, I think."

"But if you'd had some friends, it wouldn't have been so hard."

"It's always hard," Penny said. "But enough about me. What have you been up to? Now that I've dumped the whole sad story of my life on you, I'd think fair was fair."

She looked at him expectantly and Shiel hesitated. Her frankness had startled him, but it deserved to be met with honesty. Only how was he supposed to talk about what had happened to him?

You don't have a wife.

"It's my wife," he said finally. "Annie. She..."

And then it all came out in a rush. The loss and his fear that he was losing it, how his memories felt too real to be false, but so far as the world was concerned, Annie Shiel — or Lancaster, take your pick — had never existed. Except in his mind. What was left of it.

3

"Maybe I can help you," she said when he was finally done.

"You *believe* me?"

Her lips formed a moue. "Well...I believe that you believe." Shades of Randy, Shiel thought. *I can see you believe what you told me...* The difference being that Randy had known Annie. Should have known her. But he didn't.

Shiel shook his head slowly. "How could you help?"

"With the paper."

"You're going to do a feature on me? 'Man Loses Imaginary Wife?'"

Penny laughed. "I'm sorry," she said, touching fingers to her lips. "No. Nothing like that at all. I'm thinking of the Tombs—the records section."

"It won't do any good. I told you, the police have already checked everything—hospitals, schools, the works."

"Okay," Penny said. "But let's say somebody *is* erasing all evidence of your wife's existence—"

In other words, Shiel added, let's pretend you're not crazy.

"—they can only go so far. They can erase records of her birth and schooling, her job history, but the paper? How can they wipe out facts that are right there in plain black and white?"

"I don't know," Shiel said. "They've been doing pretty good so far."

"Still it's worth a try. C'mon. Do you have a car?"

"Yeah."

"Well, let's take a drive out to Baxter Road and see what we can come up with."

Shiel paid their bill and led the way to where he'd parked the Pinto. The parking meter had run out but there was no new ticket under the wiper. What do you know, Shiel thought. A small miracle.

"Was your wife ever in the news?" Penny asked as she buckled up her seat belt.

"We're just ordinary folks," Shiel replied. "Ordinary folks don't get in the news unless they win a lottery or go head on with a tree in a car crash."

Last night's nightmare flickered momentarily behind his eyes. Head on with a tree. Right. He shivered, remembering. If Penny noticed, she made no comment.

"There'd be a birth announcement at least," she was saying. "Maybe she was in the Girl Guides and had her picture snapped at a parade, or some guy took a shot of her with the year's first tulips or something like that. Filler stuff—you know? Human interest."

Shiel shook his head. "Nothing like that—not that I know of."

"We'll just have to see what we can come up with then."

The conversation turned to her life in Toronto as Shiel took them up Nicholas Street, then onto the Queensway, heading west towards the newspaper's building in the west end. They arrived at Baxter Road, parked and made their way down to the Tombs. Two hours later they came up for air and stepped back out into *The Citizen*'s parking lot, no further ahead than they'd been before.

Shiel kicked at a crumpled-up coffee cup and watched it skitter between the cars.

"Nothing," he said bitterly.

He shoved his hands deep into his pockets and stared out across the parking lot. Over on the Queensway, the traffic whipped by. He felt as though each passing vehicle was taking another piece of his sanity with it. Someone got into a car a few rows over, started it up and drove away. Everyone had someplace to go, something to do — probably someone to do it with. They hadn't lost an imaginary wife. Oh, no. They lived in the real world.

Penny touched his arm. "I'm sorry, Mike."

"That's okay. It was a long shot, right?"

"You shouldn't just give —"

"Up?" he demanded. He turned to look at her. "Why not? Why the fuck not?" He tapped a finger against his head. "Something's wrong in here — that's the real bottom line. I remember Annie. I remember six years of living with her. But she never fucking existed, did she? I mean, how could she be real and there not be one single trace of her anywhere?"

"I...I don't know what to say."

Shiel's anger drained from him, leaving him with only an emptiness inside. He looked away again, back to the traffic on the Queensway.

"There's nothing to say," he said finally. "Listen, thanks for trying. I really appreciate it. Can I give you a lift somewhere?"

Penny looked as though she wanted to take it a little further, but finally she just nodded. "I left my car at home," she said. "Maybe you could give me a lift back to my place?"

"Sure. What's the address?"

4

"Do you want to come up for a coffee or something?" Penny asked when they pulled up in front of her apartment building just off Elgin Street. "You probably shouldn't be alone right now," she added as he hesitated.

"You want to take a chance hanging around with a crazy?" Shiel asked, not really joking.

"You're not crazy," Penny said. "C'mon. The place is a mess— I'm still in the middle of moving in—but it'll be better than driving aimlessly around, which is pretty well the sum total of what you've got planned, right?"

Shiel hesitated a moment longer, then killed the Pinto's engine.

"Not crazy, huh?" he muttered as he joined her on the sidewalk.

The world had taken on a surreal quality for him ever since they'd left *The Citizen*'s parking lot. At first it was just a spacey feeling inside him. But now, getting out of the car, everything was beginning to lose its definition. There were no more sharp edges—just images bleeding into each other. Looking up the street, it was hard to tell where one building began and another ended. Street signs were unreadable. Pedestrians were patches of color—all except for Penny. She was crystal clear—the center of a camera's focus, everything blurring around her.

"You don't act crazy, anyway," she said.

How about deluded? Shiel wondered as he followed her inside the building. Paranoid might fit, too.

You don't have a wife.

Led astray. Hoaxed. Hoodwinked. Fucked over. Oh, Annie...

"C'mon," Penny said.

She stood at the door of her apartment and ushered him inside. The place *was* a mess. Shiel stood looking at the array of cardboard boxes and suitcases, some still sealed, others opened with their contents spilled about the room. The place was a blur of shifting colors and images.

"Here," Penny said. She led him to the couch and cleared off a stack of books so that he could sit. "I'll go put the water on."

It didn't seem like more than a moment—a flicker of time, no longer than that between one blink and the next—before she was back, pressing the handle of a steaming mug into his hand. He looked up at her. She was still perfectly in focus.

"It's funny," he said. "Every time I look at you, I think of commercials. Beer commercials, shampoo commercials..."

Penny smiled. "Should I take that as a compliment?"

"Definitely."

The coffee was hot going down and it helped shift the room into better definition. Objects began to regain their edges.

"Well, maybe you're just remembering some of the ones I've done."

"Maybe."

Suddenly Shiel had nothing to say. What am I doing here? he asked himself. I should be out looking for Annie, trying to track her down...Sure. And where did he start? Christ, he'd done everything he could think of. Maybe he should just go home and wait for her. Maybe they'd be bringing her back. Maybe whoever had taken her was just borrowing her and if he just waited long enough at home, she'd come walking in the door, hair tossed back, wearing that funny little smile of hers.

But who was he kidding? She wasn't coming back.

You don't have a wife.

He couldn't face going back to the empty house. Couldn't face looking at all the empty places where her things had been.

Looking up suddenly, he found Penny's gaze on him and he wondered how long the silence had been dragging on.

"You want some help sorting this stuff out?" he asked, taking in the clutter with a wave of his hand.

Penny nodded. "That'd be great."

5

The afternoon got swallowed by the task. They ate microwaved frozen dinners around seven, worked some more, and then all of a sudden it was going on eleven and Shiel knew he had to get going.

"Listen," he said, standing up from the bookcase where he'd been organizing Penny's hardbacks. "I really should be heading out. Thanks for everything."

"You don't have to go," Penny said. "I mean, you can sleep in here — on the couch," she added as his brow furrowed.

Shiel didn't want to go home — not to that empty house — but it didn't seem right to be staying here for the night either.

"I've been taking up enough of your time," he said. "I'm sure you've got better things to do than to baby-sit a basket case like me."

82

"To tell you the truth," Penny said, "I've enjoyed having the company. I don't know anybody in town anymore, and I certainly don't feel up to making the rounds of the bars just to find some company."

"Like the Lafayette..."

She laughed. "I *told* you. I just happened to see you going in."

Shiel held up his hands, placatingly. "I know, I know. I was just teasing."

"Stay, Mike. You'll feel better waking up in a place that's not so...empty."

That doesn't hold so many memories, he thought. False memories, maybe, but memories all the same.

"Okay," he said. "Thanks, Penny. You've been a real lifesaver."

An odd look came over her features for a moment, then she smiled and gave her hair a shake back from her shoulders.

"Let's see what kind of bedding we can round up for you," she said.

Shiel stood by the bookcase and watched her leave the room. There was something going on with her, he thought. Something she hadn't touched on yet, for all that she'd pretty much spilled her whole life story to him. She'd never really said why she'd left Toronto, he realized. Maybe she'd come out of a bad relationship. Maybe she was missing somebody too. Not like he was — but that wouldn't make it hurt any less.

Just a couple of lost souls, he thought.

When she came back in, her arms laden with bedding, he tried to help her make up a bed for him on the couch, but she wouldn't have any of it.

"Go ahead and use the bathroom," she said. "I'll have this ready for you by the time you're done."

He borrowed her toothbrush, washed his face and stared at his image in the mirror. Should've packed a razor, he told himself as he ran a hand along his cheek. Well, it wasn't like he and Penny were going to make out or anything. By the time he was finished in the bathroom, the couch was made up.

They had an awkward moment when he returned, both of them standing there like a couple of kids saying goodnight on a first date, then Penny stepped over to him. She kissed him lightly on the cheek.

"Pleasant dreams," she said.

Then she was gone, the bathroom door closing behind her.

Right, Shiel thought.

He turned off the light and stripped down to his briefs, then climbed in between the sheets on the couch. He put his hands behind his head and stared up at the unfamiliar ceiling.

Dreams.

Dreams he didn't need, pleasant or otherwise.

But they caught up with him all the same.

6

He was floating in a hospital room—suspended up around the ceiling while spread out below him was a scene straight out of a hundred TV hospital dramas.

The room was a small windowless cubicle in an intensive care unit. The bed took center stage, wooden planks at head and foot, metal bed rails lifting eight or ten inches up along the sides. Lying in it was the star of the show.

The patient was heavily bandaged—not just his body, but all around his face as well. In a coma. He was hooked up to a ventilator—two clear corrugated plastic hoses joining in a Y-shape, then a tube going down his trachea. A green power light glowed steadily on the machine. It made a hissing sound as it pumped air through the tube.

Behind the patient's head, mounted on a wall to the side of the bed, was a monitor to read his heartbeat. Wires ran from the monitor to circular leads that were stuck on his chest, the machine giving off a beeping sound in time with the patient's heart rate. The shelf at the head of the bed held swabs, suction tubes and resuscitative equipment. Taped to the wall near the monitor was a tongue depressor.

A bag on an IV pole fed him a saline solution through an intravenous site on his wrist. His drug dose was relegated by an IVAC pump that sounded like a mouse caught in a wall every time it started up—an annoying scratchy sound. Another bag filled with hyperalimentation—it looked the color of fluorescent urine—fed him through a larger catheter attached to his neck.

The clean antiseptic smell of a hospital filled the air.

That's me, Shiel thought, floating up there by the ceiling, looking down at the coma victim.

He saw the elm tree rear up through his windshield before it shattered, felt the engine fall out onto his lap...

If I hadn't been dreaming, if I'd survived that crash, this'd be me lying here.

And then he realized that he was dreaming again. A serial dream. *The Mike Shiel Show.* Last night, when we left our hero, he was going head on with a great big frigging elm tree and it was game over, folks. But look, you tuned in tonight and our hero's doing okay. Look's like a vegetable, sure, but he's not dead yet. The ratings are still good, so why change the name of the show?

Dreaming. Jesus. But everything looked so real. The smells, the sounds, every detail crystal clear...

Wake up, he told himself. Get out of here.

But then the door opened and Annie walked in. Not the Annie he knew—full of life and always ready with a smile. No, this Annie looked like the world had just dumped everything it had on her. Her shoulders were stooped, her face pale, eyes shot with red, heavy circles under them. She moved slowly as she took a seat beside the bed, bowed her head.

"Annie!" he called to her.

She never looked up. Didn't hear a thing.

"Annie!" he cried louder. "Jesus, Annie. Look up here!"

She didn't so much as blink.

"ANNIE!"

Now she looked up, but it was only because the door had opened again. A tall man in doctor whites entered the room.

"Mrs. Shiel?" he asked.

Annie nodded.

"The nurse said you wanted to see me."

"I just wanted...she said you'd tell me if there's...if there was any news..."

"We're doing the best we can. Mrs. Shiel. All we can do is hope."

"But what's going to happen to him? What's the—" she swallowed thickly "—bottom line?"

The doctor hesitated.

"I have to know."

"We don't like to get into worst case scenarios..."

"Please."

Shiel felt his own chest tighten, hearing the desperation in his wife's voice. That's not me, he wanted to shout at her. I'm up here, Annie. For Christ's sake, if you'd just look up—

The doctor cleared his throat. "We're not sure how much cerebral damage there's been. We've got the X-rays, of course, but until he comes out of the coma, we can't really tell."

"And if there's no brain damage? What aren't you telling me?"

Again the doctor hesitated.

"Please. I have a right to know, don't I?"

"There's an almost ninety-five percent chance that he'll be paralyzed from the neck down."

The doctor launched into some medical terminology that Shiel didn't hear. The room was fading on him. He could feel himself being pulled away. A final flash of conversation rose up to him.

"I'm sorry, Mrs. Shiel," the doctor was saying. "We're doing the best we can, under the circumstances, but..."

"ANNIE!" Shiel cried.

But then the room was gone and Annie with it. He was out of that dream—

7

—and into another.

This time *he* was lying on that hospital bed, the tubes and wires connected to him. The same antiseptic smell in the air. The same hissing, beeping sounds. Not in a coma, but not able to move a muscle all the same.

Oh, Jesus, he thought, remembering what the doctor had said. Now he was going through the paralysis that the doctor had been telling Annie about.

Quadriplegia.

Wake up, he told himself. You don't need this shit. The real world's fucked up enough, without laying this on yourself.

But he might as well have been talking to one of those whitewashed walls that surrounded him on four sides. He lay there and time ticked away—slo-mo, molasses time—then finally the door opened. He turned his head, wanting it to be Annie, but it was a nurse. Long blonde hair, in clean starched whites.

No. Not a nurse. It was Penny. Dressed up in a nurse's uniform. What the hell was go—

"And how are you today, Mr. Shiel?" she asked him.

Her smile was bright and chipper, her voice husky.

"A-annie," he said. His mouth was dry, with a chemical taste in it. "Where's my...?"

"Oh, I don't think we'll be needing her right now—do you?"

She started to unbutton her blouse.

This isn't real, Shiel thought as the blouse fell to the floor behind her. She unzipped her skirt and stepped out of it, then undid the clasps of her bra, her breasts spilling free as she pulled it away from her body and dropped it on the floor as well. She wasn't wearing any panties—just a garter belt to hold up her white stockings.

"Did you ever wonder why they call this section 'special care?'" she asked him.

She had pulled back the sheets and was on the bed now, the blonde hair falling free around her shoulders, her breasts bouncing with the movement as she knelt beside him.

"Annie," Shiel tried again. "I want my wi—"

Penny laid a finger against his lips. "Hush now," she said.

She pulled aside the blue smock he was wearing and stroked his penis.

I don't want this, Shiel thought. This is bullshit. Some teenager's clichéd wet dream. A hardcore fantasy that'd be called something like *Naughty Nurse* if it was up on the silver screen. He didn't need this kind of shit. But his penis swelled under her attention, betraying him. It seemed as though the paralysis hadn't stolen everything from the neck down.

Penny touched the tip of his penis with a long nail, drawing it slowly across the skin, then she lowered her head, taking its length into her mouth.

And Shiel couldn't move. He couldn't get away. He heard the heart rate monitor quicken its beeping. He lifted his head to look down the length of his body. Penny turned to look at him, her tongue gliding the length of his penis. It glistened in the fluorescent lighting, wet with her saliva.

I don't—Shiel began.

The room flickered suddenly.

Snap.

He wasn't in the hospital any longer, but lying on the couch in Penny's living room. She was still there, tonguing his penis.

Snap.

He was back in the hospital. Now she was licking her fingers, bringing them down to moisten the lips of her vagina. He shook his head at her, but she only smiled. Rising up on her knees so that she was straddling him, she drew his penis inside her and slowly lowered herself until she'd swallowed the whole of its length. She squirmed, then began a steady up-and-down motion, her breasts jostling, the smile never leaving her features.

Snap.

In her living room. He was still paralyzed, Penny still riding him. Her eyes were half-closed now, rolling back to show their whites. Her breath was quickening.

Snap.

In the hospital. She lowered herself so that the weight of her upper body rested on her elbows, one on either side of his shoulders, hands cupping his face, breasts pressed in close against his chest, the up-down motion quickening.

Snap.

On the couch. Penny pulling him out of her. Clasping his slick penis in her hands, she pumped it, up and down.

Shiel closed his eyes. Annie's features rose up in his mind.

I'm not a part of this, he told her.

But the orgasm was building up inside him all the same.

Snap.

On the bed. He ejaculated in a wet sticky shower all over his own stomach. Penny smiling. Putting her uniform back on.

"Sleep now," she said as she wiped him off and then pulled the sheets back in place. "You need your rest."

She stroked his brow, then left the room. Shiel turned his head, only his gaze able to follow her.

"Sleep," she repeated from the doorway, then she stepped through, closed the door, and he was alone in the room again.

He stared up at the white ceiling above him. Tears blurred his sight. All he could think of was Annie and his inadvertent betrayal of her. Guilt festered inside him, making him nauseous. She deserved better than him. She deserved somebody who'd remain faithful no matter what — dream or not.

He looked down the length of his useless body — brain still booted up, but all the body's motor workings on hold. Permanent hold. He couldn't feed himself. Couldn't turn the pages of a book, if he'd wanted to read. Couldn't even take a leak by himself, not without it running all down his thighs and pooling under him, trapped between the plastic undersheet and the fleshy prison of his body.

You're dreaming, he told himself. This is just some bullshit dream.

But the hospital seemed all too real. And when he remembered — (Annie)

The way she'd looked, all broken apart, sitting there by his bed. He knew what she'd been feeling. If that had been her lying there, and him looking at her —

Sweet Jesus. She deserved somebody who could walk. Not a slab of meat, lying here in a hospital bed where anybody could just walk in and help themselves to a serving. They could do anything to him that they wanted to, he realized. Anything. And he wouldn't be able to do a thing about it.

His helplessness rose in a blinding wave, a scream riding its crest.

FOUR

1

When Shiel woke, the only part of his body that he could move at first were his eyes. They snapped open and his gaze followed the plaster swirls on the ceiling directly above him. He had a momentary panic — it hadn't been a dream, it *had* been real — but then he moved his hand, his arm, his leg. Relief washed through him. He sat up slowly, the bedding bunched around his waist, and rubbed his face.

Jesus. He couldn't live like that — locked into a bed, his body a prison. No way he could live like that. And seeing Annie, hurting so bad...Her face filled his thoughts, but then the memory of the second dream spilled into the first — Penny stripping off her nurse's uniform — and he felt guilty all over again.

What the hell was happening to him? he asked himself as he unwound the bedding from around his waist.

That was when he saw that his briefs were lying on the floor. He'd gone to bed wearing them — he was sure of that. But now they lay on the carpet, staring up at him with what looked like an incriminating smirk in their bunched folds. His penis had a post-coital feel about it — a thickness, a certain satisfaction...

He turned to look at the hallway that led to Penny's bedroom. He'd been dreaming, hadn't he? Or had Penny come out in the middle of the night and he'd only *thought* he was dreaming?

There was something very weird going on here.

He retrieved his briefs and put them on, then his trousers. Barefoot, buttoning up his shirt, he walked down the hall to Penny's bedroom. The door was slightly ajar, silently opening wider at his touch. Penny lay on her bed, sleeping in the buff, the sheets pulled down enough so that Shiel could see most of her upper torso. His gaze touched, then held a beauty mark on the upper swell of her left breast.

He knew that mark. He'd seen it only inches away from his face. Last night. In a dream.

He backed slowly away from the room, closing the door until it was exactly the same as it had been when he'd entered. Returning to the living room, he sat down on the couch and held his head between his hands. He could feel veins pumping in his temples. His heartbeat accelerating. Unreasoning panic gibbering at the edges of the morass that had become his mind.

Was anything ever going to make sense again?

He took a few deep breaths, steadied himself. Think it through logically, he told himself. If you made love with someone as gorgeous as Penny — would you forget it?

But he didn't forget it. That was the problem. He'd thought he was dreaming, but in reality he'd only been half-asleep. Dreaming that they were getting it on while they really were.

He couldn't accept that. He felt guilty enough having dreamed he was cheating on Annie, without it being real. The birthmark had to be coincidence. But there were just too many frigging coincidences.

He remembered: *There's no such thing as coincidence – only connections you haven't figured out yet.*

He got up and began to pace back and forth. Okay. Connections. If someone was pumping him up with false memories, couldn't his thinking he'd made it with Penny be one another of those same false memories? Possibly. Except that left him with the big one: Why?

Maybe he'd imagined that birthmark on Penny's breast. Well, he sure as hell wasn't going back into her bedroom for a second look. Who knew what she'd think if she woke up with him standing over her bed.

He found himself in front of Penny's bookshelf, the one he'd filled last night. Her high school yearbooks caught his eye and he pulled one down. *The Falcon.* Flipping through it brought back a hundred memories of Philemon Wright High School. Old faces, old friends. He stopped when he came to Penny's picture.

Yeah, he remembered her all right. But there was something about her...

He tried to snag the thought, but it wouldn't come. It had all been so long ago and he'd lost touch with pretty well everyone he'd hung around with back then, for all that he'd done little more than move across the river from Hull to Ottawa. Trying to remember much about someone he'd never really known was just an exercise in futility.

"Mike...?"

He closed the book with a guilty snap and turned to find Penny standing in the hallway, looking sleepily at him. She was wearing a fluffy terrycloth bathrobe and still looked like a dream. Nothing like the mousy girl in her yearbook photo.

Would you mind pulling that bathrobe down to your waist for a second so that I can check you out for birthmarks? he thought.

"Do you always get up this early?" she asked.

"Well, you know," he said with a shrug. When you're losing your mind, it's hard to give it a rest, he added to himself. "Things to do, people to see."

He replaced the yearbook as he spoke.

"But it's seven-fifteen, Saturday morning," she said.

"I've got to get to work. Busy day, Saturday, what with Christmas coming and everything."

"Do you have time for breakfast?"

Shiel shook his head. Returning to the couch, he started to put on his socks and shoes. Penny sat down in a chair across from him, pulling the bathrobe around her legs when it began to fall open.

"What's the matter, Mike? You seem very...distant this morning."

What the hell was he supposed to say? I had a wet dream about you last night — or at least I think it was a dream. Can you show me your left boob, or tell me if we got hot and heavy on the couch here a couple of hours ago?

"Just bad dreams," he said.

Fuck you, a voice spoke up in the back of his head. Back behind that sissy guilt, you were enjoying yourself.

"About Annie?" Penny asked.

He nodded. "Yeah. Partly. I dreamt I was in a coma and she was sitting by my bed in intensive care, crying her eyes out. Doctor said I was going to wake up paralyzed from the neck down."

"They go away," Penny said. "The dreams, I mean. It just takes a little while."

Shiel gave her a considering look. There was something odd about the way she'd phrased that.

"What do you mean, they go away?" he asked.

Penny looked confused for a moment, but recovered quickly. Was that a flash of guilt he'd caught in the back of her eyes?

"Bad dreams," she said. "They're supposed to be our way of working through daytime stress, and you've got to admit you're going through a lot of stress right now." She stood up. "Just let me make you something before you go — you can't head off for a day's work on an empty stomach."

Shiel watched her leave and slowly shook his head. Jesus, the paranoia cut deep. Here she was, just trying to give him some moral support, and now he was starting to suspect her of Christ knew what. Lighten up, Shiel.

He followed her into the kitchen where she was breaking an egg into a frying pan. There was already bread in the toaster.

"Listen," he said. "I'm sorry if I'm spacing out on you. It's just all part of this bad news weirdness I'm going through."

"That's okay. I understand."

"You're being a real good friend."

92

And let's not forget those hot dreams she'd providing you with, that nagging voice in the back of his voice added.

Penny turned from the stove to look at him. "I want to be your friend," she said.

2

This is the perfect domestic scene, Shiel thought as he sat down to breakfast with Penny. Only problem was he had the wrong woman sitting across the table from him.

It made him wonder…what would have happened if he'd never met Annie…if before that day he'd gotten together with Penny? Married her out of high school, maybe — that would make them a couple for going on to fifteen years now. Would he still be working at Hot Deals, or would he have gotten a straighter job? Maybe they'd be living in the suburbs, blanding out with their neighbors, their station wagons and two-point-four kids. Maybe they'd be divorced by now.

It was a ridiculous chain of thought, because it broke down right at square one. He'd never even paid any attention to Penny back then. And he *had* met Annie. He wouldn't be who he was today without her. The changes in him had been subtle, but he knew he was a much better person now than he ever would have been if he'd never known her.

That was why he *knew* she was real. He was here, the way he was, because of her. No matter how much the evidence piled up, he refused to accept that she was just some figment of his imagination. No way, pal.

He looked up to find Penny's gaze on him. The expression in her eyes was hard to read. There was an empathy present, but something else that wasn't as easily readable.

"I guess I must come off sounding like a real loser," he said, "the way I've been carrying on since we met yesterday." He found a smile to take some of the self-deprecation from his voice, but it wasn't one of his best.

The smile she gave him back had a bittersweet turn about it. "No," she said. "You just sound like you loved your wife very much."

"Love," Shiel said. The way she'd used the past tense sent a anxious pang straight through his heart. "I still love her."

"I know you do."

"Were you ever married?" he asked.

Penny shook her head. "I only ever cared — really cared — about one guy, but he went and married somebody else."

"And nobody since then? I can't believe you're not settled down with someone."

"I've just never met anybody else that was right. See — that's part of the problem with my big 'improve Penny' program. It was great for my self-esteem, but it makes me wonder if my mother wasn't partly right all along. All the guys who hit on me only want one thing. The nice guys, they just figure they don't have a chance because I've *got* to have a boyfriend, or I'm too glamorous for them...

"And it's all just nonsense. I'm not into glamour — not really. I keep in shape, I try to look my best, because I don't want to slide back into what I was like when I was a teenager, but what I'm really looking for is someone to settle down with, a guy that I can have some quiet times with. Good times. The kind that when you grow old together you can look back on and know that you didn't waste your life."

Like his life had been with Annie.

Her expression was so wistful that Shiel's heart went out to her. Wasn't it weird, the game plan that the world handed you? She didn't get anywhere as a kid because she looked like a lump; now that she looked like a million dollars, she still couldn't get anywhere. He knew that if he wasn't already married —

Something in her eyes stopped him cold. It was almost as though he could hear —

(You don't have a wife.)

— her saying it.

He pushed his plate to the center of the table. "I really have to get going," he said. "Sarah's never going to forgive me if I leave her to fend for herself another day — especially not on a Saturday. This close to Christmas it really gets to be a zoo in the store."

"I'll try to come up with something while you're gone," Penny said. "To find your wife, I mean. Would you like to have dinner here when you've finished work? Nothing fancy."

"I..." Shiel rubbed a hand along his unshaven cheek. "I really should get back to the house tonight." And get away from you for a bit, he realized. He'd been spending so much time with her that it was beginning to feel like they were having an affair. Especially after last night's dream.

"I'd like to see your place sometime," Penny said.

Shiel glanced at her. The opportunity for him to make the invitation lay wide open. No pressure. She wasn't pushing it. But it was there all the same.

He thought about the empty house. About being there by himself tonight while the hours dragged by. Weighing that against last night—

(it was only a dream—she's only trying to help)

"Okay," he said. "You're on for dinner. And after that we can take a run by the place."

And if it gets all hot and heavy? that nagging voice asked.

Screw you, he told it. I can control myself. She's just a friend.

That's how it always starts, the voice told him before he shut it off, refusing to listen to it anymore. Penny looked so happy—how the hell was he supposed to turn around and just tell her no again? No can do.

But he thought of Annie.

He hoped she'd understand. He just couldn't face being alone. Being alone made it too easy to feel like he was losing it. Dropping off the deep end and there was no bottom.

"I've got to go," he told Penny.

3

With typical incongruity, Sarah was listening to CBC's *Morningside* when he arrived at the store. There she was, all decked out in her punker's gear—black leather jeans, a torn Jake Hamer Band T-shirt, spike heels, her hair a crest of black spikes—listening to Peter Gzowski talk about the intelligence of Guernsey cows. Shiel loved the show himself. Gzowski was laid-back and charming, interviewing anyone from politicians and movers in the business world, to authors and people dealing with social issues; always intelligent, but never highbrow. But Sarah and Guernseys?

When he came in she was leaning on the front counter, listening intently, lips dark with black lipstick shaping a smile as Gzowski read from a letter in which a Maritime farmer was talking about how his Guernsey was easier to train than his dog. Sarah looked up as Shiel stepped through the door.

"Hey, what do ya know? The prodigal son returns."

Shiel locked the door behind him. There was still a half hour before opening time, but Sarah already had the lights on, the cash float in the till, and was ready for business.

"How'd it go yesterday?" he asked.

Keep it normal, he told himself. If you keep things on an even keel maybe everything'll straighten out. Annie'll call up around noon for their daily phone chat, or maybe drop in to have lunch with him in the back.

Is that too much to ask?

"Wild times, Mike. You missed a lady who came in and got all pissed off because we don't carry vacuum cleaners."

With the bins and racks loaded with the latest albums, cassettes and CDs, it was hard to miss what the store sold.

"You're kidding—right?"

"Uh-uh. Had to escort her out, still ranting away at me. We can, and I quote, 'expect a call from the Better Business Bureau.'"

"Wonderful."

Sarah gave a negligent shrug. "Ah, she'll never do it."

"Here's hoping. Are the orders ready to go out?"

"All except for the imports—I thought you'd want to do 'em yourself."

Shiel nodded. "I'll go phone them in," he said as he started for the rear of the store. He paused at the door leading into the back with its "Employees only" sign. Under it someone had scrawled "So keep out or die."

"What's *Morningside* doing on today?" he asked. "It's Saturday."

"I was too busy yesterday morning to listen to it so I taped it up."

"Figures."

Shaking his head, Shiel went into the back room. He spent the next half hour until opening time on the phone with the Hot Deals warehouse in Toronto, then settling down to do yesterday's cash report and the bank deposit. Throwing himself into his work, he

96

managed to keep his head clear of everything except for the tasks immediately at hand. When Sarah unlocked the front door, he joined her on the floor. Clipboard in hand, he stood by the counter and went over the import order with her.

The *Morningside* tape played on behind them, but Shiel wasn't really paying attention to it. It was only when Sarah went to help the first customer of the day, then he actually heard what Gzowski was talking about. Teenage suicide.

Shiel felt as though a giant hand had slipped inside him and was tying his intestines into a knot. His legs went weak and he had to sit down on the stool behind the cash. It was that or fall down.

Suicide.

Now he remembered.

4

He was ten months out of high school and already working in records, except he was just a clerk at one of the old Treble Clef stores — a local company that got swallowed by the big franchises that eventually moved in from Toronto and took over Ottawa's music retail scene. Round about then — at the front end of the seventies — there was nothing cooler than working for Treble Clef. He was at the Sparks Street Mall location, changing the sale prices on the weekend specials back up to their regular value, when who should walk in but Billy Simmons.

In high school, Billy had a real bad rep. Acting tough, talking tougher. He came from Deschenes, which had always produced the toughest kids around, and more than one teacher predicted that if — and it was a big if — he ever finished high school, he'd be in prison within a year. Instead, he'd ragged them all. Came out with top marks and ended up with a scholarship.

Shiel had hardly recognized Billy when he came in that day. The greased back hair was gone; so was the leather jacket. He was wearing jeans still, but they were clean — not a grease stain on them — and a preppy Ottawa U sweatshirt.

"Jesus, look at you," Shiel had said. "What happened? You look like someone dropped you in a tub of Mr. Clean."

"I'm moving up in the world, Mike m'man. Don't want to grow old in a record store, making minimum wage for the rest of my life, like some folks I know will."

"Yeah. Up yours too."

Billy grinned — that shit-kicking look of his that Shiel knew so well. They'd hung around some in high school, enough so that Shiel took his lunch early to go shoot the breeze with him for awhile. A lot can change in that first year after high school. With ten months behind them, they had enough gossip to catch up on to last them through Shiel's whole lunch hour.

"Ran into Patty down on Rideau Street the other day," Billy said. "Panhandling — can you believe it?"

"I thought she got accepted at Quelf. Wasn't she going to be a veterinarian?"

Billy shrugged. "Guess she just dropped out."

"Well, she's doing better than Andy Rothwell. He's become a Scientologist. Stopped me on the street the other day and tried to convince me to come in for a personality test."

"Yeah. Or what about Penny Moore?"

"Who?"

"The Lump — remember her?"

"Oh yeah. What about her?"

"Swallowed a bottle of her old lady's sleeping pills and bit the big one."

"She's dead?"

"That's what usually happens when you stop breathing. First time she was ever a success at something, I guess. And remember Candy?"

"I'm supposed to forget her?"

The conversation had gone on, Penny Moore's suicide just one more statistic, covered in a line or two, then forgotten.

Dead.

Swallowed a bottle of her old lady's sleeping pills and bit the big one.

Penny Moore was dead.

So who the hell had picked him up at the Laf yesterday and taken him home with her?

Shiel leaned weakly on the counter, his features ashen. He felt like there was a great pit opening up under his feet and he was tottering on the brink of it, ready to fall in.

"Mike?"

He lifted his head and turned slowly to look at Sarah, dimly realizing that she'd been calling his name for some time. Staring at her, seeing himself in her worried features, he could tell just how weirded out he had to be looking right now.

"Are you okay?"

Sure I'm okay. Just spent a day and a night with someone who's been dead for a couple of decades, my wife's —

You don't have a wife.

— vanished without a trace, like she never was, but yeah. I'm okay. It's just the rest of the world that's fucked up. I'm right in step.

"I..." He cleared his throat. If only things would stop spinning. "I've got to lie...down..." Before I fall down. Into that hole that's sitting there under me, ready to suck me away.

Sarah helped him into the back room and onto the battered old couch that they kept back there. Shiel stretched out, hugging himself to stop the shakes that were trying to pry him loose from the tenuous grip he had on reality and drop him down that bottomless pit.

"Mike, I...There's no one on the floor..."

He managed to lift a hand to wave her back out. "G-go on..."

"Do you want me to call an ambulance?"

He shook his head — almost couldn't stop, once he'd started. "I just need — to lie d-down..."

Plainly worried, Sarah backed out of the room. The store was filling with customers.

Oh man, Shiel thought, pressing his face against the back of the couch. *Who* is fucking with my head?

5

It took Shiel a half hour to get himself straight again. When he finally felt he could stand up without the world shifting too much underfoot, he went into the bathroom and washed his face, drying it with a paper towel. He stared at his reflection.

You're a mess, he told it.

But he was down now. The shakes were gone. His head wasn't spinning any more. Not that anything made any more sense than it had previously, but he felt that he could face the questions once more without his body betraying him. Survival of the beast, he thought. That's what made the human animal so successful — given time, it could adapt to just about any situation.

Even this. Even losing it.

He went to his desk, pulled the telephone closer and dialed 411. Once he got Penny's new listing from information, he started to dial her number, the cradled the receiver.

Hang on, he told himself. Let's do this one step at a time. What's calling her going to prove? She was real. Flesh and blood. Maybe she wasn't Penny Moore — just someone who bore a certain resemblance to the girl they'd called the Lump in high school and was playing a game with his head — but she sure wasn't going to admit that. Not on the phone. Maybe not even in person.

He needed some facts. Something to back up his memory. Because his memory wasn't proving too reliable these days. Not as the evidence piled up to make a mockery of everything he believed was true. He remembered having a wife, but everywhere he turned that was denied. So why should it be any different with this conversation he remembered having with Billy?

Never mind that he *knew* he was remembering it right.

Never mind that he had a wife.

Let's play the game by its new rules.

Putting on his jacket, he stepped out onto the floor. There were a half-dozen customers looking through the bins — nothing Sarah couldn't handle until their part-timer Lawrence came in at noon.

"Mike...?" Sarah began when she saw him.

"I'm okay. Really. Listen, I hate to do this to you two days in a row, but I've got some shit to work out. Do you mind holding the fort for awhile?"

"Sure. Larry's going to be in soon and we've already got the orders phoned in. But, Mike, you don't really look so good. Are you sure — "

"I don't feel so good, either."

"If there's anything I can do..."

"You're doing it already."

He gave her a shaky grin and left the store before he had to do any more talking, taking with him the chorus of the song playing on the store's sound system as he went. Toyah doing a version of the old Martha and the Muffins hit "Echo Beach." That line about it being far away in time followed him all the way to the public library on Laurier.

FIVE

1

Two hours of staring at a microfiche reader in the library's reference section on the second floor finally gave him something. Not what he was looking for, but something. It was buried in the local news section of a newspaper dating from the early seventies — just a paragraph with a small headline that read "WEST QUEBEC GIRL ATTEMPTS SUICIDE."

Attempts.

That was the operative word here.

So maybe he hadn't heard Billy correctly. It was an old memory, after all. Years had gone by. Except, if he closed his eyes and concentrated, he could almost hear —

First time she was ever a success at something...

— Billy's voice.

Where do you draw the line? he wondered. The facts were there on the screen in front of him. Penny hadn't died — she'd only tried to kill herself. He'd met her, talked to her, spent some —

(carnal)

— time with her. What was real and what wasn't? What he remembered, or what he could see sitting there on the screen with his own eyes? Flesh and blood. He remembered the touch her hand —

(stroking his penis)

— as she took his arm coming out of the Laf yesterday. That was real. Those words on the screen in front of him — they were real, too.

Echo beach. Far away in time.

If it wasn't for Annie...if it wasn't for this conspiracy that was spiderwebbing all around him, trying to convince him that she'd never existed...he wouldn't even be questioning this. But there was Annie. She was real.

He pushed himself abruptly away from the fiche reader, startling the two students seated on either side of him, and fled the reference room, the library.

But the questions weren't as easily escaped. Walking the streets, with the first winter bite of the wind knifing through his thin jacket, those questions followed him, relentlessly dogging his steps, howling at the walls he was trying to build up in his mind to keep them out. He walked aimlessly, until he found himself outside of Penny's apartment building. He walked around back to its parking lot and found the red Toyota parked in a resident's spot. Same license plate number. Had to be Penny's car. Why wasn't he surprised?

Shoulders hunched against the wind, he set off eastward until he reached the canal and couldn't go any further. He stood at the railing, hands deep in his pockets, and stared down at the debris and mud that had been left behind when the canal was drained for the winter. Pieces of people's lives. Castoff things. Nothing important. Pop cans. Garbage. Things that were used once, then thrown away.

Something's using me, he thought. Right now, somebody's got a game plan and a scorecard, and I'm just a piece they're shuffling around the board. And when they're done with me, I'll be down there with the rest of the crap that gets thrown away when its served its purpose and no one's got any use for it anymore.

Question was, when?

A better question was, why?

"Mike?"

He wasn't surprised to hear her voice come from behind him. He didn't turn around, didn't bother answering.

It was funny. He'd gone through a lot in the past few days—from questioning his sanity, through rage and a sorrow so deep that it couldn't even begin to be appeased. But right now he didn't feel anything. Just an emptiness inside, an emptiness so profound it sucked the meaning from words. It made all conversation pointless.

"Mike?"

But there was power in a name.

(Annie)

Too much power.

He turned finally, slowly. With his back against the rail he looked at her. How had she done it? How had she made his wife disappear — literally erasing Annie from existence?

There was no answer in her features. She stood a few feet away, still gorgeous, but her shoulders were hunched — the body language wailing defeat — and her eyes had a desperate haunted look about them that Shiel understood, though he couldn't have put it into words. It was a look of loss. Loss of hopes. Of dreams. Of meaning.

"We have to talk," she said.

What should we talk about? he wondered. Free Trade? The new Eurythmics album? Holiday plans?

"Please," she said. "Come back to the apartment with me. It's too cold to stand here and talk."

Shiel regarded her for one more long moment, then he shrugged and pushed himself away from the railing. He fell in step beside her, hands still deep in his pockets, but there was a tingle in them now — an answering voice to the red rage that was slowly bleeding into his mind.

He thought of Annie.

He thought of what he'd been put through.

He thought of how it would feel to have that smooth white neck of Penny's between his hands.

Of squeezing her throat until her skin went blue and those pretty eyes began to pop from their sockets.

Of what she thought she could possibly say to make any of this any better.

So he let her take him home again.

In case she could bring Annie back.

But the anger continued to bleed into his mind until he was walking through a red haze.

And his hands ached, their muscles were so tense.

For the first time in his life he understood what it felt like to want to kill someone.

It was a kind of madness, that feeling. And the worst thing about it was that it felt so sane.

So terribly, terribly sane.

2

When they reached her apartment, Shiel sat down on the couch, not even bothering to remove his jacket. He slouched on the cushions, hands clasped on his lap, knuckles whitening. He watched Penny remove her coat, tracked her as she went into the bathroom. After a few moments, he heard the toilet flush. The water run in the sink. When she came back, the high-class model look was gone.

She sat down opposite him, slouching as well. She wore faded jeans and an old sweatshirt. Behind the glasses she was wearing now, her eyes weren't nearly the same startling blue he remembered them to be. Tinted contacts, he realized. But even without her makeup, in the old clothes and with her glasses on, she was still a knockout.

She could have anyone she wanted, he thought, so why was she messing around with him?

"Where's Annie?" he asked.

She just sat there, chin down, looking at the carpet.

"I said..."

She looked up and his words trailed off. She looked so lost that his heart went out to her — never mind what she'd been putting him through.

"That's not so easy to explain," she said.

His empathy for her fled. Wrong answer, he thought. His gaze settled on her neck. The muscles of his hands spasmed slightly. He clasped them tighter.

"Don't dick around with me, Penny. Before we get into anything here, I want her back."

"It's not that simple."

Shiel half-rose from the couch. What the hell had she done with his wife? All he could envision was Annie lying in a grave somewhere. The red haze grew stronger. His hands twitched.

"If you've—"

Her own hands lifted, palms outward. "Your wife's fine. No one's hurt her. No one's touched her. She's not even...involved in any of this, except peripherally."

Her words deflated him and he sat back down on the couch. Why should I believe you? he thought. But he did. Something in her tone, something in her face, told him that her plain statements were nothing but the truth.

Annie was safe.

She existed. He wasn't going crazy. Everything was going to be fine.

The red haze left his gaze. His hands stopped twitching.

But looking at Penny, he knew that however true it was that Annie was all right, nothing was going to be fine again.

"What the fuck's going on, Penny? Why're you playing around with my head?"

No anger in his voice now. Just weariness. He was so tired. After being wound up so tight, for so long, he was starting to unravel now.

"I never meant to," Penny said. "I thought it was all going to be so simple. I always loved you, Mike — back in school — but you never paid any attention to me. You didn't hurt me like the others, but I didn't exist for you either."

"You sure picked a hell of a way to get my attention."

How come I'm just sitting here, talking with her? he asked himself. Like we're just shooting the breeze, going over old times. Like nothing's the matter. How come I'm not shaking her until she tells me what I've got to know?

"This," Penny said, waving a hand limply about the room in a gesture that took in more than their immediate surroundings, "isn't here to get your attention. I tried that before — right after high school — only I didn't do too good a job of it."

"The suicide attempt."

"It wasn't an attempt, Mike. I thought my mom'd come home and find me in time, but she was late from work that day. I thought she'd take me to the hospital and have my stomach pumped and I'd be okay. I thought you'd hear about it and know I was doing it for you and you'd come to me. I was reaching out for you, Mike."

Shiel heard Billy Simmons's voice in his head, underpinning what she was saying.

Swallowed a bottle of her old lady's sleeping pills and bit the big one.

"I really blew it that time," Penny was saying.

Billy hadn't been talking about attempts.

First time she was ever a success at something, I guess.

"I was reaching out," Penny said, "but in the wrong direction. Instead of getting you, I got this." Again that gesture, encompassing the apartment and more. "An echo of what I could have had if I hadn't been such a fool. If I hadn't been so scared to just do something with myself, for myself. If I hadn't been such an emotional cripple."

"What...what are you saying?" Shiel asked.

But he knew.

Swallowed a bottle of her old lady's sleeping pills...

She was saying—

...and bit the big one.

—that it hadn't been an attempt.

"This is bullshit," he said.

Penny shook her head. "I killed myself, Mike. I thought it was all I had left. I didn't mean to die. I just...just wanted to make a statement, I guess. I was reaching out, but there was no one there to reach out to. I went too far. And then it was too late."

Shiel just looked at her. Things were becoming clear now.

Easy, he told himself. Don't spook her. You're not nuts, but she sure as shit is. He didn't know how she'd done it, but she'd managed to spirit away Annie, Annie and everything that gave evidence to the fact that she'd ever been real. He had to play her easy now, get Annie back. And then...

The anger was back, but it had no real focus. He pitied her too much to want to hurt her. He had to get Annie back and then get Penny some help.

"You don't believe me, do you?" she said.

Shiel didn't know what he was supposed to do in a situation like this. Did you play along, or did you try to talk some sense into them?

"You...you've got to admit—it sounds a little off the wall."

That sad smile of hers was back. "I know what it sounds like, Mike. I know just what you're thinking: This girl needs help. I've got to act real nice to her and get my wife back, and then see that she's put away in a nice padded cell where she can't hurt anybody else, herself included.

"I wish it was true."

Was he that transparent? Shiel wondered.

Penny was watching him, her eyes brimmed with emotion, the sad smile faltering. Shiel tried to swallow, but his mouth was too dry to collect any saliva.

"I...I don't believe in ghosts," he said finally.

Penny nodded. "Ghosts and phantoms—it all sounds so flaky, doesn't it?"

Shiel just looked at her. He couldn't believe they were having this conversation.

"But this whole world is a ghost," she said. "It's all a lie, Mike. It's a world that's just like the one we came from, except your wife never existed in it. It's my world, the world the way it should have been."

"What are you saying? That you...created the world?"

She was in worse shape than Shiel had thought.

She nodded. "I had to wait until the time was right—until you could join me."

Shiel started to get an uneasy feeling. He remembered his car going out of control on the ice, the elm tree looming up from the side of the road as the car skidded towards it.

"I thought it'd be perfect," Penny said. "Nobody'd be hurt. We'd finally be together, just like I always knew we should be. But I forgot about you. I forgot that *you'd* remember her, even if nobody else did."

Looking at her, you'd never think she was this weirded out, Shiel thought. She looked sane. She delivered her lines so reasonably. But when he focused on what she was saying—

I'm not the only ghost here.

—when he remembered the skidding car and the tree. That stopped him.

"What the hell are you saying?" he asked.

"That car crash, the intensive care unit you dreamed of?"

A sick feeling settled in the pit of Shiel's stomach. He closed his eyes and a vision of his Pinto sliding on the black ice shot into his mind. That great big frigging elm tree filling the windscreen just before he hit...

"They weren't dreams, Mike."

The nausea spread, a cold unreasoning panic chittered in the back of his head. He could feel the ventilator hose going down his windpipe. He could hear the machine's internal hissing as it pumped air into his lungs...

"That was the real world."

An antiseptic sting in his nostrils. The scratchy sound of the IVAC pump as it fed drugs into his bloodstream and the incessant beep of the monitor reading his heartbeat...

Bullshit. It was bullshit. He stared at her, slowly shaking his head, not even aware of the motion. For Christ's sake, he wasn't insane, *she* was.

"I waited and waited for the right moment to bring you here," Penny said, "here to my world."

"You're out of your—"

"This is the dream, Mike. But we can make it real. We just have to want to."

"I..."

"We're here because I wanted this...I wanted it so bad..."

3

Shiel stood up. He crossed the room to the window and stared out at the street below. When he shut his eyes, he could feel himself lying down in that hospital bed, connected to the life support systems. Gibbering fears chewed at his reason.

It wasn't true.

He stared at the street. It was real. This apartment was real. The woman behind him hadn't committed suicide. He'd never crashed the Pinto. But Annie...

He could hear her voice, coming as though from a great distance. The sadness, the pain in it.

"Mike..."

It couldn't be true.

But if this world was real, then where was Annie in it? Could he believe in a world from which she'd been erased as though she'd never existed?

You don't have a wife.

I do.

This is the dream...

It had to be.

He turned from the window to look at Penny, anguish written in every plane of his features.

"How...can it be...possible...?"

His voice was a ragged croak. He could feel the walls closing in on him. If he shut his eyes, the sounds and smells of the hospital flooded his senses. He lay helpless there.

"How...?"

Penny shook her head slowly. "I don't know, Mike. I took those pills and I lay down on my bed, waiting for my mom to come home. And then I just drifted away. When I opened my eyes again, I was here."

"In...in this place?"

"Not this apartment — this world. It was like I was being given a second chance. I think this is a place where we go when we aren't ready to accept our deaths. A kind of echo of the real world. When you've died, when it wasn't your time to die, but you did anyway, it's like there's all this leftover stuff — all those months and years, all the pieces of your life that you didn't get to live — it all gets distilled into a kind of energy that you can use to make a place like this.

"There are probably hundreds of thousands of worlds like this — one for every person who died before his or her time."

"I...I'm dead...?"

"Not yet. You're in a coma. And like the doctor said in your dream, when you come out of it — if you come out of it — you're going to be a vegetable. Or you're going to be a head attached to a body that doesn't work any more."

A quadriplegic. Helpless.

"How...how can you know this?" he asked.

She shrugged. "I'm connected to you, Mike — I think of you all the time — so when the...accident happened, when I knew there was finally nothing left for you back there, I brought you here. I thought you'd be happy — that we could be happy here. I thought that when you finally let go of your body in that world, you'd be here with me and we could make a new life together. I didn't realize that you'd remember your old life so strongly."

Annie.

"There's nothing left for you back there, Mike."

Annie.

"Even if you don't die — what kind of a life would it be?"

There'd be Annie.

"Everything will be changed. You'll be just a burden on...on your wife."

But we had a pact, Shiel thought. We swore an oath. We exchanged rings in the church and when the priest spoke —

(for better or for worse, in sickness and in health)

—we both said "I do."

He left the window and sat down on the couch again, cradling his head in his hands.

"Mike...?"

He looked up at her.

"I know it wasn't right what I've done — manipulating you the way I have — but you can't go back. It doesn't have to be with me, but you've got to stay. How can you return, knowing the kind of half-life that's waiting for you there? At least here you can make a new life for yourself — be what you would be if you hadn't hit that tree."

"But it's a lie."

"Isn't a lie better than what reality's got to offer you now?" Penny asked.

"When I dreamt of you coming to me, dressed as a nurse...Did that really happen?"

Penny nodded.

Jesus.

"But that was me," Penny said. "Manipulating you. I'll leave you alone from now on, Mike. I promise. We can be friends, or not. You don't ever have to see me again if you don't want to. Just don't go back. There's nothing for you there."

"There's Annie."

"And if you're not a vegetable, then you'll probably be paralyzed from the neck down, so what good would you —"

"Do you *know* that?"

She shook her head. "But you heard what the doctor said. And if that does happen, what will you have to offer her?"

Shiel slowly shook his head. "You don't understand. We love each other. If it was her — if it had happened to Annie — I'd be there for her. That's what it's all about. It doesn't matter how bad things get, so long as we're there for each other. If I stayed here, I'd be making a lie of everything we had between us."

"Can you even begin to imagine what your life will be like if you go back?"

"No. I won't pretend that I can. I know it'll be harder than anything I could imagine. But at least it'll be real."

Penny said nothing. Her eyes held her sadness. The lines of her body spoke her weariness. She looked away from him, off into unseen distances. Shiel closed his eyes and the smells and sounds of intensive care were back.

"If you go back," Penny said, "you'll think this was all just a dream. But it wasn't, Mike. It was real, too. It was how things could have been."

Shiel could sense Annie's presence in the hospital room, sitting beside his bed. Her love for him was so strong, it had physical weight.

It was like a lifeline, calling to him.

Calling him back to his ruined body.

Calling him home.

"I can't stop you from going back," she said.

"I don't know how to do it," Shiel said.

Penny's gaze returned to meet his. "Just let go," she said.

4

Shiel did as she said. He caught hold of the lifeline that was Annie's love, and let go of the world he was in. It was like falling into a pool of shadows, everything darkening, everything losing its definition, its connection to him.

He felt the hospital bed under his body. He heard the beep of the monitoring machine, the sound of the IVAC pump. An antiseptic odor stung his nostrils.

His eyes were closed, but he could still see Penny. It was like looking at a television screen, the last scene of a made-for-TV movie before the final fadeout and the credits came rolling up. He wasn't *there* anymore.

"I really loved you," she said. "I never meant to cause you any hurt."

But he was gone now and she spoke to an empty room. He'd crossed back over, out of her life again.

No.

He'd never really been a part of her life. Except in dreams. Her dreams.

He saw her bow her head and finally set free the tears she'd been holding back until he was gone.

The screen in his head faded to black.

The Face in the Flames

Donna Hoban was scared.

She huddled against the birch, the white bark flaking off as she pressed her face against it. Her legs were jelly-weak with no strength left in them. Though it was mid-July and a hot muggy night, she was chilled to the bone. Her dress was clammy where it clung to her body, her hair damp against her scalp. The cold was inside her, a preternatural chill that left her shivering.

She was twenty-two and a star — if you could count three singles and an LP on the UK Independent Charts as fame. But that was there. And then. This was now. Her fingers twitched, but there was no guitar to hold the chord shapes. Only the night and the fear.

This was a fear she couldn't deal with. It didn't come from a sea of faces — the butterfly flutter in the pit of her stomach just before the first chords roared out and the stadium's spotlights stabbed the darkness to find her strutting across the stage, Fender strapped on and hanging low. This was a stark terror that poisoned her like a snake's venom. It came from something cold and dry, with eyes like fire, something that moved with a sound like reptilian scales rasping one against the other.

It was more than imagination. She'd *seen* the thing with her own eyes, felt the weight of its gaze piercing her soul like a bug pinned to a board. She'd seen it and fled with no thought but escape. Fled until she could run no more and crouched gasping here against the tree. The fear made breathing an effort. It constricted the air in her lungs and stifled each breath she dragged in. Pretending it was baseless just didn't work.

She glanced at Tom, sprawled a half-dozen feet from her, his features washed out by shadows, and cursed him. Trees reared dark and threatening on all sides — both protection against what stalked the night and malignant in their own right. Their branches twisted like grasping claws. The moonlight dripped between them like a volcanic glow. The wind hissed through the leaves, a sibilant whisper that she could almost understand.

No one had forced her to come. She just hadn't believed. She'd thought it no more than a lark. But that was until...

She shuddered.

Something moved in the meadow, beyond the trees. She bit at her lip and pressed her face harder against the tree, scraping her cheek raw as she tried to clamp down the scream that was rising in her throat.

She was going to die.

Hearing that furtive sound, knowing the creature that made it, sent her fear skittering to new heights. The half-indifferent, half-amused attitude she'd worn through life dropped away like the lie it was. She did care about living. She didn't want to die.

She thought of all those times sitting around in flats and rehearsal halls, moaning about being bored. Bored, but safe. The refrain to a Chris Spedding song went through her head, the words keeping time to the pulse of her blood in her temples. Something about being bored, bored by the same-old everyday.

And you hung onto the 'everyday,' drawing out those four syllables. She used to sing that song with her first band, then played it with Spedding one night in a little club in Soho during her first week in England. She'd been in heaven that night.

The memory had risen unbidden and froze now in her mind. She listened to the stalker rustling its way through the knee-high weeds, could picture the saurian shape of its head, the hell-gleam of its eyes, and all she could think of was that Spedding song about being bored.

God! She was going insane. Some creepy-crawler best left in a Stephen King novel was about to tear her head off and all she could do was think of the stupid refrain to a stupid song.

I never meant any of it, she wanted to shout. I *do* want to live.

God damn it! She couldn't die. She turned fear-widened eyes to where Tom hunched, his face twisted with his own terror, and wished she was anywhere but here. With anybody but this man who'd brought the whole bloody mess down on their heads.

Wishes were all she had left.

She'd met Tom while taking a stroll down the Sparks Street Mall, amusing herself by trying to remember which stores dated back to the six years since she'd left Ottawa, and which were new. The day was warm, just nearing one, the humidity climbing with the temperature, the street-wide mall clogged with people on their lunch break.

Most were civil servants, but there were enough tourists scattered here and there to give the whole of it a holiday air. Clothing ranged from office gear to jogging shorts and every permutation in between. French and English came to her ears, the mixture sounding strange after her years in England. There were cameras draped over every tenth shoulder; buskers with their instruments ranging from the traditional guitar, to flutes, fiddles, even a saxophone; fruit carts and flower carts; people demanding money — everybody from winos to the blue-cloaked followers of the Process Church; Scientologists talking up reincarnation and handing out flyers asking people to "Come as you were" to their office for more information. It was like a circus — a cacophony of color, movement and sound.

Six years had passed, and nothing much seemed to have changed in Ottawa except for her. Her acoustic Yamaha had become a Custom Fender and her music had gotten weirder. The long brown hair that once framed her face had been replaced by an unruly thatch of spiked pink hair. She'd traded in her jeans and leathers for audacious forties dresses and a penchant for costume jewelry. Only her eyes had stayed the same — clear and penetrating, a bright green no matter what eye shadow she highlighted them with.

Her parents had called her a whore when they'd seen her photo on the jacket of the album, but she didn't care. The clothes and the hair — they were all in fun. It wasn't like she'd stuck a safety pin through her cheek or had her breasts tattooed. God knows, she knew people who'd done both. And there were even some who didn't regret it…

When she came to Sherman's Records — wasn't it across the street the last time she'd seen it? — she stopped in to see if they had any of her band's records in stock. She was vaguely disappointed, though not surprised, when they didn't. Her band's records were only pressed in the UK and she doubted that very many people over here were aware of them—barring those hardy souls that haunted the specialty record shops and kept up on every new British trend through reading the music papers like *Melody Maker* or the *NME*.

They were playing support for The Turn who were hotter than Soho in summer with "Fly Me" topping every chart from here to Toboken—wherever Toboken was. Donna had wanted the gig because she hadn't been back to Ottawa for so long. It was going to be weird playing here after all the hoopla back home—for England was her home now. There they had bands supporting *them*, TOP OF THE POPS, fame, fortune. She grinned. If she had more than a couple of bob in her pocket she was doing good.

Leaving the air-conditioned store made it seem even hotter outside. Caught up in her thoughts, she didn't really watch where she was going and almost tripped over an open guitar case set up in front of the Kentucky Fried Chicken Take-Out. Arms pinwheeling, she saved herself from a fall, but the case turned over and coins went in a glittering spill across the pavement.

"Shit!" she said and bent down to help the busker retrieve his earnings.

As she dropped the last handful back into the case, she straightened up to look at him. He was medium-tall and dark-haired, with one of those faces that seemed to cry out 'sensitive musician'—lean features, sunken cheeks, overly-bright eyes. He held a battered old Martin New Yorker and, taking in the compact guitar's lean lines and slotted head, she felt a moment's affection for the man. Lovely guitar. At least he had taste in instruments.

"Hey!" he said, recognition dawning in his eyes. "You're Hob! From 2 Wicked. Donna Hoban."

She grinned, inordinately pleased at being recognized. She hoped he had a pen on him if he wanted her to autograph something, because she didn't.

"And you're Cat Stevens," she said.

He frowned and squinted at her. Probably needs glasses, she thought, but was too sensitive to wear them.

Catty remark! she told herself. Remember. He's got a nice guitar. *And* he recognized you where millions wouldn't.

What did he see? With her bright pink hair — it seemed to go with the summer — and the gaudy red dress she was wearing — quite nice, thank you, even if it was thirty years out of fashion and fraying at the collar and hem — she stood out like the last of the post-punk movement that had never quite taken off in Ottawa.

"You mean you're not...?" he began.

She laughed. "I'm Hob. In the flesh. And who're you?"

"Tom. Tom Keenan."

"Ah! An Irishman. Be easy on a poor English girl."

"You're no more English than I am. I read a write-up on your band in the *NME* that said you're from Ottawa. You're playing here tomorrow night, aren't you? With The Turn at the Civic Centre?"

"Yeah." What, no autograph? "How's your day going? Sorry 'bout the mess I made."

"That's okay." He looked down into his guitar case. "Looks like about thirty bucks. Not bad for an hour's work, eh? Want to go for a beer?"

She shrugged. "Why not?"

CR&O

Four beers and an afternoon's conversation later, Donna found herself liking the busker. Their talk ranged from what it was like to live in England to the couple of years Tom had lived in Morocco, though it never strayed far from music.

"What changed your direction?" Tom asked.

"What do you mean?"

"Well, you started out as a socio-political band — you know, anarchy and the whole bit — then switched to what you're doing now. What does the press call it? 'Witchy and Weird?'"

Donna shrugged. "Peter Tiers left."

"Just like that?"

"I guess we were getting too popular for him or something."

Talking about Peter awakened a flood of memories.

She'd first met him when he was playing at The Edge in Toronto — met him backstage with Phil Canning who'd been doing a column for the *Star* then. Something had clicked between Peter and her and she'd never come back to Ottawa. She'd tagged along with the band — not really a groupie, just a part of the entourage.

New York. Boston. A swing back up to Montreal. By the time they returned to England, she was playing with the band.

They shared a vision with their music that connected into a sense of purpose when they were together. The club scene in London swallowed them. Their first single came out on Strang — an independent label working out of Edinburgh at the time that specialized in anarchy-inspired music and always sold their product for just above cost. There was a message to get across and money came second.

It was an explosive time in the British music scene. Post-Sex Pistols, but the Clash was still going strong. Reggae and dub influences were infiltrating rock'n'roll rhythms. Boy-meets-girl lyrics were becoming a thing of the past. Oh, there was still pop music. It was as strong as ever. But Punk, New Wave, call it what you will, had become a legitimate and viable child of old father rock'n'roll.

But by the time their second single came out, the vision was dimming for Donna.

She still cared about the kids. Unemployment was worse than ever. Too many people on the dole. Too many people with nothing — coming from nothing, going to nothing. No future now. England itself had been bankrupt since the end of the First World War and the economy, what was left of it, was slowly strangling the country.

There were strikes. Riots. Just this morning she'd been reading about them in the papers. Brixton in flames — the Clash saw that one coming. Chapeltown. Huddersfield. Ireland a powder keg about to ignite. Belfast on the precipice of another Easter Week.

It was no better in North America — though this being Canada, it wasn't nearly so evident. Still the Postal Union was holding the country ransom and she couldn't even send her friends a postcard.

The world was fraying at the edges. Maybe in the sixties the kids thought they could do something about it. Maybe they had. For a while. But now it was all back again. Worse than before.

She thought of the Clash singing about Brixton, and she could hear Simonon's words ring in her head, Clash power chords charging every word with menace. Or perhaps with inevitability. How many were going to choose the gun?

She didn't want to know. She wanted a way out. With only one skill to her credit, she aimed for the top of the charts. Others had done it — kids who had pulled themselves up from the streets to become superstars. Townshend. Jagger and Richards. McCartney and — No. They'd gotten to him already. Lennon's murderer had already made his choice and picked up the gun. Though what in God's name he'd thought he was doing was beyond her.

But that was the way of the world now. There were too many madmen in the streets, madmen with guns who needed little or no provocation to use them. Corporate chaos at the top of the heap, and the insane at the bottom. It all came down to the same thing. All Donna wanted was a way out. If she made it, she wouldn't flaunt it. She'd buy herself a nice safe refuge — up in the Highlands, or in Wales — and just hole up.

Peter couldn't see it that way. He was seven years her elder, had done what he could through the sixties, and was still doing it now. All it needed was commitment, he'd tell her. A belief in what was right and the willingness to reach for it. For everybody. A pipe dream, she'd told him. Their differences set them against each other, and eventually drove Peter from the band.

Their next single, the first without Peter, got to number twenty on the charts. Released on Tim Watter's Fordale label, and distributed by EMI, it was a clean-sounding, dub-influenced number. What set it apart from the thirty or so other singles released the same week were the lyrics. No longer political, they were a combination of street-talk and weird phrases that sounded like they'd been lifted straight from a witch's grimoire. Eerie. Occult. So haunting that they stayed with the listener, long after the song's last chord was just an echo. Delivered in Donna's clear voice, on top of a textured layer of electronic rhythms and chopping guitar chords, their effect was undeniable.

With EMI backing them, every disc jockey and reviewer in England had a copy on their desk before the end of the week. The reviews were mostly favorable and it got a lot of airplay. Each subsequent single did better than the one before it — the third reaching number two. When the album came out, it jumped into the top five within a week.

"I prefer the new direction," Tom said.

Donna smiled. "We do too."

"Things like 'Flame Dreamer'..."

Donna nodded, recalling the refrain.

Ever see the face in the heart of the fire?
Demon eyes grinning with vampiric desire?
In the throat of the moon, or a guttering flame,
Are you dreaming, are you waking,
when it calls your name?
Are you dreaming, are you sleeping,
will you ever be the same?

Tom leaned forward with an intense look in his eyes.

"How do you call your spirits up?" he asked.

Donna laughed. "Are you serious?"

"Aren't you?"

Her laughter fell away. Don't go all weird on me, she wanted to say. We've been having a nice afternoon. Don't go spoil it. Only the words couldn't get past her throat. Looking into Tom's eyes, she knew he was deadly serious. Her head flooded with strange images and she wasn't sure if she was attracted or repelled by them. Slowly she shook her head.

"Look," she said. "It's just a gimmick. It's all part of the image. Spooky lyrics, lots of dark lighting on stage, dramatic chords, eerie synthesizers...It's just for fun."

"I know the songs are. But behind them. The truth behind them."

She glanced at the bar's wall-clock. 5:10. She had a rehearsal at nine-thirty. That gave her a little more than four hours to get ready for it. They had to go over the set so they'd be ready for the sound check tomorrow afternoon. Looking back at Tom, she found him still watching her intently. He's got cat's eyes, she thought. They probably glow in the dark.

"I should get going," she said.

She started to get up, but he caught her by the hand and drew her back to her seat.

"Haven't you ever asked yourself, what if there is some truth behind it all? What if it's real?"

"Sure. Who hasn't? Only..."

"I can show you."

Donna's feelings swirled into a maelstrom. This is how it starts, she thought. One part of her was screaming: Get the hell away from this guy. He's a psycho. But another part that was growing stronger, repeated his question, over and over like a litany. What if it *was* real? She leaned forward.

"How?" she found herself asking. "Where?"

"Across the river. In Lucerne. Near the mountains."

He was really serious. Under the table, she fingered the soft sides of her purse, feeling for the weight of the lead-filled cosh she carried with her wherever she went.

"I've got a rehearsal at nine-thirty," she said. "Maybe some other time."

"It won't take all night. And I've got a car. We could be back by eight-thirty at the latest." He smiled. "It's perfectly safe."

Only a complete ass would agree to go. He was a perfect stranger. Well, stranger? Yes. But perfect? He just wanted to get her alone. Out in the country. Only…She let her fingers slide across the ridges of the cosh's knobbed leather end, felt its weight again. On the other hand, the whole thing was probably a lark. They'd go for a drive in the country—she hadn't been on the Quebec side in years—and she'd be back in time for her rehearsal.

"You're sure we'll be back in time?"

"Of course I'm sure. Finish your beer and we'll go get my car. I left it in a lot on Slater."

The poor starving busker, playing his fingers to the bone, Donna thought cynically, then shrugged. She lifted her mug and clinked it against his. Suddenly she felt on the brink of a wild adventure. Responsibility fell away and she was just a kid again, off on some mad spree. Tom grinned at her like a mate, and she laughed.

"To dreams," she toasted.

"And dreamers."

CRSO

The car was an old Volkswagen Beetle that had once been green, but now was more a dull orange from its rust. It rattled on the highway and, when they hit a dirt road, the dust clouded up through a hundred holes in the floor, hanging around their feet like smoke. Twenty minutes after they'd left the parking lot on Slater Street, Tom pulled up on the side of the road. He switched off the ignition and turned to Donna.

"Here?" she asked.

It seemed incongruous. The sun was still in the sky, and the sky itself was clear and blue. On one side of the road was a wide field, purple with blossoming milkweed, thatched with a hundred shades of green. Tiger lilies poked up from the ditches with brilliant orange petals. On the other side, the first outriders of the Gatineau Mountains began their march north. They were like English hills, old and rounded, only forested with birch and pine, cedar, aspen and maple.

"Over there," Tom said, pointing across the field. "Under that dead tree. There's a stone there—a special stone."

She could see the tree, if not the stone. There was nothing ominous about it. One dead tree amidst a sea of summer's wealth. She smiled cheerily, determined to keep the whole thing on the level of a lark, sure that when it came right down to the nitty-gritty, the most Tom wanted was some company. And if he tried anything weird...Well, she still had her cosh and she wasn't afraid to use it.

Tom took a rucksack from the backseat where his guitar rested, and opened the door on his side.

"You coming?"

Donna nodded. She took a deep breath, enjoying the sweet smell of the milkweed and the country air. She got out and closed the door behind her, remembering to lift it up just before pushing in. Open, the door sagged on its hinges. Joining Tom, she followed him into the field.

There was a deserted farmhouse about a half-mile to the right. Behind it were the leaning, ramshackle remnants of a barn. A few supports, thrust up like a beached whale's ribs, were all that remained of a third structure. On the left was more forest, separated from the hills by the road.

They reached the stone without incident, except that Donna wished she'd dressed more appropriately for a jaunt in the country. High heels didn't do much for traversing a field. And no matter how she tried to avoid them, she still managed to get scratched about a half-dozen times by prickles and thorns. She went to sit down on the stone—walking through a field could be hard work when the grass was almost up to your waist in places and you had more than a few beers buzzing through your bloodstream—but Tom waved her away from it.

"Over there," he said, pointing to a smaller stone.

Obediently, she sat there and watched him unload his rucksack. First came a stoneware bowl. He poured it three-quarters full of lamp oil, then added a wick on a float that bobbed in the liquid.

Wasn't the bloody sun bright enough to see by? Donna thought. They had at least another hour or so of good light.

Next came a number of curiously-shaped jars—none of them labeled. They seemed to be divided between dried herbs and powders. He selected half of them and returned the rest to his pack. Lastly, he withdrew a packet of incense cones.

He obviously meant to play the thing out to its end. Donna grinned, thinking of what the band would say when she told them how she'd spent her afternoon. "Bloody spells it was. I swear it's true. We raised the spirit of some long-dead Indian and he told us the secrets of skinning beavers. Bloody gruesome, I'll tell you, but if you ever need to know…"

She gazed up into the bare limbs of the tree, and wondered vaguely what time it was. If she was an outdoors sort of person, she could've told by the sun. Nearing evening at any rate. She looked back to see what Tom was doing.

The stone was his prop, the field his stage.

Well and fine, she thought. I'll play the audience and gasp in all the right places. So long as he doesn't try to saw me in two.

Incense burned in small clay bowls no bigger than a pence in circumference. There were five of them, set in hollows of the stone. The incense smoked upward in solid spirals until the vague breeze caught them and tugged them apart. From where Donna sat, she couldn't smell it at all. Just the milkweed—the novelty of which was wearing off. It began to cloy in her nostrils. She was getting hot as well, just sitting here. The sun, though setting, was still strong. And as usual, Ottawa Valley humidity was at its peak. Her dress clung to her skin. Maybe there'd be time for a swim, she thought. After the show's over.

Now Tom was taking the powders and herbs from their respective jars and sprinkling them along the top of the stone in the shape of a five-pointed star. The tip of each point ended at an incense burner. He finished with a circle that joined the points, then set the bowl of lamp oil in the very center of the star. Watching him work, a little chill tiptoed up Donna's spine, but she shook it off.

"I thought this sort of thing only worked at night," she said. "You know: midnight and by the light of the moon and all that."

Tom shook his head and answered her seriously.

"This is fire-magic," he said. "It works best when the sun's rising or setting."

"Oh."

He leaned forward to light the floating wick.

"I know these preparations might seem contrived," he said. "To be honest, they're not really necessary. All that's required is some method of focusing your will on the summoning. The old shaman, whose stone this was, might have danced around it, shaking rattles and drumming. This," — he waved his hand to the stone and its paraphernalia — "is just what I'm comfortable with."

Oh, really? Donna thought, then shrugged. Whatever turns you on. For her own part, she was simply enjoying the day. It might be hot — steamy hot when you came right down to it — but pleasant in a summery way. It was the kind of day, the kind of place, where you could run naked through the grass — if you ignored the prickles — and shout at the clouds — if there were any.

The wick was burning now and Donna's gaze centered on it. The chill that had started up her spine earlier —

In the throat of the moon, or a guttering flame...

— returned and wouldn't go away. It spread through her, for all that she was perspiring. And she'd never go running through the fields with Tom, she decided, naked or not...She stared at the flame, her gaze following its every flicker.

Ever see the face in the heart of the fire?

"Look," she said, forcing her gaze from it. "Maybe we should do this some other time."

"Too late," Tom replied. "Don't be afraid. Just stay where you are, and watch and learn. Don't touch anything."

Like hell I won't. She was reaching into her purse for her cosh, found the knobbed end with the pads of her fingers, then froze as the wick's flame leapt two, three inches high. And in it —

Demon eyes grinning with vampiric desires...

— was a face, smooth-shaped like a salamander's. The flames licked about its head like a golden spiked crown. Donna looked from it to Tom, then back again. Her fingers tightened on her weapon, but it seemed ineffectual now.

"Oh, God..." she began, but got no further.

Her chest was tight, her throat parched. She swallowed dryly, tried to rise, but couldn't find the strength. The image in the wick's flame held her gaze, burned into the backs of her eyes.

It's the beer, she thought. The beer and the sun. Making me light-headed. But cold fear paralyzed her and wouldn't go away.

She lost all feeling in her body, had the sensation that she was a disembodied entity, hovering just outside of herself. Her vision narrowed to the one pinpoint that was the wick's flame. And in it, the face. Oh, God! The face.

Its mouth opened and a forked tongue flicked out. She heard a sibilant whispering in her mind. All perceptions dissolved except for those hissing words—for words they were and, worse, she was almost on the point of understanding them. A reptilian odor replaced the sweet scent of the milkweed. It was like the reek of the snake house in a zoo. The saurian face grew larger, rearing until it filled her sight. Gold eyes, flecked with strange red specks, drew her gaze, drew her in. She fell into them, felt a cold-blooded body in place of her own. Her sight shattered, only to reform with bizarre perspectives. It was like being on acid, but beyond surreal, beyond the worst imaginable bad trip.

She lived a thousand memories—none of them her own. They belonged to a creature as old as the world itself was old. There was no pretending it wasn't real, that it was only the sun and the beer. The refrain of one of her own songs came back to taunt her:

See me like lizard, honey,
wizard-bane, trapped in flame...

They were just words when she wrote them, put together for their sound, meaningless. But now...

She *was* the elemental creature in the flames, wore its reptilian skin as though it were her own, saw through its eyes, felt the cold pulse of its blood through veins that had never known the warmth of a mammal's blood unless it was digested...

The experience transcended her own understanding of time. Hours appeared to rush by, then again only minutes.

She came to her own body once more, huddled in a prenatal position, legs curled up tightly against her chest, moaning softly.

Time had fled by, the summer's evening draining into night. For a long moment she thought she was blind. Everything was so dim. Flickering. She couldn't remember where she was, why she was, who she was...

The elemental's presence drew her gaze back to the stone, to the wick that still held its flame on top of it. Terror-widened eyes saw a deeper darkness gathering in the middle of the flame, a body shaping under the head, swallowing the wick.

"No," she mumbled.

Her hair was matted with grass and dirt, her face streaked with dried sweat and tears.

The darkness took shape—a now-familiar shape. She knew it from her previous vision, but this time she was on the outside. The gold orbs fixed in that long saurian skull regarded her with an unblinking gaze. Then she remembered. The memories flooded her. Trains of thought that bore no resemblance to anything human. A morality that had nothing to do with good or evil, but simply was. A fixed purpose, as fixed as the creature's stare. And the hunger. God, the hunger...

"No!"

Her voice was stronger. Somehow she was free of the creature's spell. She caught hold of the first thing that came to hand—Tom's rucksack—and flung it at the creature. Jars and vials spilled from the canvas sack to break on the stone at the elemental's feet. Taloned feet. Like some giant iguana's. Light flared as the various powders and fluids from the broken containers merged. The creature howled—a shrieking sound like a rabbit screaming in a dog's jaws—and stepped from the stone.

"Oh, Christ!" Tom cried. "What've you done?"

He grabbed her shoulder, fingers digging deep, hurting.

She shook her head, "What have *I* done? You're the fucking maniac!"

She tore free from his grip. The elemental was shuffling forward, its movements sluggish as though it were caught in a slow-motion shutter. Donna backed away.

"I didn't do anything!" she shouted at him. "The bloody thing's going to kill us."

No, she realized. Not both of them.

"You!" She thrust a finger at him. "You tried to kill me with that...that..."

Tom was shaking his head frantically.

"You don't understand," he said. "It couldn't have hurt us. It was bound to that stone—to the flame. We would have been safe, but no. You had to free it, you stupid—"

Donna fled and heard no more.

All she could think of were the creature's eyes, glowing in the dark like hungry searchlights. She remembered its lust for warm-blooded flesh, and ran. The weeds tugged at her legs. She lost first one shoe, then the other. The skirt of her dress clung to her legs, slowing her down, so she hiked it up around her waist, ignoring the thorns and sharp grass slicing at her skin.

God! Which way was the road? The car? She'd lost all sense of direction.

Dark trees reared up before her and she knew she was going the wrong way. She stood for a moment, undecided in her panic whether to plunge straight into the forest or follow its edge. She knew it reached the road at some point. But which way? Left or right? She couldn't remember. She couldn't bloody-well remember.

A sound came from behind her and she whirled, arms flailing. One fist connected with the side of Tom's head and he stumbled against her. They fell in a tangle of limbs. The touch of him repelled her. The texture of his hands seemed scaly—like she imagined the touch of the elemental would be. Dry scales. And talons. She fought free of Tom's arms and knelt gasping in the grass, gaze torn between him and watching for the thing that was surely following them. She saw only darkness in the field. Listening, she heard only their own ragged breathing.

"The car," she said. "Where's the car? Which way?"

If she could only concentrate...

He pointed back the way they'd come.

"What're we going to do?" she demanded. "Can't we...kill it or something? Does it vanish with the dawn, or silver, or...what?"

She wasn't wearing any silver today. Besides, you couldn't club a monster to death with a pair of earrings or a brooch.

"Blood," Tom said hoarsely. "It needs to kill. To feed. If you hadn't set it free..."

"I didn't set it free! And...and even if I did, I didn't know what I was doing. It wanted *me!* To feed on me. You could have warned me..."

She pressed her hands against her face. This couldn't be happening. It was like something out of a B-grade movie. So ludicrous as to verge on the ridiculous. Except...

"I thought you knew," Tom said.

She shook her head. He thought she knew. While she was writhing about on the ground, possessed by the damn thing, and all he did was sit there and watch.

"Well, I didn't bloody-well know, did I? I...I thought it was just a lark. A joke. I..."

She swallowed, trying to still the thunder of her pulse.

"Look," she said, trying to speak more calmly. "There's the car. We get to the car and we're safe, right? You said that thing needs to feed, well, maybe it'll find itself a rabbit or something. If we circle around—"

She heard it then and her breath died in her. Something moving through the grass. Slowly. A snuffling sound. A rasp of scale against scale. And the...whispering. No. That was just the wind. Just...

She turned and plunged into the forest, oblivious to the scratching branches, colliding with tree trunks more often than avoiding them. Tom was right on her heels. Spent at last, they lay where they fell, each against their own tree, and listened. Nothing. Silence. Wind. In the distance, an owl.

Donna wanted to get a move on, but couldn't find the courage to stir, nor the strength to do more than sit up. Her feet were cut and bruised and hurt like hell. She plucked at the hem of her dress, pulling it down over her knees, then realized how stupid the gesture was. Her dress was in tatters. There wasn't much left to pull down.

She tried to think. If they waited awhile, mightn't it catch something—a squirrel, a rabbit—feed, and be gone? She leaned her head against the tree and stared daggers at Tom.

"What is it?" she asked at last.

"A fire elemental—cousin to the sun. According to Amerindian lore, fire's the intermediary between the Great Spirit and man, you see. The old shaman used to call up these creatures to get...knowledge. Power."

"And according to real life?"

Even in the darkness she could see him frown.

"This *is* real life," he said. "I told you I'd show you, didn't I?"

That you did, she thought. And I, like the bloody fool I am, listened.

"You've called it up before?" she asked.

"Many times."

"And what did you...feed it?"

"I never did. I never let it free. The flame is its doorway into this world. When I was finished with it, I just snuffed the flame."

"Just like that?"

"Just like that."

Donna sighed. "Why do you even deal with the bloody thing?"

"For knowledge. Didn't it touch your mind — show you things?"

"Jesus!"

She shuddered remembering what it had shown her.

"Well, didn't it?" Tom asked.

"Just shut up, will you?"

She heard a sound, and held her breath again. Real or imagined? Furtive. Sly. Like the reptile it was. Except for those eyes. Golden orbs, flecked with red, old and wise...She shook her head, forcing the image from her mind. But now she thought she'd caught a glimmer of understanding, thought she knew why it kept drawing Tom like the proverbial moth to the flame. It stayed with you.

She shivered again, straining her eyes to see through the trees, trying to envision, sense, hear the creature's approach.

I'll wait a bit longer, she thought. Just to catch my breath. Then I'll go. If Tom wants to come, fine. If not, that's up to him. But she'd be taking his car if he didn't come and he could chat all he wanted with his bloody elemental.

Feeling like she'd just run a twenty-mile marathon, she rested her head against the tree once more. And waited.

CRSO

For a moment, Donna thought she'd been dozing. She was still chilled. Her dress was damp and clung to her like a second skin. A sound came and she snapped her eyes wide open, stared into the darkness, listened. It came again. Scale against tree.

"Tom?" she whispered.

"I hear it."

"We've got to make a run for it."

Please, God. Let us make it. She hadn't prayed in longer than she could remember. Our Father, who art in...

As quietly as she could, she got to her bruised feet. Her legs stung from dozens of scratches. Her calves ached.

"I don't think it's sense of smell is very good," Tom said. "If we move quietly..."

Donna nodded, remembering her own time inside the creature's skin. There'd been no olfactory input. Or very little. But its sight was good. And its hearing.

"We can only try," she said.

She sensed his nod and saw him as a vague shadow shape, detaching itself from a tree and creeping to her side.

"Let's go," he said.

He reached out to take her hand, but she brushed it aside. Without glancing at him, she set forth. Tom followed.

She wasn't much good at playing Indian scout. Never had been. Two steps in and a branch snapped under her foot. The sound was loud and sharp as a gunshot in the preternatural stillness. She heard the creature's advance halt, sensed it tensing for its attack. The time for stealth was gone.

It broke from the trees not a dozen yards to their left. Donna felt a scream build up in her throat, but it never got out.

"Take her!" Tom roared in her ear. "Not me!"

His hands were on her shoulders and he flung her in the direction of the creature. She scrabbled for balance, but sprawled full-length in the dead leaves and mulch. The reptilian stench was everywhere. She could see the glow of its eyes in the darkness. Fear lent speed to her next motion.

She came up off the forest floor and bolted for where she hoped the meadow was, sure the creature was hot on her trail. When she burst into the open field, the milkweed drowned the creature's reek, though it remained present, underlying the milkweed like an off-key harmony.

She ran across the field until pain stitched her side, then fell again. The weeds seemed to swallow her. She crushed them under her. Her hands grew sticky with liquid.

Blood! she thought.

Another scream tore at her throat, but she stilled it just in time. It was only the juice of the crushed milkweed.

Get up, she told herself. You've got to get up and run. Get to the bloody car before that bastard Tom does and drives off without you.

Chest heaving, she lumbered to her feet. Her blood was pounding in her ears. Its roar was so loud that it was all she could hear. But she could still see. By the moonlight.

First Tom's shirt flapping behind him. He'd torn it on something. And on his heels, the elemental. Given the choice of two targets, it had chosen the brighter motion. Tom's white shirt had given him away.

The creature appeared to glow as it closed in for the kill. Gone was the sluggish movement it had shown near the stone. It must have been drugged with sleep or cold, she thought. Or the transference from whatever place it came from to this world. That, or something in Tom's rucksack—in the flare when it had broken over the stone—had slowed the creature. Now it closed the difference between itself and its prey in a sinuous rush.

Five feet separated them. A foot.

Then the white shirt vanished under the creature's attack, the weeds hiding the scene from view. Sight, but not sound.

Tom's scream was an inhuman wail that she never wanted to hear again. It tore at her sanity, peeling back ten thousand years of civilization to leave her shuddering like one of her primeval ancestors must have in those lost times. She put a fist in her mouth, biting back her own cry. But when the sound of bones being chewed came wafting across the field, her reserve broke in a flood.

Her scream echoed Tom's—long and wailing.

She saw the elemental lift its head from its kill, swore she could see the blood on its talons, on its jaws.

For all that the creature had just tasted blood, she knew it wasn't going to vanish as simply as Tom had said it would. She remembered its hunger. It would be after her now. She knew it would come for her, that it was pointless to resist for she couldn't hope to defend herself against it. But with the surety of her death upon her, she wanted nothing more than to live. She would fight it to the very end. She would—

The stone! A memory fired her will and she exploded into motion. If she could reach it before the elemental…Where was the bloody stone?

Then she saw it, or rather the tall outline of the dead tree, not fifty paces from where she stood. The tree, and under it, the stone with its sorcerous wick's flame still flickering in the bowl of lamp oil on its granite top.

She ran as she'd never run before. Her flight from the wood had been no more than a stroll, compared to the way she raced through the clinging weeds. She could feel the creature's breath on her shoulders, feel its claws tearing at her flesh, but knew it wasn't real. Not yet. She didn't dare look back to see where it was. All she could do was propel herself towards her goal. The running pain came like a sharp knife now, thrusting in and out of her side.

Survive! she told herself.

The word lanced through her, dragging in its wake an echo of Peter's voice.

"Survival," he'd said to her once. "That's what it's all about, Hob. The kids on the street — on the dole, with no jobs, no future. A crisis wherever you turn. The whole bloody world's coming apart at the seams. Ireland. The Middle East. Brixton. We're all trying to survive, Hob. And that's the truth. But let's never do it at the cost of somebody else's survival. That's what all these small gigs are about. Wake the kids up. Let them see that if there's going to be a change, they've got to be a part of it. It's not a matter of taking their precious few bob and living in luxury while they're in rags. The dream, Hob! Never lose it. It can lead us to heaven. Lose it…and what've you got?"

Oh, Peter, she moaned. I've lost it. And now I'm going to die.

As she reached the stone, the creature landed on her back. But before the talons could do their damage, before the jaws sheered through neck muscles to sever her spinal column, she flung out her hand and closed her hand around the wick's flame.

She cried out once as the creature landed on her — dry scales scraping her skin, hot fetid breath on her neck — screamed again as the flame burned her hand. But she killed its light, quenched it with her flesh, and the weight on her back was gone.

Numbly she lay across the stone, unable to believe she'd survived. If she'd spilled the oil onto the flame before snatching the wick out of it…Opening her hand, she let the wick fall to the ground, moaning softly as it pulled away from her burned flesh.

Right hand, she thought dazedly. I can still pick with it — still play my guitar.

Then she fell off the stone, rolled onto the ground, staring up into the night skies, deep and velvet, riddled with stars.

"I'm alive," she murmured, scarcely able to believe it. "Oh, God. I'm alive!"

She sat up and every muscle protested. Looking around, there was neither sight nor sound of the elemental. Only the smell remained. And it was fading.

She stood up on trembling legs, pressing her burned hand against her stomach. With the other she explored the cuts on her shoulders as best she could, grimacing with pain when it touched the open wounds. They weren't too deep. Still her hand came away red with her own blood.

But she was alive.

Looking neither right nor left, she set off across the field to where the car was parked. When she reached the VW, she fumbled with the door catch on the driver's side and half-fell into the seat, sighing with relief when she saw that the key was still in the ignition. She leaned against the car seat for a long moment, trying to steady herself. She couldn't have faced having to search what was left of Tom's body for the keys. When she thought of his white shirt disappearing into the grass, the creature on top of him, the sounds…

The cuts on her shoulders were beginning to sting. Suppressing another series of shudders, she pushed down on the clutch and turned the ignition. She tried not to think of what awaited her in Ottawa.

The band'd be frantic and there'd be hell to pay trying to explain what had happened to the authorities. And there was still the gig tomorrow night. She didn't know if she could face it. But there was a contract and music was big business…

She shook her head. Except it wouldn't be for her. Not anymore.

First thing she'd do was try to get hold of Peter. What would she say to him? She knew. She'd tell him she'd found the dream again — never mind that it had taken a nightmare. And knowing Peter, the past two years'd fall away and they'd be just like they'd been before. Except for her. After tonight...Well, maybe she'd grown too.

The motor coughed into life. She took a last look at the meadow. The feeling in her chest had finally loosened. The horror wasn't so much fading, as being shunted aside. It was the only way she could deal with it. She flinched as she put the car in gear, her burned hand throbbing. Then, pulling a U-turn, she headed back to Ottawa.

She didn't flick on the headlights until she was well past the field. And even then she had to blink away the image that seemed to be reflected on the road when the lights hit the asphalt. Like a face...

She turned on the radio, twisting the dial until she found a rock 'n' roll station. They were playing a John Lennon song. Something about a wheel going round and round...

L'esprit de la Belle Mariette

And when the veil was torn
from my eyes,
there were shadows within shadows,
and despair...

—Henri Cuiscard

I remember Le Café de la Corne where it lies in the old quarter of Hull. From its door one can see modern skyscrapers, stark and well-lit, above the old houses of Rue Laval. The street itself is dark though, as dark as the café was that night I found it, drawn down an alleyway from Rue Principal by the sound of Quebecois music and the joyful clapping of the café's patrons. Inside, the air was heavy with smoke and low conversation. I made my way to an empty seat at a table where a young lady sat. She was too enrapt in the music to pay heed when I asked if I might join her, so I simply took a seat.

The *serveuse* brought me a black coffee and I sat sipping it, gazing alternatively from my bemused companion to the two old men on the small stage. One played accordion, the other a fiddle. The fading strains of their last tune were still reflected in my companion's eyes — sparkling eyes, alive with wonder and a certain bittersweet longing. I wondered what sorrow lay behind their false gaiety.

Her face was bewitching in the half-light thrown by the candle on the table between us. Her cheeks were flushed, lips pursed, brown hair soft against brow and cheekbones, falling to sweep her

135

shoulders. She was slender, wearing clothes that had seen better times. Her skirt was worn, its print faded, and her sweater threadbare. The only relief was a brightly colored scarf that was tied loosely about her neck.

As the last memory of the music faded, her eyes lost their sparkle. Her features took on a sorrowful mien. I was drawn to her in that moment, as much by pity as by her simple beauty. Comforting words crowded my mind, but before I could speak them, a haunted look touched her face and she arose abruptly from the table. Threading her way through the crowded café, she paused at the door to look back. Her gaze caught mine and a sudden smile lit her face. Then she was gone.

Hardly realizing what I was doing, I rose and followed her, but when I reached the street, it was empty. The air was chill. The streetlights were dim, alleyways crowding the street's cobblestones with shadow.

I was quiet when I returned to my seat inside, thoughtful as I sipped my coffee. There had been something disturbing about the young woman that I could not put my finger on. I have never been given to seeking companions in cafés, nor chasing women onto the street. Yet I would have followed her and I could not explain why. We were strangers. I knew nothing of her. Yet her smile, when she stood by the door, had been deep and warm. A young woman's smile to her lover. An old friend's adieu.

Lost in my thoughts, I started when the accordion struck up the opening chords of a new tune. The musicians had returned to their stage.

The fiddle soon joined the accordion and a pleasant melody cut across the conversation of the café's patrons. Across from me, the young woman was seated once more, though I had not seen her return. The gaiety had returned to her eyes and she drummed her fingers on the tabletop, in time to the music. She looked up at me and smiled, but her eyes lost a little of their sparkle and for a moment I could see the traces of a mystery hidden in their depths.

"*Je suis désespérée,*" she said. Her voice was so low that I had to lean across the table to hear her. "*Il y a des démons dans les ombres...quand la musique est silencieuse.*"

Demons in the shadows...

136

Her words were so unexpected that I could think of nothing to reply.

"*Je m'appelle* Mariette," she added. "*Et vous?*"

"Peter," I said. "Peter Rowland."

"Pierre," she repeated softly. Her gaze met mine. "*C'est beau, la musique...Un sentiment de sécurité.*"

I had never thought of music having a feeling of safeness. I thought of what she had said at first, that there were demons in the shadows when the music was still. I meant to ask her what she meant by such an ambiguous statement, but she was caught up in the music once more. Her cheeks were flushed, her eyes twinkling. The accordion began a merry jig and her foot tapped the hardwood floor, accentuating the 6/8 beat.

Another tune followed it, a slow reel this time. The strains played by accordion and fiddle took on a different quality, an air of benediction and safety that I was hard put to understand. I felt as though I was wrapped in a benevolent cloak of music. It hid me from my enemies. I felt safe. They would not find me here.

I was surprised at the turn my thoughts had taken and tried to put them aside. I had no enemies, nor need to hide from anyone. I glanced at Mariette as the music stopped. Before I could speak, she placed her hand on my arm.

"*Venez,*" she said, rising from the table.

I followed her out of the café to stand with her under a streetlamp. Her hair was golden in the soft light, but her eyes were wide with fear. She pointed to where the dark mouth of an alleyway encroached upon the dimly-lit street.

"*Le sorcier* Yscuin," she said as I looked.

There was movement there. Slyly and stealthily, the darkness appeared to gather in intensity at the entrance to the alley. My pulse quickened and fear rode hard on its quickening rhythm. I imagined something horrific in those shadows, something malevolent. I knew I was being foolish, yet at the same time the fear I felt was so that I could not put it aside.

"*Il est trop tard,*" I heard Mariette say.

Her hand clasped my arm tightly, then suddenly its pressure was gone. I turned to find myself alone once more. The street was empty. The shadows were nothing but shadows. The fear that had clawed at my stomach slowly subsided.

I shook my head and took a deep breath before turning to reenter the café, then stopped, cold with shock. I had thought that Mariette had returned to the café, but the café was gone. I shuddered and took an uncertain step forward. My fear had returned. I knelt on a trembling knee to touch the charred foundation that was all that remained of a building that had obviously burned down many years ago.

Something like a frenzy of madness exploded in my head. I staggered to my feet. There had been a café there, a young woman that I had spoken with. I had listened to music, drunk coffee…

The street was silent except for the murmur of distant traffic on the neighboring avenues. I spun about, staring at the dim streetlights, the cobblestoned surface of Rue Laval. The bordering twenty-storied government complexes loomed above me from a few streets over, their brightly-lit windows like so many eyes, mocking my confusion and my growing despair.

I ran to the nearest house and pounded on its door. After what seemed a lifetime of waiting, a burly man wrapped in a housecoat answered the door. He opened it a crack to stare at me.

"*Que voulez-vous?*" he demanded.

"The café!" I realized I was shouting and fought to regain some measure of control. "Do you know the café?" I asked. My voice still sounded unnecessarily loud and harsh to my own ears.

"*Oui, monsieur,*" he replied. A strange look passed over his eyes. "It was destroyed by fire some years ago—a tragic accident."

"But I was just in…"

Understanding dawned on him. "Monsieur," he said quietly, opening the door wider to usher me in. He settled me down on a worn couch in his living room and offered me a glass of brandy that I accepted with thanks.

"This very night," he said, "it is the eve of the fire, *monsieur,* and strange things have been know to occur on it. You are not the first to…Last year there was a young woman who spoke of meeting a gentleman in that café." He shrugged. "Who can say why you have seen what you did?"

"But I was there," I insisted. "It was so real." I felt calmer now. The brandy warmed me and helped to dispel the choking fear that sent me tottering to the brink of sanity. "And there was a young woman…Mariette. She said her name was Mariette and…"

My voice trailed off. No matter how real it had seemed, it was plainly obvious that I had been the victim of an hallucination. Too much overtime at the office, perhaps. Living like a hermit. Lonely. I had created the entire series of events. The café. The young woman. It had only seemed to be real.

"Le Café de la Corne," my host mused aloud. "The Café of the Horn. It was run by a man from Brittany — Yscuin ar Bras. He was said to be *un sorcier* — a magician, a sorcerer. There were many strange rumors surrounding him. It is said that the fire was caused by his summoning *les demons*…that they overcame him, destroyed him…"

Yscuin. Demons. I remembered what Mariette had told me and shuddered. I could have known none of this, yet what I had experienced tonight could not be real. That was impossible. To believe that it had been real would open the door into madness. I looked to my host. Tell me it was not real, I pleaded silently.

His gaze met mine and there was a pitying look in his eyes. "And, monsieur," he said. "Yscuin had a daughter — a daughter named Mariette who was said to have perished with him in the flames…"

CR80

I have not forgotten Mariette, nor that night, in the years that have followed. Remembering what I learned that night, I searched where I could for information on Breton sorcerers. The horn, I discovered, is a symbol of fertility, a suitable motif for a Breton sorcerer's café as the sorcerers of Brittany were known to practice certain fertility rites as part of their worship. Le Café de la Corne, I have come to believe, was not so much a café, as a place for ar Bras and his companions to gather for meetings and conduct their rites.

As to the safety in music, I ran across a reference to that in an old book that I bought at a flea market in Stittsville. The book is Edgar Miller's *Tombs and Barrows* and on page 138 it tells of —

> …an elder race of sorcerers. Many of the barrows that lie near the Channel are supposed to house their remains and on certain nights they come forth to conduct unholy rites. Only music can keep these sorcerers at bay and on such nights the cots and inns of Brittany ring with the sound of gavottes and reels, from dusk until dawn.

Burned cots and the charred remains of inns stand silent testimony to these fanciful tales of the local people. These, they say, are the fate of those who fail to keep the music playing on those nights. And a person, ensnared by the ghosts of those slain by the sorcerers, can never know peace.

I believe the folk tales of the Bretons, for I have not known peace. My only desire is to come to Rue Laval and find the café untouched by flames once more. I believe that Mariette sought an end to her father's evil ways. Somehow she secreted the musicians into the café, while her father was below, busy with his rites. It was enough to put an end to her father and his companions, though not enough to save her.

Each year, on the eve of the café's burning, I return to Rue Laval, looking for her, but always in vain. A new building now stands where once the café did. Not even the old foundations remain. I stand for long hours in front of it and, sometimes, I hear a voice echo softly against the strains of accordion and fiddle.

"*Il est trop tard,*" I hear Mariette say, though I am alone on the cobblestones.

It is too late, too late...

His City

(with Robert Tzopa)

Great art is the expression of a
solution of the conflict between
the demands of the world without
and that within.

—Edith Hamilton, *The Greek Way*

The old McKeown place is still there, if you want to have a look at it. Just take Hwy 15 south of Portland and turn right at the Sunoco. The McKeown place's maybe a mile, mile and a half down Harlem Road, an old two-story lathe and stucco that's got the look of rotting fruit about it. Paint's peeling, stairs are sagging. Front lawn's kept nice and proper, though. That was Mother McKeown's pride and joy. Even after the accident you could drive by and see her trimming her rosebushes, big as small trees.

A young couple from the city bought the place up this spring. Word has it they'll be fixing it up. They already made a start on the old shed this summer. Gave it the works. New shingles. Pine planking on the sides. Spanking new windows – stained glass in the top panes.

I heard the place went for $15,000, give or take a hundred. The land's worth it. Nicely treed. Got more raspberry bushes than you might know what to do with. Fred Sampson and Willie B. cleared them out this summer while the new folks were in the city. Sold enough to keep themselves stinking drunk for one weekend. Willie B. drove by last week and said he saw the pair of them out in the fields, white plastic berry containers in their hands.

141

Should'a seen their faces, he told us all later. He slowed down to have himself a good long gawk and couldn't stop laughing. They were just going from bush to bush, picking the few shriveled berries that were left.

I wonder what they thought of that place, once the spring came. When they bought it the ground was still frozen and covered with a nice thick blanket of snow — pretty as a picture, if you didn't look too long at the house. But once the freeze broke and the snow left, they must have had them a surprise. Dead cats and chickens lying half-rotted in pools of mud. So much garbage and litter you'd think the county'd moved the dump there. It'd be enough to turn your stomach. And the inside of that place...

Let me tell you, it's hard to believe that anyone could abide living in there. But the thing is, there were people living in there right up until the end of February. Squatters that just sort of eased on in there after what happened to the McKeowns. The hydro'd been cut off since before Christmas and they wouldn't have had any running water, what with the pipes froze up and all. But they stayed on until the realty company had 'em thrown out.

But I was telling you about the inside. The cellar was filled up with about two feet of water and God knows what was floating around in it. The rooms were all small, dinky little holes, with big gaping troughs in the plaster and the paint peeling off in long strips. There was garbage everywhere. Looked like they'd open a can of beans or whatever and just chuck it in a corner. Sgt. Maveety claims he counted 136 empties in the kitchen alone. 40-ouncers. Hard to say who left more — the McKeowns or the squatters.

Weirdest thing I can remember about that place, the time or two I was in there (and that was before Ernestine left old man McKeown, before the accident), was this hallway upstairs that ran between the west bedroom and the landing. Fifteen feet of hall, with a door on either end and nothing else but a trapdoor high up in the ceiling that led to the attic. That's where old man McKeown used to lock up the kids when they got a little too big for their britches.

Word has it that, after the accident, old man McKeown locked the oldest boy Stuart in there for better than a week. Stuart was never a big lad. He came out of there all pasty-looking and real quiet, bones sticking out from not having eaten for all those days.

He was always going to be a painter, Stuart was. I've seen a drawing or two of his and they weren't bad, for a fourteen-year-old. Hell, I could even recognize a place or two in some of them. The old boarded-up *schoolhouse. Tom Billy's barn. They say he only ever did the one painting after the accident, but I never did get to see that. Probably still in the house, thrown in a heap with some of the rest of the garbage if the new couple haven't pitched it out yet.*

CRSO

Finished.

He stepped back and studied the painting critically, gaze flitting from the stretched canvas to the square of his window, comparing the two. In the canvas, the asphalt streets narrowed into a distant point. Buildings reared up from the sidewalks, burnished concrete giants with windows of mirrored glass. He'd painted it like it would look after rain. At night. The fluorescent lighting of the buildings spilled out of the windows and made a glistening sheen on the pavement.

The painting had presence. It was as though it, too, were a window, only looking out on a different world. A static world. Not a movement. Not a car. Not a bus. Not a pedestrian on the wet sidewalks. As empty of life, as cold and narrow-bound as his own heart. Devoid of emotion as he'd been since that day when...

He looked out the window, leaving the thought unfinished. The unkempt apple trees kept watch on the far side of the back lawn. Untrimmed branches were choking each other and suckers swarmed up their lower trunks. Beyond the orchard, was a hayfield gone wild. In the middle of the field a rusted thresher. There was a hornet's nest wedged in between the cylinder-head covers. Mice nesting in the padding of the old leather seat. A wind rippled the hay, like a wave that ran the length of the field.

If he didn't look directly at it, at those waves of yellow and the rust island, he could sometimes see his brother. Not as he had been. Not the red-haired, freckled six-year-old that had shared a bowl of Cheerios across the table from him that morning. No. He needed a photograph to see the kid like that again. What he saw out of the corner of his eye was what had come out of the thresher. Sometimes it just lay there, the red seeping from it to puddle in amongst the fresh-cut stubble. But sometimes...

Sometimes he heard his brother coming up the stairs. Not taking them two at a time, his running shoes slapping against the hardwood. No. More a wet sound, as something dragged itself slowly, step by step, up to the landing. And whenever he heard that sound, all he could do was stare at the closed door of his room and wait to see if this time it'd slam open, knock some more plaster off the walls, and Johnny'd be there. Or at least what was left of him.

He waited, but the door never opened. And he never moved. He never went to look. He'd just sit there, feel a trickle of urine start down his legs, throat wound so tight that nothing could come out. Not even a whimper.

There would be nothing left of Johnny, not after the thresher got through with him. Only his eyes would accuse. "You were supposed to be taking care of me that morning, Stu." Supposed to, but he hadn't. He'd been farting around with Billy Franklin in the front yard, lobbing an old baseball back and forth that was held together with white hockey tape.

He hadn't been paying attention to Johnny who was just a pain in the ass little kid anyway, didn't know that he'd wandered around back to where Jake Chassel (Chassel the Asshole, they used to call him) was cutting the summer's first hay for the old man with a beat-up old thresher. No. He didn't know and neither did Jake. Johnny decided to play hide-and-go-seek in the hay and the thresher was it. He must've hidden there too long, started to run to late, got his foot caught in the hay and tripped.

Jake never saw him. He was too busy tipping back a mickey of Five-Star Canadian Whiskey, more than likely, though that never came up at the inquest. He'd heard, even above the roar of the thresher, the sound when the blades caught Johnny, but by then it was too late. There wasn't a whole lot left to do anything with by then.

Stuart looked away from the window and back to his painting. Miss Jennings had given him the paints and canvas — before the accident. She said he had talent. Sure. It took a lot of talent to let your kid brother get eaten by a thresher. Hell, there wasn't another kid in school who'd managed that.

Everything the window reminded him of dissolved when he returned to the painting. There was no hayfield in it, no thresher. No kid brother. Just the stark street with its buildings and sidestreets, clean lines that you could follow with your eye and never have to stop and think about threshers that couldn't tell the difference between a six-year-old and hay. You didn't have to think about your old man downstairs, drinking away the welfare check, nor the old man's mother who divided her time between her rosebushes and staring out the window of her room and never said a word. You didn't have to think about the old man coming up the stairs blind-drunk and kicking the crap out of you, or locking you in the hallway.

He stared at the painting and knew that if he lived in that city, none of that would make any difference. He wouldn't have to listen to the wet sound of his brother's feet squish on the stairs...

He'd found one of Johnny's runners two weeks after the accident. It was lying by the barn, the bloodstains as rusty as the thresher. He hadn't stopped to think about how it had gotten there — didn't want to know — didn't want to run across a hand or a foot or God knew what else, because if they'd missed his running shoe when they were sliding him in that bag, what else might they have missed? No. He'd just sit in his room, work on his painting and stare at the half-completed buildings and the wet street and wish there was some way he could be there, or anywhere, just not here.

He leaned closer to the painting, his eyes only inches from the raised ridges of the daubed oils. He put out a hand, leaned closer still. And then, as though his mind had finally found the roots of irrational thought that let the unreal be real, he found himself slipping forward, felt pavement under his feet and was blinking in the glare of fluorescent lights. He gazed wide-eyed at shop windows blaring SALE! and the lines of displayed goods that had only been daubs of paint when he'd been filling them in. The smell of turpentine and paint, the rank stench of the house and its garbage, faded, and the smells of the city took over.

The wet asphalt had its own odor, a mix of wet stone, something metallic and stale gasoline. From a bakery down the street came a waft of fresh-baked chocolate-chip cookies and bread. When he went down to have a look, there was no one in the store, but all the baked goods were laid out, row on row like they were at the grocery store in Portland, only these weren't individually packaged with a best-before date on them. They sat on metal trays and —

Stuart turned from the bakery window to look back down the street. A chill ran up his spine. With his back against the window, he slowly slid down to his haunches. Looks like he really was a McKeown. Right in there with his old man drinking and talking to

145

the garbage heaped against the kitchen wall, Mother McKeown in her room or with her flowers, his brother who played tag with a thresher. Welcome to the family, Stu. The whole bunch of them crazy as loons.

Because he couldn't see his room anymore. All he could see, towering around him like monolithic playing blocks, was his city. He was looking in the opposite direction from his viewpoint as a painter, looking out of the painting as it were, except his room wasn't there. The city just went on. Wet streets, the huge buildings. A theatre marquee read "NOW PLAYING: PENNIES FROM HEAVEN." There was a Cole's Bookstore beside it. A Fat Albert's across the street. ("THE FUSS IS ON US.") A shoe store. A women's clothing shop. A record store with a big poster of The Rolling Stones in the window. H&R Block. It was his city. A side of it he hadn't seen, but his city all the same, because when he looked to the right, he saw all the stores and buildings he *had* painted. He saw as well —

It was there and gone so quickly that he wasn't even sure that he had seen something. Just a movement in his peripheral vision. (Like when he saw Johnny out of the corner of his eye — but he pushed the memory away. It had no place here. Not in his city.) He stood up and decided that, if he had gone loop-de-loop, he might as well check things out a little. It was hard to take any of it seriously and, when he compared it to what he'd left behind...well, there really wasn't any comparison.

He headed down the street to where he'd half-seen something duck behind a building. At the corner he paused, looking down another unfamiliar street. (He'd only painted one. Everything else was virgin territory.) This was what a madman's city would look like, he thought. It would look perfectly normal. There'd just be intimations of something else. Sliding motions and things you almost heard. (A wet slooshy footstep?) He whirled, looked back. There was nothing. But further down this new sidestreet, a shadow ducked into an alleyway.

He ran down to the corner, his shoes slapping on the wet pavement. He tried not to think of what that sound reminded him of, but the image rose up all the same. Johnny coming up the stairs. Except that was there. Away. He was in his city now and not Johnny, not the old man, not even Mother McKeown could touch him. There was just whatever-it-had-been, ducking down the alleyway.

146

He paused between the buildings, considering the alley's composition with a painter's eye. There were three garbage cans on the right, halfway down. Two were lidded. The third stood gaping, its lid leaning against the red brick of the back alley. The lighting was dimmer — as it should be. All it lacked was a big tom, perched on a trashcan lid.

He caught a flicker of movement in a puddle at his feet, realized it was a reflection, then fell down in terror as a black shape flew by his head with a shrill cry. He rolled into a sitting position, gaze going up. There, caught in the glare of the sidestreet's lights, he saw it. A raven. It swooped down, just missing a lamppost, then winged on down the street.

His city was supposed to be empty, Stuart thought. He wasn't so much frightened as angry as he got to his feet, patted his wet jeans ineffectually, then set off in pursuit of the bird. He watched it dip its wings in a mocking salute just before vanishing around another corner. Breath coming sharply, Stuart followed. When he reached the corner, he paused, following the bird's flight as it headed down the street he'd painted. It wasn't supposed to be here. He wouldn't let it be here. Not in his city.

It wasn't so much the bird's intrusion as what it reminded him of. It wasn't an urban creature. It didn't belong here. It came from miles of corn and hayfields. Places where your kid brother played tag with a thresher and the old man got drunk and talked to garbage. A place where Mother McKeown kept an endless vigil, watching nothing. A place where you were becoming too much like all of them. Watching nothing. Talking to walls. Staring at that damned thresher and remembering...The raven was like an unbidden thought, a tormenting reminder. And it didn't belong here.

He came to a sports shop and went in, chose a ten-speed Raleigh that made the one-speed piece of junk he had at home seem like the one-speed piece of junk it was. Rolling it out of the store, he headed down the street after the raven, switching gears awkwardly, gaze locked more on the bird than where it was leading him. He shouted himself hoarse, pumped until he thought his legs would fall off, but still the raven led him on.

The buildings weren't so tall anymore. Trendy downtown stores became seedier, lost their glitter. There were pawnshops here. Feed & Seed stores. An empty market, the fruit and vegetables rotting on their stands. Used instrument shops. Second-run movie theatres with triple bills. There was litter in the streets, like the garbage back home that the old man strewed about and let lie where it fell, that Mother McKeown didn't see and that he didn't care about.

The older buildings gave way to factories and industrial outlets. He passed a John Bull farm machinery factory with averted eyes. The industrial area, in its turn, gave way to an expanse of fields and bush lots, then to neat suburbs, which in turn gave way to rural homes and farms. Finally he was pedaling down Harlem Road and he saw his own house. The raven entered it by the kitchen door.

He threw his bike down by one of Mother McKeown's rosebushes, looked through the orchard and saw the old man sitting on the thresher, his head bent over its controls. He was asleep or drunk. Or both. Feeling sick, he kicked open the door and ran up to his own room. The raven wasn't there. And neither was his painting. The easel stood empty, awaiting a fresh canvass. Stolen! Either his father or Mother McKeown had taken it!

The object of his anger switched, quick as thought. The raven had led him here to show him this. Not to torment him. He tried his grandmother's room, but though the painting wasn't there, there was another on the wall. Mother McKeown lay sprawled across the floor, recognizable only by her thin limbs and the faded print dress she invariably wore. What was left of the rest of her was splattered on the wall like a piece of surrealistic art, except its medium was blood and the pockmarked traces of shotgun pellets, not paint, and —

Stuart stumbled numbly from the room. He pressed his face against the rotting plaster in the hall, unable to think, unable to move.

And then he heard it — a soft, wet sound that came from the hallway where the old man used to lock him up. Stuart didn't have to look to know what was there. But he went to the door, turned the handle and let it creak open.

There was his painting, leaning against a wall. In the dark — God! If it were only darker! — was what remained of his brother. Johnny turned a familiar accusing eye to Stuart, ran his paintbrush along his arm and turned back to the painting. The raven was perched on top, talons cutting through the canvas. It pointed to a streetlight and, dutifully, Johnny began to paint it red.

"No!" Stuart screamed.

He lunged forward, hands spread out before him, and for the second time that day, went through the painting. He sprawled onto asphalt, scraping his face, knocking the breath out of him. Everywhere he looked, the city appeared as though through a red gauze. He heard a rumble — a screech of metal against stone. Turning, he saw a rusted thresher lumbering down the road towards him.

He tried to get up, but something caught at his leg. Looking down, he saw his feet were entangled in hay that was sprouting up through jagged cracks in the asphalt. He shredded his fingernails as he tried to drag himself free. Up on the thresher, he saw Jake Chassel, head tilted back, Adam's apple bobbing as he chugged back a third of a bottle of Five-Star.

That was the last thing Stuart saw.

ক্ষ্ফ০

I suppose Stuart's running off was what finally broke old man McKeown, though Lord knows he didn't show the boy much affection when he was around. Leastways, that's what the official word was. The boy ran off and old McKeown loaded up his 12-gauge, went upstairs and blew away his mother — God rest her soul. Then he went back down, reloaded, sat himself down in the seat of the damnable thresher and calmly blew himself away.

Oh, they had a look around the old place for the boy, but they never turned him up, dead or alive. Sgt. Maveety had to take the news to the boy's mum, Ernestina. (She was a Brown from up Renfrew way before she married McKeown and knew a fair bit about both farming and drinking, which was why she left McKeown when she did. She just "couldn't take no more," she told my Emma. "Woulda took the boys, but he'd've followed me clear 'cross the Rockies to keep 'em. I didn't want any more trouble.") I guess Sgt. Maveety's visit was the last bit of trouble she was going to get from the McKeowns.

The boy wasn't there and never turned up, so the official report read just like I told you. But I don't know. They say a crazy man can be pretty smart, in his own way. McKeown might've hid that boy's body anywhere, if he did kill him. Then again, Stuart could still be hiding out in the bush somewhere. Hard to say. I like to think that he did take off and he's doing well somewhere. Guess we'll never know.

I do know I don't like passing by the McKeown place. Folks have said they've seen Mother McKeown's face in the window, from time to time, or caught a glimpse of her working at one of her rosebushes which are still doing fine. And what with not knowing whatever happened to Stuart...Maybe I'll feel better about the place once the new folks have it fixed up. But then again, maybe they'll find Stuart's body boarded up behind a wall. Hell. I don't even want *to know.*

From a 24" Screen

Pritchard wished they wouldn't do it. He checked his watch again —
10:05 PM, July 5 — and looked back at the *TV Times*. The Saturday,
July 5, listing spelled it out in plain black & white:

10:00: (4) (6M) THE RETURN OF THE SAINT.
Simon Templar poses as an Austrian diplomat when
a young woman asks him to investigate the disappearance
of her father.

So what was this baseball game doing on the tube? If he'd wanted
to watch a bunch of jocks batting a ball around, he wouldn't have
turned to channel 4 (8 on the converter) at 10:00 p.m. when the *TV
Times* clearly said that —

He looked at the screen again, his jaw suddenly slack. The batter
had reversed his bat, pointing it at the pitcher's mound. A spurt of
flame burst from its end, incinerating the pitcher. The camera panned
back to show the whole of the playing field.

The outfielders knelt by small mortars, lobbing shells into the
opposing team's benches. More than half missed their mark.
Explosions rocked the spectators' stands. The infielders were firing
away with some sort of — waddaya call 'em? — lasers. A guy came
running in from the benches. The camera zoomed in on his face as a
bullet took him between the eyes.

Pritchard became aware of the commentator's voice then. It was calm, but sharp across the roar of gunfire and screams.

"Finally some action here, late in the third inning. Can we get a replay on that last one, Frank?"

A quick shift on the screen. Pritchard watched the guy run in from the benches again, this time in slow motion.

"Johnny Hanser, number 33," the sportscaster continued matter-of-factly. "This is only his second season and it looks to be his last. But when you've got a pro like 'Longtom' Wilier behind the trigger, a rookie of two seasons hasn't really got a—"

Pritchard stared, unable to believe what he was seeing. What kind of a weird flick was this anyway? He turned his face as the tiny hole sprouted in Johnny Hanser's forehead, trying to forget what the back of the guy's head would look like when the bullet came out. Bruger had been talking about it at the office just last week, smiling as he described all the gory details.

Pritchard reached for the converter to switch the channel. His eyes darted back to the screen as his fingers found the controls. The stands were in flames now. Panicked fans swelled into the playing field in a wave of terror.

The opposing team made a sortie from their benches. Lines of machine-gun bullets kicked up puffs of dirt between the first and second bases. He heard the sportscaster's unruffled voice as though it came from a great distance.

"They've definitely got a chance if they can drop Collers on third. But the outfield's keeping up a good covering fire and—They got him! Collers is down! Now with Jones's and Tanrider's crossfire opening up the pitcher's mound it looks like we've still got a ballgame! But first a word from our sponsor..."

The scene on the screen switched abruptly to a mountain slope where two husky men in jeans and plaid shirts were effortlessly maneuvering a glider onto a railed runway that ran the length of the slope. To one side, a third man and three well-endowed women stood watching them. There was a case of Labatt's 50 on a picnic table behind them. Pritchard hardly paid attention to the beer commercial.

He took another look at his watch, wondering if this was *Saturday Night Live* or something. The dial read 10:10. He had the right station. So what the hell was this show? Maybe it was one of those made-for-television specials. Except the violence was too graphic. And some of those guys had guns that looked like they came straight off the set of *Star Wars*. There was something about the sportscaster's face that bothered him as well. He'd seen it somewhere recently…

The commercials were over. Pritchard's hand stayed on the converter, his eyes glued to the screen. The sportscaster's face returned to fill the screen. His tie was loose. There was sweat on his forehead. The clamor in the background sounded all too much like a full-scale war.

"Well, waddaya think, Eddie?" the sportscaster asked. His gaze seemed to leap out at Pritchard, impaling him with its intensity. "Beginning to enjoy it now?"

Pritchard started, almost answering before he caught himself. For a moment there he'd thought —

"Hey! Eddie Pritchard! I'm talking to *you!*"

Pritchard stared at the screen, dumbfounded. Involuntarily, his finger flicked the on/off switch on the converter. The screen went black. He looked at his hands and found he was shaking uncontrollably. He swallowed dryly, Adam's apple bobbing, and reached for his coffee.

The cup was only half-full, but he was shaking so badly that he managed to spill most of it over his knees. He sat the cup down on the coffee table with a loud clunk. Ignoring the spreading stain on his pants, he looked at the darkened screen.

Eddie Pritchard. For Christ's sake! *He* was Eddie Pritchard.

He could feel his body temperature dropping as a chill shivered though him. Something like a cold hand squeezed his heart.

It was simple coincidence, he told himself. It was a movie, nothing more. It wasn't like he was the only Edward Pritchard in the world. There were at least three others in the phone book — one on Rachel, another on Riverside Drive, the third on…

He shook his head. What the hell was he making excuses for? It was just some movie. He'd probably picked up PBS by mistake and they were showing the *Monty Python* series for another fundraising drive. But when he looked at the converter the channel indicator was plainly on 8, which made it the CBC in Ottawa, channel 4.

He took a deep breath to steady himself. He reached for his coffee and was able to finish it without spilling any more. Screwing up his courage against an unreasonable fear—it was *just* a movie—he switched the TV back on.

The screen burst into life.

"But, Simon..." a blonde woman said, holding onto The Saint's arm.

Simon Templar smiled winningly. He looked away from her, across a lonely heath where a house stood shadowed on the horizon. "They won't know," he said. "I've seen to—"

Pritchard turned the set off. His hands shook so badly that he knocked the converter to the floor. He buried his face in his hands, unable to face the screen that stared at him like a dark eye from across the room. He remembered the sportscaster's face now. It'd been there when—

"Oh, Jesus, Jesus..."

The first time he'd been sitting in his car at the corner of Bank and Sunnyside, waiting for the light to change. As it turned green, the kid in the inner lane gunned his car, cutting him off. He'd gone blank for a moment, then saw two men kneeling on either side of the road, blasting the kid's car in a withering crossfire, semi-automatic rifles bucking against their shoulders.

He remembered grinning, enjoying it because he'd always wanted to see something like that. The kid was getting his just rewards, never mind that Pritchard had done the same thing himself a hundred times or more. But then someone behind him honked. His vision blurred, then cleared. Ahead he saw the kid's taillights disappearing over the hill down to Lansdowne Park. And there'd been this guy standing in front of Elaine's Irish Disco with the strangest look on his face. The sportscaster...

Then there'd been the girl on Elgin Street—tight jeans, Danskin top, hair bouncing down to her ass. That same guy'd stepped out of Aziz's Bakery and emptied a full clip from the smoking barrel of 5.56mm 63A belt-fed Light Machine Gun into her. She'd fallen in a tumble of slack limbs, her body jerking as the bullets riddled her.

The sharp acrid odor of gunsmoke bit at his nostrils. He heard the bullets ricocheting down Elgin Street. And there'd been that voice, the guy's voice, right in his ear.

"You're gonna enjoy it. Wait and see..."

Thompson in the office next door playing that damn cassette machine of his. Born Again Christian sermons. The same droning voice going on and on, over and over. And then he'd heard the sermon change. The preacher twisted the familiar words into mockeries of themselves. He'd sat there chortling to himself, imagining the look on Thompson's face as the preacher started cursing. He jumped when he heard the muffled explosion. His pens rattled on his desk and he heard another voice — that guy on Elgin Street — saying, "It's getting better. Really."

He was phoning long-distance to Toronto — using the government phone, of course — when he heard the operator scream. The gunshots echoed tinnily through the receiver. And the voice cutting in again —

Pritchard held his head between his hands. His veins in his temples were throbbing. He didn't seem to have the strength to walk down the hall and get some painkillers from the medicine cabinet. Damn things never worked anyway, no matter what anyone said.

"Oh, Jesus."

❦

Sunday, July 6.

After four weekends of rainy Sundays, it seemed a little weird to wake up to crystal blue skies and sunlight so bright it shimmered on the street. Pritchard finished his coffee on the porch. He'd brought some research papers home that he'd planned to edit today, certain it was going to rain. But with a day like this, damned if he was going to work on them now.

It wasn't like he was behind or anything. He was doing in one week what his predecessor barely finished in three. But that was the Silly Service for you. It sometimes seemed that the government wanted you to work as slowly as possible — just keep those man-hours high and the money flowing into the department's budget.

He took a walk down by the canal, watched the roller skaters skidding into the railings, groping and giggling. Joggers followed the paths with those healthier-than-thou looks on their faces. There were girls tanning on the grass. He passed a loud-mouthed kid demanding an ice cream from his fat mother who was in a T-Shirt at least two sizes too small for her that read "Foxy Lady."

Humming under his breath, he relaxed and enjoyed the sun. He never thought of the baseball game last night. Never thought about

155

all those other weird things he'd been seeing and hearing. The sun was too bright. The day too fine. Weirdness was relegated to some dim corner of his mind — distant and separate from the moment.

He passed a couple of kids. Their transistor radio was blaring out the Stones' new single "Emotional Rescue."

Damn, but it was a fine day.

CRSO

Wednesday, July 9.

"So I said, 'Screw you, too,' and you know what he said?"

Pritchard shook his head. He topped his beer and set the bottle down so that the label faced outward. He was only half-listening to Peter, his attention more on the sway of the waitress's hips as she walked back to the bar. He looked up at the television set above the bar when she was out of sight. There was a baseball game in progress. He remembered Saturday night with a sudden chill and looked away.

"He says, 'If you're inta scabs, don't...' Hey, Ed? You listenin'?"

"Sure, Pete."

Pritchard took a long pull from his beer and set the glass down carefully in the circle of foam on the table. All he could think of was these weird violent flashes that kept coming to him. Here, then gone. That was the weirdest part of it. They vanished as quick as they came, returning only when something cued them in. Like that friggin' TV set in the corner.

"You ever want to see someone die?" he asked suddenly, looking up to meet Peter's puzzled eyes.

Peter frowned. "I dunno, Ed. Waddaya mean? Like when someone pisses me off an' I wanna punch him in the head?"

Pritchard stared at him, appalled. Jesus, he thought. What am I saying? He shook his head emphatically.

"Naw. I don't know what I was thinking about, Pete. Say, when're you guys going on strike?"

"End of the month, unless those suckers come up with somethin' better'n seven percent over two years. Seven percent! I mean..."

But Pritchard wasn't listening. He saw that sportscaster standing behind Peter with a Magnum .44 in his hand. He aimed the gun at Peter's head, finger tightening on the trigger...

Thursday, July 10.

It was happening all too often now. The fear that he'd lost his mind was a steady undercurrent setting his nerves constantly on edge. He remembered each incident with a frightening clarity, all the gory details. But he couldn't be crazy. That only happened to wackos, or people under too much pressure. He had an easy job, a good social life…

He was supposed to take Julie to Theatre 2000 tonight. They were running *Killing Time*—a punk play, for Christ's sake. He wished the projectionists' strike was over so that they could go to a decent movie.

Thinking of Julie took his thoughts down a corridor of his mind where a door opened into…the weirdness. He had an image of her there, lying on the ground with her throat cut, and couldn't get it out of his mind. Her throat was cut, and the razor was all bloody in his hand, and that voice was whispering, "You're enjoying it too, aren't you? *Aren't* you?"

He stood in the bathroom and stared at the mirror. I don't look like a wacko, he thought. He rubbed his chin, knowing he could use a shave, but somehow he couldn't bring himself to take the razor from the medicine cabinet. All he could think about was Julie and her nagging him about one thing or the other and the razor lying there and she probably deserved it anyway…

She answered the phone on the fifth ring.

"Hi, Julie. Yeah, I'm okay. I was calling about that. Listen, I've got work piled up around my ears and ended up having to take some home tonight. Yeah. Well, Dr. Chandler's supposed to make a presentation at a meeting tomorrow morning. For 8:30. Yeah. I should've told him that. Yeah, me too. Okay. No, Saturday night'd be fine. See you then."

He cradled the phone, staring at it. He heard a noise coming from the living room and looked down the hall. The TV was on. He heard an announcer's voice—one of those talk show hosts that was always yapping through a toothy grin. But he hadn't turned the set on and that voice was the same voice as…

"Hey, Eddie! You with us? Bill, tell the audience and Eddie what he could win this week on *You've Got a Chance*."

"Well, Joe. How about a complete set of English Tupperware..."

Pritchard lunged to his feet. As he reached the door to the living room, the sound died away. He stood in the doorway, regarding the dead screen with revulsion. A headache was building up in the back of his head, throbbing with all the insistent force of a jackhammer banging away at the back of his skull. He stumbled to the bathroom for the Anacin, stared at the razor lying on the second shelf between his shaving cream and Old Spice aftershave.

"All my men wear..."

Or was that English Leather?

His straying thoughts focused sharply on the tiny strip of blade that protruded from his razor, as though there were nothing in the world except himself and that tiny length of steel. He fumbled for the bottle of painkillers on the third shelf, knocking eye drops and a plastic Scope bottle into the sink. He took three pills and swallowed them dry. Backing from the medicine cabinet, he made his way to the bedroom and flung himself lengthwise across the bed.

"I dunno, Ed," he remembered Peter saying when Pritchard told him about his new apartment. It was the lower half of a house on a nice quiet street in Centretown. "I heard about that place. The guy that lived there was a wacko, you know what I mean? A real friggin' class-A weirdo maniac. I mean, jeez. They found three stiffs there, all cut up. There musta been blood everywhere."

"It's been repainted."

Peter only shook his head. "Yeah, but it's still there. Under the paint. I couldn't hack it, Ed."

"You know where I can get a three-bedroom apartment for $150 a month anywhere else in this city? The landlord almost gave it to me rent-free, he was so happy to have someone take it."

"But..."

"And talk about classy."

Peter looked away, his face troubled. "I dunno, Ed. I dunno. But listen. You start getting weird ideas, you get the hell out of there. Fast. You know what I mean?"

"Pete..."

"Hey, I'm serious, man. That other guy—what's his name?"

"Williams. Joseph Williams." Pritchard, like everyone else in Ottawa, had read the front page coverage in *The Citizen* when they'd busted Williams.

"Yeah. Him. You read what he said at his trial? Said the house made him do it. The place is haunted. Like in that King book."

"Oh, Jesus. Give it a break." Pritchard smiled. "He was copping an insanity plea, for Christ's sake. You ever heard of a haunted apartment, Pete?"

"I dunno. But that guy was wacko alright."

಼ೞಲ

Pritchard rolled over on his back to stare at the ceiling. Well, he was certainly getting weird ideas. He thought of Julie again, thought of the razor. It'd be easy. Just click it out of it's handy-dandy plastic handle. It'd cut deep, too. A little messy, maybe. He could almost see...

"Jesus!"

He sat up, fear turning his stomach acidic. He could hear that friggin' announcer's voice in his head.

You're beginning to enjoy it now...

He moped his brow, trying to still the pounding of his heart. He heard the TV go on. The sound of gunfire drew him into the living room and this time the TV stayed on. He lowered his shaking body into a chair. Watching the screen, his face was bloodless, his hands gripping the chair's arms.

There was some kind of circus or Ice Capades special on, only these guys dressed up as clowns were mowing down the skaters with machine guns. One clown turned to face the camera and the picture moved into a close-up. The painted face was familiar, even under the heavy makeup. The red grin against the white greasepaint leered at Pritchard. He shrank back as the clown winked, then turned away, machine gun bucking in his hands. Pritchard felt like screaming, but all he could do was watch.

You're beginning to enjoy it now...

಼ೞಲ

Friday, July 11.

He'd had dinner. He could remember that. The dirty dishes were still piled up in the sink. He'd seen them there when he'd gone in to wash off the nice—Oh, God. The knife.

After dinner what? He'd been watching the TV again. There'd been these guys in weird masks—like they sold in Bill's Joke Shop, the rubber ones that fit right over your head so that you could look like a wax-doll Nixon or werewolf or something. And they'd been cutting up a...He shrank from the memory. He'd been watching TV—just watching—but he'd blacked out for a moment or...He looked at his watch. Christ. It couldn't have been more than 7:30 when he'd turned the set on and those guys had cut in, right in the middle of the opening credits for *The Two Ronnies*. And then...The guy in the mummy's mask had just sort of opened up and everybody'd been cutting and he'd felt the knife in his own hand...

The knife. And the blood on it. He'd washed it off in the sink without really thinking what the hell he was doing. He stared at it where it lay on the kitchen counter. He'd never seen that knife before. It was the kind you'd see in an old horror flick—a long butcher's knife with a worn wooden handle, the kind a hunchback or psycho'd carry...

Pritchard backed out of the kitchen. What if he'd killed somebody? What if he'd gone out in the streets and butchered somebody with that knife? He made his way to the door of the bathroom. The painkillers were still there on the sink. But to get them, he'd have to go in front of the open medicine cabinet and the razor was still there and there was Julie...

Blindly, he pushed himself away from the door, stumbling for the bedroom. As he fell across the bed he heard the TV go on again.

"Eddie...Eddie..."

The voices sang his name as though it were the chorus of a commercial. He burrowed into the pillows, hands pressed against his ears.

You're beginning to enjoy it now...

"No! No, I'm not!"

You're beginning to enjoy it now...

CR8O

Saturday, July 12.

The jangle of the telephone's ringing cut harshly across the still morning. Pritchard looked at the digital clock-radio by the bed. 10:43

a.m. He reached for the phone, tucked it under his chin, and lay back on the bed.

"Hello?"

"Ed? It's Julie. How's things?"

Julie, he thought, picturing her suddenly. The razor was still in the medicine cabinet.

"Uh..."

"I tried to call you at work yesterday, but you weren't in. You weren't at home either 'cos I tried a few times. Where've you been, lover-boy? Or should I ask *who've* you been with?"

He heard the edge in her voice, grating on his nerves like a fingernail on a chalkboard. Lay off, he thought. Then what she'd said struck home. He hadn't been to work yesterday? Had he even gone in on Thursday? Christ, he couldn't remember. Couldn't remember the phone ringing either...if he'd even *been* home. He remembered the knife...

"You still there, Ed?"

"Uh, yeah. I'm still here. I've been sick, Julie. Never heard the phone ring, I guess."

"Well, how are you feeling today?"

"A little better."

"Are you still up for tonight, then?"

"Tonight?"

Oh, Jesus, he had a headache again. But the painkillers were in the bathroom with the razor and this was Julie on the phone and he was having weird thoughts.

The place is haunted, he could remember Peter saying.

"Yeah, tonight. Or have you got someone else coming over?"

"No, no. There's no one coming over. I guess I'm still a little under the weather, you know?"

"Mmhmm. Maybe I should come over and nurse you back to health. What do you say?"

"Come over? Here?"

All he could think of was the razor lying in the medicine cabinet and he was having weird thoughts. But he wasn't a wacko. Not him.

"Ed, is there someone with you right now?"

"No. Really, Julie."

161

The TV went on just then. He heard soft instrumental music drifting in from the living room. It was probably one of those nature shows like *Wild, Wild World of Animals*. He could hear an announcer's voice now, muted with the distance. How come those guys always sounded the same? Except this one sounded different. Familiar. Pritchard shook the thought from him. But maybe they were going on safari today. Hunting...

"Well, do you mind if I come over?" Julie asked. "I mean if there's no one there and you're not *expecting* anyone..."

"Uh, sure...sure. Come on over." What was he saying?

"But you're beginning to enjoy it now," the voice from the television whispered.

He shook his head numbly.

"I'll see you in an hour or so then. Okay?"

"Uh, sure."

He cradled the phone, staring at it as though it were responsible for all his troubles. Julie was coming over. And the razor was still in the bathroom and — Christ! The knife in the kitchen. Where had the blood come from? What if he'd really killed someone?

You're really enjoying it now...

"No, I'm not!" he shouted. "For Christ's sake, will ya leave me alone?"

He pushed himself up from the bed, stumbled past the living room — I will *not* look in — and went to get the paper. He sat on the front porch scanning the headlines with a mixture of anticipation and fear. But the worst that was there was whether or not Parliament was going to go through with such-and-such-a-bill, and the ambassador-of-so-and-so had gotten ill at a garden party. A girl in a red swimsuit stared up at him from the front page. Underneath a caption read: "Fun at the beach. At least some local beaches are still safe..."

Relief/disappointment welled in him.

He looked up and down the street. His upstairs neighbor came down his separate stairwell on the right side of the house. Pritchard nodded to him.

"Nice day, eh?" He tried on a smile.

"Yeah, it's okay. Say, do you think you could turn your TV down a little after 11:00? I don't mind it on weekends so much, but I gotta work during the week, you know what I mean? It's kinda hard to get to sleep with that thing blaring up through the floor."

"Sure, sure. No problem."

"Say, what were you watching last night anyway? It sounded like the *weirdest* movie."

You start getting weird thoughts, you get the hell out of there…

Pritchard shrugged, feeling the sweat bead on his brow. "Uh, I'm not sure. Didn't catch the title."

"Yeah, well try and keep it down, okay?"

Resentment rushed through Pritchard. Then he saw a girl step out from around the corner of the house, her eyes rolling, a machete upraised in her hands. He looked away before it fell.

"I-I'll try," he managed.

"Well, see ya 'round."

Looking up, he watched his neighbor walk off down the street. The girl with the machete was still there, smiling at him. She lifted the blade, ran a finger along the blood on it and put that finger in her mouth, still smiling…

"You should try it," she said, only her voice was the sportscaster's voice.

A sour taste raced up Pritchard's throat. He bolted for his door, slamming it behind him. Standing in the hall, he held the newspaper rolled like a club in his hand, his fingernails gouging ragged holes in it.

"Hey, Eddie!" the smooth-voiced narrator/sportscaster/clown called from the living room.

Numbly, Pritchard dropped the paper on the floor and shuffled in. He sat down in the chair that faced the TV screen.

"Hey, Eddie! Long time no see."

The clown stared out at him, grinning hugely.

Pritchard thought of Julie coming over. There was the knife he had to throw away and the razor, because…

"You're really beginning to enjoy this now, aren't you, Eddie?"

The clown laughed as he spoke.

"No," Pritchard mumbled weakly. "I'm not. I'm really not."

"Hey, Eddie. Don't be a partypooper. I've got a — whoops. Time for a commercial. Be right back, Eddie, so don't go away."

"No. I don't want to see anymore…"

The clown's face dissolved. A commercial began—a man and a woman on a sailboat, the wind lifting their hair, the sun golden on their perfect tans. Pritchard scrabbled for leverage on the arms of his chair, trying to push himself up, but the clown reappeared as soon as he was standing.

"Hey! No fair, Eddie. Come on. Stay and watch."

Compelled by the voice, Pritchard fell back into the chair. He watched a string of meaningless commercials that slowly shifted in tone from hucksters selling deodorant, to grim men in black suits offering a multitude of deadly products.

"Gladstock Hardware, for the finest weaponry money can buy."

"Why go to a doctor when you can use Homemedic? Quick, reliable service with no questions asked."

"Public or Corporate corruption got *you* down? Try Rentassassin for sure relief!"

Then came a station identification by the woman who'd been outside his house licking the blood from the machete. When the clown returned, his painted smile was crimson and wide.

"You enjoying yourself, Eddie?"

Numbly, Pritchard nodded. He stared at the screen, unable to do anything but watch. His legs shook violently and he grabbed the arms of the chair so tightly that his knuckles whitened.

There was something he was supposed to do. Something he had to remember.

He worried at the thought but it kept drifting away.

There was something...

"You know who I am, Eddie?"

The camera panned back to show a full-length view of the clown. He had his machine gun in his hand. The camera focused in on a close-up of the clown's white-gloved fingers as he undid the safety on his weapon. Pritchard could feel the blood pounding in his head. His shirt stuck to his back. A headache throbbed behind his temples.

"You know who I am, Eddie?" the clown repeated.

His greasepaint was drying and began to flake from his face. Pritchard's eyes were locked on the clown's face and he was rigid with terror. Recognition dawned on him, still distant, but coming. He knew that face, knew it from so many horrifying vignettes, but he could recall another time he'd seen it, in black and white, a photo somewhere, perhaps in a newspaper.

The doorbell rang.

Julie!

Pritchard tried to move, to tear himself from the chair, but he couldn't free himself.

The doorbell rang again.

Don't come in! he pleaded silently. Something terrible's going to happen.

He heard the doorknob turn.

"Do you know me, Eddie?"

"No," he croaked, but he knew. He remembered the photo in the newspaper and the caption under it. "Joseph Williams, the Centretown Butcher." But the guy was supposed to be in a loony bin somewhere. They'd locked him up and threw the key away.

"Oh, they did that," the clown murmured.

Pritchard tried to scream a warning to Julie. His throat was thick with fear and all that came out was an inaudible gurgle. Helpless under the clown's will, he couldn't move. But if he didn't free himself, the clown was going to make him do something — something terrible that he was going to enjoy…

"No, Eddie. You're not going to enjoy this. But I am. I like to see people die, Eddie."

The camera zoomed in to show a close-up of the clown's face. Most of the makeup had flaked off. The man's wild red-rimmed eyes burned into Pritchard's.

"Ed?" he heard Julie call. "Ed? Are you home?"

He found himself rising. He knew where he was going. To the bathroom to get the razor on the third shelf of the medicine cabinet. He had to, because Julie was here. He paused in the hallway to look at the door. Julie stood there staring at him. His gaze focused on her hairline where he could see traces of dried-up white greasepaint. He looked down at the machine gun in her hand, took a step back as her finger tightened on the trigger.

Pritchard felt the bullets hit him, a spurt of gunfire that tore a soundless scream from his lips and drove him back against the wall, arms pinwheeling for balance. The last thing he heard was Joseph Williams laughing on the TV screen.

CR80

165

Julie Curtis frowned at the front door and knocked again. She could hear the TV from where she stood. So why doesn't he answer the door? she thought. She tried the handle. Finding the door unlocked, she pushed it open. Her eyes widened as it swung inward.

Pritchard lay in a grotesque sprawl in the hallway. His eyes were blank and fixed on the television set where some woman was extolled the virtues of Tide detergent. His face was twisted into a grimace of absolute terror.

Julie took a few steps forward. Kneeling at Pritchard's side, she reached out with a trembling hand. As she touched his cheek, his head rolled face-down on the floor. She drew back her hand with a start. Shock smothered the scream that was building up in her throat. Her face drained of color. Peripherally, she was aware that the commercial on the TV had ended. A new voice was speaking. Its insistent tones drew her out of her paralysis.

"Hey, Julie! Long time no see."

Slowly she turned to face the TV set. She saw the clown first, then Pritchard. They were both dressed in white coveralls. Pritchard held a bloody razor in his hand. They were both smiling.

"You're really going to enjoy this," the clown said.

Bordertown

Bordertown: An Introduction

Fifty years from now, Elfland came back.

It stuck a finger into a large city, creating a borderland between our world and that glittering realm with its elves and magic. As the years went by, the two worlds remained separate, co-existing only in that place where magic and reality overlap. A place called Bordertown.

CRSO

That's the original premise as set up by Terri Windling, the creator and editor of the "Bordertown" series, with creative input from Mark Alan Arnold, and later from Delia Sherman. Once Terri had roughly sketched in the background, she let the rest of us in to play. (By us, I refer to the authors who filled the first volume of the series with their stories: Bellamy Bach, Steven R. Boyett, Ellen Kushner, and myself.) And we had some fun, because the "shared world" of Bordertown was different from other shared worlds. It had an edge, and a relevance to the here-and-now, that went beyond the image of a Mohawked elf in leathers, riding through a gritty city street on a chopper.

The imagery was certainly fun – part Child ballad, part MTV – but what made Bordertown important to those of us who transcribed its stories, and to those of us who read them, was that it presented us with an opportunity to address modern concerns in a contemporary manner, while still getting to bounce riffs off each other's stories (in the best tradition of a musical jam), not to mention giving us a chance to play with the faerie of

169

Elfland and the curious juxtapositioning of its magic against the gritty reality of Bordertown's rock'n'roll clubs, back alleys, and city streets.

Because, for all the distance in time from the present day, for all its magic which remains so shimmeringly impossible in our mundane world, Bordertown is still about the here-and-now. For all their trappings, the stories are about us, living in this world, as much as they are about the inhabitants of Bordertown.

Stick

Then to the Maypole haste away
For 'tis now our holiday.

—from "Staines Morris"
English traditional

Stick paused by his vintage Harley at the sound of a scuffle. Squinting, he looked for its source. The crumbling blocks of Soho surrounded him. Half-gutted buildings and rubble-strewn lots bordered either side of the street. There could be a hundred pairs of eyes watching him—from the ruined buildings, from the rusted hulks of long abandoned cars—or there could be no one. There were those who claimed that ghosts haunted this part of Soho, and maybe they did, but it wasn't ghosts that Stick was hearing just now.

Some Bloods out Pack-bashing. Maybe some of the Pack out elf-bashing. But it was most likely some rats—human or elfin, it didn't matter which—who'd snagged themselves a runaway and were having a bit of what they thought was fun.

Runaways gravitated to Bordertown from the outside world, particularly to Soho, and most particularly to this quarter, where there were no landlords and no rent. Just the scavengers. And the rats. But they could be the worst of all.

Putting his bike back on its kickstand, Stick pocketed the elfin spell-box that fueled it.

171

Lubin growled softly from her basket strapped to the back of the bike—a quizzical sound.

"Come on," Stick told the ferret. He started across the street without looking to see if she followed.

Lubin slithered from the basket and crossed the road at Stick's heels. She was a cross between a polecat and a ferret, larger than either, with sharp pointed features and the lean build of the weasel family. When Stick paused in the doorway of the building from which the sounds of the scuffle were coming, she flowed over the toes of his boots and into its foyer, off to one side. Her hiss was the assailants' first hint that they were no longer alone.

They were three Bloods, beating up on a small unrecognizable figure that was curled up into a ball of tattered clothes at their feet. Their silver hair was dyed with streaks of orange and black; their elfin faces, when they looked up from their victim to see Stick standing in the doorway, were pale, skin stretched thin over high-boned features, silver eyes gleaming with malicious humor.

They were dressed all of a kind—three assembly line Bloods in black leather jackets, frayed jeans, T-shirts and motorcycle boots.

"Take a walk, hero," one of them said.

Stick reached up over his left shoulder and pulled out a sectional staff from its sheath on his back. With a sharp flick of his wrist, the three two-foot sections snapped into a solid staff, six feet long.

"I don't think so," he said.

"He don't think so," the first of the Bloods mocked.

"This here's our meat," a second said, giving their victim another kick. He reached inside his jacket, his hand reappearing with a switchblade. Grinning, he thumbed the button to spring it open.

Knives appeared in the hands of the other two—one from a wrist sheath. Stick didn't bother to talk. While they postured with their blades, he became a sudden blur of motion.

The staff spun in his hands, leaving broken wrists and airborne switchblades in its wake. A moment later, the Bloods were clutching mangled wrists to their chests. Stick wasn't even winded.

He made a short feint with the staff and all three Bloods jumped as though they'd been struck again. When he stepped towards their victim, they backed away.

"You're dead," one of them said flatly. "You hear me, Choc'let?"

Stick took a quick step towards them and they fled. Shaking his head, he turned to look at where Lubin was snuffling around their prize.

It was a girl, and definitely a runaway, if the ragged clothes were anything to go by. Considering current Soho fashion, that wasn't exactly a telling point. But her being here...that was another story. She had fine pale features and spiked hair a mauve she was never born with.

Stick crouched down beside her, one hand grasping his staff and using it for balance. "You okay?" he asked.

Her eyelids flickered, then her silver eyes were looking into his.

"Aw, shit," Stick said.

No wonder those Bloods'd had a hard-on for her. If there was one thing they hated more than the Pack, it was a halfling. She wasn't really something he had time for either.

"Can you stand?" he asked.

A delicate hand reached out to touch his. Pale lashes fluttered ingenuously. She started to speak, but then her eyes winked shut and her head drooped against the pile of rags where she'd been cornered by the Bloods.

"Shit!" Stick muttered again. Breaking down his staff, he returned it to its sheath.

Lubin growled and he gave her a baleful look.

"Easy for you to side with her," he said as he gathered the frail halfling in his arms. "She's probably related to you as well as the Bloods."

Lubin made querulous noises in the back of her throat as she followed him back to the bike.

"Yeah, yeah, I'm taking her already."

As though relieved of a worry, the ferret made a swift ascent onto the Harley's seat and slipped into her basket. Stick reinserted his spell-box, balanced his prize on the defunct gas tank in front of him, and kicked the bike into life. He smiled. The bike's deep-throated roar always gave him a good feeling. Putting it into gear, he twisted the throttle and the bike lunged forward. The girl's body was only a vague weight cradled against his chest. The top of her head came to the level of his nose.

For some reason, he thought she smelled like apple blossoms.

CRSO

She woke out of an unpleasant dream to a confused sense of dislocation. Dream shards were superimposed on unfamiliar surroundings. Grinning Blood faces, shattered like the pieces of a mirror, warred with a plainly furnished room and a long-haired woman who was sitting on the edge of the bed where she lay. She closed her eyes tightly, opened them again. This time only the room and the woman were there.

"Feeling a little rough around the edges?" the woman asked. "Try some of this."

Sitting up, she took the tea.

"Where am I? The last thing I remember…there was this black man…"

"Stick."

"That's his name?"

The woman nodded.

"Is he…" Your man, she thought. "Is he around?"

"Stick's not much for company."

"Oh. I just wanted to thank him."

The woman smiled. "Stick's great for making enemies, but not too good at making friends. He sticks —" She smiled. " — to himself mostly."

"But he helped me…"

"I didn't say he wasn't a good man. I don't think anyone really knows what to make of him. But he's got a thing for runaways. He picks them up when they're in trouble—and usually dumps them off with me."

"I've heard his name before."

"Anyone who lives long enough in Bordertown eventually runs into him. He's like Farrel Din—he's just always been around." The woman watched her drink her tea in silence for a few moments, then asked: "Have you got a name?"

"Manda. Amanda Woodsdatter."

"Any relation to Maggie?"

"I'm her little sister."

The woman smiled. "Well, my name's Mary and this place you've been dumped is the home of the Horn Dance."

"No kidding? Those guys that ride around with the antlers on their bikes?"

"That's one way of describing us, I suppose."

"Jeez, I..."

Looking at Mary, Manda's first thought had been that she'd ended up in some old hippie commune. There were still a few of them scattered here and there through Bordertown and on the Borders. Mary's long blonde hair — like one of the ancient folk singers Manda had seen pictures of — and her basic Whole Earth Mother wardrobe of a flowered ankle-length dress, feather earrings and the strands of multi-colored beaded necklaces around her neck, didn't exactly jibe with what Manda knew of the Horn Dance.

In ragged punk clothing, festooned with patches and colored ribbons, their bikes sporting stag's antlers in front of their handlebars, the Horn Dance could be seen cruising anywhere from the banks of the Mad River to Fare-you-well Park. They were also a band, playing music along the lines of Eldritch Steel — a group that her sister had played with that had mixed traditional songs with the hard-edged sound of punk, and only lasted the one night. Unlike Eldritch Steel, though, the Horn Dance was entirely made up of humans. Which was probably the reason they were still around.

Eldritch Steel's first and only gig had been in Farrel Din's The Dancing Ferret and sparked a brawl between the Pack and the Blood that had left the place in shambles. Farrel Din, needless to say, hadn't been pleased. The band broke up, lead singer Wicker disappearing, while the rest of the group had gone their separate ways.

"What are you thinking of?" Mary asked.

Manda blinked, then grinned sheepishly. "Mostly that you don't look as punky as I thought you guys were."

"I'm the exception," Mary said. "Wait'll you meet Teaser, or Oss."

"Yeah, well..." Manda looked around the room until she spotted her clothes on a chair by the door.

She wasn't so sure that she'd be meeting anyone. There were things to do, places to go, people to meet. Yeah. Right.

"Do you need a place to stay?" Mary asked.

"No, I'm okay."

"Look, we don't mind if you hang out for a few days. But there's a couple of things I'd like to know."

"Like?"

175

"You're not from the Hill, are you?"

"Why?"

"Runaways from the Hill can be a problem. Up there, they've got ways of tracking people down and we don't need any trouble with elves."

"They're not like the Bloods up on the Hill," Manda said. "But like I told you, I'm Maggie's little sister. We grew up in Soho."

Mary smiled. "And so you know your way around."

"I lost my shades—that's all. Those Bloods were out to kick ass and when they caught a glam of my eyes, that was it."

"Stick told me—three to one are never good odds."

Manda shrugged. "I'm not a fighter, you know?"

"Sure. And what about your folks—are they going to come looking?"

"I'm on my own."

"Okay. We just like to know where we stand when irritated people come knocking on the door—that's all." She stood up from the bed, then fished in her pocket, coming up with a pair of sunglasses. "I thought you might like another pair—just to save you the hassle you had last night from being repeated."

"Thanks. Listen, I'll just get dressed and be on my way. I don't want to be a pain."

"It's no problem."

"Yeah, well..." She hesitated, then asked: "Where can I find Stick?"

"You don't want to mess with him, Manda. He's great to have around when there's trouble, but when things are going fine he just gets antsy."

"I want to thank him, that's all."

Mary sighed. "You know the old museum up by Fare-you-well Park?"

"Sure. That's his place?"

Mary nodded.

"The *whole* thing?"

"That I couldn't tell you. I've never been there and I don't know anyone who has. Stick doesn't take to visitors."

"Well, maybe I'll wait and check him out on the street some time."

"That would be better. I've porridge still warm, if you want something to eat before you go."

The idea of porridge first thing in the morning reminded Manda of too many mornings at home. She'd never even liked porridge — that was Mom's idea of a treat. But her stomach rumbled and she found a smile.

"That'd be great."

Mary laughed. "Look, don't mind me, Manda. The Hood always says that I've got a bad case of the mothering instinct. Why do you think Stick drops off his strays with me?"

"Who's the Hood?"

"Toby Hood — our bowman."

Manda shook her head. "There's a lot about you folks I don't know."

"Well, if you shake a leg, you'll be able to find out some — we're just getting ready to ride. If you want, you can come along."

"No kidding?"

Wouldn't that be something, riding around with the Horn Dance?

"Well...?" Mary asked.

"I'm up, I'm up."

She threw aside the covers as Mary left the room and got out of the bed to put on her clothes. There was a mirror by the dresser. Looking in it, she studied her face. The bruises were already fading. She didn't feel so sore either. That was one good thing about having elf blood — you healed fast.

Riding with the Horn Dance, she thought. She gave her reflection a wink, put on her new shades, and headed out the door.

CR80

"This sucks, man."

Fineagh Steel stared out the window onto Ho Street, his back to his companion. When he turned, the sunlight coming through the dirty windowpane haloed his spiked silver hair. He was a tall elf, with razor eyes and a quick sneer, wearing a torn Guttertramps T-shirt and black leather pants tucked into black boots.

Slouching on a beat-up sofa, Billy Buttons took a long swig of some homebrew, then set the brown glass bottle on the floor by his feet. Taking out a knife, he flicked it open and began to clean his nails.

"Hey, I'm talking to you," Fineagh said.

Billy eyed the current leader of the Blood, then shrugged. "I'm listening. What do you want me to say?"

Fineagh's lip curled and he turned back to look out the window once more. "Stick's got to go."

That made Billy sit up. He ran his fingers through his black and orange Mohawk, scratched at the stubble above his ears.

"Hey," he said. "It was their own fault—bashing on his turf."

"Our turf," Fineagh said sharply. "It's *our* turf. And anyone that comes into it takes their chances. If you were to listen to Stick, you'd think the whole damn city was his turf."

Maybe it is, Billy thought, but he didn't say the words aloud. There was something spooky about Stick—you just didn't want to mess with him. But Billy was in the room with Fineagh right now and he wasn't into messing with Fineagh either.

"So what do you want to do?" he asked.

Fineagh left the window and went to where his jacket lay on the floor by the door. From the inside pocket he took out a vintage Smith & Wesson .38. Billy's eyes went wide.

"Where the hell did you get that?" he asked.

"Lifted it—in Trader's Heaven."

"You got bullets?"

"What do you think?"

"Does it still work?"

Fineagh pointed it at Billy. "Bang!" he said softly.

Billy jumped as though he *had* been shot.

"Oh, yeah," Fineagh said. "It works all right. We're talking primo goods here. Every bullet guaranteed to fire."

Billy stared at the weapon with awe. The hand guard, the gleaming barrel, everything about the gun made him shiver. It was obviously in mint condition and probably stolen from some High Born's collection if it actually worked this close to the border. Most guns didn't.

"Where are you going to take him down?" he asked. "On the street?"

178

Fineagh shook his head. "We're going to beard ol' Choc'let in his den, my man. Maybe when we're done we'll turn his place into a club—what do you think? We'll call it Fineagh's Palace."

"How're we going to get in? That museum's like a fortress."

"We're going to play a tune on Stick's heartstrings," Fineagh said with a tight-lipped smile. "There'll be this runaway, see, getting his poor little head bashed in, right there in front of ol' Choc'let's digs..."

CRSO

"Your sister's a drummer, right?" Yoho asked.

Manda nodded. "She plays skin drums."

Yoho was one of the Horn Dance's riders, a big black man with a buzz of curly dark hair and a weight-lifter's body. Manda had been introduced to them all, but the names slid by too quickly for her to put a face to every one and still remember it. A few stuck out.

Oss, with his Mohawk mane like a wild horse and wide-set eyes. Teaser, all gangly limbs, hair a bird's nest of streaked tangles and his jester's leathers—one leg black, the other red, the order reversed on his jacket. Mary, of course. Johnny Jack, another of the riders, a white man as big as Yoho and as hairy as a bear. And the Hood, dressed all in green like some old fashioned huntsman, a tattoo of a crossed bow and arrow on his left cheek and his hair a ragged cornfield of stiff yellow spikes.

"What about you? Do you play an instrument?"

Manda turned to the girl who'd spoken. A moment's thought dredged up her name. Bramble. One of the band's musicians. A year or so older than Manda's sixteen, she was a tall willowy redhead, with short red stubble on the top of her head; the rest of her hair hung down in dozens of beaded braids.

"I used to play guitar—an electric," Manda said, "but someone lifted my spell-box and amp. I can't afford another, so I don't play much anymore."

Bramble nodded. "It's not so much fun when the volume's gone. I know. I got ripped off a couple of years ago myself. Went crazy after a month, so I waitressed days in The Gold Crown and played nights on a borrowed acoustic until I could afford a new one."

Teaser rattled a jester's stick in Manda's face to get her attention. "So are you any good on yours?" he asked.

"Well, Maggie said we'd put a band together if I can get a new amp."

"We could use an axe player right now," Bramble said. "The pay's the shits, but I've got a spare amp I could lend you."

"But you don't even know me—you don't know if I'm any good."

"Bramble's got a feel for that kind of thing," Mary said.

"And I've got a feel that we should be riding," Yoho broke in. "So are we going, or what?" He thrust a patched and ribbon-festooned jacket at Manda. "Here. You can wear this today. Consider yourself an honourary Horn Dancer."

"But—"

"You ride with us, you need the look," Yoho replied. "Now let's go!"

In a motley array of colors and tatters, they all crowded outside to where the bikes stood in a neat row behind their house.

"You can come on my machine," Bramble said.

Manda smiled her thanks. "What's this all about?" she asked as they approached Bramble's bike. "What is it that you guys *do?*"

"Well, it's like this," Bramble said. "On one level we're like any other gang—the Pack, the Bloods, Dragon's Fire, you name it. We like each other. We like to hang around together. But—have you ever heard of Morris dancing?"

Manda nodded. "Sure." When Bramble gave her a considering look, she added: "I like to read—about old things and what goes on...anywhere, I guess. Across the Border. In the outside world."

"Well, what we are is like one of those old Morris teams—that's why we're set up the way we are—the six stags, three white and three black. Oss is the Hobby Horse. Teaser's the fool."

"And Mary?"

"She's like the mother in the wood—Maid Marion. Robin Hood's babe."

Manda smiled. "I've heard of him."

"Yeah. I guess he's been around long enough.

"Anyway, what we do is..." She gave a little laugh. "This is going to sound weird, or spacey, but we're like Bordertown's luck—you know? The dance we do, winding through the city's streets, the music…it's all something that goes back to the Stone Age — in Britain, anyway. It's really old, all tied up with fertility and luck and that kind of thing. We make our run through the city, at least every couple of days, and it makes things sparkle a bit.

"We get all kinds of good feedback — from old-timers, as well as the punks. And it makes us feel good, too. Like we're doing something important. Is this making any sense?"

"I…guess."

"Are we riding or jawing?" Yoho called over to them.

Bramble laughed and gave him the finger. "Come on," she said to Manda. "You'll get a better idea of what I was talking about just by getting out and doing it with us."

"What would happen if you didn't make your ride?" Manda asked.

"I don't know. Maybe nothing. Maybe the sewers would back up. Maybe we'd all go crazy. Who knows? It just feels right doing it."

Manda climbed on the back of Bramble's bike. "I think I know what you mean," she said. "I always got a good feeling when I saw you guys going by. I never caught any of your gigs, but — "

"Yeah. There's a lot of bands in this city. It's hard to catch them all."

"But still," Manda said. "Ever since Mary asked me if I wanted to come along — I've felt like I've just won a big door prize."

"*The Wheel of Fortune,*" Bramble said.

"What?"

"It was an old game show."

"You mean like on television?"

"The entertainment of the masses — in the world outside, at least. Did you ever watch it?"

"No. Did you?"

"Yeah. A friend of mine had a machine that recorded the shows. It was great. We used to watch all kinds of weird stuff on these old tapes of his. But then someone ripped it off."

The bikes coughed into life, up and down the line, cutting off further conversation. Bramble kicked her own machine awake. The bike gave a deep-throated roar as she twisted the throttle.

"Hang on!" she cried.

Manda put her arms around the other girl's waist and then suddenly they were off. Before they got to the end of the block, she found herself grinning like the fool's head on the end of Teaser's jester's stick.

CXEO

Sitting in The Dancing Ferret, the two men made a study in contrasts. Farrel Din was short and portly, smoking a pipe and wearing his inevitable patched trousers and a quilted jacket. A full-blooded elf, born across the border, he still gave the impression of a fat innkeeper from some medieval *chanson de geste*. Stick, on the other hand, was all lean lines in black jeans, boots and a leather jacket. With his deep coffee-brown skin and long dark dreadlocks, he tended to merge with shadows.

The men had the club to themselves except for Jenny Jingle, a small elfin pennywhistle player, who sat in a corner playing a monotonous five-note tune on her whistle while Stick's ferret danced by her feet. From time to time she gave the men a glance. She knew Stick by sight, though not to talk to. Trading off between waitressing, odd jobs and the occasional gig in the club, she saw him often enough, but tended to spend the times that he came into The Ferret amusing Lubin who had developed a firm interest in Breton dance tunes.

Stick wasn't one that you could cozy up to. Though he seemed to know just about everyone in Bordertown, the only people one could definitely call his friends were Farrel Din and Berlin, and she spent most of her time working with the Diggers or hanging with the old blues players like Joe Doh-dee-oh.

Farrel Din and Stick seemed to go back a long way, which was odd, Jenny'd thought more than once. Not because Farrel Din was a full-blooded elf and Stick was definitely human — and not that old a human at that if appearances were anything to go by — but because Stick seemed to remember the times before Elfland returned to the world as though he'd been there when it had happened.

She finished the gavotte she was playing with a little flourish and Lubin collapsed across her feet to look hopefully up at her for more. Watching them, Farrel Din smiled.

"Seems like just yesterday when we put this place together," he said.

"It's been a lot of yesterdays," Stick replied.

He nodded as Farrel Din offered to refill his glass. Amber wine, aged in Bordertown, but originating in Elfland's vineyards, filled his glass. They clinked their glasses together in a toast, drank, then leaned back in their chairs. Farrel Din fiddled with his pipe. When he had the top ash removed from its bowl, he frowned for a moment, concentrating. A moment later, the tobacco was smoldering and he stuck it in his mouth.

"There's a Blood out on the streets with a gun," he said around the stem.

Stick gave him a sharp look.

"Oh, it's the real McCoy—no doubt about that, Stick. The sucker'd even work across the border. Mother Mandrake had it, only someone lifted it from her booth yesterday. She didn't see it happen, but she had a bunch of Bloods in that afternoon."

"Who told you this?" Stick asked.

"Got it from John Cocklejohn. He was in to see Magical Madness playing last night."

"Wonderful. Any idea who's got the gun now?"

Farrel Din shook his head. "But there's an edgy mood out on the street and I think there's going to be some real trouble."

Stick stood up and finished his wine in one long gulp.

"That's no way to treat an elfish vintage," Farrel Din told him.

"I've got to find that gun," Stick said. "I don't mind the gangs bashing each other, but this could go way beyond that."

"Maybe they'll just use it for show," Farrel Din said hopefully. "You know how kids are."

"What do you think the chances of that are?"

Farrel Din sighed. "I wouldn't take odds on it."

"Right." Stick gave a quick sharp whistle and Lubin left her dancing to join him. "Thanks for amusing the brat, Jenny," he told the whistle player, then he left, the ferret at his heels.

Jenny blinked, surprised that he'd even known her name.

At his own table, Farrel Din put down his pipe and poured himself some more wine, filling the glass to its brim.

Aw, crap, he thought. He wished he hadn't had to tell Stick about the gun. But there was no one else he could think of that could track it down as quickly, and what they didn't need now was the trouble that gun could cause. Not with tensions running as high as they were. So why did he feel like the gun was going to come to Stick anyway, whether he looked for it or not?

Farrel Din frowned, downing his glass with the same disregard for the vintage that Stick had shown earlier. Maybe he could dull the sense of prescience that had lodged in his head. Since leaving Elfland, the ability had rarely made itself known. Why did it have to come messing him up now?

He poured himself another glass.

CR℘

Manda had a glorious time that day. The Horn Dancers took turns having her ride on the back of their bikes and she wound up renewing a childhood love affair with the big deep-throated machines. She'd always wanted one. She'd even settle for a scooter if it came down to that, but given her druthers, she'd take one of these rebuilt machines—or better yet, a vintage Harley like Stick had.

Johnny Jack had given her a mask at their first stop so that she could *really* feel a part of the Dancers. It was like a fox's head, lightweight with tinted glass in the eyeholes so that her silver eyes wouldn't give her away. The mask had just been collecting dust, he assured her when she tried to give it back to him with a half-hearted protest. Whether that was true or not—and Manda was willing to lean towards the former if he was—she accepted it greedily.

Masked and with her ribboned jacket, Morris bells jingling on her calves, she happily joined in on an impromptu dance at the corner of Ho Street and Brews, hopping from one foot to the other along with the rest of them while Bramble played out a lively hornpipe on a beat-up old melodeon. Then it was back on the bikes and they were off again, a ragged line of gypsy riders leaving a sparkle as real as fairy dust behind in the eyes of those who watched them pass by.

That night the Horn Dance had a gig at The Wheeling Heart, a club on the outskirts of the Scandal District that was in a big barn-like warehouse. Manda was too shy to play, but she enjoyed standing near the stage in her new gear and watching the show. The audience was fun to watch, too, an even mix between pogoing punks and an older crowd doing English country dances. By the end of the second set there were punks with their leathers and spiked hair doing the country dances, and old-timers pogoing. The main concern seemed to be to have fun.

Manda was still feeling shy as the band started its third set, but she was itching to play. That always happened when she saw a good band. Her fingers would start shaping chords down by her leg. When Bramble came to ask if she'd join them on some of the numbers she knew, it didn't take a whole lot of urging.

"The Road to the Border," "Up Helly-O," "The Land of Apples," "Tommy's Going Down to Berks."

The tunes went by and Manda grinned behind her fox's mask, even joining in on the singing when the band launched into "Hal-an-Tow." Listening to the words, she realized that the song pretty well said what the band was all about.

> *Do not scorn to wear the horn*
> *It was the crest when you was born*
> *Your father's father wore it and*
> *Your father wore it, too*
>
> *Hal-an-tow, jolly rumble-o*
> *We were up, long before the day-o*
> *To welcome in the summer*
> *To welcome in the May-o*
> *For summer is a-coming in*
> *and winter's gone away-o*

It didn't matter what time of year it was, Manda thought, as she chorded along on the chorus. The song wasn't just about the change of the seasons, but about day following night, good times following the bad; how there was always a light waiting for you on the other side — you just had to go looking for it, instead of stewing in what had brought you down.

Bramble laid down a synthesized drone underneath a sharp rhythm of electronic drums. Yoho was playing bass. Teaser hopped around in front of the stage, waving his jester's stick, while the rest of the band crowded around a couple of microphones. The Hood sang lead. Manda smiled as he began the third verse.

Robin Hood and Little John
Have both gone to the fair-o
And we will to the merry green wood
To hunt the bonny hare-o

Hal-an-tow, jolly rumble-o...

The music had a sharp raw edge to it that never quite overpowered the basic beauty of the melody. Voices rose and twisted in startling harmonies. Manda found herself jigging on the spot as she played her borrowed guitar. There was a certain rightness about the fact that it was the same canary yellow as her own Les Paul.

God bless the merry old man
And all the poor and might'-o
God bring peace to all you here
And bring it day and night-o

The final chorus rose in a crashing wave that threatened to lift the roof off of the club. Punkers and old-timers were mixed in whirling dervish lines that made patterns as intricate as the song's harmonies. When the final note came down with a thunderous chord on the synthesizer, there was a long moment of silence. Then the crowd clapped and shouted their approval with almost as much volume as the band's electric instruments.

"I knew you'd be hot," Bramble said as she and Manda left the stage. "Did you have fun?"

Manda nodded. She bumped into Teaser who thrust his jester's stick up to her face.

"Says Tom Fool—you're pretty cool," he sang to her, then whirled off in a flutter of ribbons and leather.

The two women made their way to the small room in the back that the club had set aside for the band to hang out in between sets. Manda slumped on a bench and tried to stop grinning. She laid her foxhead mask on the bench beside her, her silver eyes flashing.

"See, we don't have elf magic," Bramble said, plonking herself down beside Manda, "so we've got to make our own."

"What you've got's magic all right."

"Want a beer?"

"Sure. Thanks."

"I've talked to the others," Bramble said. "They were willing to go along just on my say-so, but now that they've all heard you, it's official: you want to gig with us for awhile?"

Manda sat up straighter. Absently chewing on her lower lip, she had to look at Bramble to see if it was a joke.

"For true," Bramble said.

"But I'm not..." Human, she thought. "Like you. It could cause trouble."

"What do you mean?"

"Well, like —"

Manda never had a chance to continue. The club's owner poked his head in through the door. "Hey, have you seen Toby? There's a guy outside looking for him to —" He broke off when he saw Manda. "What're you doing in here?"

"She's with me," Bramble said.

"Uh-uh. No 'breeds in my club. You. Get out of here."

Bramble frowned and stood up. "Lay off, George. I said she's okay.

"No. You listen to me. The Bloods got their own places to hang out and I don't want them in here. This is a clean club. If I wanted to deal with the crap that the gangs hand out, I would've opened The Heart in the middle of Soho. She's out, or you're all out."

"You're acting like a bigot," Bramble told him, "not to mention an asshole."

But Manda laid a hand on her arm. "It's okay," she said. "I was just going anyway."

"Manda. We can work this —"

Manda shook her head. She should have known the day was going too well. Everything had just seemed perfect. Under the club owner's baleful eye, she stripped off the ribboned jacket and laid it on the bench beside her mask.

"I'll see you around," she told Bramble.

"At least let me get the Hood and —"

187

Manda shook her head again. Blinking back tears, she put on her shades and shouldered her way by the club owner.

"Manda!"

When she was out on the dance floor, Manda broke into a run. By the time Bramble had gathered a few of the band to go outside to look for her, she was long gone.

"This is crap," Bramble said. "I'm out."

"What do you mean you're out?" the Hood asked. "We've got another set to do still."

"I'm not playing for these bigots."

"Bramble, he's got a right to run the kind of club he wants."

"Sure. Just like I've got the right to tell him to stick his head where the sun don't shine. We're supposed to be putting out good vibes, right? Be the 'luck of the city' and all that other good stuff? Well, I liked that kid, Hood, and I *don't* like the idea of being around people who can't see beyond the silver in her eyes."

"But—"

"I'll pick up my gear at the house tomorrow."

"Where you going now?" Mary asked.

"To see if I can find her."

"I'll come with you," Johnny Jack said.

Bramble shook her head. "You guys go on and finish the gig, if that's what you want to do, okay? Me, I just want to think some things through."

"I've got an idea where she might have gone," Mary said.

"Where's that?"

"Stick's place."

"Oh, great. That's all we need. To get him pissed off."

"Bramble, listen to me," the Hood tried again, catching hold of her arm.

Bramble shook off his hand. "No, you listen to me. Didn't you see how that kid took to what's supposed to be going down with us? She fit right in. I have a feel for her, man. She could be something and I want to see her get that chance."

"Okay," the Hood said. "Go look for her. But don't turn your back on us. Let's at least talk things out tomorrow."

Bramble thought about that. "Okay. If I find her, I'll be by tomorrow."

"We've got a commitment to fulfill here," the Hood went on. "For tonight at least. We don't have to come back."

"We shouldn't be in a place like this at all," Bramble muttered under her breath as she headed for her bike. "Not when it turns out they're a bunch of racist wankers."

ରୁ৪০

Manda didn't think it could hurt so much. It wasn't like she'd spent her whole life with the Dance or anything. So what if it had seemed so perfect. It wasn't like she'd ever fit in anywhere. Not with the kids her own age, not with Maggie's friends, not with anyone. Some people just weren't meant to fit in. That's all it was. They got born with a frigging pair of silver eyes and everybody dumped on them, but who cared? That was just the way it goes sometimes, right?

Yeah, sure. Right. Screw the world and go your own way. That's what it came down to in the end.

Be a loner. You could survive. No problem.

A brown face surrounded by dreadlocks came into her mind. It was good enough for Stick, wasn't it? Sure. But how come it had to hurt so much? Did it hurt him? Did he ever get lonely?

She was crying so hard now, she couldn't see where she was going. Dragging her shades from her eyes, she shoved them in her pocket and wiped away the flow of tears with her sleeve.

Maybe she'd just go ask Stick how he did it. She hadn't even had a chance to thank him yet, anyway.

Still sniffling, she headed for the museum by Fare-you-well Park.

ରୁ৪০

Around the same time as the Horn Dance was leaving the stage in The Wheeling Heart, Stick pulled his Harley up in front of the museum. Cutting the engine, he stretched stiff neck muscles, then put the bike on its stand.

"End of the line," he said.

Lubin left her basket to perch on the seat. Wrinkling her nose, she made a small rumbly noise in the back of her throat.

"Yeah I know. It's long past supper."

189

What a night, he thought.

Pocketing his spell-box, he chained the bike to the iron grating by the museum's door and went up the broad steps. Lubin flowed up the steps ahead of him. By the time he reached the door, she'd already slid through her own private entrance to wait for him inside.

"Get the stew on!" he called to her through the door as he dug around in his jacket pocket for his keys.

He was just about to fit the key into the lock when he heard it.

Oh, crap, he thought. Not again.

Turning, he tried to pinpoint the source of what held just heard — a young voice raised in a high cry of pain. Now who'd be stupid enough to mess around this close to his digs? It was bad enough that he'd spent the better part of the day and evening unsuccessfully trying to run down a lead on Farrel Din's rumor, without this kind of shit.

The sound of the fight came from an alleyway across the street. Stick took out his staff and snapped it into one solid length as he crossed the street. Packers or Bloods, somebody was getting their head busted because he was not in a mood to be gentle with bashers tonight.

He slowed down to a noiseless glide as he approached the mouth of the alley. Hugging the wall to the right, he slipped inside. Bloods. Bashing some kid. It was hard to make out if it was a boy or a girl; a runaway or one of the Pack. He didn't stop to think about it. His staff shot out in a whirling blur, hitting the closest Blood before any of them even seemed to be aware he was there.

The one he hit went down hard. The rest scattered towards the back of the alley.

Stick smiled humorlessly. Seemed they didn't know the alley had a dead end.

He moved after them, sparing their victim a quick glance before going on. Looked like a Blood — a small one, but a Blood all the same. Now that didn't make much —

"Hey, Stick. How's it hanging?"

Stick's gaze went up. The Bloods were making a stand. Well, that was fine with him. There were seven — no, eight of them. He shifted his feet into a firmer stance, staff held out horizontally in front of him. As he began to cat-step towards them, the ones in front broke ranks. Stick had no trouble recognizing the figure that moved forward. Fineagh.

"Times hard?" Stick asked. "Haven't seen you getting own your hands dirty for awhile. I thought you just let your bullyboys handle crap like this."

"Well, this is personal," Fineagh replied.

Stick gave him a tight-lipped smile. "Pleasure's mine."

"I don't think so," Fineagh said. Taking his hand from his pocket, the Blood leader pointed the stolen .38 at Stick. "Bye-bye, Choc'let."

Oh, man. He'd been set up like some dumbass kid who should know better.

He started for Fineagh, staff whistling through the air, but he just wasn't fast enough.

The gunshot boomed loud in the alleyway. The bullet hit him high in the shoulder, the force of the impact slamming him back against the brick wall. His staff dropped from numbed fingers as he tried to stay on his feet. A second bullet hit him just above the knee, searing through muscle and tendon. His leg buckled under him and he sprawled to the ground.

"You always were just *too* damn good," Fineagh said conversationally. He kicked the staff just out of reach of Stick's clawing fingers, then hunched down, eyes glittering with malicious pleasure. "Never could deal with you like we could anybody else. So you had to come down, ol' Choc'let on a stick—you see that, don't you? We got a rep to maintain." He grinned mockingly. "Nothing personal, you understand?"

Stick saved his breath, trying to muster the energy for a last go at Fineagh, but it just wasn't there. The wounds, the shock that was playing havoc with his nervous system, had drained all his strength. He kept his gaze steady on the Blood leader's eyes as Fineagh centered the .38, but that didn't stop him from seeing the elf's finger tightening on the trigger. He could see every pore of Fineagh's pale skin. The silver death's head stud in his ear. The spill of dark laughter in his eyes…

Though he tried not to, he still flinched when the gun went off again.

CRSO

Manda hitched a ride with a friend of Maggie's that she ran into on Cutter Street, arriving at the museum just in time to see Stick enter the alleyway. She was at the far end of the street, though, and paused, not sure what to do. She could hear the fight. Stick wouldn't want her getting in the way. But when she heard the first gunshot, she took off for the alley at a run, speeding up when the sharp crack of gunfire was repeated.

Lubin reached it before her, streaking across the street from the museum to disappear into the mouth of the alley.

When Manda got there, she caught a momentary glimpse of Stick's sprawled form, the circle of Bloods around him, Fineagh with the gun...

Just as Fineagh squeezed off his third shot, Manda saw the ferret launch herself at the elf's arm. Her teeth bit through to the bone, throwing off his shot. The bullet spat against the wall, showering Stick with bits of brick. The gun tumbled from Fineagh's nerveless fingers to fly in a short arc towards Manda, hitting the pavement with a spit of sparks. Hardly realizing what she was doing, she ran forward and claimed up the weapon.

Fineagh screamed, trying to shake the ferret from his wrist. It wasn't until one of his companions reached for her, that Lubin dropped free to crouch protectively over Stick. Fineagh aimed a kick at her.

"D-don't do it!" Manda called nervously. The gun was a heavy cold weight in her fist as she aimed it down the alley.

The Bloods turned to face her.

Fineagh's eyes narrowed. He clutched his wrist, blood dripping between his fingers, but gave no sign of the pain he had to be feeling.

"Hey, babe," he said. "Why don't you just give me that back — maybe we'll leave you in one piece."

Manda shook her head.

Fineagh shrugged. "Your funeral."

As he started towards her, Manda closed her eyes and pulled the trigger. The gun bucked in her hands, almost flying from her grip, but her fingers had tightened with surprise as the weapon jerked. That was the only thing that kept her from losing it. Her shot went wild, but the Bloods no longer seemed so eager to confront her.

"Hey, come on," one of them said to Fineagh. "Let's get out of here."

Billy Buttons stepped up to the lean elf's side. "Nabber's right. We got what we came for, Fineagh. Time to blow."

Fineagh turned to him. "You want to leave her with that piece?"

"I just want to get the hell out of here."

Biting at her lower lip, Manda listened to them argue. She didn't know what she'd do if they charged her. How many bullets did this thing have left anyway? Not that she was sure she could even hit anything, no matter how many bullets there were.

Fineagh glared at Billy, at the ferret guarding Stick, at Manda.

"Sure," he said finally. "We're gone."

Manda backed away from the mouth of the alley as the Bloods approached, standing well away from them as they stepped out onto the street.

"I won't forget," Fineagh said, pointing a finger at her. "I *never* forget."

"Come on," Billy said. "Let's get that wrist looked at."

"Screw the wrist! You hear me, babe? Fineagh Steel's got your number. You are not going to like what I'm going to do to you next time we meet."

"You...you can just..." Manda was so scared, the words stuck in her throat.

Fineagh took a step towards her. "I ought to rip your—"

He stopped when she raised the gun. She hoped desperately that they couldn't see how badly she was shaking.

Fineagh gave her an evil smile. "Later, babe. You and me."

He turned abruptly and led the gang away.

Manda waited until they turned the corner, then ran back into the alley.

"Easy," she said soothingly to the ferret. "Good boy. Don't bite me now. I'm here to help."

Help. Right. She almost threw up when she looked at the mess the bullets had made. There was blood everywhere. Stick was so pale from shock and loss of blood that she didn't think he'd have any trouble passing himself off as a white man if he wanted to. The light in his eyes was dimming.

"F-funny...seeing you...here..." he mumbled.

Manda swallowed thickly. "Don't try to talk," she said.

She laid the gun down on the ground and knelt beside him. Lubin made a suspicious noise and sniffed at her, then backed slowly away, growling softly. Manda closed her eyes and took a deep steadying breath. Leaning over him, eyes still closed, she began to hum monotonously. The sound helped keep her head clear for what she meant to do.

She sustained the drone for a few moments, then laid her left hand gently on Stick's thigh, covering the wound, her right on his shoulder. Here was one thing that silver eyes were good for. Elf blood. She stopped humming as she concentrated fully on the task at hand. The part inside her that was connected to her elfish heritage reached out and assessed the damage done to Stick's body, mended the broken bones, reconnected arteries and nerves, healed the flesh, all the while taking the pain into herself. Not until the least of his cells was healed, did she sit back and take her hands away.

Stick's pain, curdling inside her, rose up and hit her like a blow. She tumbled over on her side. Her body, drained of the energy she'd used to heal Stick, tried to deal with the pain, shutting down all but the most essential life systems when it couldn't. She curled into a fetal position as a black wave knifed through her, sucking away her consciousness.

Lubin crept up to Stick, sniffing at where his wounds had been, then put her nose up against Manda's cheek. She whined, but there was no response from either of them.

CRSO

Bramble pulled up in front of the museum and parked her bike beside Stick's. She put it on its kickstand, disconnected her spell-box and walked up to the big front door. There she hammered on the broad wooden beams for what seemed like the longest time. There was no reply.

"Aw, crap," she said.

She knew Stick was here — or at least his bike was. But what were the chances he'd take Manda in even if she had come knocking on his door? Thinking of what Stick was like, Bramble realized that it wasn't bloody likely. Okay, so where else might she have gone?

Back to the Horn Dance's house? Even more unlikely.

That only left the streets.

194

Bramble tried the door again, then sighed. Heading back to her bike, she kicked it into life. It looked like she was in for a night of cruising the streets. But she wasn't going to leave the poor kid out there on her own — not feeling as messed up as she'd obviously been when she'd fled The Heart.

She revved the throttle a couple of times, then took off, heading for Soho's club district.

CR$O

The sound of Bramble's engine as she drove off roused Stick from a dream of a warm soft place. He'd felt as though he'd been lying somewhere with a beautiful earth goddess, his whole body nestled between her generous breasts. When he opened his eyes to find himself lying in the alley, it took him a few moments to remember where he was and how he'd come to be here.

Bloods. Bashing a kid. Who'd turned out to be a Blood. All part of a trap. And he'd gone charging in like an idiot and got himself shot.

He lifted a hand to his shoulder. His jacket had a hole in it and it was sticky with blood, but there was no wound there.

He peered down and looked at his thigh. Same story. Only there he could see the scar. How the...?

That was when he saw her, lying there on the pavement, the kid he'd helped last night, all curled up in a ball. Half elf — and with an elf's healing ability, it seemed. That's what it had to have been. He had a dim recollection of her facing down the Bloods.

Somehow she'd got hold of Fineagh's gun and sent the whole crew packing.

"You're really something, kid," he said.

He looked for the gun and saw it lying just beyond her. Reaching over, he hefted it thoughtfully, then pocketed it. Lubin nuzzled his hand.

"Yeah, yeah," he said, ruffling her fur. "I remember you going one-on-one with Fineagh. Got myself a regular pair of guardian angels, don't I?"

He got slowly to his feet, marveling that he was still alive. Retrieving his staff, he broke it down and replaced it in its sheath. Then he picked up the girl and headed for home.

"This is getting to be a habit," he said, talking to himself more than to her, for she was still unconscious. "Only this time I'm taking care of you myself — I figure I owe you that much."

Not to mention that Fineagh wasn't likely to forget this. Stick knew that both he and the girl were looking to be in some serious trouble and it was going to be coming down all too soon.

CRSD

Stick awoke, stiff from a night on the sofa. He groaned as he sat up and swung his legs to the floor. Don't complain, he told himself. It sure beats lying dead in an alleyway with a bullet in your head.

Pulling on his jeans, he padded across the room to the doorway of his bedroom. His guest was already up and gone. Finding a shirt, he went to see if she'd left the museum or was just exploring. He found her on the ground floor, gazing with awe at a full-size skeleton display of a brontosaurus.

"Jeez," she said as he approached her. "This place is really something."

"How're you feeling?"

"Okay. A good night's sleep is all I usually need to recover from something like last night."

"Yeah," Stick said. "About last night. Thanks."

Manda grinned. "Hey, I owed you one." She looked back at the display. "Do you really have this whole place to yourself?"

From the outside, the five-story museum looked like a castle. Inside, the first four floors held natural history displays, everything from dinosaurs to contemporary wildlife — contemporary to the world outside, at least, for there were no examples of the strange elfish creatures that now inhabited the borderlands. All the natural sciences were represented. Geology, zoology, anthropology. Manda had spent the morning wandering from floor to floor, captivated by everything she saw. Her favorites, so far, were the Native American displays and the dinosaurs.

The fifth floor was where Stick lived. It had originally contained the museum's offices and research labs. Now most of the rooms stored the vast library that Stick had accumulated — books, music recordings, videotapes and DVDs; a wealth of pre-Elfland knowledge unmatched this side of the Border. A few rooms served as his living quarters.

"Except for Lubin," Stick said, "I've pretty much got the place to myself."

"Well, now I know why you know so much about the old days," Manda said. "But it does seem kind of decadent."

"What do you mean?"

"Well, there's all this neat stuff in here. It doesn't seem right to just keep it all to yourself."

"So what do you think I should do—open it to the public?"

"Sure."

Stick shook his head. "It wouldn't work."

"I know *lots* of folks who'd die to see this stuff."

"Sure. And when they got bored? They'd probably trash the place."

Manda gave him a funny look, then thought about what was left of the various pre-Elfland galleries and the like that she'd seen.

"I guess you're right." She ran a hand along a smooth phalanx of the brontosaurus. "It seems a shame, though."

"This place had a use after Elfland came back," Stick said. "The Bloods that wanted to go into the outside world used to come here to learn a thing or two about the way things work over on the other side of the border. So that they could fit in better—at least those that didn't want to be noticed."

"Really?"

"Um-hmm. That's why I've got power—there's a generator that runs off a big spell-box that they left behind—and a lot of technological stuff works in here where it wouldn't out on the street."

"You mean those TV sets and stereos and other equipment up on the top floor are for real?"

Stick nodded.

"Wow. I'd love to check out some of that stuff. I've only read about them before."

"Come on," Stick said. "I'll show you how they work." He bent down and held out his arm so that Lubin could slip into its crook, then led the way upstairs.

"Would you look at all this stuff!" Manda cried in the music room. She pulled records from the big bookshelf racks that lined the walls. "Jimi Hendrix. David Bowie. The Nazgul." She looked up. "Is this stuff really as good as it's supposed to be?"

"Better."

Manda's mouth formed a silent "Wow."

"Listen," Stick asked as he turned the stereo on. "Have you got a place you can stay? — some place out of the way, I mean. Like across the border?"

"I..."

Well what had she been thinking anyway, Manda asked herself. That she was just going to be able to move in here or something? Jeez, it was really time that she grew up.

Stick saw the disappointment cross her face.

"I'm not throwing you out," he said. "You seem like an okay kid and I owe you."

"That's okay. I can go. I've got lots of places to stay."

"You're taking this wrong. See, the thing is, Fineagh — you know Fineagh?"

Manda nodded. "Sure. At least I've heard of him. He's the Bloods' latest leader."

"He's also the guy you put down last night."

Manda blanched. "Oh, boy."

"Right. So the problem is, he's going to come looking for us, and this time he'll bring every frigging Blood he can lay his hands on. I've got a feeling that they're going to lay siege to this place, and it'll be going down today."

"Can...can they actually get in?" Manda asked. She thought of what the museum looked like from the outside — an impregnable fortress.

"Well, the place's got a certain amount of built-in security, left behind by the elves who used it, but there's no way it could stand up to a concentrated assault."

"So what are we going to do?"

Stick smiled. "Well, I want to get *you* someplace safe for starters."

"No way."

"Listen, you don't know how bad it's going to get when — "

"I did pretty good last night, didn't I?"

"Yeah, sure. But — "

"And besides," Manda added. "I really want to hear some of this music."

"Listen, kid, you —"

"Manda."

"What?"

"My name's Manda."

"Okay. Manda."

Before he could go on, Manda laid down the stack of records she'd pulled out and walked over to where he was standing.

"I'm not a hero," she said, "but I can't just walk away from this."

"Sure you can. You just —"

"Then, why don't *you* just walk away?"

Manda couldn't believe it. Here she was arguing with Stick, like were they old pals or something. This was just too weird.

"That's different," Stick told her. "I've got a responsibility."

"To what? To this place that no one ever gets to see? To the people out on the streets who let you help them, but that you never let help you?"

"You don't know what you're talking about," Stick said.

But listening to her, hearing the conviction in her voice, he found himself wondering what had ever happened to that sense of rightness he'd felt when he was her age. There was nothing he didn't have an opinion on back then — and a damn strong opinion at that — but somehow the years had drained it away. Where once his head had been filled with a pure sense of where he was going and what his place in the world was, he'd fallen into living by habits. Still doing things, but no longer sure just exactly why he was doing them.

Such as patrolling the streets like some comic book superhero…

He was so still, his face squinted in a frown, that Manda figured she'd gone too far.

"Listen," she said. "I didn't mean to mouth off like that. You can do whatever you want — I mean, it's your place. If you want me to get out of your way, I'll go."

Stick shook his head. "No," he said. "You're right. Doesn't matter where you go, sooner or later you're going to have to settle this thing between Fineagh and you — same as I do. It might as well be now. But I'll tell you, Manda, we don't have a hope in hell of getting out of this in one piece — not if he musters as many Bloods as I think he will."

"Do you want to split?" Manda asked.

"Can't."

She grinned. "Well then, let's listen to some rock and roll."

She held up a record jacket with a full-face photo of a handsome curly-haired man. She was attracted to the group's name as much as the photo — mostly because of the time she'd just spent downstairs in the dinosaur display. The group was called Tyrannosaurus Rex.

"Are they any good?" she asked.

"Yeah. They're great. Do you want to hear it?"

Manda nodded. She rubbed her hair nervously, making the mauve spikes stand up at attention. Way down inside, she was about as scared as she could get. What she really needed right now was something to take her mind off of what was going to be coming down all too soon. A little time was all she needed. Sure. And then she'd just face down Fineagh and his gang all by herself.

Music blasted from the speakers then, a mix of electric and acoustic instruments that pushed the immediacy of her fears to the back of her mind. After a short intro, the lead singer's curiously timbered voice sounded across the instruments, singing about a "Woodland Bop." By the time the second chorus came, she was singing along, Lubin dancing at her feet.

Stick left them to it while he went to see to some weapons. The gun they'd taken from Fineagh last night was out of bullets and his staff just wasn't going to cut it, not with what Fineagh was going to bring down on them.

CR80

Bramble spent a fruitless night, going from club to club, stopping on street corners, asking after Little Maggie Woodsdatter's younger sister Manda from everyone she met. She didn't have much luck.

Dawn was just pinking the sky when she finally ran down a rumor that was just starting to make the rounds of the Soho streets. Hearing it, she headed straight for home.

Mary was the only one up when Bramble came into the kitchen.

"Any luck?" Mary asked.

Bramble shook her head.

Mary sighed. "About last night," she said. "You know what the Hood's like. He's really into fulfilling obligations."

"Yeah. I know. But—"

"Anyway," Mary broke in. "We won't be playing there again —
not even if we wanted to."

"Why not?"

"After the gig, the Hood collected our bread, then he decked
George. 'That's for the kid,' he said. Left him with a beautiful shiner."

Bramble smiled. "I wish I'd seen that."

"Oh, I'm sure he'll be more than happy to give you a complete
blow-by-blow rundown if you ask." She eyed Bramble thoughtfully.
"So now what are you going to do? Are you still planning to pack it
in?"

"No. Just before I got here, I heard a story that's making the
rounds. Something about Stick and some kid facing down Fineagh
and bunch of his Bloods. Whatever happened, the Bloods are
planning a full-scale assault on Stick's place this afternoon."

"What's that?"

The sound of their conversation had woken a few other members
of the band. The Hood sat down at the table with them, while Teaser
and Johnny Jack fought a mock battle for the tea pot. It was the
Hood who'd spoken.

Bramble gave them what details that she'd been able to pick up.
By the time she finished, most of the band was awake and had joined
them.

"This kid with Stick," Johnny Jack asked. "You think it's Manda?"

Bramble nodded.

"It makes sense," Mary added. "She was asking about him
yesterday morning."

The Hood looked around at the rest of them. "Anybody here *not*
want to get involved?"

"She seemed like a nice kid," Oss volunteered.

"And she *is* an honourary member of the band still," Johnny
Jack added.

Mary shook her head. "But what can *we* do?" she asked. "We're
not fighters."

"Oh, I don't know about that," Yoho said. "I've been known to
kick some ass."

Mary sighed. "You know what I mean. How could we possibly
stand up to the numbers Fineagh can put together?"

There was a long silence. One by one heads turned to look at the
Hood.

"Hell," he said after a moment. "It's simple. We just dance 'em into surrendering."

"Come on," Bramble. "This is serious."

"I *am* being serious," the Hood replied. "The only thing is, we're going to need a wizard."

CR80

It was shaping up even worse than Stick had imagined it would.

"What are we going to do?" Manda said, joining him at the window.

Behind them, the needle lifted from an LP by Big Audio Dynamite and the turntable automatically shut off. Neither of them noticed. All their attention was focused on the street below that fronted the museum.

Bloods rounded the corner and came down the street in a slow wave. There were easily more than a hundred of them, bedecked in jeans and leather, silver eyes glittering in the afternoon light. Their hair was a multi-colored forest, ranging from elfin silver through every color of the spectrum. They were armed with knives and cudgels, broken lengths of pipe and chains, traditional elfin bows and arrows. The front ranks had sledgehammers and crowbars. They were making it obvious that, one way or another, they'd be cracking the museum open today.

The Bloods alone were bad enough. But word had spread and the various other gangs of Bordertown were showing up in force to watch the show. The Pack, in their leathers. Dragon's Fire, down from the Hill, looking soft beside the real street gangs. Scruffy headbangers and Soho rats, runaways and burn-outs.

Staring down at the crowd, Stick had visions of the bloodbath that was just a few wrong words away from exploding. He checked the load of his pump shotgun. With a quick snapping motion, he pumped a shell into place. Inside the museum, he had no doubt as to its reliability. But outside, beyond the elfin spells that kept the building and its contents in working order, he knew he'd be lucky if one shot in three fired.

Manda swallowed hard.

"Scared?" Stick asked.

She nodded.

"Me, too." When she looked at him in surprise, he added: "It might not be too late to get out the back."

"And do what?"

There was that, Stick thought. No matter where they went, they were going to have to face Fineagh sooner or later. Taking off now just meant the museum was going to get trashed and they'd still have the Blood leader on their case. Making a stand here — maybe it was just suicide. But there didn't seem to be any other option.

"Did you ever get lonely?" Manda asked. "You know, just being here by yourself all the time?"

"I went out a lot. I've got friends. Berlin. Farrel. And besides, Lubin's good company."

The ferret was crouched on the windowsill in front of them. Manda gave her soft fur a pat.

"Yeah, but you don't exactly hang out a lot when you *did* go out," she said.

"How would you know?"

"Hey, you're famous, Stick."

He sighed. "That's the kind of thing that got me into this in the first place. Always being the do-gooder." He gave her a quick look. "Okay. So maybe I get a little lonely from time to time. I guess it just comes with the territory."

"You've helped an awful lot of people — did you never find one of them you liked well enough to be your friend?"

The look of an old hurt crossed his features, gone so quick Manda wasn't sure she'd even seen it.

"It's not that simple," he told her. "See, I've got to keep some distance between myself and the street. Without it, I can't do my job properly."

Manda nodded. "After being in here with you today, I can tell you're not as scary as you make yourself out to be down there." She nodded to where the gangs were gathering. "But how'd this get to be your job?"

"Kind of fell into it, I guess. The kids didn't have anyone looking after them and the gangs just started getting too rough on them. Hell, I'm no shining knight — don't get me wrong. But someone had to look out for them. Only now…" He shook his head. "I don't know how it got so out of control."

Manda looked down. She could make out Fineagh, standing at the head of the Bloods. He seemed so small from this height that she felt she could just reach out and squeeze him between her fingers like she might a bug.

"I guess we should...get down there," she said.

Stick nodded grimly. "Maybe I can shame Fineagh into going one-on-one with me—winner take all."

"Do you think he'd just—" Manda interrupted herself before she could finish the question. "Look!" she cried.

But she didn't have to point it out to Stick.

Forcing a way through the spectators came a familiar band of bikers. It was the Horn Dance. An open-backed pick-up truck followed the path the bikes made. That was the portable stage and power generator that they needed for their amps and sound system.

The bikes pulled up at the front steps, forming a semi-circle around the truck. The truck stopped, its cab facing the museum doors, its bed directly in front of Fineagh.

"What are they trying to pull?" Stick muttered as the band members began to strap on instruments.

The whine of feedback and the sound of guitars and synthesizers being tuned rose up to their window.

"I think they're trying to help," Manda said.

"We'd better get down there," Stick said.

He strode off, Lubin at his heels, going so fast that Manda had to trot to keep up with him.

CRSO

"Did you get it yet?" the Hood asked Farrel Din.

The wizard sat frowning behind the amplifiers in the bed of the Horn Dance's pick-up. He looked at an old bumper sticker that was stuck to one of the wooden slats that made up the sides of the bed. It read, "I'd rather be Dancing." Well, he'd rather be anywhere, doing anything, he thought, than be here.

"Farrel?" the Hood prompted him.

"I'm thinking. I always have trouble with the simple spells. They're so easy that they just go out of my mind."

"Well, if you know some big smash-up of a one, go for it instead. We could use just about anything right about now."

204

Farrel Din sighed. "I never could learn the big ones," he admitted.

"We should have gotten a different wizard," Bramble told the Hood.

"Nobody else seemed to have a better idea before we went and asked Farrel."

"Sure, but—"

"Will you go away and let me think!" Farrel Din shouted at them. "Why don't you start playing or something and as soon as I get it, I'll let you know."

"If you get it," Bramble muttered.

Farrel Din sighed, and returned to his task.

It was such a stupidly simple spell, surely even *he* could remember it. Couldn't he? It had been such a favorite—long ago, before Elfland ever left the outside world in the first place. But there hadn't been much call for it in the last few centuries and he'd never been much of a wizard anyway. Why else did he run The Ferret? He'd always been better serving up beers than serving up spells.

Up front, Johnny Jack was arguing with Fineagh. The Blood leader wasn't ready to just wipe out the Horn Dance—they were too popular for him to risk that—but he was rapidly approaching the point where he just wouldn't care anymore. He hadn't expected so many of the other gangs to show up either—but screw them as well.

The Bloods were ready to take on anyone.

"Listen, you jackass," he told Johnny Jack. "I'm giving you two minutes to get this crap out of my way, or we're just going through you—understand?"

"Everybody tuned?" the Hood asked from the bed of the pick-up.

He'd been keeping a wary eye on the Bloods and knew that they couldn't hold off much longer.

Farrel Din, he thought. Get it together and we'll play your club for a month—free of charge.

"We're rooting to toot," Teaser called to him.

"Then let's get this show on the road!" the Hood cried.

CR&D

Stick and Manda stepped out of the museum's front door at the same time as the Horn Dance kicked into the opening bars of a high-powered version of the "Morris Call". The sheer volume of sound stopped them in their tracks. The Bloods looked to Fineagh for direction, but the rest of the crowd immediately began to stamp their feet.

"All right!" someone shouted.

Shouts and whistles rose up from the crowd, but were drowned by the music. Bramble kept an eye on Fineagh, then turned to see how Farrel Din was doing, all the while playing her button accordion. The portly wizard was hunched over, muttering to himself.

Great plan, Hood, Bramble thought. She turned back to face the crowd. Most of the punkers and runaways were dancing—their usual combination of shuffled country dance steps and pogoing. The Rats eyed the Bloods, ready to rumble. Everyone else seemed to be trying to figure out if they'd come to a free concert or a street fight, with the crowd from the Hill hanging back as usual—wanting to be a part of things, but nervous of a free-for-all.

Stick started down the steps, Manda and Lubin trailing a few paces behind. Fineagh's eyes narrowed as he took in Stick's shotgun. The Horn Dance broke into a medley of "Barley Break" and "The Hare's Maggot."

"Come on!" the Hood shouted at Farrel Din.

"Easy for you to say," the wizard replied. He counted on his fingers, shaking his head. "No. That's shit into gold. Maybe...?" He squeezed his eyes shut, trying to think, while the music thundered on.

Stick moved along the side of the truck, the shotgun held down by his side. With his finger in the trigger guard, he only needed to swing it up to fire.

Bramble tried to catch Manda's eye. If Stick and Fineagh started in on each other it wouldn't make any difference if Farrel found the spell of not. But Manda's gaze was locked on the tall Blood leader who awaited their approach. The Bloods began to press closer to Fineagh. Those armed with bows, notched arrows.

Stick stopped when he was a few paces away from Fineagh.

"Kill the music," Fineagh said, nodding at the band.

"Not my party," Stick told him.

Fineagh turned to his followers, but before a command could leave his lips, Farrel Din sat up in the back of the truck.

"Got it!" he cried.

He jumped up and ran over to Bramble, tripped over a power cord, and fell against the willowy redhead. The two went down in a tumble. Bramble was carrying the tune. When she fell, her accordion made a discordant wheezing sound. The band faltered at the loss of the melody line.

Farrel Din grinned into Bramble's face. "Play 'Off She Goes,'" he said as they disentangled themselves.

"But—"

"Trust me. Just play it."

Bramble nodded to the Hood. The band stopped trying to find the tune they'd lost as she broke into the jig. She played the first few bars on her own, the others quickly joining in when they recognized the tune. While they played, Farrel Din stood directly in front of Bramble, eyes closed in concentration. Hopping from one foot to the other, he waved his fingers around her accordion in a curious motion, all the while singing something in the old elfin tongue.

The effect was almost instantaneous.

Anyone not already moving to the music, immediately began to dance, whether they wanted to or not. Rats and Bloods shuffled in time to the lilting rhythm. Those in the crowd who were already dancing moved into high gear, happily swinging partners and generally having a grand old time. In the back, the crowd from the Hill looked embarrassed as they flung themselves about, but like everyone else, were unable to stop themselves.

The Bloods fought the glamour, but the spell, combined with the music, gave them no choice. They lifted one foot, then the other, keeping time with the beat, frowns on their faces. Only Fineagh, through the sheer stubbornness of his will, stood still.

Fineagh and Stick.

Jigging on the spot, Manda couldn't believe that they weren't affected. Even Lubin was dancing—though the ferret loved to at any excuse so perhaps that didn't count. But then Manda saw that even the two men's feet were tapping slightly.

"This doesn't stop anything, Choc'let," Fineagh said. Fires flickered in his eyes.

Stick shrugged. "It doesn't have to be like this — you could just walk away."

"Can't."

"You mean, you won't."

The hate in the elf's silver eyes became a quicksilvering smolder. Stick knew they were both moments away from falling prey to the glamour in the music.

"Give it up,"' he said.

Even if he said yes, Manda wondered, how could they trust him?

But the Blood leader had no intention of giving up. One minute his hand was empty, in the next a throwing knife had dropped into it from a wrist sheath. The blade left his hand, flying straight and true for Stick.

Stick brought up the shotgun and knocked the knife from the air. Leveling the gun, he pulled the trigger. The shell was a dud.

A second knife appeared in Fineagh's hand at the same time as Stick pumped a new shell into place. The boom of the shotgun was lost in the thundering music, but Fineagh's chest exploded as the load hit him. He was lifted into the air and thrown back a half dozen feet, dead before he hit the ground.

The band's music stopped as suddenly as though someone had pulled the plug. Hundreds of eyes stared at the blood-splattered remains of the tall elf. The sound of Stick's pumping a new shell into place was loud in the abrupt silence. He leveled the shotgun at the ranks of Bloods.

"Anybody else what a piece?" he asked. "Now's the time to make your play."

Nobody moved.

With their leader dead, gone with him was the mania that had brought them all to this point. The Bloods were suddenly aware of just how dangerously outnumbered they were.

"Hell, no," Billy Buttons said finally. "We're cool."

Turning, he shouldered his way through the Bloods. Long tense moments passed, but slowly the Bloods followed him, leaving Fineagh's corpse where it lay.

"That...that's it?" Manda asked softly.

Stick looked at her, then at the Horn Dance and the crowds still gathered.

"It's not enough?" he asked.

Manda swallowed. "Sure. I mean..."

Stick nodded. "I know."

With that, he turned and retraced his way back up the museum's steps, the shotgun hanging loosely in his hand.

Lubin ran ahead, disappearing inside before him. Stick paused at the door to look back.

"Come visit," he said. "Anytime."

Then he too was gone.

The door closed with a loud thunk.

Manda stared at it, but all she could see was the pain she'd discovered in Stick's eyes. Damn him! Didn't he realize that it didn't have to be like this? He had friends. The Horn Dance had turned out to help him. Farrel Din had. She was here. Tears welled up in her own eyes and she wasn't sure if they were from feeling hurt, or for him.

She started to move for the door, but Bramble appeared at her side. She caught Manda's arm.

"But I want...I should..."

"Not a good time," Bramble said.

"But..."

Bramble pulled a couple of notes from her button accordion, then softly sang.

There was an old woman
tossed up in a blanket
ninety-nine miles, beyond the moon
And under one arm
she carried a basket
and under t' other she carried a broom
Old woman, old woman, old woman, cried I
O wither, O wither, O wither, so high?
I'm going to sweep cobwebs
beyond the sky
but I'll be back again, by and by

She ended with a flourish on the accordion and gave Manda a lopsided smile.

"I don't understand," Manda said.

"Clean your own house, and let him clean his. You heard what he said. He *did* ask you to come visit him...anytime."

"Sure, but—"

"But now's not 'by and by,'" Bramble said. "Come on. Give the Horn Dance a chance. We've got a captive audience—what with Farrel's spell. We could use your licks, kiddo."

Manda looked up at the museum's fifth floor. Was there a movement at the window?

But then she realized that Bramble was right. While Manda wasn't sure what she wanted from Stick, it had to come at its own pace. She'd give him a bit of a grace period, but if he didn't wise up soon, then he'd find her camped out on his front steps.

"Hey!" Yoho called from the back of the truck.

Manda looked up at him and saw he was holding out Bramble's canary yellow Les Paul. She followed Bramble up onto the back of the truck and took the instrument with a smile of thanks.

Someone had already removed Fineagh Steel's body. Bramble led the band in a rousing version of the "Staines Morris." Teaser and Mary moved amongst the crowd, showing the steps. Manda was about to start playing when Johnny Jack caught her by the arm.

"I think you're forgetting something," he said.

He held out her foxhead mask and the ribbon-festooned jacket.

Manda propped the Les Paul up against its amp and put them on. Then she slung the guitar on and joined the tune with a flashy spill of notes. Bramble gave her a grin.

Leaning into the tune's chords, Manda looked out at the sea of bobbing faces. The Rats had left soon after the Bloods. The crowd that remained didn't need Farrel Din's glamour to join in. And neither did she, Manda thought, jigging on the spot with Johnny Jack. The music was good and the people were good. Maybe it was about time that she stopped backing away from things and took the plunge. If she couldn't do it herself, how could she ever expect to set an example for Stick?

She glanced up at the fifth floor again, and this time, while she didn't see Stick, she could see Lubin dancing on the windowsill. Smiling, she turned her attention back to the music.

Berlin

Offering dragons quarter is no good,
they regrow all their parts & come on again,
they have to be killed.

—John Berryman

ONE

Long after midnight and there was no escape.

Three Bloods caught Nicky in the free flophouse he ran for the Diggers down in Tintown — that part of Soho to which the hobos tended to gravitate. They had silver Mohawks shot through with orange and black streaks, ice stones glittering in their ears, black leathers. The two males held Nicky on the floor while the third took a small metal container from her pocket. She held it in front of Nicky's face and gave it a gentle shake.

Shucka-shuck.

"Got something for you, Nicky," she said. Her thin-lipped smile never reached her eyes.

Nicky struggled in his captors' grip, then froze when a new shadow filled the doorway of the room. A tall Blood stood there, but he wasn't a punk. His long silver hair fell to his shoulders and his clothes were pure elfin cut, made from some sleek and glimmering material that there was no name for this side of the

211

border. A High Born. Not a Bordertowner, but straight out of glittering Elfland. He took a step into the room.

Nicky's blood went cold when the candlelight picked out the tall Blood's features.

It was Long Lankin, the murdering knight. Nicky had only seen him once before when Tam Sharper pointed out the High Born to him at an outdoor concert in Fare-you-well Park. There was something in the Blood's hawklike features and cold eyes that would never let you forget him, once you'd seen him.

Shucka-shuck.

Nicky's gaze flickered back to the woman and the container she held.

"There's a new kind of pearl in town, Nicky-boy," she said.

Her name was Ysa Cran and she ran a gang of Blood pushers who could provide you with whatever you wanted — smoke, fairy dust, coke, pearl, they had it all.

"I don't..." Nicky began.

"Oh, everyone knows," Ysa said. "Nicky broke his habit. Nicky dropped the pearl. Nicky's a fucking saint."

She popped open the little metal container and shook its contents into the palm of her hand. Pink and mauve flakes glittered in the candlelight.

"See, it's something new," Ysa said. "Not quite pearl, but not quite anything else either. Straight from Elfland, Nicky-boy. And it's going to be good for business, you know? The business you're taking away from me, you and the Diggers, trying to clean up everybody's act. It's called shake, Nicky-boy, and its going to be all over the streets in a few weeks. We're doing, like, a test run tonight. And you know what's really fine about this?"

Nicky swallowed thickly, but made no reply.

"It's one hundred percent addictive, Nicky-boy." This time the smile reached Ysa's eyes. "You just gotta try it and you're hooked. And that's the secret of this biz, Nicky-boy. Repeat customers." She gave the Bloods holding him a nod. "Open his mouth."

"N-nuh—"

The Bloods had Nicky's mouth open before he could spit out a word. He struggled frantically in their grip, but they were too strong for him.

"You can smoke it," Ysa said conversationally. "You can powder it up and snort it like pearl. You can swallow it. You can stick it up your ass, Nicky-boy. Any way you take it, it's a straight mainline back to that place you left behind when you dropped the pearl. Remember, Nicky-boy? Remember how it felt to be on top of the world, fucking-A?"

There were tears in Nicky's eyes as she cupped her hand and funneled the shake into his mouth. He gagged, trying to spit it out, but she rubbed his throat with smooth cool fingers and he swallowed reflexively.

"You can let him go now," she told her companions.

The two Bloods dropped his arms and Nicky sprang to his feet, lunging for her. She batted him casually aside and he skidded across the floor. Her companions moved towards him, but she shook her head.

"He's flying now," she said.

And it was true. Nicky lay where he'd fallen. From behind them, Long Lankin stepped over to the boy and rolled him over with a shiny black boot. Nicky's eyes were glazed. Spittle trickled from a corner of his mouth.

"You see, Corwyn?" Ysa said. "You feed this shit to a townie and they're gone before it's halfway down their throat."

Long Lankin nodded. "And the most amusing thing is that they will actually pay to have this done to them."

Nicky lay staring up at them, trying to focus, trying to get up, but he was long gone. Flying high. Fucking-A.

"Well?" Ysa asked the High Born. "Do we get the contract or what?"

Long Lankin nodded. "Exclusive—for three months. The first shipment will be delivered by the end of the week."

Ysa tried not to let her satisfaction show. "Sounds good."

"But finish up here first," Long Lankin said. He gave Nicky a last look, a vague smile flickering in his silver eyes, then he turned and left the room.

The Bloods waited till they could see him on the street below, walking away from the building, before they really let loose with some whoops.

"All *right!*" Nabber shouted. "Ysa—you've got the balls, that's all I can say."

Teddy Grim nodded. "Dealing with Lankin—that's like dicing with the dragons, man. But, hot shit, you pulled it off!"

Ysa just grinned. She screwed the top back on the little container of sample shake and knelt down beside Nicky.

Shucka-shuck.

"How's it going, Nicky-boy? You met God yet?"

She ran the long nails of one hand down his cheek. Silver nail polish glittered in the candlelight.

Nicky stared up at her, eyes focused now, but blurred with tears. The shake was burning through him—it was good, oh Jesus, it was so good. But there was a part of him that remembered. He'd been a junkie with nothing going for him till the Diggers pulled him back. He'd gone through hell breaking the hold the pearl had on him. Vomiting his guts, day after day. Cramps and seizures. Shaking. Headaches sharp as amps feeding back at full volume...

And then he was clean.

Two years he was clean. Two years he worked helping others through that hell. Helped the Diggers clothe and feed the hobos and runaways, the lost and the lonely. Helped talk down the junkies, dry out the alkies. Helped the people who were going to throw it all away because they were hurting, or burnt out, or the hundred other reasons that people could find to kill themselves. And now...

He could hear Ysa's voice, though she wasn't speaking.

There's a new kind of pearl in town...

Oh yeah. Didn't he know it? The shake was riding through his body like an old friend. He could feel the pearl glow, and behind it, kicking in every few seconds, speedy little rushes that made him feel like he was coming. Flying high. Long gone.

One hundred percent addictive...

He couldn't do it again. He couldn't go through it again. He'd already been to hell. He couldn't go back. He...

Shucka-shuck.

Ysa shook the container, a mocking glitter in her silver Blood eyes.

"Here, Nicky-boy," she said, and she stuffed the shake container into his pocket. "You're going to be needing this."

She stood up. Nicky couldn't take his eyes from her. Goddamn Bloods. She looked so good. Goddamn Bloods. One like Ysa Cran could seduce you just by looking at you. He hated her. He wanted her.

She could see it all in his eyes and all it did was make her laugh. "I don't fuck junkies," she told him. "I just fuck 'em around, Nicky-boy."

Nicky lunged up to a sitting position. The room spun, the candlelight turning into a kaleidoscope of pulsating colors, before everything settled down. Teddy Grim moved towards him, but Ysa waved him off.

"Nicky-boy's not going to hurt nobody," she said. "Are you Nicky-boy?"

Nicky struggled to his feet and stood swaying on a floor that breathed slightly, in a room that strobed with color. The Bloods were brilliant flares of black and silver and orange.

One hundred percent addictive...

Cold turkey.

He couldn't do it again. No one could do it again. He staggered across the room towards the window.

"Hey, Ysa," Nabber began. "Maybe we'd better —"

He and Teddy Grim started to move towards Nicky, but before they could cross the room, Nicky threw himself at the window.

The glass shattered. It sounded like bells. The shards that cut him didn't really hurt. They were just opening his body so that his blood could breathe. Wind was rushing by his ears. Everything was moving so fast. The whole world was moving. The ground was waiting to embrace him. It'd keep him safe from Ysa and Long Lankin and from the hell that'd be his if he tried to drop the pearl again...

Falling was a speed rush and slow motion, all at the same time. When he hit the ground he had one stunned moment of shocked realization. I'm dea —

And then everything was gone.

"Hol-ee fuck," Nabber said.

The three Bloods looked out the window. It was a three story drop to the street below. Nicky's small body lay in a twist of strange angles.

"Come on," Ysa said finally. "Let's burn this place down. The Diggers are going to have to realize that they're out of the helping people business. People get helped, they're worth shit to us, right?"

Her companions nodded.
"So let's do it."

CRØD

Later, out on the street, while the Diggers' free flophouse went up in flames, Ysa stood over Nicky's broken body. Hobos and runaways were shuffling and staggering around them, milling in a panic while the building burned. Gray smoke rose up to meet the lightening skies of the coming dawn. Ysa took a flat piece of lacquered wood from her pocket and glanced at the dragon embossed on it, black against red, before flipping it onto Nicky's body. Teddy Grim gave her a questioning look.

"Maybe they'll think one of Dragontown's tongs did him in," she said.

Teddy Grim, and then Nabber, smiled in appreciation. Laughing, they headed for the club district and one last round of brews.

TWO

There were just the two of them now.

Everyone else had crashed by the time a gray dawn came crawling in over Soho. They sat on the rambling front porch of the Diggers' House—the main house that sits in a rubbled lot equidistant from the Canal and Soho's club district, just a spit away from New Asia. Two of them, still following where the music led them. Up all night, playing the blues.

Berlin had a vintage Martin New Yorker six-string. Its tiny body fit comfortably in the curved hollow between her lap and breasts, while the neck was wide enough so that her fingers didn't get tangled, but not so wide that her small hands couldn't shape the chords. She was playing an easy-going G progression, violet eyes closed, head bobbing just slightly to the rhythm. Her hair was thick—a dark brown with green tints—and pulled back from her face with a pink scarf that made it stand up around her head like a halo.

Well, if the good die young
I said, the good die young

216

She was singing, her voice surprisingly gruff and deep for her small frame and nineteen or so years. Joe Doh-dee-oh was accompanying her on the harmonica, leaning back against the porch railing across from her, a smile in his dark eyes.

He looked to be in his late seventies, an old black man playing the blues. He wore a checkered shirt and faded jeans held up with bright red suspenders. His hair was a salty white, his brown wrinkled skin was a roadmap of all the tunes he'd played through the years. He knew them all, and a few more besides.

> Now if the good die young
> Then I gotta be just as wicked as they come
> — uh-huh
> I gotta be
> Just as wicked as they come

He sang along on the last line, then brought the harmonica back up to his mouth, chording on it while Berlin's fingers did a walking riff up the neck of her guitar. By the time Berlin hit the final G chord, a double bar at the tenth fret, Joe was wailing a long finishing note.

"Whoo-ee," he said, cradling his harmonica on his lap. "That's an old one."

Berlin grinned. "Learned that from Poppa Lightnin' — could that man play."

Joe didn't say anything for a moment. Poppa Lightnin' had died a long time ago — in the World beyond Bordertown — maybe only a decade or so after the Change. He gave her a curious look.

"He made some good records," Joe said finally.

"I suppose he did. Hey, remember this?" She broke into a version of "Cold, Cold Feeling."

"Know it? I coulda wrote it," Joe told her. "I've been there, Berlin. Makes for a good song, but you don't much care for it when it's going down."

He brought up his harmonica, but before he could join in, Berlin laid her hands across her guitar's strings. In the sudden silence, they could hear the creak of wooden wheels.

"Brandy's up early," Joe said.

Berlin nodded. "Too early. I got a bad feeling, Joe..."

217

They held off playing as Brandy Jack came walking around the side of the house. He walked with a shuffling limp, an old skinny hobo in battered hand-me-downs, hair as white as Joe's, but looking washed-out against his pale skin. Beside him a big mongrel pulled a small wagon that held all of Brandy's worldly possessions. Tin cans and found things; magazines, a couple of old Reader's Digest books and a lot of paperbacks with the front covers torn off; rags and mismatched clothing, a lot of it too big or too small for him; a broken harmonium and a ukulele that still worked; a bit of everything to reflect the varying aspects of his fifty-five some years.

The dog was called Noz and he had a small beanie on his head with a propeller that still turned. Berlin hoped that Brandy had just heard their music and come to play a few of his old Music Hall songs.

"Hey, Jack," Joe called. "Glad you're back."

Brandy shook his head mournfully. Even on the sunniest day he wore a hang-dog expression.

"Dig out your old uke there, Brandy," Berlin said, "and sing us a couple."

Brandy shuffled to a halt when he was at the foot of the steps going up to the porch. Noz sat down in his harness, his short tail thumping the dirt.

"Seen the sky?" Brandy asked.

Berlin and Joe looked up. It was growing steadily lighter, but the dismal gray was here for the day.

"Over there," Brandy said, pointing west. "Something's burning in Tintown. Something big."

"Burning...?" Joe began.

Berlin hopped over the rail and landed lightly on the ground, backing up until the house no longer hid her view of the western skies.

"Shit," she said.

"What's up, Berlin?" Joe asked.

"Shit!"

She ran up the stairs, disappearing inside the house. Moments later she was outside once more, a jean jacket thrown on over her faded T-shirt, her jeans tucked into a pair of black leather boots. A knife hung sheathed under each armpit, under the jacket.

218

"That's one of our places that's burning," she told Joe as she wheeled a small battered scooter out of the shed that leaned up against the side of the house like a drunken companion too unsteady to stand.

Tugging a small spell-box free from one of the jean jacket's many inner pockets, she inserted it into the scooter and turned the engine over. The starting motor ground a couple of times, then the machine coughed into life.

"What do you want us to do, Berlin?" Joe asked, joining Brandy at the bottom of the stairs.

"Wake Hooter. Keep a watch on the place."

"What about the rounds?"

Berlin frowned. In another hour or so it'd be time to take out the big wagon and make the rounds of the restaurants to collect what freebie food they could get for the free supper the Diggers provided every night. It was Berlin's week to take the wagon out.

"If I'm not back in time, get Casey to take it out."

"Casey's not going to like that," Joe said. "She's always complaining that—"

Berlin just shook her head. Gunning the engine, she took off, the scooter's rear wheel spraying dirt behind it until she hit the pavement.

Joe looked at Brandy, then shrugged. "Guess Casey'll just have to complain some more," he said as he went back up the stairs.

∞∞

There was a big vintage Harley parked in front of the burnt rubble of the Diggers' free flophouse in Tintown when Berlin arrived. She parked her scooter beside it, putting the little machine on its kickstand. A large ferret sat on the Harley's saddle, it's weasel-like body stretched out on the leather as it watched Berlin pocket her spell-box.

"How ya doing, Lubin?" she said and gave the ferret a pat before joining the tall black man who knelt by something at the front of the building.

The area was eerily quiet. There were usually a lot of hobos up and about by now, cooking coffee and what breakfast makings they had. Runaways hanging around—Soho Rats looking for a handout from those who weren't much better off than they were themselves, but still always seemed to make do. But Tintown was empty. The only smoke going up to the sky coming from the big ruined building.

"Christ," Berlin muttered. "What the…?"

Her voice trailed off as she reached the owner of the Harley and saw what he was kneeling beside.

"Oh, Jesus — Nicky!" She dropped to her knees in the dirt beside the limp broken body, tears welling up behind her eyes. She touched his cold cheek with a trembling hand, then turned away.

"Stick?" she asked softly, her gravelly voice huskier than ever.

"Easy, Berlin," he said. "There's nothing you can do."

He took her in his arms as she began to shake. Tears erupted, and Stick just held her close, letting them soak into his shirt. He stroked her hair until she finally pulled away, sitting back on her heels, violet eyes dark with pain.

"What happened?" she asked, her voice firmer now.

Stick sighed. He stood up and turned away, looking out over Tintown and beyond. His dreadlocks hung like fat fuzzy snakes down his back. When he turned back to look at her, his coffee-colored skin was pulled tight across his face.

"I think Nicky took a jump," he said at last.

Berlin shook her head. "No way, Stick. He had everything going for him now. All that shit was so far behind him that — "

Stick silently handed over a small metal container.

"What's that?"

"I found it on him."

Berlin opened it up and shook some of the pink and mauve flakes into the palm of her hand. She licked a finger and went to touch it to the flakes, but Stick caught her hand.

"Bad idea."

"Well, what is it?"

"Looks like a kind of pearl, but there's something about it makes me nervous."

Berlin looked at the dope, then slowly funneled it back into the container.

"There's no way Nicky'd go back," she said.

Stick nodded. "That's what I thought. Found this lying on his chest."

He passed over a lacquered marker chip with a Dragontown chop on it—what some of the old folks used to use as a calling card. Berlin studied the black dragon against the red background and shook her head.

"I don't recognize the chop," she said.

"Neither do I—but it's definitely a calling card."

"One of the tongs?"

"Doubtful," Stick said. "It might be someone else trying to set it up to look like the tongs're involved."

"Bloods?"

"Hard to say at this point, Berlin."

Berlin stuck the marker in her back pocket. "Then I guess we'd better go about finding out."

"What about Nicky?"

"Nicky? I…"

When she looked back at that small broken body the tears wanted to come all over again.

Berlin swallowed hard. "Can you bring him to the House on your chopper?"

Stick nodded. "We can't go off half-cocked on this, Berlin."

Berlin looked from the smoldering rubble to Nicky.

"Fuck that," she said. "Somebody just declared war, Stick."

"Diggers don't go to war," Stick reminded her.

"But Berlin does," she said softly. "And maybe somebody forgot that."

Stick sighed. "And maybe that's just what they want you to do."

Berlin lifted her gaze from Nicky's body. "Thanks for being here, Stick."

Stick looked as though he had something more to add, then he just shook his head.

"Yeah," he said.

Gently he cradled Nicky's body in his arms and carried it back to his Harley. Balancing it on his gas tank, he followed Berlin's scooter back to the Diggers' House.

THREE

The Diggers go back a long way.

Most people who remember them think of 1967 — Haight Ashbury in San Francisco, Yorkville in Toronto. The Summer of Love. Be-ins and Love-ins. Free music in the parks. The Diggers ran houses that provided free shelter, food, medical advice and counseling for the kids who had dropped out, but had nowhere to go, no one else to turn to.

The original Diggers date back to 1649, in England. They were a radical offshoot of the Levellers — the extreme left wing of Oliver Cromwell's army. Christian communists, they didn't believe in private property and were contemptuously called "the Diggers" when they tried to communally farm some poor unused land in St. George's Hill, Surrey. Forcibly removed, it took over three hundred years for their name and hopes to be revived in the sixties.

Since then they have resurfaced from time to time — most notably during the food riots in New York City at the beginning of the twenty-first century. More recently they appeared in Bordertown, answering an unspoken need as the city's population continued to swell with a constant influx of runaways and down-and-outers escaping the World and its ever-increasing capitalistic concerns.

Berlin thought of all that as they buried Nicky in the graveyard behind the Diggers' House. A different kind of digging. Instead of scruffing about, looking for handouts to feed their charges, and buildings to bed them in, they were planting one of their own. Digging in the dirt. The world's common treasury that was more abused every year. But that was what happened when people thought they could own land. The world's most successful cultures, at least in an ethical sense, had always been those that understood that the land was only theirs on loan.

She was the last to leave when the short nondenominational service was over. Stick gave her some time on her own by the graveside, then returned from the House where he'd been talking with a couple of the other Diggers.

"I didn't know him too well," he said after awhile.

"I did."

"How'd you meet?"

"I was the one that brought him in — talked him down, saw him through the first rough weeks when he was dropping the pearl. I never thought he'd..." Stick touched her shoulder, but she shook her head. "I'm okay. I'm all cried out, Stick. Now I just want to find the fucker who did this to him."

Hooter was the Diggers' current medic. When they brought Nicky's body back to the House, it had only taken him a few moments to find the telltale flaring in the dead boy's pupils. Nicky hadn't ODed, but he'd definitely been pearl diving when he died.

"Sometimes they just go back to it," Stick said quietly. "It's not nice and it's not pretty, Berlin, but it happens."

"I know. And I know the kind it happens to. Nicky wasn't like that. By the time he was finally clean, Stick, all he could feel was relief. He was the best we had to handle anyone who was making the break for themselves. He *hated* dope — any kind of it. Believe me."

Stick looked down at the raw earth of the grave and sighed. "Okay. I'm going to do some poking around — see what I can come up with. Can you be cool till then?"

Berlin shook her head. "*I'm* tracking them down, Stick."

"Bad move."

She turned to face him, eyes dark with anger. "You're treating me like a kid and I don't like it."

"Think of what you're about to do. The Diggers are tolerated at best, but only because they don't get political. They don't get involved. They're not aggressive. You start shoving your weight around, Berlin, you're just going to make things worse. You want your food sources cut off in Dragontown? You want some Blood gangs or Packers to come down on you and trash your Houses? Who's going to defend them? You? All by yourself?"

"If I have to."

"But you don't have to. I can do this thing for you. Christ, it's what I do."

"You don't understand," Berlin said.

"Hey, all of a sudden I'm—"

"Will you listen to me? You're out on the streets, sure, and you help a lot of people — my people, street people, whoever's in trouble. I can appreciate that. But then you go back to your fancy museum with all its conveniences and shut the door on the world. It's not the same out here. We're living right on the front lines with the people we're trying to help."

"Now don't—"

Berlin cut him off again. "I'm not saying there's anything wrong with what you're doing, Stick. I know what'd happen if you opened your place to the streets—the museum'd get trashed. And you're doing more for those who need help than just about anybody else, but it's still not the same as being a part of it. Can you understand that? It's not just revenge I want. I've got to know *why* this is suddenly happening. Who's got it in for us and why."

Stick nodded. "Okay. I get the picture. You want to come with me or go it on your own?"

"No offense, but I think I'll go it on my own."

She looked up to meet his gaze. Stick laid the palm of his hand against her cheek.

"There's not many of us left," he said. "You be careful. Let me know if you need anything."

Berlin nodded.

"Be seeing you then."

He turned and strode off, leaving her by the grave feeling very much alone. Not until she heard the deep-throated roar of his Harley starting up and then taking off, did she walk slowly from the grave herself.

FOUR

There was music on the roof.

Stick heard it when he shut off his Harley, a jaunty version of "Tamberwine's Jig" on tin whistle and electric guitar that came drifting down from the museum's rooftop garden. Locking up his bike and pocketing its spell-box, he went up the six flights of stairs to find Amanda Woodsdatter and Jenny Jingle in the garden amusing Lubin with their music. The ferret danced on her hind legs, keeping perfect time to the 6/8 rhythm of the jig.

The girls brought the tune to an end when they saw Stick.

"You don't look so good," Manda said.

"It's not been a good day," Stick agreed.

224

Silver-eyed and mauve-haired, Manda leaned against the balustrade in a polka-dotted mini-dress that matched the canary yellow of her Les Paul. She played lead guitar for the Horn Dance, but spent a good deal of her spare time hanging around the museum acting the part of Stick's surrogate daughter, much to Stick's amusement. Leaning her guitar against its small portable amp, she picked up a thermos to pour Stick a mug of tea.

"Did you find out where the fire was?" she asked.

Stick nodded. "Someone torched the Diggers' place in Tintown."

"Are you serious? Was anybody hurt?"

"A guy named Nicky who ran the place."

"I've met him," Jenny said.

She pushed Lubin away from her knee which the ferret kept nudging in an attempt to get her to continue the music.

Unlike Manda who was a halfling, the whistle player was a full-blooded elf who worked part-time at Farrel Din's place down in Soho. She wore her hair in a half-dozen silver braids from which hung tiny bells that jingled whenever she moved her head and a pair of shades with pink plastic frames. Her T-shirt was one that Stick had given to Manda advertising a long-gone rock band called the Divinyls.

Stick took his tea from Manda with a nod of thanks. Slouching down in an old wicker rocker, he put his feet up on Manda's guitar case and sighed.

"Well, Nicky's dead now," he said heavily.

"Dead?"

"I just got back from burying him."

The girls exchanged horrified looks.

"God," Manda said. "What a horrible way to go."

Stick shook his head. "He didn't get caught in the fire. He was on the pearl and took a drop from one of the windows."

"That doesn't sound right," Jenny said. "I know he used to be a junkie but he dropped the pearl a long time ago. There's no way he'd go back."

"That's what Berlin said, too. She's taking it pretty hard. But we found some shit on him — weird shit. Some new kind of pearl, looks like."

He filled in the rest of the details with a few terse sentences. When he was done, they all sat around without speaking for a long while. Lubin gave up on Jenny and came to collapse on the arm of Stick's chair. He ruffled the thick fur at the nape of the ferret's neck and looked out across the rooftop garden to Fare-you-well Park and beyond.

"Well," he said finally. "Time's wasting. I've got to head over to Dragontown to check up on that marker."

"I know someone who might be able to help you with that," Jenny said.

"Who's that?"

"My teacher — Koga Sensei."

Something flickered in Stick's eyes.

"Shoki," he said quietly. "I hadn't thought of him."

Jenny looked puzzled. "Who or what's Shoki?" she asked, but Stick was already turning away.

"Not this time," he told Lubin as the ferret rose to follow him. "Manda?"

Manda called Lubin back. Stick nodded to them from the door.

"Don't hold supper for me," he said.

Then he was gone. Jenny and Manda looked at each other.

"Sometimes," Jenny said after a few subdued moments, "he really spooks me."

"He just gets a little intense, that's all," Manda said.

Jenny nodded. "Poor Nicky. I wonder how it happened. He was the last guy I'd expect to get hooked again."

The gray skies above them seemed drearier than ever. The air held a sudden chill. Manda shivered.

"Let's go inside," she said.

Together they packed up their things and brought them down to the living quarters on the museum's fifth floor.

ᏚᏰᎦᎾ

Koga Sensei lived behind his dojo which was on the second floor of a building that also housed a Trader's shop. The store was run by an old Japanese couple and took up most of the main floor. Stick glanced at the goods for sale in the window — everything from Japanese noodles and gaudily-wrapped imported candies to elfin herb-pouches — then went up the stairs.

He recognized the girl who answered the door as another of Farrel Din's waitresses. She wore an oversized red T-shirt with the word "Tokyo" emblazoned on the front and her black Mohawk sprang up to attention in a swath of spikes, adding six inches or so to her diminutive stature. Stick gave her a quick slight bow.

"I am pleased to see you again," he said to her in fluent Japanese. "Would it be possible for me to speak with Shoki-san at this time?"

"I'm sorry," the girl said. "But I don't, uh…speak Japanese."

"Who is it, Laura?" a male voice asked from inside.

"It's Stick," she called back over her shoulder.

She stepped aside as the owner of that voice came to the door. Koga Sensei was compact and muscular, taller than Laura but still a head or so shorter than Stick, casually dressed in loose white cotton trousers and a collarless shirt. He ran a hand through his short dark hair.

"Stick," he said softly.

Stick gave him a brief bow which Koga returned.

"Shoki-san," he said.

"That's not a name I usually go by."

Stick shrugged. "It's the name I know you by."

"Yes. Well." Koga glanced at Laura, then sighed and stepped aside. "Will you come in?"

Stick took off his boots and, leaving them by the door, walked past the Sensei. In the center of the room, he knelt, back straight, weight on his ankles, hands on his knees.

"What's going on?" Laura whispered to Koga. "I thought you two were friends."

"We know each other," Koga replied.

"You've seemed pretty friendly other times I've seen you meet."

Koga nodded. "But this appears to be a formal visit, Laura."

"I don't get it. And why's he calling you Shoki?"

The only other time that Laura had heard her lover referred to by that name had been in quite unpleasant circumstances. Shoki was the Demon Queller. She'd been a demon at the time.

"We go back a long way," Koga replied. "But there are…differences between us from those times that have never been resolved." He stopped her next question with a raised hand. "Serve tea, Laura."

227

"So now I'm your geisha girl? Shit, when you revert to the old ways, you really revert, don't you?"

Koga smiled. One of those, not-now-let's-fight-about-it-later smiles.

All right, she smiled back. Later.

"I'll let you get away with it this time," she said aloud.

She kept her voice low so that only Koga could hear her. Giving him a poke in the stomach with a stiff finger, she put her palms together in a prayer position and hurried off to the kitchen with a geisha's quick mincing steps. Koga rolled his eyes, then walked over to where Stick was sitting. By the time he sat down across from his guest, his features were composed again.

"This is an unexpected pleasure," he said. "I'd given up ever having you visit me in my home."

Stick gave a small shrug. "Had some business that couldn't keep."

Koga nodded. They waited in silence then for the tea to be served. Laura pulled out a low table and set it between the two men, serving them their tea in small handleless cups of bone china. Not until they were finished with their first cup and they each had a second in front of them did they get to Stick's business.

Sitting off to one side, Laura watched them, struck by how much alike they seemed at this moment. She listened attentively as Stick explained the Diggers' problem, then muttered under her breath something about "slaves and geishas" as she fetched some ink, parchment and a brush so that he could quickly sketch the dragon symbol from the marker that had been left behind on Nicky's body.

"Why is it that one need only mention drugs and dragons and immediately it is assumed that the problem originates in New Asia?" Koga said when Stick was done.

"Maybe it's got something to do with your yakuza and tongs," Stick replied.

"There are other dragons—"

"I'm only interested in this one," Stick said, breaking in.

Koga nodded. "All right. I think it belongs to the Cho tong—Billy Hu's people. At least it used to. I've seen this motif on some of the dishware in their gaming rooms."

"Didn't think you gambled," Stick said.

"I don't. But I like watching sometimes."

"Okay. Thanks."

Stick started to rise, but Koga reached across the table to touch his arm. "You never forget, do you? What will it take for you to forget?"

"Can you bring Onisu back?"

Koga shook his head. "I had no choice."

"You think I don't know that? Why the hell do you think we're still on talking terms?"

"I just thought...if enough time went by..."

"Don't kid yourself, Shoki—there aren't that many years." He gave Koga a brief nod, then rose from the table. Standing, he towered over both Laura and the Sensei. His gaze went to Laura. "Thanks for the tea—you served it real well for a *gaijin*."

Before Laura could reply, he was outside, the door closing on him. She could hear him on the landing, putting on his boots, but she waited until she heard him go down the stairs before she spoke.

"What was all that about?"

Koga shook his head. "Like I said before—an old disagreement."

"But who's this Onisu he was talking about? Why's he so pissed off, Koga?"

"Onisu was Stick's wife, Laura—a long time ago."

"And she's...is she dead?"

Koga nodded. "Shoki killed her."

"But you're..." Laura couldn't finish.

"I know," Koga said. "Believe me, Laura. I know."

Laura began to feel that this was a secret she wished she had never learned about.

"Was she a...a demon? Like I was?"

"No." Koga moved to sit beside her. He took her hands in his. "There are dragons," he said, "that are here as caretakers for the world, Laura. Dragons of earth and fire, water and air; guardian spirits. They live in mortal flesh and some small sphere of the world falls under their protection. But sometimes those guardians become rogues—do you understand? They become what you might have become if you hadn't learned how to control *your* demon."

"Stick had a wife that was a dragon?"

Koga nodded.

"Then what does that make Stick?"

Koga was silent for a long while. When he finally spoke, his voice was so low that Laura had to lean close to hear him.

"I don't really know," he said. "I just know that once he was my friend."

"How could you do it?" Laura asked him. "How could you kill her?"

Koga shook his head. "You don't understand. I did it for him. She was his responsibility—just as he was hers. But he couldn't do it. I had to do it for him."

Laura remembered the demon she had been and how she'd prayed that if she couldn't be saved, that Koga would kill her so that she wouldn't hurt anyone else. She shivered. It wasn't a memory she liked to call up. Glancing at Koga, she saw that he too was remembering. She drew his head against her shoulder.

"I think I understand," she said.

Koga made no reply. He just drew her closer, accepting her comfort.

FIVE

It was a high lonesome sound.

Berlin sat on the back porch of the Diggers' House, playing one of Joe Doh-dee-oh's harmonicas that could hit the high notes her own voice never could. The last of the afternoon drained away as she sat there playing—not really thinking, just remembering. And waiting. After awhile, she put the harmonica down and lit up a thin cigar.

She was waiting for the day to pass. She was waiting for the night to come, when Dragontown would come alive. Joe shifted in the chair behind her, but she didn't turn her head.

"It's a long lonely road," he said finally.

Berlin blew out a stream of blue-gray smoke, then studied the glowing tip of her cigar. "What is?"

"Getting back. Getting even."

"What makes you think I want any more than just to know what's going on and stopping it?"

"You just wouldn't be Berlin, then. Is Stick helping you out?"

She shrugged. "He's looking, I'm looking."

"And whoever gets there first wins the prize?"

Berlin turned slowly. "What are you trying to say, Joe?"

"Nothing. It's just...we had a good thing going here, helping people and everything. I liked the feeling that I was being of some use to somebody, even if it was just to runaway punks and bums."

"That doesn't have to change."

"But nothing's going to be the same anymore, either," Joe said.

"I didn't make the first move."

"Nobody's blaming you, Berlin. I'm just talking. Thinking aloud."

Berlin tossed her cigar into the dirt below the porch. "Thinking's bad for you—remember? You told me that. Anyone who thinks too much, they can't play the blues."

"I'm not talking music, Berlin. I'm talking about what we're going to *do*, what we're going to *be* when this is all done."

Berlin sighed and stood up. "We're going to be changed—but that's not necessarily a bad thing, Joe. We're still going to be helping people."

"What people? We had a half dozen hobos here for the free supper tonight. And that was it. People are scared. Talk's already going around that wherever the Diggers are is not a good place to be."

"That's why I've got to be doing something now."

She left the porch before he could reply, going to the shed where she wheeled out her scooter. The sun was almost down now, sinking below Bordertown's western skyline. The rubbled lots around the House grew thick with shadows. She looked back at the House. Joe was right. There'd been almost nobody at the free supper tonight and they didn't have *anybody* crashing for the night.

It sure made things quiet.

She started up the scooter. The purr of its engine sounded loud in the stillness. She gave the throttle a rev, then set off across the dirt yard towards the street. Just before she could turn onto the pavement, a small figure detached itself from the hulking shadows of an abandoned delivery truck and waved her down.

Berlin used one hand on the rear brakes to bring the scooter to a stop, palming a throwing knife in the other. She put the knife away as soon as she saw who it was.

"Hey, Berlin," the figure said.

"Hey, Gamen. How's tricks?"

Gamen was one of Sammy's kids, living up with the rest of them at the old Lightworks building from which Sammy ran the Pack. You could find Sammy's kids all through Soho, and ranging out into Trader's Heaven and Riverside—scruffy little Packers in rags and tatters, scrounging a living from the streets or wherever they could. They turned up at the Diggers' Houses from time to time, though Sammy frowned on that. The Diggers let anybody crash, and Sammy wasn't big on his kids mixing with the Blood runaways that showed up as regularly as any other kind of kid on the streets.

"I heard about the burn in Tintown," Gamen said.

She turned her big sad eyes on Berlin. There weren't many could turn Gamen down when she was asking for a handout—not with those eyes.

"It was a bad scene," Berlin agreed. "Listen, if you're hungry, we've got plenty of eats tonight. Go back up to the House and ask Joe or Hooter."

"I'm not here for eats," Gamen said. "Sammy sent me."

Berlin's eyebrows went up. "What's Sammy got to say?"

Gamen scuffed at a lip of broken pavement with a dirty shoe. "Well, I seen something in Tintown and when I told him, he told me to come and tell you. Nobody else, just you."

"What did you see, Gamen?"

"A High Born. I saw a High Born on the back streets of Tintown just a little while before the fire started up."

Berlin regarded her steadily. A High Born. In Tintown. It wasn't totally preposterous—but she had to take into account the source of the information. Sammy was a pure townie bigot. He hated Bloods. It could be just like him to make trouble between the Bloods and Diggers, because he wasn't that big on the Diggers either. He'd lost a kid or two to the Diggers—not enough to make them his enemy, but enough so that he wouldn't mind them having a little war with the Bloods.

"Did you *see* this?" Berlin demanded. "Or did Sammy just tell you you did?"

"Come on, Berlin. I wouldn't shit you."

The big eyes met her gaze without blinking. Berlin sighed. With those eyes—especially on a streetkid—there was no way to tell if Gamen was lying or not.

"Okay," Berlin said. "Thanks for the tip, Gamen. Tell Sammy I owe him one."

"What about me?"

"I thought we were friends," Berlin said. "Friends don't owe each other."

Gamen thought about that for a moment, then her grimy face brightened. She gave Berlin a quick salute before vanishing into the deepening shadows. Berlin sat on her scooter, the engine still idling, while she thought about what this new information could mean. A High Born in Tintown. And pearl came straight across the Borders from Elfland. If only she could trust Sammy's reasons for passing the info on...

She thought it all through one more time, then shook her head. There just wasn't enough to go on. Putting the scooter into gear, she pointed it towards Dragontown.

CR&D

Berlin knew her way around Dragontown. She knew the twists and turns of its narrow streets. She understood the safe blocks and those that were off-limits even to her. She could read the pulse of the streets and the Dragons that patrolled them in gangs of twos and threes. But the vibes were wrong tonight.

She could feel angry eyes watching her from the teahouses and shops she passed by. The paper lanterns seemed greedier than ever with their light tonight, leaving dark pools of shadow that spilled beyond the mouths of alleyways to eat away at the streets. There was a high buzz of anger in the air that grew into an ever-stronger whine with each Dragon she passed. It wasn't until she ran down Locas in the gaming district that she found out what was going down.

"What chew doin' here, Berlin?" Locas demanded, dragging her off the street into an alley. "Chew crazy or somethin'?"

Locas was a thin dark-skinned youth, half Chinese and half Puerto Rican. He lived in the barrios out past Fare-you-well Park borough, but usually spent his evenings cruising the streets of New Asia.

Berlin shook off his grip. She'd left her scooter chained up in an alley out by Ho Street, before entering Dragontown on foot.

"You think *I'm* crazy? What the hell's going on here, Locas?"

"Oh, man. Don't chew *know*? Word's out on chew, babe. Chew gone lobo on us. Calling in the bulls from uptown. Word's all over the street. Chew know the uptown fuzz don't bother with us — not 'less they got somebody to point out who's who an' what's what."

"People are believing this shit?"

"Hey, we're not talkin' one rumor here, babe. We're talkin' everybody sayin' the same thing 'bout chew."

"Well, everybody's wrong. Come on, Locas — you think I'd turn *anybody* in?"

"I tol' 'em chew wouldn't — but there's too much talkin' goin' down, Berlin. Chew stay here too long tonight an' the uptown bulls gonna get your pretty little head delivered to 'em in a box, chew know what I'm sayin'?"

Berlin leaned weakly against the alley wall.

"Jesus Christ," she muttered. "The whole friggin' world's turning upside down."

"Ain't that the truth. Chew gotta split, babe. Chill right outta here."

Berlin nodded. "Okay. I get the picture. I'm gone. But before I go, can you tell me something?"

"What chew want, Berlin?"

"Who's this belong to?"

She pulled out the lacquered wood marker and dropped it into his hand. Locas sidled up to the mouth of the alleyway, gave it a quick look, then returned to her side.

"It's an old marker," he said. "Used to belong to Billy Hu's people — chew know who I mean? We're talkin' tongs here, babe. What chew want with them?"

It was too dark to see his features, but Berlin could read the suspicion in his voice.

"You heard about our house in Tintown?"

"It's a fuckin' shame. Nicky was okay."

"Somebody left that on Nicky's body."

Locas weighed the marker in his hand, then passed it back to her.

"Somebody's makin' trouble, an' not just with chew," he said finally.

"I've got to talk to Billy Hu, Locas. Can you set up a meet?"

"I'll see what's brewin' — talk to some people."

"I'd appreciate it," Berlin said. "This is shaping up into a major fuck-up."

"No shit. Everybody's gettin' a hard-on for chew, babe, an'..."

His voice trailed off. Berlin turned to see what he was looking at and watched them fill up the entrance of the alleyway. Dragons. Four, no five of them.

"Get out of here," she told Locas.

"Hey, Berlin. I—"

"Blow!"

As he started to shuffle away, Berlin shifted slightly into a loose *yoi*, or ready, stance and faced the Dragons. She really didn't need this. She had to be careful — not hurt them too badly, because that'd just make this whole mess worse — but they weren't going to be operating under any such limitations.

"You got a lot of nerve," one of the Dragons said, "showing your ass around here."

He was enough in the light so that Berlin could recognize him. Jackie Won. Half the gangs in lower Dragontown answered to him. Beautiful, she thought.

"You've been hearing a lot bullshit, Jackie," Berlin replied. "Let me go before someone gets hurt."

Jackie laughed. He looked at his companions. "You hear that? She's afraid of hurting us." His hard gaze returned to Berlin. "We're not afraid of a little pain — 'specially not when you'll be the one feeling it."

Berlin didn't bother replying. Stay cool, she told herself. Don't get mad. Don't go tearing them apart. But there were five of them and they were already fanning out. There was no way she could take all five *without* tearing them apart.

"Two things," she said quietly. "And I want you to remember them both. Whatever you heard on the street about me's bullshit."

"This is so scary," Jackie said with a grin. "What's the other thing, dead meat?"

"You don't fuck around with Berlin."

They never saw her first move. She just flowed to one side of the alley, grabbed up a couple of garbage can lids, flung them like discs at the Dragons, then leapt up to the fire escape that was hanging above her. Two Dragons went down as the lids spun into them. The other three rushed forward and she dropped down amongst them.

She drop-kicked the first, trying to hold back, but she heard his thigh-bone snap under the impact of her foot. The next she took out with a lightning blur of punches that left him wheezing and choking on the ground. When she turned to Jackie, he was already committed to a whirling kick.

She came up under his attack, a pointed fist firing into his groin. As he started to fall, she flipped him over her back, then came up to face the first two she'd taken out with the garbage can lids who were now back on their feet. A low growl came up from her diaphragm—a rumbling sound that turned into a panther's cough. The two Dragons looked as though they were going to stand their ground, but as soon as she took a step towards them, they both fled.

A pinpoint of heat burned in the center of Berlin's head, licking at her thoughts like a fire. Her eyes glimmered eerily as she studied her downed foes. She took a step towards the nearest one, then stopped. Bowing her head, she took one deep breath after another until the heat cooled, until the light in her eyes died, until the rumbling sound in her chest fell still.

Close. She'd almost lost it. She'd…

She looked down into Jackie's shocked eyes. There was a flicker of fear behind his pain. Perfect. Now the Dragons were really going to be after her ass. She broke eye contact with him and headed deeper down into the alley at a gliding walk. She was going to have to disappear for awhile. It was that, or go after all the gangs in Dragontown before they came after her.

SIX

Ysa Cran laughed like a pearl diver.

She sat at a table in The Underground, a live music club on Ho Street just down the block from The Dancing Ferret. Drag 'em Down were on stage, blasting through an uptempo version of "Sucking Down the Future." Nabber slouched beside her, boots up on one chair, head tilted back against his chair's headrest. There was an empty beer pitcher on the table in front of them. They each had a joint of Bordertown Blue smoldering between their fingers.

Teddy Grim returned with a new pitcher of beer. Shoving Nabber's feet off the chair, he sat down. Ysa passed him a joint.

"I still can't believe it," he said. "I always heard Berlin had a temper, but I didn't think she'd let go so easily."

"She just never had the right people pushing her," Ysa said. "That's all. Tomorrow we'll start spreading the word around in Riverside and the Scandal District—just like we did in Dragontown. Then no matter which way she turns, she'll burn."

Nabber filled their glasses from the new pitcher.

"So are we hitting their main digs tonight or what?" he wanted to know.

Ysa shook her head. "Why bother? The Dragons'll probably trash the place for us, seeing how Berlin's been kind enough to add fuel to our rumors." She grinned. "She took out Jackie Won, hey? I'll bet those Dragons are just burning to rumble."

"So what are *we* going to do?" Nabber asked.

Ysa gave Teddy Grim a knowing look. "Looks like the Nab here's developed a real taste for torching townies."

"Hey, we didn't burn anybody."

"So we were unlucky. We'll just have to bar up the doors and windows when we hit their place near the Market tonight."

"There's going to be bulls hanging around there," Teddy Grim warned.

The cityguard pretty well stayed out of Soho and the areas like it, giving them up as already lost, but Trader's Heaven was a whole other story. Half of Bordertown's economy depended on its Market. There were beat cops as well as plainclothes bulls constantly patrolling the Market and its immediate vicinity.

"Hell," Ysa said. "We're on a roll. They're just going to have to stay out of our way."

The band on stage kicked into "Rip It Out" with the heavy metallic whine of their lead guitar soaring over the deep throbbing rhythm.

"Give 'em hell," Ysa yelled.

The music drowned her out, but the lead guitarist caught her eye and gave her a wink before settling into the chopping chords that underpinned the lead singer's lyrics. Ysa turned to her companions.

"I just love this shit," she said, taking a long drag from her joint.

SEVEN

Two days now and it was just getting worse.

Stick sat in the Museum's Native American hall, staring at a display of Hopi kachina masks. He should never have gone to Koga's. It hadn't started there, but it might as well have. That's where it had all come home for him. Seeing Koga again, in that kind of environment. Koga, the Sensei and man. Shoki, the Demon Queller.

It brought back too many memories. Past failures, present failures. Onisu, dead and gone. But reborn in Berlin. Or maybe it was just Onisu's madness taking root in Berlin. It didn't make a whole lot of difference.

It was two days since Berlin had disappeared in Dragontown, but the streets were full of rumors of her. All of Bordertown was ranked against her now. They were saying that she'd gone lobo long before anybody made a move against her. They were saying that the fire in Tintown had been the start of a justified retribution for the shit she was bringing down on the city. On her own head.

Stick was hearing it so much, he almost believed it himself.

She'd taken out a few Dragons that first night. Later word had it she'd wasted a pack of Wharf Rats who'd cornered her down in Riverside the following afternoon. Two of those died. Later still, she'd taken out a gang of Bloods who'd run into her out by the Old Wall.

Stick stroked Lubin's fur. The ferret lay still in his lap, eyes open, but not focused. Stick wondered if she was staring into the same bleak vistas he was looking into.

Somebody'd hit the Diggers' place by the Market a couple of nights ago. All the Diggers had left was their main House in Soho, but that was vacant now — taken over by a mixed gang of Dragons and Bloods who'd trashed the place. They were supposedly waiting for Berlin to show up, but nobody really believed she would. It was just something to do.

And if all of that wasn't bad enough, now there was word of a new drug hitting the streets. Shake. Twice the flash pearl was and you didn't have to mainline it. Stick remembered the container he'd found on Nicky's body. Had to be the same shit. Everything tied together, but he was damned if he could make the connections. All he knew was Berlin was over the edge and he was going to have to track her down.

He looked up as Manda came into the room and beside him.

"When did you get in?" she asked.

Stick shrugged. "An hour or so ago."

"Still no luck, I guess."

That depended, Stick thought, on how much he really wanted to find Berlin.

"No luck," he agreed.

"It's just getting worse, isn't it?"

Stick thought of a dark night, of the silver flash of a katana as the blade swung home, of cradling Onisu in his arms. He hadn't been able to cry then. Koga, kneeling on the other side of his wife's body, had wept for both of them.

"I've got to talk to her," he said. "Maybe it's not too late."

"Too late for what?"

Stick looked bleakly at Manda, then passed Lubin over to her.

"I don't want the past to be repeated," he said. "Because this time I'll have to do it myself."

"Stick, what're you talking about?"

He nodded at Lubin. "Take care of her for me, will you?"

"Sure, but..."

He was walking away before she could finish, leaving only the echo of his footsteps in the empty hall. Manda looked at the kachina masks lining the walls and shivered.

ʘʖ

There was one place Stick hadn't looked. He drove out there now, the big Harley eating up the blocks. It was out past Tintown. The rubbled lots were empty — had been since the fire. The tin shanties still stood, dotting the lots here and there. There were some canvas tents. In other places sheets of corrugated iron had been pulled over roofless basements for more permanent shelters. But none of the hobos were around.

Stick drove on, out to the old freight yards.

Before the Change came, and Elfland came creeping over the city making it a Borderland, this had been the heart of the city's transportation. But the trains stopped running, the decades took their toll, and the heart of the city's railway network had been turned into a dump. Now, after years of neglect, you could no longer see the rails for the refuse. Only the old freight cars still stood, scattered here and there like beached whales in a sea of garbage.

Rats made their home here—the animal kind that Lubin was trained to hunt in an earlier age, not the kids from Soho. There were other residents as well. Die-hard hobos had carved camps deep inside the dump. Some of the 'bos took over the odd freight car that was still mostly in one piece, scavenging carpets and furniture and you name it to turn them into regular homes. But the area got its name from a third inhabitant—the real rulers of the dump.

The place was called Dogtown now.

Stick pulled up at the edge of the dump and killed the Harley. Pocketing his spell-box, he stayed astride the big bike, patiently waiting. He knew the procedure. If you weren't dumping trash, you waited.

They came bounding out from the heaps of garbage, huge mastiffs and rat-earred little Border collies. German shepherds and Dobermans. But mostly they were mongrels, tough lean dogs with the blood of a hundred lines running in their veins.

They circled the bike and Stick didn't move a muscle, didn't speak a word. One or the other and they'd be all over him. He just waited, breathing through his mouth so that the stink of the dump wouldn't make him gag. None of the dogs came too close, but it wasn't because they were afraid of him. They knew the procedure too. They were waiting, just as he was.

It might have been a half hour later that Stick caught movement out of the corner of his eye. The figure that finally shuffled through the circle of dogs was an old 'bo. His skin was browned like leather from the sun, his hair as fine and white as spiderwebs floating down to his shoulders. His clothes were so patched it was hard to tell what the original material had been. His feet were bare, the soles tougher than any workboot. He had a bag over his shoulder that rattled as he moved. When he got near to Stick, he just stood there staring at him.

"I just want to talk to her," Stick said. "That's all."

"Talk to who?"

Stick put a hand in his pocket — moving very slowly when one of the mastiffs took a few stiff steps towards him — and withdrew a tin of chewing tobacco. He tossed the tin over.

"Berlin," Stick said. "I just want to talk to her, Pazzo."

The 'bo studied the tin for a moment, then slipped it into his bag. Without a word, he turned and started off on a faint trail that led through the garbage. Stick took a few quick shallow breaths, then started after the old man. The dogs flowed in a wave all around them, never quite touching Stick, but so close he could feel the heat of their bodies.

Pazzo led them on a long meandering route through Dogtown, stopping sometimes to add something to his bag, muttering to himself, but never looking straight at Stick. The dogs seemed to count every shallow breath Stick took. The reek was overpowering. The air was thick with it, thick with flies too. He saw rats on the tops of some of the heaps, but they burrowed into the garbage at the sight of the dogs, moving so quick Stick wasn't even sure he'd seen them half the time.

It took awhile, but finally they entered a narrow ravine between two towering mountains of refuse and Stick blinked at what he saw. He'd never been this deep into Dogtown before, never dreamed this existed.

Encircling a glade like a circle of wagons in an old B-western were a number of freight cars, dwarfed by the steep towers of garbage all around them. Inside the circle, grass and bushes grew, flowering vines crawled up the freight cars. Somehow, the air was clean. The dogs went racing ahead, leaving Stick and Pazzo to follow at the old 'bo's pace. Stick heard the sound of guitar music. As they came around the bulk of the nearest freight car, he saw Berlin sitting by a fire with a number of hobos.

Brandy Jack was there and Joe Doh-dee-oh. One of them had probably fetched Berlin's guitar for her, but he couldn't guess which one. She finished the tune she was playing, a slow rendition of "Dogtown Blues." Stick wondered if she'd known he was coming and was playing that tune for him. He'd always liked it. She'd probably written it and just never admitted it to him.

Pazzo kept on going and the other 'bos drifted away from the fire as Stick approached. He leaned against a big iron barrel and looked down at Berlin. She looked back, her eyes giving nothing

241

away. Stick held her gaze for a long time before he settled on a log across the fire from her.

"So what's doing, Berlin? You declaring war on the city?"

"Nice to see you too, Stick."

"Come on, Berlin. What the fuck's going on?"

"City's declared war on me."

"Bullshit."

Her eyebrows went up. "Oh? And what would you call it?"

"I think you've stepped across the line."

She doodled a few riffs on her guitar, not looking at what she was doing, not looking at anything. When her gaze finally focused on him, her violet eyes burned with an inner flicker.

"Somehow I didn't think you'd fall for all the shit that's been spread around, Stick. You've disappointed me."

"What the hell am I supposed to think? You've been running wild, throwing your weight around...Christ, you never even talked to me about it."

"What's to say? I read you now, Stick—loud and clear."

"Talk to me, Berlin. What's going down?"

"You blind?"

Angry words swarmed in Stick's throat, but he looked away, staring into the fire until they'd been burned off.

"So maybe I'm blind," he said. "Talk to me."

"Someone's working a frame on me—it started with the Diggers, but it looks like I'm all that's left."

"Who's working the frame?"

"Don't know. All I know is it's coming straight across the Border, looking for my ass."

Stick sighed. "That doesn't make any sense."

"I didn't say it would."

"And it doesn't explain your taking on half the gangs in the city. You have a responsibility, Berlin. And you're abusing it."

"Fuck you, Stick. I'm staying alive—that's all. We're not all like you—willing to get gutshot rather than ripping out their hearts when they try to cut you down."

"You're—"

"And besides—we don't all have little halfie healers hanging around, ready to fix us up if we *do* get gutshot."

"Manda's not my—"

242

"Come *off* it, Stick. Face the facts. I'm not you. I can't be you. I don't want to be you. Nothing personal, understand, but I got my own ways of handling things. You want to get down to nitty-gritties? How many people have you killed?"

"I killed them naturally, not—"

"Jesus, I can't believe I'm hearing this. Dead's dead, Stick. I'm not out hunting—people are hunting me. They come for me, they've got to know I'm not going to stand back and let them take me down without giving it my best shot. Now maybe you think handfighting a couple of punks in an alley's okay, or shooting them down like you did Fineagh Steel awhile back, but we've all got to play the cards we're dealt. The hand I've been dealt—it's just not that simple."

"I don't know you anymore."

"Maybe you never did, Stick."

"If you don't stop this, I'm going to have to come after you."

For one moment Berlin's eyes softened. "I'm not Onisu," she said, her voice gentle. "You've got to stop fitting me into her life."

"Don't bring her into this."

"I'm not—you are. You think I'm stepping over the line, but what you're really afraid of is something you never dealt with a long time ago, Stick. I'm Berlin—okay? I'm not a Stick clone, I'm not an Onisu clone. I'm just me. And for some reason, a lot of people want to hurt me."

Stick stood up. "Come back with me," he said. "We'll deal with them together."

"What're we going to do? Go to an uptown court? Get serious, Stick. This's got to be dealt with on the streets—where it began. I've got find the suckers who started this and stop it with them. That's the only way it's going to end. I've got to have them in my hand and show the gangs that I'm not what they're hearing I am."

"I'm going," Stick said. "Either come with me—"

"It's all black and white, right? I'm either with you or against you?"

"—or I've got to come back to get you. I'll give you till midnight."

Berlin shook her head. "I'm not coming with you, Stick. Not now, not later. And I won't be here when you come back."

"I'll find you."

"I know you will."

She watched him go. Her fingers found a slow blues riff, but for once she was fumbling the notes. If Stick had turned then, he would have seen her eyes flooding with tears. But he never looked back.

CRSO

Manda heard Stick come in and went looking for him. She found him on the rooftop, sitting on his knees in a *seiza* position with a sheathed katana on the ground within easy reach of his right hand.

"Stick?" she said softly.

When he made no reply, she walked around in front of him and knelt down so that she could look into his face.

"Did you find her?"

His face was as still as the kachina masks downstairs.

"You're scaring me, Stick."

His gaze slowly focused on her.

"I found her," he said softly. "I just wish to Christ I hadn't."

Manda looked down at the sword in its sheath of lacquered wood. A chill catpawed up her spine. "What are you saying, Stick? Did...did you kill her?"

He shook his head.

"But I will," he said. His voice was just a faint whisper now. "God help me, I will."

EIGHT

The pain went through her heart like a razor.

Berlin sat hunched over her guitar, hugging its body against her as she fought to hold back a flood of tears. The fire crackled and spat in front of her. Out past the freight cars she heard a dog howl.

"Dogs got his smell—they can get him for you."

She looked up through a blurry veil to find Pazzo crouched down beside her, anger clouding his eyes. She shook her head numbly.

"It's not his fault," she said. "He's trapped—we all are. This is just something we should have looked to a long time ago. See, he never dealt with it, Pazzo. He just hid it—locked it away and never dealt with it. But you can't do that. You've always got to deal with it — if you don't do it when it happens, when maybe you've got some choice, then *it's* going to decide its own time to bust loose."

Pazzo didn't really know what she was talking about. "He shouldn't've made you cry."

"He's a hard man — that's how he kept going. He just got hard and stayed that way. I think it's the kid he's got staying with him — I think she opened a crack or two in his armor and now it's all falling out. Falling apart."

Pazzo shrugged. Digging about in one patched pocket, he came up with a clean handkerchief that he gave to her.

"Thanks."

"You've got another visitor."

Berlin tried to find a smile. "I'm just a real Miss Popularity today, aren't I?"

"You want to see him?"

Berlin nodded, then blew her nose when Pazzo shuffled off. He came back a few moments later with Locas in tow.

"This guy makes you feel bad..." Pazzo began.

"I'm okay, Pazzo. Honest."

Locas waited until the old 'bo left them alone, then sank down on the log that Stick had so recently vacated. "Shit, Berlin. Chew got some weird friends."

"That include you?"

"Fuckin' A." He grinned, white teeth gleaming against his dark skin, until Berlin couldn't help but smile back.

"Did you have any luck?" she asked.

Locas shrugged. "Okay. Sammy's no problem. He's got a hard on for whoever's dumping this shake on the streets an' if chew can deliver 'em, he'll back us."

"What about the Dragons?"

"Well, Jackie Won'd take your balls — just sayin' chew had any. But they'll be there. Billy Hu's sendin' somebody to look out for the Cho interests — I think it's gonna be Hsian."

"At least he's honest. What about the Bloods?"

"There'll be Bloods an' Wharf Rats there — a little bit of everybody, all lookin' to take a piece of chew, just sayin' chew can't deliver."

Berlin nodded. "And can we?"

"John Cocklejohn tracked 'em down. Lady chew want's called Ysa Cran. She's tight with someone from across the Border, but the word don't say who. Chew gotta deliver her, Berlin. There's no way me an' John can handle her. She's feral, man."

A faraway look came into Berlin's eyes. "Oh, I can deliver her."

"Chew know her?"

"I know where to find her."

"Then what chew waitin' for?"

"Nightfall. What time did you set the meet for?"

"Midnight. In the old station."

"Be there, or be square," Berlin said softly.

Locas shook his head. "Chew got some weird ways of puttin' together words, Berlin."

NINE

The wizard couldn't help her.

"It's not that I won't," Farrel Din told Manda. "It's that I can't."

They were sitting at a back table in The Dancing Ferret. The club was quiet, drifting in the lull between the lunch and dinner crowds. By mid-evening, once the band was on stage, the place would be so crowded there wouldn't be standing space or a moment's quiet. Right now Manda could hear the tinkle of Jenny Jingle's bells as she moved about across the room, sweeping.

Farrel Din sighed. "This has been a long time coming."

"What do you mean?"

"It's not my story to tell."

"Okay. But *why* can't you help me?"

Farrel Din regarded her for a moment, then set about cleaning and refilling his pipe.

"My kind of magic doesn't work on someone like Stick," he said once he had the pipe going.

A cloud of smoke drifted up above his head.

Manda nodded slowly, remembering. There'd been a time when the wizard had put a spell on the Horn Dance's music. It had affected everyone who could hear it except for Stick and the elf he was trying to avoid killing at the time. He hadn't been able to avoid it.

"Is there anyone who can help me?" she asked.

"Shoki."

"Who's Shoki?" She had a dim recollection of hearing the name before. It seemed that Stick had mentioned it once. "Where can I find him?"

"I can bring you to him."

Manda turned at the sound of the new voice to find another of The Ferret's waitresses standing by their table.

"I couldn't help overhearing," Laura said.

Manda waved off her apology. "That doesn't matter. Not if you know who he is."

"I live with him."

Manda glanced at Jenny, still sweeping. "He's Koga? The Sensei?"

Laura nodded.

Manda reached out and squeezed Farrel Din's hand where it lay on the tabletop.

"Thanks," she said.

"Can I get the time off?" Laura asked.

Farrel Din nodded. "Just be careful. You're stepping into a gray area. Sometimes the more you try to help, the worse things get."

"I can't let him kill Berlin," Manda said, rising from the table. "I don't know what's wrong with Stick, but I'm not going to let him do this. Not to her. Not to himself."

There were times, Farrel Din thought as he watched them leave, that he wondered why he'd ever crossed the Borders to stay here. Elfland had its own dangers—there was no denying that—but Bordertown was such a mix of differing cultures, each with its own beliefs and particular guardians, that the city could never let up its balancing act between various disasters. All it had to do was lean too far, one way, or the other...

CR8O

Koga was dressed in what Manda took to be some sort of ceremonial outfit when they arrived at his dojo. He wore a kimono and hakama of black silk, with a white silk under kimono and a dark red obi, or sash. On his shoulder was his family crest, a circular ka-mon worked in white silk stitches. The big room was empty except for him. He was seated in a seiza position and appeared to be waiting for them. Two swords, a katana and the smaller wakazashi, rested in a small wooden frame in front of him.

Laura removed her shoes and flowed into the room ahead of Manda. When she stepped in front of Koga, she knelt on the matted floor and gave him a short bow before sitting up, back straight as a board.

They were acting like Sensei and student, instead of lovers, Manda thought. For some reason that bothered her. She fumbled with her boots and got them off, but didn't try to copy Laura's entrance. She shuffled across the floor and stood awkwardly above them for a moment, then sat down. It was hard to get comfortable. She didn't feel that she should slouch, but just a few moments of trying to copy their straight-backed posture made her muscles ache.

Koga inclined his head briefly to her. "How can I help you, Amanda?" he asked.

You mean you don't already know? she thought, but she kept that to herself. They were obviously going through some kind of ceremonial thing. If Koga was the only one that could help her with Stick, she didn't want to blow it by rocking the boat.

"It's Stick," she said, and then plunged into her story. When she was done, Koga told her about Onisu and Stick and the part he had played in Onisu's death.

"So he thinks Berlin's this Onisu?" Manda asked.

"That is simplifying it, but, yes."

"And when he came to you...?"

"I think he came for help. Any punk in Dragontown could have identified that marker for him. Instead he came to me. You must understand. Stick is no longer who he is — he is who he was. That is why he came to me. Farrel Din and I are the only ones who were there when it all went down."

"I'm confused," Manda said. "These dragons..."

"They are guardian spirits. Dragons are what we name them in New Asia — that's why the street gangs call themselves Dragons. They see themselves as Dragontown's protectors."

"But Berlin and Stick...they're *real* dragons?"

"They are guardian spirits, yes. They have a great responsibility, being the earthly representations of the elements. The powers they have may not be abused. Their work is done in subtle ways — not

248

on a grand scale as poets and storytellers would have it—but in small things."

Manda tried to think it all through.

"What if he's right?" she said finally. "What if Berlin's really stepped across this line?"

Koga shook his head. "I talked to one of her friends. Berlin's called a meeting tonight between the various factions of Bordertown to plead her case. That is not the action of one who has turned her back upon her responsibilities."

"Does Stick know this? That'd change everything, wouldn't it?"

"The same source told me that Stick and Berlin have already spoken today, but Stick is hearing only an echo of the past—he is *in* the past."

Manda rubbed her face with her hands. "So what happens? What can we do?"

"Not we. This is my responsibility, Manda. I have to stop him." As he spoke, he took the long katana from the wooden rack in front of him and laid its sheathed length across his knees. "You will excuse me now, please. I need time to meditate."

Manda shivered. This was too much like Stick sitting up on the museum's roof.

Laura caught her arm. "We'd better go," she said.

"But—"

Laura shook her head. Drawing Manda to her feet, she collected their footgear and led the way outside.

"He's going to kill Stick!" Manda wailed once they were out on the stairs. "That's not the kind of help I came for."

"Believe me," Laura said. "Killing Stick is the last thing Koga would want to do."

"And what if there's no other way to stop him?"

Laura didn't have an answer to that.

"I'm staying right here," Manda said, "and when Koga leaves, I'm going with him, whether he wants me to or not."

"We're both going," Laura said. Koga was good, maybe the best that Bordertown had for this kind of a thing, but Stick was good too. How good, she didn't know. She hoped they wouldn't have to find out. But if it came down to a fight, she was damn sure going to be there in case Koga needed her.

Manda sat down in a slump at the top of the stairs. "I feel like I've just sold Stick out," she said.

Laura sat down beside her and put an arm around her shoulder. "The past's there waiting to betray us all, Manda. You didn't have a thing to do with it."

"Tell that to my heart."

Laura didn't have an answer for that either.

TEN

The room was as dark as her soul.

Ysa Cran paused in the doorway. She lived on the top floor of an abandoned brownstone that squatted near the Old Wall. She had a thing about coming home to a dark apartment, so she always had a lightbox going, night and day. She could afford it. She had only the best. Guaranteed to last forever or until she trashed it, whichever came first.

Her building was spelled with safeguards—it had to be. This was where she kept her stash. This was where she could be who she was, alone, no masks, no need to strut. No one came here. The safeguards would let nobody in but one person, and that was Ysa Cran. Even a High Born like Corwyn couldn't get through unless she let him. The safeguards came from straight across the Border and were keyed to her and her alone.

But now the lightbox was out. The room was dark. And she wasn't alone. She knew that without having to step across the threshold. Someone was in there, waiting for her. Someone who knew where to find her. Someone good enough to get through the safeguards. She loosed a heavy length of chain from around her waist and let one end fall to the floor with a clank.

"Ysa Cran, Ysa Cran," a husky voice called from out of the darkness. "No one loves her, Blood or man."

Ysa's silver eyes narrowed and she took a firmer grip on the chain. She took a step forward and the lightbox came on—not in a flash, but slowly, erasing the shadows one by one, until Ysa could see the small figure in blue jeans sitting in a chair waiting for her.

"You're dead meat, Berlin," she hissed.

Berlin didn't move except to shake her head. "Everybody's got it in for poor Berlin and we know why, don't we? Ysa Cran, Ysa Cran, nobody loves—"

"Shut up!"

"What's the matter, Ysa? That bring back bad memories? I know all about you—living up on the Hill, had the best of everything, but somehow something got left out, right? You're like those stories they like to tell about Bloods out in the World—you got no soul."

"You don't know shit."

"I'm not saying you didn't have it hard," Berlin said. "but we've all had some hard knocks, Ysa. That doesn't mean we go around fucking everybody else up. What's the matter? You figure the world owes you something? You figure that Ysa Cran's better than everybody else and she doesn't have to bust her ass like the rest of us do?"

Ysa started forward, the chain coming up, but something in Berlin's eyes stopped her. There was a red flickering there, behind the violet. Something inhuman that had nothing to do with the hills across the Border.

"You..." her voice trailed off.

"No, you made the mistake, Ysa. And now you've got to make it up."

Ysa stared at her. She'd heard about the meeting that had been called tonight in the old train station. Berlin was going to be there to set everybody straight. Oh, they'd had a good laugh about that— Teddy Grim, Nabber and her. What was Berlin going to do? Hand over her ass on a silver platter? Because there was no way anybody was going to listen to shit from Berlin—not after the job she and her boys had done on her rep. Only now Ysa began to understand what was going down. And looking into the fires that burned in those violet eyes, she got her first inkling of just what they'd been fooling around with.

"Listen," she tried. "I never knew you were one of...one of them."

"You think that matters now? You think that's going to bring Nicky back? Or those kids you burned in the house by the Market? Or the two Rats I had to take down by the river?"

"No, it's just—"

251

Berlin cut her off with a shake of her head. "It's time to pay the piper, Ysa. You know how it goes?"

Ysa began to back out of the room, but Berlin was too fast for her. She was out of the chair, around the Blood and blocking the door, before Ysa even started to get away. A flicker of a hand and Ysa's wrist went numb. The chain dropped with a clatter to the floor. Another flicker, this time a foot, and Ysa crumpled down on top of the chain, her whole right leg numb.

"Who's your connection?" Berlin asked. "Who's passing the dope to you?"

A wrist knife appeared in Ysa's hand. She made an awkward lunge with it, but Berlin just flowed back out of reach. Her left foot seemed to float in the air as she stepped back. The knife went skittering across the room. Ysa clutched a broken wrist to her chest, biting back the pain.

"Who is it, Ysa?"

"Are you...kidding? I open my mouth and I'm dead."

"What do you think we're doing here—playing a game?"

Berlin feinted another kick. Ysa flinched, but Berlin could tell that this was one thing she wasn't going to get out of the Blood. It was lying there, hidden behind her silver eyes. A locked door that no amount of pain was going to open.

"Okay," she said. "I guess that name's going to be your private little treasure. I just hope it sees you through the night."

"What...what do you mean?" Ysa asked, but she already knew. It was all going to go down at the train station.

"You're clearing my name."

"I..."

"That's not open to discussion," Berlin told her. "You're clearing my name, period. And don't think you can weasel out of it once we're there. I've got backing like you wouldn't believe on this."

But Ysa was already calculating her chances. She could plead her innocence—Christ, who was going to believe Berlin at this point of the game? Who was even going to take the time to listen to her?

"Sure," she said. "Anything you say."

Berlin smiled. "You're so easy to read, Ysa. Maybe you should ask me about my backing before you go off half-cocked, thinking you're going to squeeze out of another scrape."

"Okay. What's your backing?"

"Dogtown's coming to the meeting. You still think you're not going to spill your guts? You still think they're going to take me down when I've got that pack guarding each door and my ass?"

She watched the spirit finally break in Ysa's eyes, but it gave her no pleasure. Like she'd told the Blood earlier, it didn't bring the dead back.

Reaching down, she pulled Ysa to her feet by the scruff of her leather jacket and propelled her out the door. Ysa staggered against a wall, trying to keep to her feet. The one numbed leg barely held her weight. Berlin never gave her a chance to steady herself. She just kept shoving her along. Down the stairs. Out through the foyer. Onto the street. Down to the train station.

They heard the distant sound of the Mock Avenue Bell Tower ring the half hour. Midnight was only another thirty minutes away.

It'll all be over soon, Berlin thought. Except for one thing. She still had to deal with the spectre of somebody else's past.

She still had to deal with Stick.

ELEVEN

Midnight came and went.

Stick lifted his head slowly and gazed across the museum's roof. A bat moved in his field of vision, a quick silent swoop, then it was gone. He closed his fingers around the katana's lacquered wood sheath. His mind moved in the past. He saw a red-eyed rogue dragon and a man clad all in black silk. He watched the blade rise, then come down, as quick and smooth as the bat's flight. Blood sprayed. The night was suddenly filled with its hot scent.

Squeezing his eyes shut, Stick rose silently. He thrust the katana into his belt and and left the rooftop at a gliding walk. Down through the museum he went, one more ghost in a building over-filled with ghosts.

On the street outside he paused, nostrils widening to take in the still night air. Bordertown held its secrets close to its vest, but unerringly, he turned and drifted down the street, making for the old train station that bordered Dogtown. Behind him, low to the ground, Lubin padded silently in his wake, but he never noticed the ferret.

He was still moving through the past, trying to reach a point in it before the figure in black silk buried his katana in dragon flesh. He quickened his pace, grinding his teeth as he loped down the silent streets. It was long past time for him to shoulder the responsibilities that he'd once shirked. He wasn't sure how it had come to be that he could return to the past, that he could give Onisu the freedom now that in another life he hadn't been able to. All he knew was that this time he wouldn't fail her. No matter what face she wore. He would do what had to be done.

CRSO

The old train station.

Inside, Bordertown was listening to Ysa Cran's confession. Out front, dogs and gang members patrolled, each studiously ignoring the other, each aware of the others' every move. Behind, on the old tracks, a single figure stood. Dressed in black silk, Shoki the Demon Queller waited, katana and wakazashi thrust into his silk obi. Huddled nearby, Manda and Laura waited as well, but without the armed figure's calm.

A step sounded and a fourth figure stirred, moving in the shadows that cloaked the back of the train station. It was a bag lady, wreathed in patched layers of clothes, her treasures gathered around her like a clutch of garbage bags standing on a street curb waiting for the garbage collectors that no longer served this part of the city. Her head swiveled slowly, taking in Shoki, the two girls, then she turned to see what they were looking at.

The darkness almost swallowed him, brown skin, black clothes, dreadlocks and all. He paused, gaze settling on Shoki. When Shoki gave him a brief bow, Stick lifted his hand to the hilt of his katana. There was a sharp click as he unlocked the blade with his thumb, pulling it a half-inch free of the wooden sheath.

"I've come for her," he said softly. "I've got to do it myself this time."

Shoki made no move towards his own weapons.

"She has been long dead," he said.

Stick shook his head and began to close the distance between them.

Manda couldn't stand it any more. She jumped up from where she was sitting, but Laura hauled her back down. Manda glared at her.

"If we don't do something," she hissed, "one of them's going to get killed."

Laura put an arm around Manda's shoulders, as much to keep her down as to comfort her. "Right now, the worst thing we could do is get in the way."

"But…"

"I don't like it anymore that you do, Manda. Believe me."

Manda started suddenly as something touched her, then looked down to find Lubin crouched by her feet. She patted her lap and the ferret flowed up on to it, shivering.

"Yeah," Manda said softly, stroking Lubin's fur. "I know just what you're going through."

Stick and Shoki stood with just a few feet between them. Within striking distance.

"Listen to me," Shoki said. "The past is gone. If you go on with this, *you'll* be crossing the line."

Stick blinked. He was still in the past, but pieces of the present were beginning to superimpose themselves on what had been, on what he knew he had to do.

"Berlin's clearing her name right now," Shoki went on, pressing the momentary advantage. "It was all a mistake."

Stick shook his head as if to clear it.

"I'm not here for Berlin," he said. "I'm here for Onisu. Get out of the way."

"I can't," Shoki said.

Nothing gave Stick away. There was no narrowing of the eyes, no shift in his stance. But Shoki knew Stick was moments from drawing his katana. And once drawn, there'd be no turning back — not for either of them. It would be decided in seconds. A duel between masters such as they would be over almost before it began.

Shoki centered his balance. He closed his mind, allowing the years of practice to rise up and take control. When he finally made his move, it would be fueled by instinct. His body would know the correct move at the correct time before his mind could even begin to consider it.

He knew a moment's sadness, but before either of them could move —

"Stick!"

Instinctively — and for all the disagreement between them — they flowed into new stances, each facing outwards, protecting the other's back. Shoki's eyes widened slightly. What he saw was a circle of dogs. The circle began directly in front of him, then fanned out on either side until the lines left his range of vision. Stick saw the dogs, too. But he also saw the one who had called his name.

The bag lady had moved from the side of the train station to stand in front of him. Out of the shadows, she was easily recognized — if not by Stick, at least by the others.

Berlin.

She had a dark cloak over her shoulders. Her hands reached out from under it, holding a Kabuki mask of a woman's face. The cheeks and brow were a deathly white, the lips red, the eyes painted with long stylized strokes. Slowly Berlin pulled it on.

"Onisu," Stick breathed.

"*Hai,*" the masked figure replied. Yes.

Stick took a step towards her, fingers tightening on the hilt of his katana.

"Forgive me," he said.

"There is nothing to forgive."

The katana whispered against the lacquered wood of its sheath. Berlin's cloak billowed as she moved an instant before the katana was completely clear of the sheath. The sword blurred in the night air to cut deeply into the cloak's undulating folds. The mask went skittering across the pavement, landing face-up to stare at the sky. Berlin let herself fall, the cloak collapsing around her, covering her completely as she touched the ground.

After that one stroke, Stick stood as though carved from granite. He stared at the Kabuki mask.

Sensing the beginning of Stick's movement, Shoki had begun to turn. When he saw what happened, the aspect of the Demon Queller left him and Koga stood in his place. It was Koga — the man, the Sensei — who plucked the katana from Stick's nerveless fingers. He noted that the blade was still dry.

Stick walked slowly over to the Kabuki mask. Kneeling beside it, he picked it up. He stared at it for a long moment, then held it against his chest and bowed his head.

Manda and Laura rose from where they'd been sitting, Manda clutching Lubin close to her. All around them the dogs watched silently.

"Koga," Laura called. "Berlin. Is she...?"

But when they looked at where she'd dropped, they saw the cloak move. Folds of cloth fell aside. Berlin flowed to her feet and held the cloak open so that they could see the clean slice where the katana had cut through the fabric.

"Jesus, I played that close," Berlin murmured. "Another inch and that hole'd be in me."

She let the cloak flutter to the ground at her feet.

Stick turned at the sound of her voice.

"Hey, tall, dark and ugly," she said.

Stick laid the mask down. "Berlin, I..."

She shook her head. "You don't have to say anything. We've all been there, at one time or another. Question is, are you okay now?"

"I've been better, but yeah. I'm okay. Thanks." He turned to where the others were standing. "All of you. I mean that. I was really...someplace else."

He rose to his feet as Koga approached, the katana outstretched in his hands. Stick took the blade with a brief bow and returned it to its sheath. For a long moment the two men faced each other, then Stick moved closer and the two men embraced.

"Been a long time, man," Stick said.

"Too long," Koga replied.

When they stepped back, Berlin rubbed her hands briskly together. "Well, I won't say it hasn't been fun, but I've got to run. It's time I got a new House going — the Diggers were just starting to make a difference, you know?" She gave a sharp whistle and the dogs exploded into motion all around them, heading back to Dogtown. "But I still wish I had the name of the sucker who started all of this. I don't like having enemies hiding across the Border, never knowing when they'll strike again."

"It's better than having them inside yourself," Stick said.

Berlin nodded soberly. "I guess so."

"Do you need any help or anything?" Manda asked her.

Berlin shot Stick a glance, then she grinned. "I can always use a hand. Best thing you could do is get that band of yours to play a benefit or two—just to get the Diggers on the road again. Do you know 'The World Turned Upside Down?'"

Manda shook her head.

"Leon Rosselson wrote it—long time ago now. You guys should learn it. It's an angry song, but an honest one. Like the blues are sometimes, you know?" Berlin pulled one of her thin cigars out of an inside pocket of her jean jacket. "Anyway, if you can do a benefit..."

She lit up, ground the wooden match under her heel, and started to walk away, still talking. Manda kept pace at her side, Lubin asleep in her arms. Stick, Koga and Laura took up the rear.

"That's Berlin," Stick said. "She's always got some scheme on the go."

Koga put his arm around Laura. "Good thing," he said.

Stick nodded. "Yeah," he agreed. "Damn good thing."

May This Be Your Last Sorrow

It was Joe Doh-dee-oh who told her about the gargoyle that perches on a cornice of the Mock Avenue Bell Tower, how if the clock in its belfry ever chimed the correct time, the gargoyle would be freed from his body of stone.

"I'm sure," she'd replied.

She waited for the teasing look to come into Joe's eyes, but all he did was shrug, as though to say, "Well, if you don't want to believe me..."

CR8O

I'm nobody really; any glitter I've got's just fallout from people I know. Borrowed limelight. But that's okay. I never wanted to be anybody special in the first place. I like being part of the faceless audience — the people that attend the theatres and concerts, that sit in the dark and appreciate the skill of the performers. I read the books without any urge to write one myself. I'm the one who goes to the galleries, not by invitation on opening night, but later, when the anonymous people come to steal a glimpse of what made the artists' spirits sing so fiercely that they just had to find a way to give it physical dimension.

You'll find me in the back of a club, sitting by myself and enjoying the band, instead of trying to talk over the music to describe my own next project. I'm the one you see walking through a museum with the big goofy smile on my face because everything's just so amazing. I'm not full of ideas about what I'm going to do; I'm appreciating all the wonderful things that have already been done.

I think there's too much emphasis put on having to be Someone, on making something out of nothing. It's not a road that everybody can follow. It's not a road that anybody should have to want to follow.

I'm not making up excuses for having no talent — really I'm not. I don't know whether I've got any or not; all I know is I'm short on the inclination.

You know the old argument about whether talent comes from your genes or your environment? Well, I give lie to both. See, my mom's Deeva. You never heard of her? She was the "Elf Acid House *chanteuse*" as her recording company liked to put it. That was because, when the Change came, she was the first to take the visuals from across the Border and use them in her music and videos.

There was a time when all she had to do was just think about putting out a new recording and it'd go triple-platinum. She was the first of the post-Madonna dance artists who did everything — wrote, sang, produced, played all the instruments with nothing sampled, not even the drum track. She directed and choreographed her own videos, too. At the peak of her career she was a one-woman industry, all by herself. Amazing, really, when you think about it.

And my dad? He was Ned Bradley — uh-huh. *That* Ned Bradley, the one who played Luke on *Timestop for Chance*. It's funny. I thought music'd make way bigger impression in a place like this than a TV series would, but I guess I understand. I've gotta admit the show was pretty cool. I mean, he started shooting *Timestop* way before I was born, so it's like, really old stuff. The first show aired twenty years ago, right? But I could still relate to all those kids. It'd be so weird if reincarnation really worked and you could remember it the way they could. I think that's what made it so popular. It didn't matter what historical era they used for the background on any particular year, the continuity was so fascinating and the cast worked so well together that they just made each episode sing.

Anyway, so there's like more talent in my house when I'm growing up than anyone could know what to do with. Not just my parents, but all their friends, too. I guess the biggest disappointment to my parents was that I didn't show much of an aptitude for anything.

My mom must have tried to teach me to play a half-dozen instruments. She'd get real mad and tell me I wasn't applying myself; she wouldn't listen when I told her I loved music — just to listen to, not to make. That's something so alien to her that she must've just tuned it out. I mean, she still can't listen to a new recording — doesn't matter what style of music it is — without her fingers twitching and her wanting to head down to the studio to lay down a few tracks herself.

My dad's another story. I'm not unattractive, but I'm not as pretty as Deeva is, either — who really is? My mom sure isn't. She's just Anna Westway until she does that amazing makeup and puts on her Deeva wig, you know? I like her better as Anna Westway, but who's going to listen to me? Anyway, my dad tried to get me into commercials and bit parts in shows that his friends were producing — stuff like that — but it never took. I wasn't Deeva. I have no camera presence. Zip. Nada. Which my dad just *couldn't* believe.

You see, when my dad's doing his thing — doesn't matter whether it's on the big screen or a dinky little TV set — he just commands your attention. I think the thing that really proves his talent was how he managed to never overshadow whoever was in a scene with him. With as riveting a screen presence as he had that wasn't exactly an easy thing to pull off.

Anyway, needless to say, I was a big disappointment to them both. They tried to get me interested in anything creative — writing, painting, sculpting — but none of it took. It was kind of embarrassing for them, I guess, but what could I do? I'm just me; I can't be anybody else. I wouldn't know how.

My parents kind of gave up on me by the time I turned thirteen. They didn't turn mean or anything, they just sort of forgot that I existed, I think. Mom was working on a comeback; my dad got a part in *Traffic* — yeah, he plays the holograph man. Great part, isn't it?

That was about the worst year of my life. It wasn't just the way things were at home. I was having the shittiest time in school, too. You know what I think is really weird? It's how everyone thinks that rich people can't have real problems. It's like, if you've got all that money, you can't possibly be hurting emotionally.

When I first started high school, people thought I was pretty cool, considering who my parents were, but that wore off real fast when I wouldn't like, get them free tickets to some concert, or introduce them to that kid in Dad's new show, Tommy Marot — you know, Mr. Heart-throb? I like to be quiet, but they just figured I was stuck up — with nothing to be stuck up about.

So that's why I ran away. There was nothing for me at home, nothing for me at school, nothing for me anywhere except here. I don't think my parents even know I'm gone. I used to check the papers, during the first few weeks, but there was never anything about Deeva and Ned Bradley's kid having turned up missing. No mention at all. I guess they were kind of relieved to be rid of me, that's what I think.

Why'd I pick this place? I dunno. Not because it's so cool. I mean, I still get a kick out of seeing elves and everything, but that's not really why I came. I think it was because I heard that this was a place where people left you alone.

And I love it here, I really do. It was tough at first, but I'm staying with the Diggers now and they're really nice — especially Berlin. And Joe, even if he does tease me sometimes. So long as I pull my weight, I'll always have a place to crash and something to eat.

Nobody bugs me; nobody's trying to make me be something I'm not. If I don't want to talk, they don't get in my face about it. They just let me go my own way.

What I like the best is the clubs and galleries, though. It's like all the best talent from the outside world and across the Border's been distilled into this magic potion. You take a sip, and it just takes you away. Who needs drugs in a place like this? I get high on the music and the art; that's the real magic, I think. Something about being this close to the Border hones this edge onto anything that's created in its shadow.

And I like the way nobody's pushy; they just leave you alone. That's the way it should be. People should just let you have your own space.

So I know I did the right thing. Really. I just wish I didn't feel so…lonely sometimes, you know?

I think you're the only one who really understands.

CR80

The stone gargoyle on top of the Mock Avenue Bell Tower watched the small figure climb down from the belfry. He enjoyed her visits, even if they always left a melancholy pang, deep in his stone chest.

When she got to the bottom rung of the ladder, she disappeared from sight. He shifted his gaze over the edge of the cornice, waiting until she stepped out the tower door far below. Her slim shoulders were bowed under her tattered jacket, her unruly tangles of hair hanging in her face to hide the tears that had been welling up in her eyes before she left the belfry.

He watched as she dried her eyes on the sleeve of her jacket, straightened her shoulders and then marched off down the street.

If he could speak, he would advise her to approach another human the way she did him. But he couldn't speak. And if he could, he doubted she would listen anyway. But he would still try.

She needed a friend. Anyone could see that, if they only took the time to look beyond her bravado.

The belfry clock chimed twelve although it was only the middle of the afternoon.

Was there ever such a bittersweet, forlorn sound? the gargoyle wondered as he had far too often in the two hundred years he had kept watch over the city from the bell tower.

What might have been a sigh shivered his stone skin.

I think you're the only one who really understands, she'd said.

He did understand. He understood all too well.

Science Fiction

A Tattoo on Her Heart

The world is too much with us.

—William Wordsworth

Myth is the natural and indispensable
intermediate stage between unconscious
and conscious cognition.

—Carl Jung,
from *Memories, Dreams, Reflections*

Night fell and the tribes hit the street.

Their yelps and howls filled the night air — a cacophony of mock
beast sounds to match the beast masks that they wore. Underpinning
the dissonance was the insistent rhythm of palms dancing across
skin-headed drums, of hands banging sticks against each other, or
against cans and sheets of metal. Mouths lipped whistles and flutes
to cast out brittle handfuls of high skirling notes. Fingers plucked
chords from oddly-shaped guitar-like instruments, or else drew
bows across tightly-wound strings to wake weird yowls and moans.

The sound Catherine-wheeled between the tumbled-down
tenements — a full moon madness of disconnected noise that hurt
the ear and made melody nothing more than a vague memory. But
then, slowly, the dissonance resolved into a kind of music. The

dervishing whirls of masked figures that twisted and spun amidst the rubble became a set dance with patterned steps. Torches were cast into metal drums, the oiled paper and debris inside flaring to heights of two meters and better. The bobbing masks of the dancers appeared almost real in the sudden flickering light. Wood and metal frames, plastic and papier-mâché coverings, the decorations of feather and coiled wires, shells and bottlecaps, lost their manmade origins and became mythic.

Jorey crouched in the shadows at the mouth of an alley, her home-made fetish clutched in one hot sweaty hand. Wide-eyed, she watched them.

Wolf and eagle, rat and salamander, bear and pigeon. And more. Raccoon and cricket, snake and cat, roach and sparrow. And still more.

Totems dancing in the dead streets of the city.

The tribes were calling up the past.

Not the past that had been—the truth of unemployment and hunger and overcrowded cities and fouled air and melting polar caps and limited nuclear exchange—but the past that lived in their hearts that told of how things might have been.

Of how things should have been.

A past where the shaman called up totems to lead the people out of their hell-bent demolition course to self-destruction; a past where the tribes at least had listened.

CR&D

It was all make-believe, Auntie liked to say. It was all lies. But it kept them happy. And that was why the jackets allowed the tribes their revels. That was why they never came down out of their towers, weapons in hand, to put them down. Citizens didn't get hurt so long as they weren't on the streets on a revel night.

Jorey had been intrigued by the tribes from the first time she was old enough to sit perched high on a windowsill and looked down on the dancing figures, the thin wail of their music rising up from the street to where she sat. It woke something in her. A need. A yearning. Nothing that could be put into words, but she knew instinctively that no matter what Auntie said, there was something important happening on the streets on a revel night.

"How do they know when it's going to happen?" she would ask Auntie.

There was no fixed night for a revel. Sometimes the moon was full, sometimes not. Sometimes weeks went by between them, sometimes they came two nights in a row.

Auntie only shook her head.

"You ask me," she said, "the jackets spray something in the air — that's what makes it happen. They see the hopeless anger building up until its going to spill out of the streets and into their towers. So then, before it gets out of hand, they just lock up their citizens and let the night swallow the tribes with its craziness. It's a kind of safety valve."

"Did you never want to...you know, go out yourself...?" Jorey asked.

Auntie gave her a withering look. "I'm poor, girl. Not crazy."

"But —"

"And I don't want to find you sneaking out some revel night. We're people. Human beings. Not animals."

CR&D

Jorey slept in a locked room at nights and Auntie kept the key. But that didn't matter. Auntie had her own lies about the past and how things were. Jorey was her fourteen-year-old niece, but what was true once, wasn't necessarily so anymore. Times had changed. There were no longer any schools or malls or playgrounds — not if poverty stole away your citizenship. Jorey spent most of her days on the street and one of the first things she learned was how to pick a lock.

So now she was out here on revel night. Watching. Hoping.

She didn't have a totem, so she didn't have a mask. At least not a proper one. But she'd gone down to the clay field behind the old plastics factory and smeared white clay in her short hair, twisting and pulling out strands until they stood out straight from her head like a hedgehog's spikes. She'd dabbed it on her cheeks and temples as well — white stylized streaks like a street version of some vid singer's glamour lines.

Studying her reflection in a piece of broken glass, she realized that she actually looked like a dried up old weed, about to be blown apart by the wind. But it didn't matter. It was still a kind of mask.

And then there was her fetish.

⚮

Ricia said you needed a fetish to call your totem to you.

"Get yourself a little plastic bag," she'd told Jorey, "and fill it with bits of everything that means anything to you. You have to make it a focus — a distillation of everything that makes you *you* — so that the totem can find you when you call it to you."

Ricia was two years older than Jorey. She was a tall, striking young woman with mocha-colored skin and actually had a job — six hours a week at one of the restaurants in the towers. She watched the servitor belt, kitchen-side, guarding against the anomalies that the computer sometimes tossed out in place of a food order.

"Auntie says there's no such thing as totems," Jorey told her. "She says the revels are just something the jackets came up with so that we don't go too crazy."

Ricia only laughed. "What does she know?"

Being old didn't automatically make you wrong, Jorey thought.

"Doesn't make you right, either," Ricia said, knowing Jorey well enough to as much as read her mind.

⚮

Jorey's fetish bag was a used WaterPure tablet package. In it she'd put a tiny book wafer about riverside animals filched from the library; a hair from a horse's mane that came from the head of a doll that Auntie had given her; three real wooden buttons she'd found on the street; nail parings from the last time she'd trimmed her nails; a sliver of shimmery metal that Moakes swore was a true Shuttle Remnant and for which she'd traded two food credits and a cotton shammy; little bits of animals — a pigeon feather, the shiny delicate back of a cockroach, a dried rat's tail — not because she wanted any one of them for a totem, but because they were a part of her life; one tear, dropped onto a swatch of brightly-colored cotton; the tip of an aloe leaf that Ricia had given her; and her prize possession — a cat's eye alley that Auntie said had once belonged to Jorey's father.

What would it call to her — just saying totems were real?

Clutching the fetish, she looked out at where the tribes were still dancing in winding spiral lines between the fires, instruments sending up a wild clamor that, while it was recognizably music now, was a kind of music you'd never hear on a citizen vid. And they were singing, too. A boisterous, almost feral vocalizing that was wordless, but eloquent with meaning.

It woke a buzzing in her head — a not-quite whine that was more pleasant than not. The buzzing was immediately followed by a strange, indescribable sensation that skittered up her spine like scurrying roaches. Moakes had described tripping on wire to her once and this, she realized, was what it must be like.

A feeling of dislocation from her body settled over her so that it was as though she was floating just above her body, apart from it, but a part of it still.

Her mind seemed to expand so that it encompassed not only her immediate surroundings, but went whispering and peeking and peering for blocks around her. Part of her viewed the group mind of the tribes as they reveled; part of her looked in on those like Auntie who hid away in their rundown buildings, minds closed against the strange reveling sorcery that rode the city air; and part of her — that part not yet connected to the revel, because she was still without a totem, she supposed — found the source of the revel.

A half-dozen jackets, hidden in a nearby building, black clothing making them almost invisible in the shadows except for the gleam and wink of the embroidered silver thread on their stylized jackets that shaped the symbol of the citizen security force of which they were members. Five of them — two women, three men — kept watch, gleaming weapons in hand. The sixth was bent over a machine on which tiny lights flickered and strobed. He adjusted dials and knobs with deft graceful movements of his slender fingers, looking for all the world like a syntharp player, standing center stage on a vid, concertoing and symphanying, an entire orchestra sampled and hidden away in the small flat black box that lay on his lap.

They all wore earplugs, though Jorey could hear no sound.

Auntie had been right, she realized, the thought coming to her in a detached, almost disinterested fashion. The revels did have their origin in the towers. But what stopped people like Auntie from hearing whatever it was that the jackets were calling up with their odd little machine?

Maybe you had to want to hear it?

Maybe you needed a totem?

But I hear it, she thought.

She *did* hear something. The revel spirit of the tribes had filled her, hadn't it?, until her body strained and trembled to join the whirling figures in their winding dance. Her throat could feel the sting of their song as it escaped her lips, her hands beat a rhythmic tattoo against her thighs...

She had wanted to hear it.

Could the technology of the towers be so refined that it could read people's minds? Or was it like Auntie had said the time Jorey asked her why the citizens let the rest of them live the way they did—eking out a hungry and poor existence in the dead streets of the city.

"They see us," Auntie had explained, "but we just don't register."

That was why Auntie and those like her didn't join the tribes in their revels. They heard whatever it was that the jackets' machines pumped into the city air on a revel night, but it just didn't register.

And that was why the tribes didn't pay any attention to the source of a revel night, to the black jacketed man standing over his machine as it called up the dance.

Her consciousness narrowed until she was back near her body again. A masked figure stood over her—the weird features of a fly on top of a woman's body. Jorey fled back into her skin, wanting to bolt from the strange apparition, but wanting to stay at the same time. The figure reached out a hand to her, bug-head dipping low, the glass-glitter of her multi-faceted eyes casting weird patterns of light into the alleyway.

"Come on, Jorey," the figure said.

She recognized Ricia's voice. She took her hand from her fetish and let the plastic bag bounce against her chest as Ricia drew her to her feet.

The dance lay inside her—its steps and its tune. A pattern that was now indelibly etched into her mind, tattooed on her heart. It didn't matter that it had its source in a small flat box manipulated by the clever fingers of some jacket. It was a part of her now and she made it her own.

Laughing, she let Ricia lead her onto the street and there —

She just danced.

CRISO

It was in the early hours of the morning that she finally collapsed where she'd been dancing, exhausted, but happy. She slept more peacefully than she'd ever slept before, feeling safe and warm though a cold wind was frosting its way down the street. When she woke, dawn was a pale wash of yellow in the smoggy sky.

She found herself surrounded by the tribes. They were recognizably her neighbors now, masks set aside, humanity returned. As they rose from their makeshift beds, there was a sense of camaraderie in the air that was as unfamiliar as it was heady. People talked and joked among themselves as they gathered their masks and instruments and slowly made their way home.

"It's always like this," Ricia explained, as she walked Jorey back to Auntie's. "We're always so…close. Sometimes it lasts for days before the feeling fades. I wish it would never fade."

Jorey nodded. An indefinable exuberance still whistled and hummed in her veins.

"But then there's always the next revel," Ricia said with a bright smile as they reached Auntie's door. She looked at Jorey, then added, "Did you find your totem?"

Jorey nodded again.

"Don't tell me," Ricia said before Jorey could speak. "Surprise me at the next revel."

Then she was off, heading down the street, dodging the refuse and rubble with a practiced stride, her mask swinging in one hand, tapping her flute against her thigh with the other.

Jorey watched her go. She fingered her fetish, smiling.

Auntie had been both right and wrong. The revels did originate in the towers, from the machines of the jackets, but it didn't turn people into animals. The city did that. The hunger and the poverty, the emptiness and uselessness of their lives…that was what pushed people apart until they lived in worlds where they barely registered to themselves, little say had time for their neighbors.

The revels connected people to each other again. It didn't make them animals; it reminded them of their humanity.

Jorey didn't doubt that all the jackets had in mind with the revels was to create a safety valve — just as Auntie had determined. Something to keep the poor in line so that their frustration and hunger and pain and anger wouldn't become so furious that they would rise to storm the towers. But the people had taken those nights and made them their own. Somewhere between jacket machine and tribal mind, a token — a promise — had been born, and on revel nights it blazed from candle flicker to solar flare.

It was a good thing. All it lacked was a way to keep the connection going beyond a revel night.

Had she found her totem? Ricia had asked her.

Jorey smiled and went inside to wash off the clay from her face and hair. When she'd scrubbed herself clean, she set about making her totem mask.

Under her hands, it came to life. Carved wood and plastic for its features, wire coils for hair. Painted lips.

A human face.

Raven Sings a Medicine Way, Coyote Steals the Pollen

Increasing, now, not diminishing.
With their voices, for me they are calling,
With their voices, for me they are calling,
Ya'e neye yana!

—Frank Mitchell,
from *A Navajo Horse Song*

The third day of her fast, hunger no longer troubled her.

The burning lands stretched for as far as the eye could see, the red-brown dirt cracked and dry under a blistering sun. She regarded the unchanging landscape from under eyelids dusted with cornflower pollen, breathed the sharp dry air with short shallow breaths. Her cheeks and forehead were daubed with streaks of ash that made gray patterns against the dusky copper of her skin. Her hair was drawn back in a braid interwoven with feathers, rattlesnake rattles that sounded when she moved her head, and tiny beads dyed yellow, red and green. A water gourd rested by her left knee, under the neat pile of her discarded clothes; by her right knee was a small traveling pack. She allowed herself to drink twice each day—once when the sun rose, once when it set. Between the rough stone of the mesa from which she studied the burning lands and the nakedness of her lean flesh was a ceremonial blanket that she had woven herself. There were patterns of ash above each of her breasts, more on her stomach. A design created from variously colored sands was on the stone between her gourd and pack.

She was waiting for the spirits to find her, that they might converse.

This was how it was done in the old days, she assured herself, though she had no way of knowing how she knew. When she first began to question what she perceived as the empty way of her people, a voice came to her and spoke in her dreams. It told her of the lost times before the stars fell, of the spirits, but told her nothing of how those times had come to be lost, or why the spirits spoke no more. An endless parade of seasons had walked the lands beyond the desert since the Old People left the burning lands. There were no shaman now, no medicine singers. The people that survived could not afford to seek out the old ways that fed the spirit rather than the stomach. It took all their strength to eke out a living from the desolate land; there was none left over to chase ghosts or seek spirits.

But the spirits were still out there in the burning lands. She knew that. As the stoneworks of the Old People survived atop mesas and along the hidden arroyos where the water no longer flowed, so did the spirits survive as well. It needed only patience to wait for them to notice her. It needed only time.

Night came and she drew the stopper of her water gourd as the sun dipped below the horizon, bobbed back up in an optical illusion worthy of the Trickster, then sank once more, this time for good. She hoisted the gourd, tilted it, let the warm water trickle down her throat. Setting the gourd down, she began to dress against the growing chill of the night. The shirt and skirt she put on were of unbleached cotton. Over them she wore a long jacket dyed a bluish-black from the leaves of the chiilchin, the sumac. Her feet she left bare. When she was dressed, she took a tiny clay pot from her pack and shook out the coal in it onto the makings of a fire that she had readied before the sun began its journey across the sky this morning. It was as she was blowing the fire aflame that she realized she was no longer alone.

An old man stood watching her, a dark old man made all the more shadowed by the twilight; a spirit. She knew he was a spirit because, while he was not of her people, he still knew her name.

"Little Raven," he said. "Is there room by your fire for an old man?"

When Raven nodded, he moved forward on silent feet and crouched by her fire. He glanced at the patterns of ash and pollen on her face, then at the design of colored sand and nodded. Raven's hands returned to her pack to come up with a handful of dried hemp leaves that she offered to him. This too was something the voice in her dreams had told her she must do. Her own people used the hemp to make ropes, but the stranger did a curious thing with it. He crumpled up the leaves and stuck them in the bowl of a small clay pipe that he lit with a glowing twig from the fire. His cheeks moved as he sucked the smoke into his lungs. Raven stared awestruck when it issued from his nose and mouth. She shook her head slowly and her rattlesnake rattles sounded softly from her braid.

"Which spirit are you, Grandfather?" she asked.

The old man smiled, his teeth gleaming in the firelight. "I'm no spirit—just an old man."

"But you know my name."

The old man's smile grew wider. "With hair so dark, what else would your people call you?"

"Hola," Raven said with a shrug. I don't know. Except that all her people had black hair, but she didn't bother to mention that. Spirits, her dream-voice had told her, did not like to be corrected and she'd already done so once as it was.

"Are you looking for spirits?" the old man asked.

Raven nodded. "I've been fasting for three days now, but you are the first person I've seen."

"Do you think the spirits care whether you meet them with a full stomach or an empty one?"

Raven made no reply. Her dream-voice had told her that the spirits would try to confuse her when she met them. That was their way. Besides, the fasting had been her own idea. "I've seen lizards and a snake, and once a coyote crossing the desert below," she said instead.

"Smoke with me," the old man said, "and I will tell you a story of what happened to Coyote one day." He handed her the pipe.

Raven took it dubiously. It was all very well for spirits to breathe smoke, but what would it do to an ordinary person? Still, she didn't see how she could politely refuse, so she raised the stem to her lips and took a little puff. Immediately she began to cough.

277

"Draw it deep into your chest and hold it there," the old man said. "This is sacred smoke and it won't harm you if you use it sparingly."

Raven did as she was told. The smoke burned her throat and hurt her lungs. Her eyes teared. But she took three lungfuls before she handed the pipe back to the stranger.

"How do you feel?" he asked.

"A little...dizzy."

"That will pass."

The old man finished the pipe, then tapped the ashes into the fire. He stowed it away under his shirt and regarded her from across the fire. His eyes are like a bird's, Raven thought. Glittering and bright. Her dizziness had passed as he'd said it would, but she was beginning to feel strange now, as though some mystery of the desert night had entered her heart and was whispering to her as her dream-voice did, only softly, so that she could hear the voice but not make out what was being said.

"One day, long before the stars fell," the old man said, "Malii the Coyote Man came upon a hogan standing alonein the desert." And then he proceeded to tell the story.

CR§O

There were all manner of wonderful things in that hogan—fresh fish, though there was no water nearby; carved masks hanging on the walls, each depicting a different creature; tortoise drums and beadwork, turquoise as big as a man's head, weapons and tools, ceremonial blankets woven from turkey feathers...wonderful things. But what Malii fancied most was a pair of moccasins. They came from the far northern forests and were made from moosehide, decorated with crow feathers and porcupine quills.

"Give these to me, friend," Malii said to the stranger who lived there.

"I can't do that," the stranger replied.

"But you've got so many wonderful things—you don't need them as well."

"They are old moccasins," the stranger said, "almost worn through. If you were to wear them on the rocky ground they'd be of no use to you in a week. Choose something else instead."

But the moccasins were all Malii wanted. "If you won't give them to me," he said, "at least let me spend the night here."

The stranger agreed.

That night when his host was sleeping, Malii rose from his blankets and stole the moccasins. He put them on and ran far out into the desert, out over the sand so that they wouldn't get worn. He ran for as far as he could go, until he could run no further. Then he lay down to sleep. When he woke, he was back in the stranger's hogan. The stranger looked at the moccasins on Malii's feet.

"What are you doing with my moccasins?" he demanded.

"Nothing," Malii replied. "I don't know how they came to be on my feet. I think they must like me and want to be with me instead of hanging on your wall."

The stranger frowned and took the moccasins back. Malii frowned too, but he hid it from his host. He planned to stay another night, and he did, but that night was a repetition of the one before and he woke in the stranger's hogan again.

"I don't like this," the stranger said. "Still, if the moccasins like you so much, I suppose I should give them to you. But they have a medicine in them — lightning lives in their leather. Don't wear them too often — only when you want to make a fire. Then you must dance and the lightning will spring out of them to light your wood."

Malii hurried home with his new possessions. When he neared the hogans of his people, he put them on so that they would see what a fine gift he had been given. They would all marvel and make much of him — something Malii expected as his due. So he put the moccasins on, but there was no desert where he lived. At the first step he took, the lightning sprang from them to light the grass all around him. Malii grew frightened as the grass burst into flame on every side and started to run. But the quicker he ran, the fiercer the fires grew. His people saw him coming and thought that he meant to burn the village down until Malii finally managed to get the moccasins off. They immediately burst into flame then and all Malii had left of his gift was a pile of ashes.

CREO

"After this," the old man finished, "Coyote Man's people looked at him in a strange way whenever he came near, and they did so for a very long time."

Whether it was the sacred smoke, or the old man's way of telling a story, Raven saw it all befall before her closed eyelids — Malii and the stranger, the moccasins with the lightning springing from them. When the old man fell silent, she sat quietly for awhile longer until she suddenly realized that the story was over. She opened her eyes to find the old man watching her with a smile, his bird-bright eyes glittering in the firelight.

"Did that happen to you?" she asked.

"No, no," the old man replied. "That's a story the Old People used to tell, a long time ago before the stars fell. I'm old, but not that old. Do I look like a coyote to you?"

"Hola," Raven said. I don't know. She was finding that conversing with the spirits was even more confusing than her dream-voice had warned her it would be. Perhaps it had something to do with the smoke....

"You look unhappy," the old man said.

Raven sighed. "I expected more."

"A longer story?"

"No. It's just...hola. I thought I would learn something of the old ways." She had been looking down at the fire, but now she lifted her gaze to meet his. "I believe there's more to life than growing crops and hunting. That there is meaning to our living, to the land around us, to what we take from it and what we give it back. The Old People knew something my people don't. They had something we lack."

"Perhaps they had mystery."

"What?"

"Or perhaps they were curious enough to ask."

"And that's all?"

"I'm just an old man who lives in the desert, Little Raven. I saw you sitting here and I was curious as to what would bring one of the New People here to sit so quietly, day after day, doing nothing, when the rest of her people are always busy, busy, busy. Indeed it wasn't always so."

"What do you know of the Old People?" Raven asked, eagerness touching her voice again.

The old man shrugged. "Old People...New People. They come and go and come again. That's all I know. But because you have the same name as a cousin of mine, I will teach you a Blessingway — a sacred song that I remember from long ago. Would that do?"

Raven nodded happily. The old man rose to his feet and began a shuffling dance on the opposite side of the fire. His voice, when he began to sing rang out in the desert night air, clear and piercing. The words clung to Raven's memory like burrs and with each chorusing "Ya Ha Hey, Ya Ha Hey" her spirit soared. The old man appeared to change shape as he danced, but she wasn't sure if that was something real that she saw or something left over from the smoke she had shared with him. The outlines of various birds and beasts seemed to be superimposed over his. Her head bobbed to the rhythm he woke so that her snake rattles sounded in time to the shuffle of his feet. She grew sleepy, listening, and her eyelids drooped. The last thing she remembered before she tumbled down to lay outstretched on her blanket, was that his voice sounded very much like her dream-voice when he spoke into the sea of her drowsiness, saying:

"Be the new hataalii of your people, Little Raven. Be their singer and their medicine woman. All people, old and new, need a Blessingway."

Then she slept.

The old man shuffled to a halt and walked slowly over to her, still singing, but softly now. "Yale neye yanai," he murmured, finishing his medicine song. "Yehe! Jiyei." Bending over her sleeping form, he licked the pollen from her eyelids, then turned and disappeared into the night.

Raven woke with the old man's song humming inside her. Filled with eagerness, she packed up and broke camp, hurrying back to the hogans of her people. As she went she imagined the looks on their faces when she taught them what she had learned. They wouldn't be so quick to tease her now; they wouldn't be so quick to smile. Once they heard the song, once they learned the dance, they would finally look at her with respect. She grinned, happy at the thought. Her feet began the shuffling steps of the dance and the song came bubbling up her throat. She remembered every step, every word. She knew instinctively the rituals that must accompany the song, the ceremonial dress, how the hogan must be prepared, the blanket hung over the door, the sand paintings that must be done, the bright cloth headband that she would wear....

The sharp yip, yip, yip of a coyote barking in the distance brought her to a sudden halt. She flushed as she remembered the old man's story. She was doing with her gift what Malii had done with his. Kneeling in the desert sun, she bowed her head. The sun was hot on the nape of her neck, the sand hot and gritty against her knees. She drew a flat stone out of the sand and opened her pack. In the center of the stone she placed a small mound of hemp leaves, then with pinches of pollen, made a circle around it. Standing quickly, she backed away, holding her pack by its strap.

"I'll remember now!" she called out. "I won't forget again, Grandfather Malii, I promise!" The burning lands were silent until a wind came up and scattered the leaves and pollen across the sand. Raven smiled. She would remember. It was hard to be wise when one was as young as she was, but she would try. As she turned and continued on her way, she heard the coyote bark again, but this time its yip, yip, yip sounded more like the "Ya Ha Hey!" of the Blessingway.

The Lantern Is the Moon

Wisdom entereth not into a malicious mind,
and science without conscience is but the ruin of the soul.

—Francois Rabelais

All that I have to say, is, to tell you
that the lanthorn is the moon; I, the
man in the moon; this thorn-bush, my
thorn-bush; and this dog, my dog.

—William Shakespeare,
from *A Midsummer Night's Dream*

Not a sound, Bethany. It'll do no one any good if they catch us now — except for the Feras, and they don't need our help.>

Bethany nodded, only just suppressing the sudden increase in her heart rate at the thought of those awful creatures.

She shifted her attention back to the maze of wiring under her fingers. Was it the pink line from the computer's vid-link to that black one...there? Or was it the yellow?

Her hair, once the soft green and auburn of the berryblossom tree, was black now and fell down her back in a long braid.

(<Witch's hair, Bethany,> Fryfe had cautioned in Zoth. <Best you cut and dye it soon.>)

She wore a gray standard-issue ComCorp jumpsuit, and with her trim figure, could easily pass for a young male tech. Except for the braid of hair, hanging long, black on gray.

("I won't cut it, Fryfe, so stop your grumbling.")

(<Witch's hair.>

(They dyed it black. In Zoth. Long enough ago that it seemed like forever.)

The computer consoles murmured around them, an unbroken automated drone that grated on the nerves after awhile. Bethany tried to shut it out with little success.

She had one green eye, the other gray. And though she could be taken for a Trader from a distance, she'd been born on D'Mast. More specifically, she was a Delen — golden-skinned, with her red-green hair and six fingers per hand.

("Where's their sense of balance, these five-fingered starmen?" she had to ask Fryfe once.

(<In metal ships and the dark between the stars, Bethany. Best you remember that.>)

Fryfe sat on her shoulder — a small, brown-furred rodent with a long tail, huge liquid eyes green as stastones, and a small horn in the center of her brow. She was a Tane, also native to D'Mast.

<The pink one, Bethany-love,> Fryfe told her. <The pink to the black.>

Bethany shrugged and reached down.

ᘓᘍ

The Traders, reaching back to memories of Terra and a time before the Corporations took to the starways, called the Delen witches, for that was how they appeared with their strange powers and the rodent Tane that rode on their shoulders like old Terran familiars. The Delen, when speaking with Traders, called themselves the Chosen of Hecate.

The problem, Fryfe never tired of telling Bethany, was that the ComCorp Traders had only a merchant's soul. Like the Feras, those shadowy creatures of the Between, there was no poetry in the souls of the scowling starmen. They were little better than hucksters, selling their technology for mineral wealth — technology that held no interest to any D'Mastian.

At first only the ComCorp anthropologists were interested in the native population. They puzzled over a culture that, by their standards, had been stagnant for thousands of years — if D'Mastian histories could be believed. But, dutifully, the anthros learned the D'Mastian language, so similar in structure to some of the more complex tongues of their homeworld, and puzzled over the curious resemblances.

The language itself was subtle and loosely regulated, the word orders circular, the grammatical inflections vague. Its cadence was such that, no matter how musical it sounded coming from the natives, the Traders stumbled over it, their tongues constantly tripping over harsh sounds that they knew were wrong.

The D'Mastians, on the other hand — at least those who bothered — could learn Terran Basic in a matter of weeks.

What puzzled the anthros most were certain names in D'Mastian that were identical to those of old Terran mythologies. Particularly intriguing was Hecate, though in retrospect, this was most likely because Dr. Hesting, the head of the ComCorp anthropological studies on D'Mast at the time of the Traders' first landfall, was writing a thesis on the White Goddess and her various aspects in alien cultures. The anthros would scratch their heads, puzzling over this name and that word, trying to recall all they could of the three-faced goddess myths of their homeworld.

"Crete?"

"No. Greece."

They would key questions into their computer consoles and come up with:

...A DAUGHTER OF PERSES AND ASTERIA {DETAILS AVAILABLE}...SEE LUNA, DIANA, PROSERPINE...and... PRESIDED OVER MAGIC AND ENCHANTMENT...and ...REPRESENTED AS HORSE-HEADED, DOG-HEADED, BOAR-HEADED {DETAILS AVAILABLE}...SEE MORRIGAN...SEE GRAVES, ROBERT...

Or, if they touched on the history banks:

...IRRELEVANT...SEE MYTHOLOGIES.

It was when the anthros went out among the general populace with their mobile research probes that the psientists became interested, for in their testing, the Delen registered a higher psi rating than any race so far encountered by the Amalgamated Corporations of Terra. Why, the psientists wanted to know, of the two races that inhabited D'Mast, did the Delen have such a high psi rating, while the normal D'Mastians — who looked much like Terrans, particularly those of the eastern block of their homeworld — registered below norm?

("Can't they feel the Feras?" Bethany asked when she first learned of the Traders' ignorance. Even that simple question made her shiver.

(<They're only duffers,> Fryfe replied tartly. <Thin-souled and mercantile. They hoard life's knowledge, but have yet to learn that reason is not the same as wisdom.>)

D'Mast was a broad, sprawling planet, once again the size of the Traders' homeworld, but with only a fractionally greater gravitational pull. ComCorp scientists puzzled over that incongruity for years without finding a solution. It had two major continents, Clann and Zoth, one to each hemisphere. Between them was the dark blue sea of Jemin.

The Traders situated their main base on the northern continent, as close to the mineral-rich Sarn mountains as the boglands would let them. They called it Reason — a rough rendering of the native name that was more correctly translated into Terran Basic as Wisdom. It was from there that the anthros trekked across D'Mast trying to puzzle out how such a simplistic, Spartan existence — one that nullified any possible progress — could have remain unchanged for as long as it apparently had.

Even more baffling were the complex rituals that were part and parcel of the D'Mastian culture. The ritualists might spend an entire lifetime studying the art of pouring boiling water over chiel leaves, or tending tiny gardens that were more rock than vegetation, or pondering an incomprehensible game played with colored sticks on patterned cloth called kren. There had been examples of similar cultures on old Terra, but none that clung so doggedly to their traditions — particularly once they were offered the fruits of the ACT's own hard-won progress.

There was a strong caste system — a worker's class, a warrior's, a scholar's — but each was of equal rank. And the ritualists were born to any one of the three. The Delen lived within those classes as well, but were not a part of them. So far as the anthros could discover, they were not a class to themselves either.

But with the discovery of such high psi ratings among the Delen, the Traders gave up trying to understand the D'Mastians. The ComCorp psientists took over from the anthros and they simply worked at convincing the Delen to give up their nomadic, unproductive existences and join the ACT's space force where their talents could be put to better use—navigating the huge starships, or mind-linking with computers. When this failed to raise one iota of interest among the Delen, the Traders were forced to resort to a more direct recourse.

Coercion.

They caught Bethany on a scouting run over the northern provinces of Zoth, for all the disguise of her dyed hair. They tried to separate her from her Tane, but the small rodent had an uncanny talent that circumvented every effort the Traders made. In the end, both Bethany and Fryfe rode north in a ComCorp flitter, bound for the experimental psience labs set up in Reason. Rather than being alarmed, they were amused by the Traders' seriousness and meant to enjoy themselves and learn what they could from the starmen.

("They can't all be bad," Bethany said. "There must be some with poetry in their souls.")

(<Care to lay a wager?> Fryfe replied.)

Once they were settled into their quarters, the questioning began. Bethany had an extensive knowledge of Terran Basic, learned in Trader-frequented bars in northern Zoth, so a language barrier wasn't a problem.

The trouble came from how the Traders tried to understand Delen psionics, an insistence on exploring what the power was and where it originated in them, rather than the why.

CRSO

Bethany sighed. Once the first wire was connected, and Fryfe could sense no alarms going off in the vast computer system, she settled down to her task.

"We'd be better off just shutting the whole thing down," she muttered.

Once she'd started, the work settled into a simple chore, as basic as the opening ring of a kren game.

Fryfe chittered scoldingly in her ear. <And where's the subtlety in that? You're beginning to sound like a Trader, Bethany my love. It's that Jard. Do you mean to *become* a Trader, just like him?>

Bethany shook her head. But where was the poetry in what she did now?

CR೮O

When Jard Simpson first came to her quarters, Bethany peppered him with as many questions about Terra and his own people as he asked about the Delen and herself. She was determined to understand the why behind their what and where, but Jard wasn't very forthcoming — not on things that mattered. He could wax eloquent about the ACT in general and ComCorp in particular; about star drives and progress and technological wonders; but knew nothing, or would at least tell her nothing, about his peoples' hopes and dreams, their aspirations beyond the mechanics of their day-to-day existence.

Fryfe grew quickly bored. When she realized that Bethany was resolved to see it through until she understood what made the Traders to be the way they were, Fryfe amused herself with curious mental disciplines that frequently had the psi sensors in their quarters overloading and the Trader techs scrambling over themselves trying to pinpoint what they were convinced were mechanical anomalies.

Weeks dragged into a month.

The Traders were kept happy with all the knowledge that they thought they were acquiring, while Bethany grew increasingly frustrated at how little she herself learned. The Traders refused to consider the basics of the relationship between a Delen and Tane, so she in turn withheld the more complex aspects of their potential — just as one would with a D'Mastian novice Delen who first joined with her Tane.

She said nothing of the ice she could create with thoughts, ice that burned the soul like a cold fire. Or how she could step from the here-and-now into the Between and from there to any place she could visualize. Or what, beyond the poetry of the alliance, was the more practical application of their relationship: to keep watch on the seams that separated the Between from the here-and-now so that the Feras remained in their gray prison.

If they couldn't grasp the conceit that the "talent" they were studying belonged to Fryfe—Bethany was merely a reservoir, powering what the Tane focused—then there was no basis upon which to build further understanding.

One month crawled into two.

And Jard's interest shifted from merely prying into Bethany's talents, to a more physical interest in her—though Bethany couldn't be sure if his desire was genuine, or merely another ploy. He kept any thoughts pertaining to that firmly locked away from the prying fingers of her psi talent. But when she spoke now, he watched her lips move more than he listened. He found every excuse to come into contact with her and then she could smell a sexual desire rising from him that disgusted her. The time came when he asked her point-blank why she wasn't interested in him.

("As if I *had* to be," Bethany told Fryfe later. "The cretin.")

"Because we're too different," she'd answered diplomatically.

"What? Physically?" Jard grinned knowingly.

"No."

"So what *is* the difference?"

"Your thinking. It's too linear."

(<Barbaric, you mean,> Fryfe chittered in her ear. <Mercantile. Fettered.>)

"And yours is...?"

"It's like..." Bethany shrugged. "Like seeing from the inside of a poem."

Jard shook his head. "What's that got to do with sex?"

Bethany grimaced.

(She remembered her first lover, Danyth, the shy ward of a chiel master in Seoth. Remembered their first night of lovemaking with an absolute clarity—undoubtedly aided by the uncouthness of the Terran and his egotistic manner.

(They were sitting on pillows, she and Danyth, the low table between them, drinking chiel served by Danyth moments before. The chiel was rich and dark, sweetened with helenroot, and served in ritual porcelain cups. In the candlelight, she read the small parchment Danyth pressed gravely into her hand:

rust-green hair falling
...strand by strand...seems
like...spring thoughts...
or a thousand birds

(Later they lay together in the chiel fields, her hair a tent about their faces, the scent of crushed chiel leaves pungent in the air. And their lovemaking had seemed like the thunder of a thousand birds winging across the skies of their hearts...)

"Everything," she replied, answering Jard. "Or nothing, if you're referring to us."

CRSO

Bethany sat back on her heels and rubbed her temples. Remembering all the connections wasn't so hard. It was the mind-link with the computer, erasing or changing every fragment of necessary information, that numbed her. Fryfe did the actual work, true enough, but the energy to power it was drawn from her. Their Trader diet of the past two months was hardly suitable for building inner strength. The recycled air of the labs tasted too chemically sweet in her lungs, so she'd never really felt she could breathe.

Fryfe kneaded Bethany's shoulders with her tiny paws, offering what comfort she could. Then they both froze.

<Traders,> Fryfe whispered in a low chitter. <Two of them.>

Bethany stifled a groan. The console was still open, the wires not yet reconnected to their original placements...

"Are they...?" she began.

<Guards,> Fryfe affirmed.

CRSO

"Could a Terran become a Delen?" Jard asked. "I mean, could someone like myself learn your talents?"

Bethany held up a six-fingered hand. "All unbalanced as you are?"

"It's got nothing to do with your hands, or the color of your eyes, or skin, or hair. It's a mental discipline. I know that much. I'm only asking if I could learn it."

"The relationship between a Tane and her Delen is a responsibility," Bethany replied. "Not the talent you understand it to be."

"Sort of like priestesses to Hecate? The Goddess?"

Goddess was only another word for world, Bethany thought, and world could be as small a microcosm as what came about when a Tane and her Delen were joined, but what was the point in trying to make him understand that at this point? First he had to understand the obligation to maintain the boundaries of the Between.

And then there was the poetry...

But all she had to do was taste his thoughts to know that he didn't care to understand either. He was only a figurehead of ComCorp, and the corporation sought only power.

"Not quite," she said finally. "It's both simpler and more complex than that."

Jard glanced at the Tane sitting on her shoulder.

"You mean I need a rat crawling around my shoulders like you've got?" he asked.

Bethany's eyes narrowed and let her mind brush against his again—not close enough to connect with it, only close enough to observe what was happening to him. Her green one began to sparkle and a sudden cold raced through the Trader's body. Every cell and fiber of his being seemed to turn to ice. He opened his mouth, but could only gasp. For long moments the tableau held, then Fryfe relented and let the power flow away. Bethany smiled as Jard collapsed back into his chair.

<It was the tone of his voice,> Fryfe muttered. <The utter disrespect...>

A klaxon alarm was shrieking in the hallway. The door to their quarters burst open and three white-suited guards lunged into the room, sidearms leveled at Bethany. One holstered his weapon, then crossed to where Jard sat wheezing.

"Sir? Are you all right? The psi-register leapt from 5 to 300 and—"

Jard waved him back, still gasping.

"I-I'm fine," he said weakly. "You can go. It was an...accident."

<Accident?> Fryfe chittered indignantly.

<Hush,> Bethany replied. She soothed the Tane, ruffling her fur.

When the door closed behind the guards, Jard had recovered enough to sit up once more. He eyed Bethany warily.

"Why did you do that?" he asked. "Better yet, *what* did you do?"

"It wasn't me. It was Fryfe. When you — "

"Cut the crap. I know that — " He held up his hands when Bethany's green eye began to glitter again. "Okay. Okay. I don't need to be shown twice."

<Oh, no?> Fryfe asked. <Boor.>

Jard was looking closely at the Tane now, a measuring look in his eyes.

"You really mean it, don't you? It's the...your companion that has the power?"

<Fear is a great weapon,> Fryfe observed. <See? Already this lug begins to learn a glimmer of respect for his betters.>

But Bethany was watching Jard's face and the look of cunning that stole across his features. She reached out with her mind to find...nothing. The Trader had closed his thoughts to her, leaving only a formless gray that held the impression of another person being present, but no longer a sense of the man himself. She linked with Fryfe to let the Tane share what she sensed.

Jard was smiling strangely.

"I must be going," he murmured.

Before either Bethany or Fryfe could gather their wits about them, he was up, across the room, and out the door.

Fryfe reached beyond the confines of the room with her mind to find the same cloudiness that had been in the Trader's mind all around them. Their quarters had been psi-sealed.

<We've made a mistake,> the Tane muttered. <They're duffers, yes. But cunning. Sly as Feras...>

Bethany nodded glumly. They'd been here too long. It was as simple as that. They should have realized that whatever poetry the starmen carried within them, they had either left behind on their homeworld, or it lay hidden in the hearts of representatives of ACT that they had yet to meet. There was nothing to learn here, where Wisdom had been corrupted into simply Reason.

But now...

They should have seen it coming. They should have seen that the Traders could never step beyond their need for power, ignoring the poetry that gave it meaning. With their cleverness, they would find a way to harness the D'Mast's Delentane to their needs. Perhaps they could even replicate the power with their technology.

She thought of a man like Jard, wielding a Delentane's talents. Without heart, without responsibility, the first time he used it, the seams would tear between the here-and-now and the Between, and then the Feras would come howling out...

Bethany shuddered. They should have realized that, given time, the Traders would discover what they wanted. They were as tenacious as a scale-backed ghenna once it caught the scent of its prey. The question now was, how much did they already know?

<Too much,> Fryfe said. <That's plain. So. We must erase all record of our presence from this place and depart.>

Bethany brightened. "When?"

<At nightfall.>

So when night came, when the first of D'Mast's three moons rose red from the eastern horizon, Fryfe, through Bethany, brought a blackout to their quarters. Then it was a simple matter to step out of the here-and-now to the Between. From there, Fryfe raided the minds of the Trader techs, discovering where the data concerning them was stored, how the computer safeguards could be circumvented, what data could safely be erased, what needed simply to be adjusted. Then it was only a matter of doing.

൶൶

The guards were coming. Two white-suits. Their breathing thick, their minds gray, untouchable.

We have to escape, Bethany thought, and quickly, but she was too weak from her ordeal with the computer to provide the energy needed for both of them to step into the Between.

<We'll hide,> Fryfe said.

But it was already too late.

Whether it was Bethany's weakness, or the sterile atmosphere of the computer rooms, Fryfe has miscalculated the distance between their foes and themselves. The guards rounded the corner and dropped into protective positions, sidearms leveled. Both wore gasmasks.

Tentatively, Fryfe reached out. But the guards were psi-sealed, their minds misty and gray.

<Bethany-love,> she said.

<Go,> Bethany told her. <While I can still send you.>

One guard unstoppered a canister. As he threw it towards them, underhanded, gas hissing from it, Bethany let Fryfe draw on her strength. There wasn't much there, not enough for both of them, but enough for...

The Tane vanished with a soft *ffhut* of displaced air. Then the gas was clogging Bethany's lungs. Her sight spun. Her head felt as though it would split. Blackness welled up, bringing with it a welcome relief.

∝∽

"Got her," Jard said, stepping around the corner.

He nodded to the guards and knelt by Bethany. Pushing back her hair, he fitted a small helmet to her head, fastened its chin-strap, and flicked a switch on its side. Tiny needles punctured her skin under the helmet, forcing psi-dampers and a truth serum into her blood system.

"Did you see her familiar?" he asked. "The rat?"

He wasn't sure he believed the Delen when she'd told him that the power was in the Tane, but after the attack on him this afternoon, he'd decided to step up the investigation. He'd been getting nowhere being pleasant.

"There was something on her shoulder," one of the guards replied. "It could've been the rat. Scurried off before the gas hit, I guess."

Jard frowned. "Wonderful. Well, it'll be around somewhere — we'll get it later. Come on. Give me a hand with her."

∝∽

Bethany was in a place of drifting smoke — like the Between, but not, for there were no Feras here. At least not the sort with which she was familiar.

She hovered there in that gray place, floating, distant to her surroundings, but close to them as well. From far away she could hear voices, but she could fix no particular meaning to what they said.

"Everything?"

That was Jard's voice, a part of her mind said. But what was a Jard?

"Wiped clean, sir. The whole bank. But just the references to the Delen and Tane. Where they *are* still mentioned, the data's been readjusted."

A second voice.

"How's that possible?"

"She was crouched in front of a control panel when we came upon her, sir."

Yet another voice.

"These people are primitives," Jard protested. "She couldn't possibly understand the workings of a computer. To do what she did, adjusting data, circumventing the machine's defenses...she'd have to have such a delicate touch and training...Have we got a 'puter-link who could do it?"

"Not planetside."

"Hmm. Is she ready for interrogation yet?"

"We've had her ready for the past five minutes, sir."

"Good. Bethany? I know you can hear me. Answer my questions, honestly and completely, and we'll let you go as soon as the drugs wear off. Can you understand me?"

Liar. Lies...lies...lies...

But Bethany answered yes. She could do nothing else.

"What are the Delen?"

"The Chosen of Hecate."

Jard sighed. "Not this crap again. Tech, can we do a deep probe?"

"We could, sir, but I don't recommend it. There's an assured thirty percent burn-out involved."

"So?"

"Well...there's always the possibility that the data you require will be in that thirty percent. We've no control over what goes. She's the first Delen we've had under, so it's impossible to compute how her mind will react."

"Wonderful." Jard turned back to Bethany. "Who or what is Hecate?"

"She is the Goddess. Her power is in sky and earth and sea— three bodies, standing back to back—but she encompasses the underworld as well. The three moons are hers, one for each of her faces. From her comes all poetry, all power. She it was who first brought the rituals to D'Mast, the rituals of body, of mind, of soul. The first teaches — "

"Okay, okay. Turn off for a moment."

Obediently, Bethany let the dark smoke enfold her mind once more.

"What do you make of this, doctor?"

The psientist who had been standing by all the while simply shrugged.

"She's under," he said. "Deep under. Whatever she tells us, *she* believes is the truth. Ask about her 'familiar.' I know her talent's being dampened, but even with the psi-lock on, it should still be there, underneath, for our instruments to measure. She's not registering."

"It's the rat." Jard frowned. "But this Hecate business bothers me. She — all the natives — describe her the same way as Terran textapes describe the Greek goddess with the same name. I want to know why."

"You've studied the myths?" the psientist asked, surprised.

"Only what I needed to for this operation. Dreary stuff." He turned back to Bethany. "Where does the name Hecate come from?"

Even under sedation, a smile came to Bethany's lips.

"We took it from the mind of one of the first Traders who landed here," she said. "It seemed like a good joke."

"You took…"

Jard's face darkened. There were entire databases of studies exploring the similarities between the D'Mastian pantheon and the gods of Terra's old myths. And now they were being told that they all came from doddering old Dr. Hesting and his thesis?

"Okay," he said. "We're done with the jokes. Tell us about the rat."

"Fryfe is a Tane, the dominant intelligent species on D'Mast. The Tane have made it their task to keep at bay the Feras which haunt the Between…"

CRSO

Fryfe was in the Between.
Drifting…drifting…

How long she was there, she wasn't sure. Temporal measurements had a way of running rampant in the Between. She only knew that it was cold. And it was dark. Darker than usual. It was always a gray place, but Fryfe was puzzled that it grew so black now. Perhaps it was because she was here alone, without warm Bethany. Alone and unable to return. There was no strength for her to draw from. She was trapped here while in the Terran labs, the starmen would be probing Bethany. Hurting her. Chilling her soft warmth.

It was so cold here...

And then she knew.

There were Feras near — dozens of the shadowy creatures.

Feras. They had no form, only vague shadow-shapes that lay in the Between like kren cloths tossed untidily on the floor. But the danger in them lay not in physical threat, but in how they could manipulate one's mind...

All the dark thoughts of ancient D'Mast had been siphoned away by the ancestors of today's Delentane and sent to this place until those now long-dead Delentane realized that something in the Between gave them a life of their own. Some said the Feras were created through the genetic manipulating of renegade Delentane. Others avowed that they simply acquired life from the dark and cold. Neither opinion changed the fact that the Feras had nothing except for this strange existence in the gray Between and a burning need to destroy anything that came into it from beyond its confines. Sometimes they broke through, into the there-and-then, but mostly the Delentane kept them in check.

If she was here with Bethany, they would never dare to approach. But they sensed that she was helpless now, without her other half. They would feed on her mind, on her soul, then they would use her death to tear a rent in what separated the there-and-then from the Between and they would ravage D'Mast, feeding more, growing stronger...

Damn the Traders for the meddling duffers they were. And damn herself for playing the clown with them until the game grew so out of hand.

She could feel the Feras ringed all about her, the cloud of their dark thoughts pressing at her mind, close and choking. She longed to use their raw strength against them. But without Bethany. Without...

A mad thought raced across her mind. Her small teeth showed as she grinned and her chittering laugh echoed and ran through the Between.

As the first Fera fouled her mind with the crawling touch of its thoughts, she drew on the creature's strength, riding its thoughts with a viciousness that she would never have dreamed to use with Bethany. The Fera fought her control, but she had already mastered its defenses and was using its strength to snare another of the creatures before it could rally. The second was easier to overcome, the third easier still.

By the time she had five under her control, her mind was buzzing with the raw potency of their strength. The other creatures fled, wailing and howling into the deeper reaches of the Between. Fryfe let them go. She had what she needed.

What she held was an alien power, but it was still power. And she could use it.

The Feras under her control fought her every step of the way, but she was too versed in the rituals of focusing to let them break free now. She wound her thoughts inward, spiraling them tight, then cast a long thread of them out into the Between. The thread wove a gleaming topaz path through the grayness, leading her to where she could come out into the there-and-then and help Bethany.

It should have been hard. The Between spread across the entire surface of D'Mast and having to keep the Feras in hand took much of her concentration. But Bethany was in Reason, and the port of the Traders was situated on an old holy place that bore another name in D'Mastian. Wisdom. The focus of Delentane poetry. It called to her like a compass point pulled to magnetic north.

Her thought-thread led her to the golden place that was Wisdom in the Between. The Feras fought her hold with renewed fury as they neared the burning glow. And then Fryfe felt Bethany — the Delen's drugged thoughts as chaotic and strange as a Fera's.

Fryfe let her mind range further, bypassing the psi-seal of the lab with the ease of a kren master sweeping an amateur's sticks from the cloth. She focused on those in the lab.

Jard. A technician. Another technician. A psientist.

<Would you like to know power?> she asked.

298

They couldn't hear her, so they made no response.

<Would you care to understand why it requires wisdom to wield?>

For without the poetry, it was simply power. And power, as any novice knew, corrupted if it wasn't tempered.

<Would you truly understand what you sought?>

Still the Traders couldn't hear, still they couldn't respond.

But the Feras howled.

And Fryfe was beyond compassion.

She hooked each Trader's mind to that of one of the Feras she was riding. Using the power of the fifth, her large eyes narrowed with concentration, she let the Feras pull the Traders into the Between while she slipped through the psi-seals into the lab and broke her own contact with the creatures.

The sudden silence inside the lab was startling in its intensity.

Then slowly sound intruded. The hum and buzz of the Traders' machinery. The soft murmur of the monitoring devices. There was no one present except for Bethany, strapped to a table, the psi-damping helmet on her head.

Fryfe scurried over to the table and ran up its leg to reach where Bethany lay. She gave Bethany's cheek a soft, quick lick, then began to chew on the straps that bound the helmet to the Delen's head.

CRENO

"Fryfe?"

The Tane perched on Bethany's chest and stared into her mismatched eyes.

<How are you feeling, Bethany, my love?>

"I'm not sure. Disjointed. Is that sky above?"

<Sky, indeed.>

"And the Traders' lab?"

<Many jhen away, Bethany. A duffer's stronghold is no place for folk such as you and I.>

Bethany sat up and Fryfe scrambled to her shoulder. D'Mast's purple-blue skies were crystalline above them. They sat in a field of kemberweed, all red and yellow, the tiny blossoms filling the air with a heady scent. In the distance, Bethany saw a chiel farmer's round holding and his chiel fields beyond it. She thought of Danyth...and then of Jard.

A frown flickered on her lips.

"What happened?" she asked. "They...drugged me, I guess."

<They wanted power,> Fryfe explained, <so I sent them into the Between where they could see it firsthand. I don't doubt but that the Feras welcomed them in their own inimitable fashion.>

Bethany smiled politely at the gruesome joke. She'd seen a D'Mastian possessed by a Fera once. The unfortunate man had torn out his own eyes before his family managed to restrain him and call for a Delentane. How much worse would the creatures' influence be in the Between?

"And now?" she asked.

Fryfe rubbed her horn against Bethany's cheek.

<Now life goes on, Bethany-love. There's a kren tournament in Stemmer. Hald is playing.>

"But the Traders...?"

<They'll still be here. They're too strong for us to be free of them—the Delentane who first met them saw that clearly enough. We played the fool for them, but no more. Never again will there be a Delentane in their labs. We will become...another myth. Life is full of myths for the Traders. Let us simply be another.>

"And Hecate?"

<What a strange sound I hear from your lips, Bethany. Hecate. Are you coughing?> Fryfe bared her teeth in a sharp grin, then grew solemn. <No, love. The Goddess will be as she was—three-mooned and nameless—and we will be her light. Did you learn nothing as a novice?>

Bethany nodded. "The Goddess is the world," she said.

<And?>

"The world is what we make it to be."

<Just so. The first lesson a novice learns. But the Traders...they look afar, for what lies within.>

Bethany had other questions, a dozen more, and then another dozen, but none of them were crucial. Not at this time. They reminded her too much of the Terrans' poking and prying. Questions were important, but how they were asked was even more important. Asked without respect, they had no meaning.

For the moment she preferred to let a poetry fill her, three-mooned and nameless.

Songwalking the Hunter's Road

The starship *Lenneth* was in a holding pattern high above the blue-green sphere that was the planet Tuorn. On its bridge, the main display panels flickered with a network of pre-warp indicators as the navs completed their last-minute course coordinates. Tallien f'Hein, the ship's psi-link to its master computer, had strapped herself into her teleweb control. From there she would guide the ship as it sped through reverspace. But while the crew awaited their final orders, Cassielle Stendra, the ship's captain, was pacing the stainless steel floor of the infirmary, trying to keep the current situation in perspective. Just because they were already behind schedule...

"So what've we got?"

She turned arched eyebrows to Kant f'Uhol, her security head, as she waited for the chief medic's reply.

"Two cases of fayne-poisoning," Benth Lawell replied. "Dream-dust."

"Just them?" She peered through a plastiglass partition into the observation cubicle where two still forms lay. One was a tall gaunt man in the yellow robes of an acolyte of the Universal Church of the Dominion. The other was a shorter figure, though just as slender. In place of the Church Warden's clean-shaven pate, he had curly brown hair that fell in a tangle to rim his fine-boned features. Attractive features, Cassie decided.

"Who's that?" she asked, indicating the latter.

"Citizen Jeran an Bodach," f'Uhol replied, consulting the computer printout he was holding. "A starbard. He boarded at Centreport, planetside, bound for Weyth in the Koth System."

"Origin?"

"Wasn't entered."

"Figures." She glanced at the black and silver object that lay on a table by the door. "That his?"

F'Uhol nodded. It was a regulation synth/arp, modified to carry a larger memory bank than was usual for an instrument its size. The heat-sensitive fingerboard control was of a black alloy, the casing and speaker grille, Vran-forged silver.

"Powered by a Luvan firestone," he said. "Say 37 or 38 DVs."

Cassie nodded. "How'd they get dusted?"

"The Warden attacked —" He consulted his printout again. " — An Bodach in the Main Lounge just after lift-off. Used a makeshift blowgun — just a rolled up piece of stammin' plastic. An Bodach didn't go under as fast as he was supposed to. He'd time to launch himself at the Warden but only succeeded in spilling the dust over the both of them. I've got it all down on vid if you want a playback."

"I think I will. Later. Anybody else get dusted?"

F'Uhol shook his head. "The stuff settles fast."

"But," the medic broke in, "you have to avoid direct skin contact with them — at least until the drug's run its course."

"Motive?" Cassie asked. "Even a guess?"

"Well," F'Uhol said, scratching a sideburn, "I'd say the Warden took him for a Kell. The Church still pays a bounty on them."

Cassie shot another glance in the starbard's direction. "He doesn't look like a Kell. He hasn't even got red hair."

F'Uhol shrugged. "They don't always. Taphen told me that the Warden went over the passengers' psi-scan. An Bodach here's got a stammin' high rating."

Well, that made sense, Cassie thought. An unbonded psi was fair game for any Warden. And if he was wrong...

"I wish our starbard the best of luck if he tries to press charges," she said. She turned to Lawell. "How long's he going to be under for?"

"Hard to say. If he were normal —"

"What do you mean *normal?*"

"Look for yourself," Lawell said. He crossed to a terminal and punched in a code. A computer-generated outline of the starbard appeared on the infirmary's viewscreen. Within the red outline was a webwork of yellow lines, with a second green web following the pattern of the yellow. "The yellow is his nervous system," the medic explained. "The green is a secondary one."

"But..."

"Wait for it. Not only does he have two nervous systems, but his cells are regenerative to an infinite degree — at least that's what the computer shows after a preliminary examination. I took a tissue sample but it's still being analyzed."

"Genetic engineering?" Cassie asked.

"Hard to say, Captain. If it is, it's beyond anything the Dominion's capable of."

"Hath!" Cassie took another look at the starbard. "So how long do you give him?"

Lawell shrugged. "To be honest, I don't know. In a normal case, say four or five hours, barring complications. The trouble with fayne is that while it affects the body initially, its real scope lies in the mind. It's like...dreaming. The difference is that, under the influence of fayne, the subject goes somewhere in his own mind and — hallucination, dream, call it what you will — the experience supersedes reality. If he was to get hurt there, or...Well, there was a study done at the Psience Institute on Tone — "

"You mean they could die?"

Visions of being grilled by bored planetside authorities, not to mention the Church, danced in Cassie's mind.

"It's possible," Lawell said.

And even if they survived and the incident was reported, it would put them so far behind schedule...

"Can we warp with them aboard in that state?" she asked.

The medic considered that. The human mind was unable to withstand long exposure to reverspace, hence starships traveling through it kept psi-shields locked in place, controlled by their psi-link and enhanced by the master computer.

"Theoretically," he said, "there shouldn't be any problem."

Cassie stepped up to the terminal and punched in a code. A voice floated down from the speaker grille above the door.

"Yes, Captain?"

"Take us into reverspace, Tally."

"Stand by," the psi-link replied.

Cassie and the others strapped themselves into the foamchairs that lined one wall and waited for the warp into reverdrive. Thinking over all that Lawell had said, Cassie found herself staring at the starbard's calm features.

"What're you thinking of?" f'Uhol asked.

"I was wondering where he was," she replied. "And what it's like in there. I mean he's a balladeer, isn't he? Just think of what he's got rolling around in his head."

F'Uhol considered that. He'd been a peace-officer on a low-tech world before signing on with Cassie and once had to lock up a whole band of Kellian gypsies before shipping them off-planet. To this day he could still recall their weird songs, at least those sung in Basic. They'd kept it up all night to the accompaniment of antique instruments and when the Tassen-bound starship's portal hissed shut on them, he'd breathed a sigh of relief. But those songs came back to haunt him from time to time. Which was one of the major reasons that the Church had outlawed the Kells. Their music had a way of awakening an inexplicable discontent in the most tenable mind.

"Well, if he's in a song," he said, "I hope he had the good sense to pick a rollicking drinking rhyme or something similar."

Cassie nodded, adding in a murmur, "If he had a choice."

Cℛℰᴐ

The forest was on the largest of a scattering of green isles, stretching in a vast sweep of oak trees, maple and wild apple, from shore to shore of the cold north seas that cradled them. It was a place where the mistletoe grew and the twilight sheltered from the day in dense thickets. It echoed with memories of a shy and ancient people and was home to the fox and hare, the wren and raven, the bear and stag. And somewhere in its deepest reaches was a bardic college, trees of learning that were safeguarded by a harping wizard. He wore a cloak he had borrowed from the Green Man and spoke only in riddles. His green-gold eyes were the gifts of a tree-wife; his red-gold hair a gift of the Moon.

His name no man knew.

Jeran an Bodach thought on that as he approached the forest, unsure of how the knowledge came to him.

Morning mist wreathed about his shoulders. He trod an unseen path that led from where his ship's keel scraped the shingles of the inlet where it was anchored, to the edge of the forest and within, straight as a bird's flight and as unmarked as a spider's web in shadow. Behind him, the grass sprang up again to swallow his footprints. Overhead, a hawk circled, its keen eyes marking him. The scent of the forest was deep and musty in his nostrils, like fresh-turned loam or a rare old book. For long moments he stood, soaking in the stillness that surrounded him, letting the silence seep through his every pore and cranny until his soul held a measure of the forest's quiet presence.

Then, from out of the woods, a jackdaw called.

<Curious,> a voice said in Jeran's mind.

Jeran only nodded.

Seen from a distance, there was no way to tell that his slender frame housed two beings: one the man that had been born to wear this body, the other the asomatous alien that had come to share it with him. Their peculiar symbiosis had proved to be mutually beneficial, Jeran had discovered, once the initial shock of it had eased into a grudging alliance. Ta'kis're-k'at, who Jeran called Tak for convenience, gave as much as he took, exchanging an awakening of psionic talents and longevity for sustenance and a host body. That their relationship had proved to be permanent no longer troubled them, once their uncertain respect for each other had subtly shifted into friendship.

"How did we come to be here?" Jeran asked softly.

The beginnings of something indefinable lay underfoot. A road? Then to where? A quest? For what? Whatever it was, they both sensed that the answer, if answer there was to be, lay in the forest before them.

<We boarded the *Lenneth* on Tuorn,> Tak began.

"Bound for Weyth."

<And then...>

"And then?"

Jeran sighed for both of them. The how and why of their being in this place remained as oblique as a mirror that gave forth no reflection.

<We're in your mind,> Tak said at last. <In one of your ballads.>

"*My* mind?"

Tak answered with a mental shrug. <Do you think I could come up with a scene like this? And what about all that mumbo-jumbo about green men and wizards?>

"The Kells," Jeran said.

<What?>

"If...if we're in my mind...in a ballad in my mind, ridiculous as that seems...we're in a Kellian ballad." Thinking of ballads and music reminded him of: "Where's Gwynolen?"

But as soon as he thought of his synth/arp, he could feel the instrument's comfortable weight hanging by its strap from his shoulder. Had it been there before he'd thought of it, or had his desire for it shaped its presence?

"This doesn't make a whole lot of sense," he offered.

He pinched his arm, then reached up to touch a low-hanging bough. The green leaves were cool to his touch, felt real. Looking back, he could see the shingled beach of the inlet, but there was no sign of the ship that had brought them here. Had it been real, or —

"Tak?"

<Ease up,> his inner companion said, sensing Jeran's sudden panic.

He concentrated on slowing their quickening pulse, dissipating the adrenaline that had rushed into their bloodstream. Their breathing returned to normal, the bunched tightness of their neck muscles loosened.

"What are we going to do?" Jeran asked.

He looked back to the shore. The morning sun was stronger now, shredding the mist that hung over the meadow they stood in. But further back, not only was the ship gone, but the mist there was growing thicker. He could no longer see the waves, nor hear their rise and fall against the shore. The faint tang of salt was gone from the air. The sea had vanished, as though it had never been.

<Let's accept, for the moment, the premise that we're in a Kellian ballad,> Tak said. <Can you tell which one?>

Jeran thought. Wild apples and mistletoe. A harping wizard. A bear, a stag and a tree-wife. A college of trees...They were familiar images, but came from many songs, were merely a synthesis of many things Kellian.

"No," he said. He tried to repress a cold chill that woke goose bumps on his skin.

<We're making a poor start,> Tak said. <You'd think with all the music you've got cluttering up your mind, that sooner or later you'd put it in some sort of order. What's the use of having it all, if you can't put your finger on—What's that?>

Through shared ears they heard the sound. It was neither wind in the boughs above, nor the murmur of the trees as they settled and shifted in their roots, but it was still air moving to make a sound.

<Music,> Tak said.

"Harping," Jeran clarified. He saw, in his mind, a green-cloaked, red-haired harper, bent over his ancient instrument to pull forth music and shake it out into the air. The sound of it echoed all around them now, full rich notes that rippled and fell, the high ones stinging sharp, the low ones deep and thrumming.

<Do you know the tune?> Tak asked.

"No. That is, it's familiar, but…"

As the music had earlier, now a sixth sense drew their gaze back along the way they'd come. Through the mists they saw a figure moving, more a flash of yellow amidst the gray than something they could clearly make out. Frozen, they watched its approach, the harp music adding an eerie counterpoint to the sense of danger they felt building up inside them. Then a Church Warden stepped from the mist and something clicked in their shared thoughts.

Where earlier conjecture had proved useless, the yellow swirl of the Warden's robes brought a rush of memory: the blowgun and the cloud of dream-dust, Tak taking control of their body and attacking, the subsequent failure and falling, starbard and Warden…

<We're tripping,> Jeran said, mindspeaking.

Tak ignored him. He saw the handgun in the Warden's hand and knew, dream-dusted or not, they could still die here. As he took charge of Jeran's skeletal muscles, the Warden leveled his weapon and fired. The heat-sear of the weapon's laser ionized the air where they'd been standing a moment before, scarring the nearest tree. The smell of burnt wood stung their nostrils. Before the Warden could fire again, Tak turned and fled into the forest, the first racket of broken branches and stamping feet dissolving into a noiseless glide as he brought all his woodlore to bear.

The harping had died as abruptly as the Warden's attack had begun. Tak could hear the acolyte enter the woods behind them. Jeran's panic, once the initial shock of the attack had eased, rose to cloud the alien's control, numbing his abilities. A branch snapped underfoot and Tak could hear the Warden adjust his pursuit accordingly. He fought Jeran's panic, but the combination of trying to keep their flight as noiseless and swift as possible while doing so, was proving ineffectual. If the Warden wasn't armed, or if they had a weapon...But Jeran couldn't abide weapons. Then Tak had a thought. Out of his memory, he drew forth the music of the unknown harper and let it fill their mind. He could feel Jeran relax and full control of the starbard's musculature and reflexes returned to him.

Grimly he sped on, keeping the Warden's position fixed as he tried to put as much distance as he could between them. How long before the fayne wore off? He shook his head, realizing that that line of reasoning was unproductive. The Warden would still be on the starship when they stopped tripping. What they had to do was either disarm the threat or continue their flight. Until some other solution came to him, he opted for the latter.

CRSO

"Listen," Cassie said. "What's that?"

"I don't hear anyth—" f'Uhol began, then broke off as he heard it too.

"It sounds like humming." Cassie looked around the infirmary, puzzled. They were only a few minutes into reverspace, but she undid her foamchair's straps. "Where's it coming from?"

Lawell pointed to the speaker grille that was wired to the observation chamber. "From in there."

They rose to cross the room, pressing their faces against the plastiglass.

"It's the starbard," f'Uhol said.

Beside him, Cassie nodded. Stepping back from the partition, she walked to the door that gave access into the observation room.

"Captain!" Lawell cried. "Don't!"

"Cassie!" f'Uhol called at the same time, but they were both too late.

Palming the door open, she stepped inside. As it hissed shut behind her, the two men heard a faint snick as it locked.

"Her master-key," f'Uhol said. He turned to the medic. "She's bolted the stammin' thing with her master-key. We've got to override it. What's gotten into her?"

Lawell turned back to the observation room and for a long moment didn't answer the security head. "Hath knows," he said at last. "Look. She's standing over the starbard." He lunged for the comm-mic and, switching it on, shouted into it: "Don't touch his skin, Captain!"

Cassie gave no evidence that she'd heard him. Listening to the soft spill of sound that came from between the starbard's lips, she felt an old memory rise to life inside her, a memory that seemed to come from her forefather's time and was old when she was born. Her eyes wore a dreamy look as she bent over the starbard, one hand reaching out to stroke his cheek.

രു൭

Tak perched in the broad boughs of a tree so wide that two men couldn't have joined hands around its trunk. The tree was one of many golden-leafed oaks that encircled a hectare of ankle-high grass. In the middle of the glade was another oak, taller than any of its surrounding sentinels, its coloring like the heart of a flame. Slouching more comfortably, between bough and trunk, Tak listened. If the forest had been still earlier, here it was positively hallowed in its quietness.

He had paused here because, while he could still sense the Warden beating the woods somewhere far behind them, ahead he sensed another presence. His psi-senses reached out but came back to tell him nothing. It wasn't until the harping started up again that he guessed who was in the glade, hidden from sight by the giant tree.

<Jeran?>

The starbard's presence stirred in their mind. Tak pumped a little reassurance into him and the stirring shifted into full awareness. Jeran's first feelings were a vague shame.

<I did it again, didn't I? Went into a funk like some—>

<At least you have the sense to mindspeak,> Tak said.

311

<You've probably got my mouth wired shut. I wouldn't blame you.>

In their mind, Tak smiled. <If the stars had wanted to make a warrior out of you, they'd have given you the body to do it with.>

<You seem to do alright with this body.>

<But I was trained. Now, had you seen my own body...>

<The Warden?> Jeran asked, not wanting to drift into reminiscences. He felt redundant enough as it was.

<We've lost him for now. Listen.>

Jeran heard the harping then. While they'd been speaking, it had been like a holograph's incidental music. Now it came rushing across the glade, filling the woods with its fierce and exultant sound.

<I know that playing,> Jeran said.

<You would.>

That was a knack Jeran had. He never forgot another musician's style. Furrowing his brow, he tried to recall the player. New goose bumps started across his skin as the harper's features came to mind. He shared the swell of memory with Tak. They'd met him in the market square of a mid-tech world in the Sarn System, two minstrels working their trade, stopping long enough to swap a few songs over some cheap local wine. That one night grew into a month of companionship, until...

<Kiern,> Jeran said. <Kiern Kennan.>

<I remember him. We met him on Polst, what? Three years ago?>

Jeran nodded numbly. <But he's dead.>

There was a long silence as Tak digested that. The young Kell had been no older than the twenty-odd years that Jeran's body gave him the appearance of.

<So he is,> he said softly. <Dead. But he left you this song.>

"This song," Jeran said aloud. "I remember it now. He called it a roadsong. Tak. How can it be him?"

Dream-dust was something neither of them had experienced before. The herenow surrounded them with sight and smell and sound. It seemed far more real than the cubicle on the *Lenneth* where their bodies lay. They weren't even aware of another reality, except in a rational sense.

<These woods are full of presences,> Tak said. <I recognize the harper's now. The Warden is still somewhere behind us. But there are others...>

312

As he spoke, they became aware of a figure standing on the edge of the glade. It was a woman in a dusty gray flightsuit that was standard Dominion issue for starship personnel. She had short-cropped black hair and her face, as she tilted back her head to listen to the harping, was familiar to both of them.

<That's the captain of the *Lenneth*,> Tak said.

"Layn'fey!" Jeran murmured. "Is the whole starship wandering around in these woods?"

Tak gave a mental shrug. <If the dream-dust got into the ship's ventilation system...>

<But wouldn't they all be in their own heads? What're they doing in ours?>

<We seem to be in your friend's.>

<That's different.>

<Is it? How?>

Jeran shook his head irritably. He looked to the ground. The lowest bough was six meters above the forest floor.

<Ah, Tak. Can you get us down?>

<Sure. What've you got planned?>

They began to descend in a quick scuttling motion, Tak working their limbs like a squirrel's as they spiraled down the tree's broad trunk. Jeran breathed a sigh of relief when at last they had firm earth underfoot.

<I thought I'd find out what's going on,> he said, then he smiled. <You coming?>

Tak grinned back in their head.

<Better make it quick,> he said. <That music your friend's making is bound to draw the Warden here.>

Jeran nodded. <First the captain.>

She turned at their approach, eyes narrowing before a cautious smile came to her lips.

"Hello," she said in Dominion Basic. "I, ah..."

<She's Urnen,> Tak opinioned.

<Do you know their language?>

<Not much different from Gessian. Want to give it a go?>

Jeran shrugged. "Hello," he said. "How did you get here?"

Tak translated the words into Urnen before they left Jeran's mouth. Hearing her native tongue from the starbard's lips, for all its strange accent, brought a comic reaction to Cassie's face.

"You..." she began, eyes round.

"No," Jeran answered, saving her the need of asking the question. "I'm not Urnen. I'm a bard, remember? The gift of tongues and all."

<Well,> Tak said. <You've made a good first impression. The worldly, knowledgeable starbard strikes again.>

<Not now,> Jeran replied a trifle smugly.

"You were dusted," the Captain was saying, "just before we warped."

"The whole ship?"

She shook her head. "Just you and the Warden. I...ah, got into skin contact with one of you and...Well, here I am. Where is here, anyway?"

Jeran jerked a hand in the direction of the central oak, behind which the harper was still playing.

"We're in one of his songs, or so Ta – Ah, so I think."

"Is it...How can it be so real?"

But the harping played the same tune that the starbard had been humming in the infirmary, the same tune that had made her forget her responsibilities and brought her here. She remembered the strange feeling of familiarity she'd felt.

"I know that song," she added. "But I don't know how I do."

"It's a Kellian roadsong. Aren't there any gypsies on Urne?"

"Not in my time."

Jeran took her hand. "Well, come and meet one."

<She likes you,> Tak said.

Jeran felt his neck redden. <How would you know? You haven't been reading her...>

<Her mind? No. It's in her eyes.>

Jeran turned to her and met her smile. Her eyes were a strange mingling of mauve and green and were watching him with a guarded friendliness. He smiled back and she squeezed his hand.

Normally wary in the company of strangers, Cassie felt a certain boldness in the starbard's presence that surprised her. But it was harmless, she told herself. After all. This was just a dream. They were tripping and the starbard was refreshing company, considering the usual sorts that hung around the spacer docks. Except Lawell had said something about him. How old was he, anyway? And hadn't Lawell also said something about if you got hurt here...

"What's your name?" Jeran asked.

"Cassielle Stendra. Call me Cassie."

How did he come to speak Urnen? Urne was a low-tech world, the smallest of three inhabited planets that circled a sun on the left arm of the Isset System. Hardly a prepossessing world, which is why she'd worked so hard to get off-planet herself. So what had he been doing there?

"My name's Jeran."

She started, then nodded. "Have you ever been to Urne?"

"Me? No."

"Then how —"

But they had reached the oak now. Its yellow and gold boughs swept above them, moving with the wind so it seemed they were standing in a fire. The harper looked up and his music trailed away.

"Jeran," he said.

It *was* Kiern. Jeran could feel his knees growing weak, his face paling. Tak steadied the drum of their pulse, brought the color back into their cheeks.

"Kiern. You…that is…"

"I died. Yes. In your arms. It wasn't too bright getting caught in that alley, was it? Did you get away?"

Cassie moved closer to the starbard. Dead? she thought.

"But…" Jeran was saying.

"Then how am I here?"

His hair was red-gold, like the oak above them, and he wore a green cloak. Remembering his first impression of the wood — a bardic college of trees and its guardian — Jeran could only nod.

"We were friends for a month, Jeran, and we shared much, for there's nothing like music to twine two souls as one. But I could never begin to explain all the Kellian mysteries in one lifetime, little say the month we had. This is the Wood Perilous — don't look so nervous. It's just a name, I'm here because I'm waiting…for many things. Mostly to walk the Dominion again, but there aren't many Kells being born and there are so many spirits waiting to be reborn."

"Here?" Jeran asked, trying to understand. "In this wood?"

"In this, or one of their own making. This one had its origin in that roadsong I taught you. I shared the tune with you so that there might be a bridge between us should you care to brave it. Now you have, and with a friend, and here we are."

<Songwalking,> Tak said smugly. <Didn't I tell you?>

Jeran frowned, cutting him off. "There's a Warden here, too," he said.

"A Warden?" The harper's brow darkened, then he shrugged and smiled. "I'm dead. Surely I can't die again. But how did he come to be here? Did you bring him?"

Jeran explained.

"So you didn't use the song?" Kiern asked.

"Not directly. Still..."

"...it brought you here nevertheless. What else can explain your presence?" Kiern nodded. "Come," he said, indicating Jeran's synth/arp. "Sit down the both of you and wake that strange beast of yours. We'll play a tune or two."

Jeran glanced at Cassie, then they sat down, drawing their legs under them.

"The Warden...?" Jeran began.

"Let the wood take care of him. Come on, now. Tune up."

Still feeling somewhat numb, Jeran complied. He adjusted his instrument and ran through a few practice chords, regulating the tone controls until the intonation was true. Cassie watched him, fascinated at his fingers' deft movements. Tak settled into a listening position in their head. Whatever Jeran might have lacked in other skills, the musicianship of their body was strictly his.

When Jeran was satisfied with the tone of the instrument's synthetic strings, he began an underlying pattern for the harp to build its melody upon. Kiern plucked, one string and then another, and the melody dropped into the wash of the synth/arp's sound like dolphins at play in the sea.

"Just so," Kiern murmured, and he began to sing:

The long road, the hunter's road,
the way the old folk ken,
winds a riddled way, I'm told,
makes strangers out of friends;
makes friends out of strangers,
mingles dark and gold,
finds beauty, offers dangers,
does the hunter's road...

Cassie listened and her thoughts went spiraling. She looked away from the players into the flame-leafed boughs above, across the glade to where the wood stood listening, mysterious and dark. Makes friends out of strangers, she repeated to herself. Does it? Is that why she felt the way she did, a sort of comfortable knowledge that they'd get along, she and the starbard? Was she on this hunter's road?

She'd always been a striver and a searcher, from her first resolve to get off-planet as soon as she could, to the years she'd spent riding the starways, searching for something, but unsure as to what. In the end, she thought it was the searching itself that had been what she'd sought. And now...Well, she still wasn't sure. She was only tripping and the feeling was good, but they'd all wake up soon enough, and then what?

Waking...Her gaze drifted along the edge of the glade, the strange mingled sound of ancient harp and contemporary synthesizer drawing thoughts from her like a bee drawing nectar from a flower, the sound of old and new entwined, notes falling like pollen from that bee's wing...Pollen to seed, seed to new growth, blossom to pollen—a circle was what the music seemed to tell her. Once those trees that ringed the glade were only seeds. Once—

She caught a flash of movement, yellow amidst the brown and green, and knew a quick fear.

"Jeran!" she called above the music.

But Tak was already taking control of their body. The synth/arp fell from fingers that no longer knew how to work it, but even Tak's speed wasn't enough. The Warden fired from the wood's edge and Jeran took a hit.

Tak blanked the pain, but his left arm was useless. It was too far across the glade to launch a counterattack, but there was nowhere to take shelter. If he could only hold the Warden off until the others got free...

"Move!" Tak shouted at the other two, using Jeran's voice.

The harper shook his head. "I'm dead," he said in a strained voice. "He can't kill me again. Not here, not now."

The laser burned the air between them, charring a long streak across the oak's trunk.

"Do you want to stick around and find out?"

317

The stranger's voice coming from Jeran's lips suddenly registered.

"Who are you?" Kiern demanded.

"Move!"

Blanking the pain wasn't doing much good. The laser had sealed off the severed veins, but the raw nerve ends were more than he could handle. The only thing keeping the Warden at a distance was that he didn't know what weapons they had, if any. He'd realize soon enough that they were unarmed and if they weren't in the woods and running by then...The world swayed in his vision.

With enough concentration he could teleport the short distance between the Warden and them. But the aftereffects of it would leave him in no condition to repair their body. If he could...His... Jeran's...his legs crumpled under him and he pitched forward. Cassie caught him just before he hit the grass.

"Help me get him out of here," she cried to Kiern.

The Warden advanced across the glade, weapon leveled, gaunt features settling into a confidence Cassie wished he didn't feel. She struggled with Jeran's weight and shot a glance at the harper to see why he'd ignored her. But Kiern was staring at the Warden, his own features twisted into the grim semblance of some wild beast.

"This circle I will not see completed," he said. "Not again."

He reached for Jeran's synth/arp.

CRSO

F'Uhol punched the control of the comm-link with the bridge.

"Tadder here."

"Is Kymms on the bridge?"

"Right beside me, sir."

"Tell him to get his ass down here with a half-dozen security men," f'Uhol demanded.

Without signing off, he turned to the door of the observation room and drew his laser pistol.

"What are you doing?" Lawell cried.

"What do you think I'm doing? I'm going to blow that stammin' lock off the door!"

"But..."

"Look, man! All Hath's breaking loose in there. Are you going to stand around gawking and whistling 'Tucker's Star,' or give me a hand?"

Lawell looked through the partition. A raw hole had blossomed in the starbard's shoulder. It looked, for all the world, like he'd been shot, the Medic thought. Cassie had slumped across his body. Now she rolled off the bunk. Lawell winced as her head hit the floor. By the time he reached f'Uhol's side, the security head had melted the door's locking mechanism and half of the door's frame and was kicking it in.

"Don't touch her skin!" Lawell called as the door gave way.

F'Uhol nodded. He had the brief thought that they should replace all sliding doors with the swinging kind they had in old holograms, at least for occasions like these. Kneeling by Cassie's side, he gingerly touched her shoulder. Having already seen how quick the drug could work, he wasn't about to repeat her mistake.

"She's out for the count," he said. "Just like them. What do you think got into her?"

"Space-cafard? Who knows?"

"What about the starbard?"

The medic moved to Jeran's side to study the shoulder wound and shook his head. "Looks like a laser wound. See how clean the edges are?" He glanced from f'Uhol's pistol to the door, then back to the wound.

"My shots weren't even near him. Besides. He got that before we broke in. What about the Warden?"

"No change there."

At that moment the security men entered with their weapons drawn.

"What's up, Kant?"

Tim'en Kymms, the *Lenneth*'s pilot, took in the slagged lock mechanism and the captain's inert body with a quick glance.

F'Uhol shook his head wearily. "Triple case of fayne-poisoning." He beckoned to the security men. "I want those two in stasis-bonds — take care you don't make skin contact. Tim'en, give me a hand with the captain, would you?"

Gingerly, they lifted her onto one of the two remaining bunks in the observation room.

"I heard about those two," Kymms said. "But how did the captain get it?"

"Touched the bard—don't ask me why—and went out like a stammin' light. Looks like you'll be captaining the *Lenneth* for the duration, Tim'en."

"Wonderful," the pilot replied without enthusiasm.

CRSO

Kiern never had a chance.

Whatever he had planned or meant to do with Jeran's synth/arp died stillborn. As he reached for the instrument, the Warden tightened his finger on the firing lever of his laser and kept it depressed. The beam of amplified light seared the air as it cut the young harper down. The stench of burned flesh made Cassie's stomach lurch, but she couldn't look away. Clutching Jeran's shoulders, she stared as the Warden loosened his finger and the laser died. The muzzle of the weapon swiveled until its sights settled on her.

"H-hath."

The word stuck in her throat.

"No," the Warden said. "Even Hath is too good for his like. Kells!"

He spat on the grass between them. The laser never wavered in his hand.

"What do you want with us?"

"With you, Captain? Nothing. I apologize for any inconvenience this affair might have caused you. I want the starbard, that is all. The Kell was simply a...bonus, shall we say?"

"But you killed him."

"We are licensed to do what we will with Kells. And a slain Kell means there will be one less in the Dominion—surely that is explanation enough? Though—" His face took on a thoughtful look, "—what a Kell's death in this fayne-born dream might mean is open to conjecture."

"You're licensed to capture them, not kill them."

"And what do you supposed we do with them after they are captured? Turn them loose so that they can spread their damnable lies against the Church once more? We are a strength in the Dominion still, Captain, so long as we do not overstep our bounds. Ridding the universe of Kells is no crime. They are gypsies—thieves, spacejackers and worse. There is not one planet authority that will vouch for them. Now, if you please. Step back from the bard."

With his weapon trained on her she could only do as she was told. Using his free hand, the Warden withdrew a small object from under his robes. Cassie caught a brief glimpse of a black meshsuit under the yellow cloth before the folds fell back into place. Then she looked at what the Warden held. The object appeared to be a ball, mostly comprised of wires. When the Warden shook it out, it took a cap-like shape that he placed over Jeran's skull.

"A psi-damper," Cassie said.

The Warden nodded. "With a few modifications. With this in place, the psi has no thoughts whatsoever—a convenient way to keep a prisoner, don't you think? Without a will, without even a thought, what can he do? It is, of course, merely a precaution. If, as it appears, that what is done in this place reflects as well in the real world, then the damper should hold him even if he throws off the effects of the fayne before I do. He won't be harmed by it, I can assure you."

"What are you going to do with him?"

Cassie was surprised that her voice remained as steady as it did. She was trying not to look at Kiern's corpse, but the more effort she put into ignoring it, the more aware of it she was. She'd never seen a man killed before.

The Warden smiled. "Our starbard here appears to be a most remarkable creature, Captain. Some sort of genetic mutation, I should think. He, or it, warrants further study—but only under laboratory conditions."

"You're going to kill him, too! There are laws—"

"There *are* laws," he agreed, "but few of them apply to the Church. Still, if questioned, I'll have to swear that he was a..." He glanced at Kiern's body. "Why, a Kell, of course."

"I'll fight that. When we return to the ship—"

"You will do nothing of the kind, Captain. I know that you seem to have some sort of affection for this creature, but I can assure you that it is misplaced. You are not even of the same race, no matter how much it might seem so. Look, if you will. Look at his wound. Does anything even remotely human heal that quickly?"

Cassie looked. Already the blackened edges of Jeran's wound were reddening, closing, forming scabs. She looked away, unsure whether the heightened queasiness she felt was due to the wound itself or the method of its healing.

"He's still a sentient being. He still has rights."

The Warden shook his head. "With the damper in place, sentient is the one thing he is not, Captain. Now please," he cut off her next protest. "If you would settle down, we can rest here at our leisure and wait for the drug to wear off."

He followed his own advice, but kept the laser trained on Cassie.

"Tell me, Captain," he added after a moment. "How did you and this Kell come to be here?"

Cassie ignored him. She sat with her legs tucked under her and stared at Jeran's face. What was going on inside his mind? Could a psi-damper be modified to such an extent that it would just wipe him out? The Warden was very sure of himself and there didn't seem to be anything she could do. If she could remove the damper, get the Warden off-guard somehow, perhaps...She continued to study Jeran's features, wondering why she couldn't just let things lie. Both Jeran and the Warden would be off the ship when they landed on Weyth and she'd never see either of them again. Especially not Jeran. Not when the Warden was finished with him.

That thought brought a tightness to her throat. She had to do something.

"I didn't go under the same time that you and Jeran did," she said suddenly. "We have your attack down on vid—an unwarranted attack on a private citizen who you can't prove to be a Kell. The Church may be allowed a lot, but hardly full discretionary power."

"Please," the Warden replied. "Do not be so infantile. I have had this particular being under study for a full Dominion year. He is hardly a citizen. Do you know that there is no listing for him in Central? The only 'Jeran an Bodach' listed was an advance scout for an exploration mission who died on an asteroid some seventy years ago. And while I will admit that he bears a striking resemblance to holo-photos of that scout, he could scarcely have remained unchanged over so many years, now could he? An Bodach crashed when he was twenty-five. Add some seventy years and that would make him ninety-five. Even with rejuvenation surgery he would still appear to be middle-aged.

"Look," he added, lifting Jeran's chin back to expose his neck. "Do you see any surgical scars?"

Cassie shook her head.

The Warden smiled. "I rest my case. And, Captain, I hope that will be the end of this line of inquiry. You will, of course, offer me all possible aid, once we are back on board the *Lenneth?*"

"Of course," Cassie said, trying not to choke on the words.

She'd rather see him in Hath. The ease with which he manipulated her, the way he and his kind bent the rules to suit their own ends, made her sick. He treated her as though she were still the naïve planet-bound girl who'd longed to be free of her world's limited options. The trouble was, underlying the worldly starship captain, she still retained many elements of that naïveté. Like the romantic impulse that had gotten her here in the first place. And when she thought of all the times she'd had Wardens and their Kellian prisoners aboard, she felt like weeping.

Certainly the Church had played its part in the history of the Dominion. It had been the unifying factor in the rebellious years, a militaristic organization that every Dominion-held system at least paid lip-service to. Its Holy Leader was a man who had died 1700 years ago, but whose mind was kept alive in the memory banks of the Church's Master Computer situated in the Turuo System.

In essence, at one time the Church *had been* the Dominion, affecting the destinies of a thousand thousand planets with its doctrines and tenets. But while its unifying strengths had kept the Dominion from disintegrating into a hundred warring fractions, in this stage of the Dominion's history, it was only grudgingly respected by most, and loved by few. Cassie, never having had much to do with the Church or its Wardens except for ferrying the odd yellow-robed acolyte between systems, had never really considered what it was, or what power it still held. But now, in only a few terse sentences, the full enormity of its activities were brought home to her. Her own ineffectualness only served to heighten her frustration.

Again she looked at Jeran, wishing she could think of a way to free them both, here and now, so that they could finish this thing in this place of fayne-dreams, so that while the Church itself would go on, they would have at least frustrated this one arm of its power. But while the object of her attention seemed oblivious to what was going on around it, in reality, Jeran was very much aware, though he was even more helpless than the *Lenneth's* captain.

The psi-damper had trapped Tak, not him. When they'd fallen, it had been Tak's mind controlling their body, Tak's mind that held the psionic power that the damper centered on. So while Jeran was free to wander through his own mind, he had no control over his musculature.

He'd listened to all that was said with a growing panic that threatened to overshadow any fear he might have had before. He had never been a particularly brave person. Independent to a degree, and fairly sufficient, perhaps, but until he'd met with Tak, he'd never been in a situation that required martial courage. Since then, Tak had taken care of those incidences. But now...now...

Jeran had never thought to feel lonely inside his own mind. There were times they shared thoughts and were to all intents and purposes one being. At other times they were two entities in the one body, conversing with each other, sharing the control of their body. To be stripped of that other being who had been with him for most of the years of his life sent Jeran's mind skittering through the dark places of his soul, starting at shadows, screaming silently, falling through endless black reaches from which there was no escape. He cared nothing about the Warden or his plans. All there was, was the soul-wrenching terror of being alone and trapped in a body that would not obey his simplest command.

It was at the very ebbing of all rational thought, as he was about to let his mind shatter into the welcoming embrace of encompassing madness, that he drew back and knew that he could not let it end in such a way. The constant reliance on Tak's strength of will, on his inimitable skills, had sapped any potential growth that Jeran might have had in similar directions. But those potentials were still there. Ultimately, it was the remembrance of Tak and all they'd been through, all that the alien had done for him — even in those days when he'd screamed and pleaded to be left alone in his own mind — that lifted him from the razor-thin edge of final defeat.

The emotion was new to him — this hardening of will, this sense of purpose — but it grew, imperceptibly at first, then by leaps and bounds, stronger. He readdressed old memories, saw that Tak had not been fearless, he had merely gone ahead, repressed his fears as best he could while he strived. There was nothing brave about a fearless man. A fearless man had no inner turmoil to overcome. As that knowledge was assimilated, the new purpose he felt became something he could use, something he could not only rely on, but should never allow to slip away again.

He let his mind drift over the situation and possibilities flew thick and fast. First and foremost—though his body wasn't his to command, the damper had only trapped the one mind. Since he still thought and felt, *he* was free. And not helpless. For he had Tak's powers still at his command, Tak's psionic strengths and abilities. The psi-damper could only work neurologically. It was not programmed for the possibility that one body might house more than one entity.

But having access to Tak's psionics and utilizing them were two different matters. He'd never learned more than some basic exercises. He couldn't teleport them to safety—even Tak had trouble with that. Jeran also had trouble simply receiving somebody's thoughts. Tak had a delicate, finely attuned touch, where he lumbered like a two-ton Gralian behemoth. Still…The captain would have some martial training. If he could cause a diversion—enough of one to give her time to release the damper—and if she recognized the opportunity when it arose…

Jeran took the equivalent of a deep breath and tried to still the jumble of his thoughts. The Warden's face shimmered in his mind's eye and he felt anger seethe inside him. What the Church had done to Kiern, not once, but twice. What it meant to do to him…

Slowly he forced the ugly emotion aside. He needed a clear mind. He needed…

He recalled Kiern's roadsong and set it humming in his mind. And as the tune soothed him, bringing some semblance of peace to his frightened anger, a plan arose. It needed only the captain's help. If she could understand. If she could take the chance he offered. They wouldn't get a second one.

CRSO

Kant f'Uhol paced the infirmary, echoing Cassie's earlier impatience. Glancing from the partition to the viewscreens where the medic's computer showed a printout of the three fayne-victims' life functions, he stopped by Lawell's seat and sat down beside him.

"What's it all mean?" he asked, indicating the screens.

The medic shrugged. "Simply that there's been no change. You have to be patient, Kant."

"To Hath with stammim' patience. We'll be warping out of reverspace in another twenty-six ship hours. What are we going to do when the Weyth authorities want to talk to the captain?"

"We'll simply explain what happened and — "

"Explain? How do we explain what Cassie's gone and done? They'll revoke her bloody papers and put her under probe to find out what came over her. Where does that leave her? Where does that leave us? I've got ten years seniority on this stammin' ship. You think I want to start all over again?"

Lawell sighed. There didn't seem a pleasant way out of this situation. They wouldn't even be able to press charges against the Church for the Warden's attack that started the whole mess. He looked into the observation cubicle where the starbard and Warden were secured with stasis bonds. They were effectively immobilized, the starbard's wound had almost closed. But that didn't help their problem at all. Unless they could rouse the captain before they warped from reverspace...

"Listen," f'Uhol said suddenly. "He's started again."

Humming came from the cubicle's speaker grille. Remembering what had happened the last time they'd heard it, Lawell reached over to his terminal and punched a button, breaking the connection. The sound was cut off immediately.

"We could say she came down with something," Lawell said. "Migraine, sleeping sickness, whatever. Once the drug wears off, there is no trace of it left in the body."

"I suppose we could," f'Uhol said. Leaning back in his chair, he made a bridge with his fingers and stared broodingly through the plastiglass partition. "And while we're at it, we could dump those two before we warp into Weyth's space."

Lawell shook his head. "They have records of their passage on Tuorn. We could wipe the ship's memory banks and nobody would miss the bard, but the Warden..." He frowned. "It isn't exactly ethical."

"Neither's spraying dream-dust around on a starship," the security head muttered. "But then, I was just indulging in a little wishful thinking."

CR&O

Sunk in depression, Cassie reviewed her situation for the hundredth time in an hour. She weighed common sense against her outraged morals, worked out plans but discarded them as quickly as they came. The Warden never let up his vigilance. He didn't even seem to blink. And he needed only to lift his laser and depress its trigger to forestall any attempt she might make. Her frustration went far beyond her initial attraction to the starbard and her subsequent worrying for him. She felt a need to strike back, to somehow make amends for her years of blind complacency, even if it was only against one Warden and not the Church as a whole. But while the need was strong and the will was there, a solution failed to present itself.

Caught in her brooding, it took her a few moments to react to the sound of harping that started up — first as an almost inaudible murmur, then a sound that grew in volume, faltering notes becoming sure, a familiar air...

The Kellian roadsong.

Slowly she turned. Her eyes went wide when she saw the Kell's harp playing by itself. Preternatural fear went through her like an electric shock, making her every hair feel like it was standing on end. Glancing at the Warden, she saw a flicker of uncertainty in his eyes. He stood, the movement swift and smooth, laser held ready, finger caressing the trigger as he searched the glade, looked back to the harp, searched the glade again. He was about to blast the instrument when something in Cassie's eyes made him turn. A strange figure flickered into life in the middle of the glade and began to advance on them.

He was like a Kell, but such a Kell as neither of them had seen before. He triggered a memory in Cassie, a vague recollection reminiscent of the roadsong itself. Horns lifted from his brow in a wide sweep, stag's horns with twelve points to each antler. He wore a cloak of leaves, was red-haired and green-eyed, and those eyes held death.

The Warden aimed and fired, but to no effect. The figure continued his advance and all the while the harp played the Kellian roadsong, played on its own, and then Cassie knew.

It was impossible, but it had to be. Somehow Jeran was responsible for this. Unable to move, he had still managed to circumvent the damper enough to create that image of the horned Kell and play the harp. She remembered his psi-rating, realized the opportunity that was being provided, and leapt into action.

She lunged at Jeran, fingers tearing at the psi-damper. But it was attached too well. Probes had channeled through Jeran's skull, their needles pouring the psi-damping fluid through his nervous system to paralyze body and mind. The Warden turned, saw what she was doing and leveled his weapon as he, too, understood.

With her fingers still entangled in the damper's wiring, she twisted her body and kicked the weapon from his hands. Then she had the damper free — its deadly machination turned into so much useless wire and circuitry. She flung it at the Warden's face and dove for his weapon, but he was on her before she'd gotten half the way. Wriggling free, she rolled to her feet and faced him, standing between him and the weapon.

She was trained, as all starship personnel were, in basic hand-to-hand combat, but she knew she was no match for the Warden. Where Dominion personnel learned martial skills as just another part of their training, a perfunctory exercise at best, the Church trained their acolytes from their formative years and on, creating ruthless fighting machines.

The Warden came to his feet with fluid grace and for a long moment regarded her. Then he moved forward, his hands a flutter of elegant motion. She blocked his initial attack, felt an arm break under one blow, her feet kicked out from under her with another. Pain seared up her arm and raced through her as she toppled to the ground. She saw him above her, yellow robes swaying, eyes devoid of emotion as he bent towards her, fingers curled for a killing blow. She knew she could do nothing to stop him, could scarcely think through her pain, when —

"Warden!"

The yellow-robed acolyte turned from his victim to face Jeran.

Eyes narrowed, the Warden advanced.

<You've done what you could!> Tak cried inside their mind. <Now leave it to me.>

<But...>

328

Jeran was flushed with the success of his efforts. Somehow it seemed to him that he could finish this thing that he had begun.

<Jeran!>

The harping still rang through the glade. For a flickering instant, Jeran listened, saw the horned figure that regarded them all with his inhuman eyes, saw Cassie lying still on the ground, her face white with shock and pain, saw the Warden coming for them with death in his skilled hands. He gave the reins of their body over to Tak and let the alien meet the Warden's attack.

Their struggle might have been liquid beauty to watch, had it not been filled with such deadly intent. As it was, they seemed evenly matched as they traded blow for blow, not the one of them landing. Then Tak, the memory of his defeat still rankling inside, began a maneuver that left the Warden dazzled. There was no human defense for it. It was as alien to the Warden's martial knowledge as Tak himself was to Jeran. He seemed to float before the Warden's eyes, to drift close like smoke. His finger's reached out to caress the Warden's chest and the tall gaunt man stood swaying for long moments until his eyes glazed. Then he pitched forward and died.

Tak stood over him, looking down with a mingling of curious emotions. There was the regret of taking a life, even such a life. At the same time he felt a certain pride that he had completed that intricate maneuver, even in this coarse body that he borrowed. Shaking his head, he withdrew into their mind, returning the control to Jeran. The starbard stared with wide eyes at the dead acolyte, then made his way to Cassie's side.

<You've changed,> Tak remarked.

<Not really.>

Jeran still felt shaken.

The alien smiled. <Still, there's an edge to your will, Jeran an Bodach, that was never there before.>

Jeran could feel his neck redden. <I...I've decided to pull my own weight.>

<So you have.>

Jeran knelt by Cassie and stared helplessly at her arm. Stroking her brow, he said to Tak, <This is really more your line.>

The alien nodded. He took charge once more. A pinch of a nerve in Cassie's neck and she went under. He set the arm and, tearing a strip from their tunic, bound it up as best he could. Then he brought her around again. She blinked and, looking up into Jeran's face, found a smile, albeit a small one.

"Guess I didn't do too well, did I?"

Jeran shook his head. "Without you, we'd still be trapped."

"Where did you ever come up with that projection of the horned Kell?" she asked.

"Projection? I..."

Jeran looked up, but the horned figure was gone. The harping had stopped as well and, when he glanced back at the oak, he saw that Kiern's body and his harp were both gone.

"I only made the harp play," he said at last.

She followed his gaze. "What happened to the body?"

"I guess he was right. He couldn't die here. Not again."

"Was he the horned man?"

Jeran thought about his first impressions of the wood. There was a harping wizard who wore a green cloak and guarded the wood, who had red hair and green eyes and whose name no man knew.

"I think he was," he said. "Partly, at least."

<Tak? What's going on?> he added soundlessly.

<You've got me. I never pretended to understand any of it.>

<But...?>

<I think we're going back. Better tell the captain that she'll follow us soon enough.>

"Captain...ah, Cassie," Jeran began. "The fayne's wearing off of us—of me, I mean. If you just stay here and be quiet, you'll be along soon enough."

She smiled. "I'm not worried. See you on the *Lenneth*."

Jeran opened his mouth to answer, but then he woke up in the observation cubicle of the *Lenneth* and couldn't move.

<Stasis bond,> Tak said. <Looks like our troubles are starting all over again.>

Jeran didn't even want to think about it.

ᘓᔓᘔ

A month later, by prearrangement, Jeran and Cassie met again in a small establishment just by the space docks in Kirwynda, Weyth's largest spaceport. Cassie slipped into the booth beside him and nodded approvingly at the simplicity of his disguise. Padding in the cheeks, straight black hair, blue contacts for the eyes, the flamboyant garb of a starbard traded in for a plain gray flightsuit. The synth/arp was stowed away in a spacer's travelsack. If they hadn't specified the fifth booth from the door, she might have passed him by herself.

"How's the arm?"

"Good as new. I didn't think you'd be here. Did you have any trouble landing?"

<Just a thirty kilometer walk to the nearest port,> Tak said.

"Not much," Jeran replied, ignoring Tak. "Did you find the shuttle?"

Cassie shook her head. "Our insurance covered it."

"How about the Church authorities?"

"They're still looking for you — 10,000 credits if brought in alive — but the furor's mostly died down. The *Lenneth*'s leaving this evening if you still want to come."

"It won't be too dangerous for you?"

"Not for me. But how about yourself?"

Jeran drew out a new identi-card and showed it to her.

<Pity we can't tell her how clever I was getting that for us,> Tak remarked. <Hacking into the 'puter and building a new history for us.>

<Maybe we will tell her,> Jeran said.

Tak sighed. <After seventy years without any serious entanglements,> he began.

But Jeran wasn't listening to him again.

"I keep thinking of that horned man," Jeran said.

Cassie put a finger to his lips. "I think you talk too much," she said, snuggling close to him.

<I think she's right,> Tak added and discreetly retired to a part of their mind where he occupied himself with some stored logistics material that he'd put away for times like these.

The Dralan: A Tale of the Shift Worlds

(with Roger Camm)

This means nothing. The open warfare recedes
to become an invisible background—so what? As long
as the Companies exist, the fighting will go on. Not
so openly, perhaps. With less discernible loss of
properties and lives, perhaps. But it will continue.
How can it be stopped?

> —from an interview with Dr. Hansd
> Wolner, Head of Corporate Studies
> at the Kolder Institute, WST* 86,
> in reference to the signing of the
> Diven Peace Pact in 2893.
> *(*West Shift)*

She awoke with a dull throbbing in the back of her head. The sun
was a yellow glare in her eyes, tinged with the greens of a thin
canopy of yew and ash, cedar, mottled oak. She blinked in its
brightness. Lying very still, she listened to the forest stir around
her.

A sense of urgency nagged at the edges of her consciousness.
She seemed to remember flickering shadows, a vague sense of
danger and —

The wind shifted to bring the sharp odor of burned plastics and melted circuitry biting at her nostrils. The hazy uncertainties focused. Her shifter! *The Prospern.* Where...?

She pushed herself up on her elbows, head swimming with the sudden movement. Dampening a rush of panic, she searched her surroundings.

The forest towered on all sides, breaking into a small clearing to her right where the remains of her shifter smoldered. The small ship's tail-bubble protruded from the smoking crater of its impact. Its pointed nose was buried in the ground. The vegetation was blackened for a dozen yards around.

She stared bleakly at the wreckage. If she'd been aboard when it had crashed...She shook her head, grimacing as new waves of pain shot through her. Rubbing her temples with shaking fingers, she tried to collect her thoughts. She'd been amusing herself with a game of solo-dars on the ship's 'puter when —

CR&O

A two-tiered warning preceded the strange shifter's sudden appearance. On board the Ravenheir porting shifter, *The Prospern*, Marta Chaykin froze. Her ears rang with the warbling high-pitched klaxon in her helmet's comm-unit, echoing seconds after the shift-'puter's warning.

She punched the viewscreen's controls into operation and activated the 'puter's defense screens with her psi-link. Half-shaped shields shimmered about *The Prospern* as the strange shifter loosed its first barrage.

Lancing rays sliced through the partial shields. *The Prospern* bucked and Marta cursed, holding onto the control panel to keep her balance. She mind-set a new pattern in the 'puter. Staring at the attacker, she watched in horror as it fired again. Displacement circuits blew in the next attack. They were in mid-shift — that gray place between the worlds. Phasing in now — where in Raven's Hell were they? A simple porting-shift, 17 STs west of Third Base would put them —

Another blast hit the already crippled shifter. *The Prospern* shuddered. They were spinning on a random course now, the strange shifter still firing. What was going on?

Marta shook her head as she took over more and more of the 'puter's blown circuits. Who was attacking them? A rival Company—even pirates—would have used a crazer like the one mounted on her own craft. The crazer's blast was such that it rendered the crew unconscious, simultaneously disrupting the 'puter's defense systems long enough for a grapple-link to be established. Nobody shot down shifters anymore. There wasn't a war going on—at least not a visible one, not on settled shifting lines—not since the Diven Pact.

The Prospern's tail-bubble took a direct hit and cracked. Shards of tail-glass spilled into the control room, showering Marta. The gray mists of mid-shift were thick in her throat, choking her. The wrecked shifter chose that moment to tear into phase. The night skies of a world—what world?—shimmered in the viewscreens. *The Prospern* plunged downward.

Marta cut off her strained link with the disabled 'puter and fought her way to her feet. Stumbling to the door of the control room, she sent out a mind-call, hoping that her one-man crew had already realized the enormity of their situation.

Abandon. Abandon. Code K double 5. Abandon.

At the door she paused long enough to snatch up her per-gun and a bandoleer of spare shells. She forced her way through the door.

The enemy's barrage continued. *The Prospern* shuddered under each onslaught. Through the door, she breathed a sigh of relief to see Hallie waiting for her. The escape flitter was already primed.

"Who's attacking—" Hallie began.

Another blast hit *The Prospern* knocking them to the floor.

Marta scrambled to her feet. "Damned if I know! Let's get that flitter going."

They were no sooner aboard, flitter-shields on full, when *The Prospern*'s engines took a direct hit. Trying to keep down the raw taste that was rising up in her throat, Marta braced herself as the flitter shot out of the wrecked shifter. She pushed past Hallie and punched the flitter's controls. The engine died and they were floating on anti-grav. The flitter's small rear screens showed the strange shifter behind them. It was knobby and gray, devoid of markings. Would engine silence convince them that the flitter was no more than debris? If so, they had a slim chance of escaping. Once they were near the ground...

For all that the anti-grav was operating on full, the ground still rushed up at a frightening speed. Forests filled the fore-screens. Marta buckled on her per-gun, slinging the bandoleer over her shoulder. She stared at the fore-screens. The forest took on sharper focus. A pre-techno world? And if so, which Company had the most shares?

"They're following."

Hallie's quiet statement drew Marta's eyes to the rear screens. The enemy shifter was approaching swiftly. A sudden slash of light cut the night air and a piece of debris two hundred yards from them exploded.

Marta cursed and strapped herself into the co-pilot's seat.

"Engines on," she said to Hallie. "Let's try to get this damn thing down before they zero in on *us!*"

The flitter's engines hummed into life. The small craft shot forward. It swept over the treetops. Behind them, the enemy opened fire once more. Lasers bit the night about them.

Hallie's knuckles were white on the controls. Body tense, he concentrated on a random course. A direct hit smashed into the flitter's shields. Though the shields held, the whole craft rocked violently under the blow.

"Down!" Marta cried. "Get us down!"

"But—"

"Down!"

The flitter's shields couldn't take another direct hit. They weren't designed for warfare in the first place. Hallie steered them into the trees, cutting the engines suddenly. The anti-grav working against the forest now — spluttered, then brought them up sharp.

They'd come down near the wreck of *The Prospern*. Marta could see it in the screens, half-buried in the ground not a hundred yards from their hiding place. Lasers still blasted around them, but with engine silence they couldn't home in on their target. She turned to Hallie and grinned, weak with relief.

"If they armed this thing," Hallie said tapping the flitter's controls, "we could give 'em a run for their money."

Marta nodded, thinking again, who were they? It seemed beyond belief that any Company would chance another outbreak of war. The very thought made her —

The flitter rocked and a blinding glare gouged her eyes. We're hit, she thought. Raven's Hell! We're hit!

The last thing she remembered was flicking the control of her ejector seat. Then the blackness came.

ᘓᘔᗱ

Staring about the quiet forest, it was hard to believe it had been the scene of such violence. Marta stumbled to her feet, leaning heavily on a tree. She saw her ejector seat a good six yards to her left — a crumpled ruin wrapped about the trunk of an old oak. Her helmet lay by her feet. She stared numbly at *The Prospern*. Had the crew of the strange shifter checked the results of their handiwork? Did they guess that she'd survived and were they, even now, looking for her? Did —

Hallie!

The thought cut through her like a knife. He'd been with her on the flitter when it was hit and…

ᘓᘔᗱ

She found him in what remained of the flitter, just beyond *The Prospern*. Whatever fate had guided her hand to the control of her ejector seat had passed him by. A piece of twisted metal, torn from the undercarriage, had almost cut him in two and…

Marta turned away, emptying the contents of her stomach on the ground beside the flitter. She knelt in the charred grass, stomach still heaving long after it was empty, the weight of her upper torso supported on trembling arms. Numb with shock, it was long moments before she realized that something, an alien intelligence, was touching her mind with —

— *searching thoughts…poised and cold…sharp and hard as steel…searching* —

A choking fear thickened into blind panic. She lifted her head, eyes rolling, and heard the low thrum of an approaching shifter. The need for action over-ruled her fear. Adrenalin rushed through

337

her, clearing her mind. She bolted for the undergrowth, turning her thoughts to —

— an itchy hind leg…curiosity as to the burned machine…a yearning for tender clover shoots —

The searching presence hovered over her. Under her hare-thoughts, Marta shivered. Sweat broke out on her brow, falling in small beads to the front of her shifter-suit. The other mind worried at her thoughts, tugging and appraising. Then, as quickly as it had come, the presence left her to fare further afield, fading abruptly.

Hidden in the undergrowth, Marta listened to the shifter circling the wreckage of *The Prospern*. She remained motionless long after the sound of its engines was gone. Then she moved deeper into the underbrush. Thorns caught at the ridges of her shifter-suit and she loosened them patiently. She'd gone no more than a mile when the presence came sweeping back. Again it investigated her hare-thoughts.

The touch was brief this time — gone almost as soon as it had come. Marta wiped her brow with her sleeve, muscles tight. With that second touch, she'd recognized the mind for what it was. Before, when *The Prospern* had been destroyed and its flitter soon after, she'd been afraid. Her enemy had been unknown. Now that she knew what she was up against, she had a name for her fear, something concrete to focus on. She wasn't sure which was worse.

Marta Chaykin was a slender woman in her early twenties, standing just under five and a half feet. Long black hair — hanging now in wet sticky strands — framed an oval face. Her eyes were deep brown, large and wide-set. With her bearing and her age, and in her dark gray shifter-suit, she looked just like what she was — a young graduate, fresh out of Ravenheir Academy.

She was a little young to be a 'Puterlink, but the psi rating on the left breast of her suit gave her a Y7 — high for her age. When her prenticing was done, she would be promoted to working the High Shifts and could forget the Low porting runs. If she lived that long.

For the presence that had come tugging at her mind belonged to a dralan — a telepath with a rating ten times her own, a psi whose mind could lock onto another's with the same ease that Marta linked her own mind to a shifter's 'puter. And, from that second brief touch, she'd caught a plain thought. The dralan wanted her, and he wanted her dead. The whys of her situation had become almost irrelevant now. First she had to survive.

She knew the basic mind-guards and shields. The trouble was that they would give her away as quickly as an unshielded mind. Which, she realized, was how they'd zeroed in on the flitter. Engine silence had meant nothing, when the dralan could home in on their thoughts. But that was then, and this was now. She knew what she was up against, if nothing else. The key here was subtlety. She had to become a part of the environment. A small animal. A bird.

Ranjol—one of her instructors back at the Academy—had been a master of such subterfuge. Once, he'd hidden under animal thoughts for a full week while the dralans of Alatea Ltd. scoured three worlds for him. She could do worse than emulate his example. And though she was alone now, as soon as *The Prospern* was discovered missing, there'd be search parties out looking.

The confidence that thought gave her didn't last long. How long would it take her own people to find her? She could be on any one of an almost infinite number of worlds that existed parallel to one another—shift after shift after...Even if they contacted her, how could she give them coordinates when she didn't even know her position herself? And then there were the personnel of the unknown shifter. The dralan. She'd have to maintain a psi silence for fear of him finding her before her own people did.

With an effort, she turned aside her negative train of thought. She was still alive, at least. Bruised, but functional. If she wanted to stay alive she had to keep moving.

CR&O

Near midday she stopped to test the comm-unit on her helmet. She switched the controls to "receive only." She went through band after band until she was rewarded with a static that cleared into intelligible speech.

" —here, as far as I can see. Any luck on your side, Jaerd? Holne out."

"Negative, Holne. Too many large life-forms to get a clear reading." Lord, Marta thought. They even have body-sensors. "Perhaps we should try further south, Kaern? Jaerd out."

"Negative as well. Return to ship. Kaern out."

The clipped speech-pattern of the final voice sent a chill up Marta's spine. In Kaern's voice she recognized the leader of the unknown shifter's crew. Kaern. The dralan.

Not long after the broadcast, she heard the faint hum of their shifter above the trees again and bolted for cover, holding fox-thoughts foremost in her mind. When they had passed on, she kept moving, choosing a direction at random.

Soon the oaks and ash gave way to wilder yew and thick stands of cedar, flanked by high pines and silver fir. Twice more — under the fox-thoughts that hid her own — Marta sensed the questing probe of the dralan's mind. The second probe came just at dusk and was so strong that she was afraid they were almost upon her.

She stood as still as one of the hawks that hovered endlessly above the Academy at Ravenheir's Third Base. The wind licked her hair across her face, tickling cheek and brow. Her helmet hung like a lead weight in her hand while she thought only of —

— *twilight...moon coming...grouse scent...hedgehog (?)...ground squirrel (!)...hunger —*

The dralan's thoughts paused, moving on only when he was assured she was the harmless beast she appeared to be. As the shifter moved away yet again, she dropped her hand to the per-gun that weighted one hip. Gripping its hilt, she felt a sense of support slowly seep through her troubled mind. The gun and a regulation blade were all she had for armament. Not that they would help her a great deal if the shifter caught her alone in the open. But if she was to meet one of the searchers...singly...

She tried not to think of what might happen then. She'd still been in training when the last of the Company wars ended with the Peace Pact signing. In theory she knew what to do. In drill she'd performed at peak requirements. But this would be different. These would be living, breathing people, capable of shooting back. Would she even be able to pull the trigger...? Hallie's face floated in her mind. Her heart hardened at the memory. Considering the question a second time, she knew that she could do it. Given the chance...

CRLED

It was still night when she came awake suddenly, her per-gun gripped in both hands before she was on her feet. She stared into

the surrounding darkness. Something had woken her, something —
She felt the dralan's probe and withdrew behind hare thoughts —
only not quickly enough. Her comm-unit crackled — she'd left it on
the band they were using — and she heard the dralan give her
position to his men. Her thoughts were cloaked now, but she knew
she'd been too late. She could sense them coming. There. A rustle in
the undergrowth.

She slipped into the darker shadows, per-gun in one hand, the
other reaching upward. Catching hold of a branch, she holstered
her pistol and pulled herself up. Her muscles bunched and ached at
the strain she put on them as she made her perch. But the tree gave
out a groan under her weight that sounded like a crack of thunder
to her ears. She poised on the branch, listening.

Again the rustling. To her left. Her per-gun swept in that
direction.

A percussion gun worked on the principal of a small charge in
the casing shell exploding when the firing pin hit it. In turn that
charge loosed the actual missile — a rocket-powered pellet with the
range of a rifle. This close, no matter where she hit her stalker, there
was no way he could survive. But she had to hit him.

There...a darker shadow. Her fingers tensed. There! Squeezing
the trigger, she heard the muffled igniting of the shell, the whisper
as it shot from the barrel, the thud as it struck its target. A scream of
pain tore the night.

She loosened her pressure on the trigger. The exhausted shell
spat out, another slipped into position. Leaning forward, she lost
her grip on her precarious perch and tumbled to the ground in a
sprawl of limbs. She kept a hold of her gun, grunting with pain. The
dralan's web of thoughts drew close — so close — weaving about her,
fixing her position. She heard another man approach.

Rising to her feet, she extended her arm, pulling the trigger. It
fell on a dud shell. She cursed the manufacturer — why couldn't
Ravenheir's factories supply ammunition for their own guns? As
she worked the ejection, the shell jammed. She must have damaged
it in the fall. Cursing, she sped off. There was no time to fix it now.

She ran. Doe-thoughts filled her mind —

—*hooves against pine needles...silent, silent...panic at man-
scent...scent of fresh blood* —

The moon was high when she'd first bolted, low when she finally collapsed in a stand of cedar. Cloaked thoughts, she cried to herself as the doe-thoughts grew hard to hold in place. She clambered into a cedar. Hidden on this new perch, she thought —

— *feathers preened…eyes wide…ears searching the telltale mole rustle…mouse scurry* —

The dralan's mind seemed to fill the woods. It swept over her time and again — went through her like a rushing wind, passing her by, swooping back, searching, searching…Under the owl-thoughts, she was near panic. But gradually the probe faded, the tugging eased. She'd won free again. But for how long?

CR&D

Somehow she slept. When she woke, it was to feel the dralan all about her. She hid under bird thoughts, animal thoughts, and knew she couldn't hold out for another day of this. Her defenses — feeble as they were compared to his — would soon falter and then she'd be at his mercy. There was a sour taste in her mouth. The panic-brink she was so near to grew closer by the moment.

She came to a sudden decision. Dropping to the ground, she sped in the direction of the dralan's searching thoughts — heading for the source. She wore fox-thoughts over her own. She broke out of the woods into a wide meadow dotted with huge scraggly junipers and there — She saw the shifter and the man lying by it and dropped to the ground before he saw her.

Think, she demanded of herself. But it was hard. Just keeping the fox-thoughts in place took almost all her strength,

She looked over the tall grass that hid her from the man. He was hunched over. From my shot, she thought. Raven's Hell! How was he even alive?

She eased back, drawing her per-gun from its holster. She gave it a thorough check. The jammed shell she pried out with her knife. Its earlier malfunctioning had simply been caused by dirt caught in the firing mechanism. From her fall. Still, she wished now that she'd bought a more efficient model on her last leave. For only a hundred more credits —

The dralan's mind-search roared about her — deafening her own thoughts. She strained to find his position. Veins popped out on her

342

brow with the effort. West. He was west. How far she couldn't quite pinpoint. But there was a shifter there for the taking—just across the meadow with only one guard. A wounded guard at that. With it she could make her escape. Then the corp-execs could figure out what was going on.

Drawing on her remaining strength, she built a barrier in her mind, sending it out before her as she edged through the grass. Once she was close enough, she let the barrier slip over the area where the man sat by the shifter. Once it held, she slipped inside and felt...silence.

The dralan was momentarily blocked. He would come running soon, as soon as he sensed this blank fold in the woods. Before that happened, she had a chance to find out the why of the attack and to escape.

She moved lightly through the grass, per-gun raised in her hand, and made her way to where the man still half-lay, half-sat. Doubled over with pain, he never noticed her approach. Two steps away, she called out.

"You!"

He looked up and reached for his own weapon, grimacing with pain. He dropped his hand as he caught the hard look in her eyes. The per-gun remained unwaveringly aimed at him. He stared at her dully.

"What—what do you want?"

A sudden fit of coughing brought blood flecks to his lips and chin. His left arm ended at the elbow, wrapped in blood-soaked cloth. They'd probably sealed the wound with a laser and...Pity came to Marta's eyes. She was the cause of his pain. She...no! They had brought it on themselves. She hardened her heart to him.

"Why?" she asked.

As she spoke, she watched the perimeters of the meadow from the corner of her eye. She expected the other two to come at any moment.

The man shook his head slowly. "You—you're the survivor?"

Marta nodded,

"A girl...nothing but a girl."

Another fit of coughing shook him. There was probably shrapnel lodged in his chest. What he needed was a medic. His fevered eyes fixed on hers.

"I'll tell you...why..." he said. "Too late for you anyway. Kaern'll...get you." More coughing, more blood. "The Companies...we're cutting their...their hold. Become too strong. Starting with Ravenheir...hoping to get you to...to fight among yourselves. We'd...pick up the pieces..."

"Who's we?"

"F—FIR—" He choked suddenly, pitching over on his side.

Marta glanced at him, turned to watch the meadow's edges. Satisfied that she was still alone, she knelt by the man—Holne or Jaerd? Didn't really matter now. Whoever he'd been, he was dead.

She shook her head, lips pursed in thought. FIR. The Federal Investigative Researchers. The government was declaring war on the Companies? That was crazy. The Companies were what kept the government solvent. Except...She nodded slowly. Except if the government controlled industry. Then they'd have everything.

She bit at her lip, thinking. She *had* to get word to Ravenheir. This was far bigger than a Company war. And if it wasn't stopped now...

She ran for the shifter, saw movement far down the meadow. They had come. She'd wasted precious seconds and now it was all ended. For glancing at the shifter, she saw that it had a palm-print lock. That avenue of escape was blocked and—

She dove to the ground as the dralan and his man opened fire. The shots whined above her head, then she was behind the shifter. Edging sideways to offer the smallest target, she chanced a long shot. The per-gun bucked in her hand and she saw one of the men fall. Then she was behind the shifter again.

She eased back on the trigger and the ejected shell spat out. Her hold on her mind-barrier fell under the dralan's superior strength and she felt the rush of his thoughts. So she'd not killed him. Only the two of them remained. She looked around. She could still make the woods, keeping the shifter between him and her line of escape, but then what? She'd still be trapped. More than likely, he'd simply go for reinforcements. She needed his ship to get off this world. It was her only chance.

She evened her breathing and let her mind open. The dralan's thoughts roared into hers, grappling for control. She let them pound at her as she fixed his position. Then, steeling her nerves, she stepped clear of the shifter, firing in the same motion.

She had time to see the dralan's amazement—he was so close. Her shot went a little to the right. He fired as she fell into a roll, missed. She shot again.

She'd hit his weapon. She watched his per-gun explode, taking away his hand. Her own weapon jammed, a plastic casing melted in the overheated barrel, but she had eyes only for the dralan. Her mind reeled under the shock of what she saw, then he was upon her. She twisted in his grip, battering him with her useless gun. And he—the one hand locked on her arm, while from the other wrist hung a mass of wire and metal. Robot? Cyber?

The ruined hand rose to strike her. Adrenalin and fear gave her the strength to pull free. She hit him again with her gun. He staggered and she rolled free. Rising to a crouch, she faced him, panting for breath, fumbling with the workings of her weapon. If she could get the damn casing out...

He stood facing her, eyes intent. She felt the sudden surge of his mind strike hers. She raised her defenses instinctively—barriers that buckled under the dralan's pressure. Her face was white with concentration.

She rose, backed away from him. He followed her, step for step. Her useless per-gun hung in a limp hand and she let it fall to the ground. She could feel herself succumbing to him. He would—Her eyes flickered from the end of his blasted arm, back to his eyes. He would have her in a moment. The battering at her mind rose into a crescendo of white noise. Her hand snaked to her belt, came away with her blade and threw it in the same swift motion.

The dralan began a sidestep he never completed. Her blade plunged into his chest, exploding with a surge of electrical fire. His eyes blanked, then he pitched forward.

Marta stood shaking and stared at his inert form, unable to believe what she'd accomplished. Slowly, she backed away. Moving to the side of the man she'd spoken to, she dragged him to the shifter and set his still warm palm against the palm-print lock. The door hissed open and she climbed in, shutting it behind her.

Collapsing into the pilot seat, she set its controls to manual and primed the engine. With trembling fingers she hit the shift-button. Not until the ship phased into mid-shift did she let out a long sigh.

Her part was done. Whatever came after this would no longer be her concern. The Company's corp-execs would decide how to deal with the FIR. And as for her — well, if there *was* a war brewing, they'd just have to fight it without her.

Keying her helmet's comm-unit into the shifter's 'puter, she sent out a call.

"Porting shift 4-A-3, repeat 4-A-3, to Ravenheir Base. Come in please..."

The Cost of Shadows: A Tale of the Shift Worlds

(with Roger Camm)

Apart from the Assassin Guilds, the prime mercenaries utilized for Company Duels and Termination Postings are the Donsyan. Although they are well versed in the use of the most sophisticated of hardware (see Chapter 11, "The Donsyan War"), their prime weapon is the sword, particularly their own *cledha* with its guardless hilt and slightly curved, single-edged blade.

This predilection, of course, is essential in Termination Postings where sophisticated weaponry has been outlawed because of the possible danger to bystanders (see The Diven Pact). It should be noted that not once has there been a recording of a Donsyan being out-listed or fined for the mismanagement of a Termination Posting—a record unmatched by any Guild.

> —from *An Donsyan: Future Man or Throwback?* by K.R. Stassing, Doctor of Anthropological Studies at the University of Man, EST* 12. *(*East Shift)*

Ranjol Hest walked the length of the bar and slid into a private booth near the rear. He swiveled his seat so that he could watch both the entrance and the aisle through the pale yellow plastic of the booth's door. His brow was beaded with sweat. There was the smell of fear about him. But with his back to the wall, and the cool silence of the booth washing over him, he began to regain a measure of composure.

The small 'puter-grid on his side of the table lit up with three words, one positioned above the other:

FOOD? STIMULANT? DEPRESSANT?

"I'm expecting a guest. We'll order food later," Ran said, surprised that his voice sounded as calm as it did.

He certainly didn't feel calm. Shas! Who would when they'd just been posted?

His voice was picked up by a small voice-keyed receiver. The 'puter-grid flickered an acknowledgment.

STIMULANT? DEPRESSANT? remained on the grid.

"A small hadji," he said.

The grid went blank. Seconds later a small green light appeared on it. Ran punched his credit code into the machine and recited his confirmation sequence into the grid. He then took his drink from the wall cavity that hissed open to his right.

The red liquid was a weak relaxant—something he normally stayed well away from. A "nerve-numb" they called it back at the lab. But Shas knew he could use some numbing just now. He'd stopped sweating, but still felt hot. His shirt was sticky against his skin. Wrinkles furrowed his normally unlined brow. He sipped at his hadji, grimacing at the thought of drinking it as much as at its sweetness, and pulled a 'puter-print from his pocket.

The fear returned as he read it.

—POSTING NOTICE...0600/212/3047/EST 32..............
PRIME BANK BIT NUMBER N0047*9*223...SERIES 4Y7.........

...SUBJECT...RANJOL HEST................................
RAVENHEIR LAB-TECH/'PUTER LINK/PSI-Y14..............
LINK-GROUP 774 RAVENHEIR THIRD BASE/UST 3D3.........
PRESENTLY ON EXTENDED LEAVE/EST 32..................
NO PREVIOUS TERMINATION POSTING.....................
PROJECTED TERMINATION...24 HOURS....................
FROM 0600/212/3047 TO 0600/213/3047.................

EXECUTOR...KRESS SAN ZAR.............................
SYOLTH GUILD/FINNER BRANCH/EST 32....................

YEARS OF SERVICE...11................................

PREVIOUS CONTRACTS...37............................

SUCCESSFUL CONTRACTS...37............................

...BONDING INSURANCE...10,000 CREDITS AT 10%............

PREPAYMENT UPON COMMENCEMENT OF CONTRACT...

BOND FORFEIT IF TERMINATION EXCEEDS PROJECTED TIMESPAN

There was no reason for it, Ran thought. Or at least none that he could think of. But someone wanted him dead and had the credits to afford a Syolth Assassin to ensure that he would be. Within 24 hours. It was within his rights to file a counter posting. But he didn't know who to file it on. Nor could he file it until tomorrow at 0600. By then he would be dead.

He stiffened at the thought; Shas! It wasn't as though he was totally helpless. He'd had a full Academy training—in armed as well as unarmed combat, psi warfare, 'puter-tamping. But even at his peak he'd have been hard put to best a Syolth. Besides, all the action he'd seen had been on Low Tech worlds where his enemies stood out as much as he did. This was *his* homeworld. The assassin could be any one of the 38 million people that lived in Capitol. Ran hadn't been in the field for a good 15 years. His reflexes were slower now. And though there were some things you never forgot, he wasn't a match for a professional operating at his peak. Thirty-seven successful contracts. What was he going to—

There was a flicker of movement at the front entrance. He tensed involuntarily, even with the hadji relaxing his strained nerves. Not even the relaxant could quite still the sudden flash of adrenalin that rushed through him. He had to get out of the booth, into the open where he could move and—

He smiled with weak relief, recognizing the approaching man.

It was the silver shimmer-suit that had fooled him—something a corp-exec might wear; not the usual drab grays and browns of a Donsyan. Ran's smile broadened into honest pleasure as he watched Trigar'n draw near.

The Donsyan's movements were fluid—a trait that a thousand shimmer-suits couldn't disguise. His lean form possessed a feline grace, the poised assurance of a hunting cat. For all that the Donsyan were mercenaries, fighters, Duelers, in the end it was that grace that set them above their fellows. No matter where you found one, on any of a thousand worlds, that sense of a hunting cat's instincts, the supple lean frame, made them stand out. And those with cause to fear, seeing such a man, knew fear.

Ran relaxed again. Trigar'n might be a mercenary like this San Zar who held Ran's contract, but Trigar'n was a friend as well. Ran's friend.

Ran crushed the 'puter-print into his fist as the booth door hissed open. Trigar'n took the seat across from him. The Donsyan's gray eyes rested momentarily on the near empty glass of hadji. His nostrils flared briefly and an eyebrow rose.

"Ran," he said warmly. His eyes flicked back to the hadji glass.

Ran knew what he was thinking. The trouble with a Donsyan was that you couldn't hide anything from them. Let one thing stand out from the norm and they focused on it. Trigar'n knew Ran's feelings about stimulants and depressants. They echoed his own.

"Too much pressure at the lab," Ran began, motioning to the glass. "I—"

"While on leave?" Trigar'n asked, plainly upset at the lie.

Ran flushed. He'd said the first thing that came to mind, never thinking of its incongruity. And for all that his ebony skin hid the flush, he could feel the heat rising there. He began to explain again when Trigar'n raised his hand.

"There is no need to explain," the Donsyan said. "If you don't want to talk about it, I won't press you. It's likely Company business and I couldn't be less interested in that."

He smiled easily and looked at his grid.

FOOD? STIMULANT? DEPRESSANT?

"Food," he said and the grid awoke with lines of fine print.

Ran stared at his friend. Company business? It could well be. But...Silently he handed Trigar'n the crumpled 'puter-print, watching him as he read. A strange thing happened to the Donsyan's face.

The tanned skin smoothed, became almost translucent. The pupils of his eyes expanded to swallow the irises. The features gave the impression of a great calmness about to explode into action.

The Donsyan fighting mask, Ran thought. He'd seen it only once before, on EST 412 when he'd first met Trigar'n.

Trigar'n stood abruptly, the motion smooth and precise. "Cancel food," he said. "Come, Ran."

"But—"

Trigar'n shook his head. "There is no safety in a public place. Even less than in your 'plex. We'll go there now. Together."

"It's not your concern," Ran protested. "Shas knows who's posted me, but there's no need for you to get involved."

Trigar'n stared at him as though he'd been slapped. The huge pupils in his eyes began to throb.

"You are my friend," he said softly, as though that were all that need be said.

ଓଃ୭ଠ

Kress San Zar watched the two men enter the apartment complex that housed his victim's private unit. He recognized Ranjol Hest from the tapes he'd picked up with his contract. But the other—the man in the shimmer-suit—was an uncomfortable unknown. Had Hest hired himself some protection? The stranger moved with a fighter's grace. That could complicate matters somewhat. The 'plex's electronic auto-alarms were all the problems he wanted.

He remained in his floater, staring thoughtfully at the 'plex's now empty lobby. Automatically, he packed equipment into the pockets of his flat-black night suit. Lastly, he snapped a small hand-axe to his belt, complementing its weight with a handful of throwing stars. The latter were poisoned and he fitted them to the belt with care. Then he sat, gathering his inner quiet, and waited.

Extraneous thoughts crept into his meditation. He fingered the haft of his axe and considered again what lay before him. It would be so much easier to cut down this Hest with a long range per-rifle. Or to set an explosive charge in his unit that would take out Hest and half of his neighbors in one fell swoop. San Zar smiled inwardly at the forbidden thought.

Sometimes he wondered if the edged-weapons-only ruling on Postings and Duels was nothing more than some bureaucrat's romantic notion of chivalry rather than a concern for the protection of innocent bystanders. If all citizens were trained in the usage of modern offensive and defensive weaponry, then they could take their own chances. It would make his own job easier at any rate. On the other hand, the chaos that would ensue would be enough to give any Com-Pol exec a migraine. And then there was the *honor* of his Guild and the fealty he owed his axe.

The weapons of a Guildsman had a soul and he, as his axe's priest, held its honor in his trust. As an Assassin, he walked a holy path. Hest's death would be a fitting sacrifice to Chadtha, the Lord of Assassins. San Zar smiled cynically. Hest's death would also free him from his current debts and keep him solvent for at least eight months.

Hest's companion chose that moment to emerge from the 'plex. San Zar's train of thought broke abruptly as he watched the lean form glide down the street, holo-lights glimmering on his shimmer-suit. The stranger reached the end of the block and hailed an auto-cab. Not until the cab's red taillights disappeared into the distance did San Zar relax.

So. The stranger had been a chance companion, not a hired defender. San Zar checked the luminous read-out of his floater's time-keeper. 2300. He had awhile yet.

෬෫

At 0400, San Zar slid from his floater and drew a gaudy party cape around his nightsuit. The cape billowed around his calves as he crossed the street. The 'plex was dark, except for the lobby lights. There lay his first obstacle. 'Puter-directed laser sight-beams wove a patternless web back and forth across the foyer.

It had been easier in the old days, before the Diven Pact, before the non-interference laws and bonds for accidental damages. The Guildmasters never tired telling of them. Still, the new generation of Guildsmen had found ways of coping with both the laws and the more sophisticated defenses. Living in interesting times. San Zar smiled, recalling the old proverb that was known on a hundred worlds.

A small piece of plastic was sufficient to jimmy open the 'plex's front door. Some things never change, he thought. Easing the door open, he dropped three deflated dummies at his feet, then lobbed thermal grenades to either side of the lobby to confuse the heat-seeking gun controls that guarded the entranceway. The dummies hissed to life size on impact. Then San Zar dove, rolling to the stairwell on his left.

As the grenades' flares died down, the lasers reoriented on the dummies. Intolerable swords of light razed the lobby, zeroing in on the small battery-operated heaters inside each dummy. Just within the stairwell, San Zar nodded to himself. It was beyond belief to him that 'plex owners still left their defenses up to older 'puters like the one in this building. He supposed they were sufficient against common thieves and the like, but...

He shrugged, concentrating on a mental floor-plan of the 'plex, and began the climb to the twenty-sixth floor. The defense was their problem. Still, you wouldn't catch him living in an older building like this. Not with what he knew.

At the twenty-sixth floor, San Zar slipped out into the hallway, just below the sighting path of the camera that was attached to the wall above head level. Reaching up, he attached two sets of alligator clips to the armored cables. From the clips, wires ran down to the small VTR unit San Zar took from his belt. He set the unit to 'Record' and withdrew into the stairwell.

He bit at his lip nervously, watching both the hall and his recording unit. This was the only weak part of his plan—the one thing he couldn't do before hand. If someone chanced to walk in the hallway just now...All it needed was one door opening, one late-arriving tenant, and he'd have to begin again. With the 'puter on alert status due to the decoys in the lobby...But it was 0421. The chance of discovery was slim.

A half-hour later, San Zar sighed with relief. He rewound the tape, set the VTR unit to 'Replay,' and snipped the wall camera from its circuit. Now, no matter what happened in the hallway, the 'plex's main 'puter would only see a replay of the quiet corridor. He had half an hour to do the job and be gone. It was time enough.

He moved quickly down the hallway to Hest's doorway. Crouching by it, he pulled a small cutter from a side-pocket and cut a small cavity in the wall beside the door. Reaching in, he delicately cut the six wires that negated the door's alarms and its link-up with the main 'puter. Now there was just the door itself.

From another pocket he withdrew a small black box and attached it to the door's hand-plate. It had been expensive. But any unit capable of over-stimulating the mini 'puter responsible for the door's hand-plate was worth its price. There was a sudden intense blaze of light. The door slid open.

Inside it was dark. The only light came from the holo-lights outside the windows of the unit's main room. Outlined against those windows was a standing figure, back to the door. A prickle of uncertainty wormed into San Zar's confidence. Something was wrong. A tic tugged at the corner of his mouth. The figure stood unnaturally still. But he could sense life in it. It was just that—

San Zar grimaced. He was too close now. He eased his axe from his belt and took a step forward.

"I've been waiting for you," the figure said without turning, halting San Zar in mid-stride.

San Zar snapped a throwing star from his belt, flung it left-handed and watched in disbelief as the figure sidestepped the attack. A silver blade flashed out and down striking the star with a sharp clang. In the same motion, the figure slashed the curtain's bindings. Absolute darkness cloaked the room as the curtains fell across the windows.

San Zar dropped night-lenses over his eyes and stepped to one side. When his eyes adjusted to the new vision he found no sign of the figure. The uncertainty he'd felt on entering was building into a sour pressure in his stomach. Nobody could move that fast. But he'd seen it and...San Zar snapped another throwing star from his belt and called out, hoping to draw an audio fix by provoking a response from the unknown figure.

"Don't even breathe," said a voice in his ear.

San Zar dove forward into a front roll, spinning around as he came to his feet, axe held before him defensively. He stared at the man in the doorway. This wasn't Hest. It was the other one. His companion. But how...?

He gave up that line of questioning as he realized his position. At this point, with his contract still open, he couldn't risk a fine for killing someone who wasn't posted. Lowering his axe, he bowed to the silent figure and made for the door.

The stranger's sword rose to block the way.

"We have unfinished business," he said.

He raised his voice slightly, canceling the alarm status on the 'puter console.

San Zar watched the stranger, trying to place him. There was something familiar about him — not a personal thing. More a racial familiarity. He took in the masklike features, the eyes that were almost entirely pupil, and understanding came to him.

"Donsyan," he murmured.

"Indeed," Trigar'n said. "Answer one question for me, Kress San Zar, and you can be on your way. Who posted Ranjol Hest?"

San Zar shook his head. "You know I can't answer that."

Trigar'n shrugged, an infinitesimal lift of his shoulders, and his sword licked out. San Zar sidestepped the attack, gaining the room he needed to throw another star. The Donsyan's sword struck it out of the air, then leapt forward to engage San Zar's axe. The assassin groped for another throwing star, then fell back before Trigar'n's onslaught. His axe caught the sword in the hook of its neck. He pulled, but Trigar'n spun his blade free. Once, twice more, the Donsyan feinted. San Zar managed to deflect the following up attacks each time, but he moved with desperation. His axe wasn't a match for the sleek blade, nor he for the lean man who wielded it.

Then Trigar'n's blade cut through the nightsuit to the flesh beneath. San Zar's axe sagged in a hand suddenly weak. The Donsyan slashed his chest twice, then knelt by the stricken assassin's side, his knee pressed against the open wounds.

"The name!"

San Zar shook his head. Blood flecked his lips.

"Give me the name and you live. If not..."

Trigar'n applied pressure with his knee and the assassin bit back a cry.

"You Guildsmen," Trigar'n said conversationally. "You enjoy your work, don't you? The game of the hunt, toying with your victims..." He leaned on the wounds again. "It is not mine to judge you, Kress San Zar. Your ways are not mine. The Blade you swear to, that you mock with your mindless yammering, I hold as holy. In truth, I do. And my service to it is not founded on hollow words. Nor is it dedicated to blood. But enough.

"Would you live to kill again, Kress San Zar? Speak and I will release you. But speak truth, man. I will know a lie if I hear one."

San Zar stared into the Donsyan's pitiless mask of a face. He knew the fine line he walked this moment. This man at whose mercy he was, upheld all that the Guildsmen merely mouthed. When the pain increased to a white hot pitch, he spat out a name.

"Ben...Ben Stalwylth."

"Why?"

San Zar rolled his eyes. "Would he tell an assassin?"

Again the pressure. "He would."

San Zar gasped. "Hest...Hest works for him. Stalwylth's been selling information to Alatea. He...he was afraid that Hest was...coming too close to discovering the truth. If Ravenheir ever found out that he was betraying them to a...a rival Company..."

Trigar'n nodded. An age-old situation. He stood and stepped aside, all in one swift sudden motion.

"You may leave," he said.

San Zar rolled to his side. Weakly, he lifted himself to his knees. He took up his fallen axe and the throwing star that lay at his feet. The Donsyan watched him with the slow unblinking stare of a panther.

"Hest," San Zar asked. "Where is he?"

"Safe."

"And you? I...I saw you leave."

A smile flickered on the Donsyan's grim lips. "And I saw your floater, saw that you were alone. It was a simple matter to leave and return through the rear entrance." The look in his eyes plainly added "fool" to his quiet statement.

San Zar nodded. Painfully he began to rise. He let his eyes flick to the open doorway, register a hairbreadth surprise. It was the oldest of tricks, but it caught Trigar'n for the brief moment he needed to—

The throwing star left his hand. Trigar'n's blade arced up and for the third time that evening caught the star in mid-flight, ricocheting it into a corner of the room. The blade continued its wide sweep and cut the assassin through the chest.

Trigar'n stared silently at the body. Ah, when would the Guilds learn the meaning of honor? he wondered. He lifted his eyes as the bedroom door opened.

"It's almost over, Ran," he said.

CR&O

Ben Stalwylth sauntered across the lobby of his hotel, at peace with the world. He left a call at the desk for his floater to be brought around, then stepped over to the Posting board as he waited for it to arrive. He had a feeling of completeness this morning. Last night's business should have been completed without complications — after all, this San Zar was reputed to be one of the best in his trade — and now that he'd thought of a way to cover his tracks for good, why he —

He stared at the board, cold fear devouring his peace.

POSTING NOTICE...0600/213/3047/EST 32.....................
PRIME BANK BIT NUMBER N0048*7*262...SERIES 8Y7............

...SUBJECT...BENDIRTH STALWYTH.............................
RAVENHEIR LAB-EXEC.......................................
RAVENHEIR THIRD BASE/WST 3D3.............................
PRESENTLY ON THREE-DAY-LEAVE/EST 32..................
NO PREVIOUS TERMINATION POSTING......................
PROJECTED TERMINATION...7 MINUTES....................
FROM 0900/213/3047 TO 0907/213/3047......................

...EXECUTOR...TRIGAR'N...{NO SURNAME}..................
DONSYAN...
YEARS OF SERVICE...UNKNOWN...............................
PREVIOUS CONTRACTS...UNKNOWN.......................
SUCCESSFUL CONTRACTS...UNKNOWN.....................

BONDING INSURANCE...NONE...................................

Donsyan.

The word cut through Stalwylth's soul like sharpened ice. He glanced at his watch. It was 0906. Behind him, he heard the sound of a sword hissing from a lacquered wooden sheath.